Whistleblower

The Senator's Wife Series
Book III

JEN LYON

Whistleblower

The Senator's Wife Series

Book III

First Print Edition

Copyright © 2023 Jen Lyon

ISBN: 979-8-9877320-5-2 (paperback)

Published by Doss About Publishing

To my English friends
—you know who you are—
who helped me muddle through.

And to the readers,
with unwavering support,
who've made this dream come true.

Chapter One

Red, white, and blue confetti was plastered to Alex's face, her eyelashes adorned with glitter. Glancing at her reflection in the sheen of aluminum lockers, she wondered if it had been there before her teammates doused her in champagne and—from the smell of it—a bottle of jack, or if she'd collected the debris after. Had it been the former, she'd just spent fifteen minutes accepting the Silver Boot on stage in front of the entirety of Wembley Stadium, along with millions of TV viewers, looking like the aftermath of a RuPaul Drag Show gone wrong—or right, depending on how you looked at it.

Perhaps she'd been lucky. Maybe the tinseled carnage had waited for the ambush celebration in the tunnel after she'd slogged her way through the post-game interviews and slipped out of the limelight. It didn't really matter. She'd spent plenty of conferences covered in mud and grass and sweat, so what was a little glitter? They'd just won the World Cup.

She stared at her bedazzled reflection as the thought swirled through her head. It hadn't quite sunk in. *They'd just won the World Cup!* It didn't feel real. At some point she was going to wake up, back in Oakland, back in her one bedroom apartment, to find she'd dreamt the entire thing. But no. She'd stood on that stage with twenty-two of her teammates and lifted that trophy. She'd listened to the fans chant *U... S... A...* to a thunderclap of approval. She'd felt a flush climb up her neck when her own name—*Grey*—had reverberated through the stands as she'd accepted the Silver Boot for the second-most goals scored in the tournament. And she'd recoiled inwardly when she'd been awarded *Player of the Match*—an award she knew should have gone to no one other than Amelia Walker.

And then there was Catharine...

1

Catharine, who'd come to watch her win the match, wearing a jersey with her name and number.

Catharine, who she'd climbed a wall to kiss in front of ninety thousand people.

Had that really happened?

The post-match interviews had quickly unveiled the surrealness of the moment, snapping Alex back to reality.

"Now, I know I'd have a lot of unhappy viewers, Alex, if I didn't ask you about the support of an unexpected fan in the stands tonight."

Alex had wanted to ask the reporter why she wasn't more interested in the seven goals she'd scored throughout the tournament. Or, if it was controversy she was aiming for, why she wasn't inquiring about the late minutes foul from Monica Ashby against Amelia Walker. The foul that had stolen the match from the Australians. A cheap shot. From a cheap player. Alex would have preferred that uncomfortable conversation, had it steered the spotlight away from her personal life.

"I think we had a lot of support in the stands tonight," Alex had opted instead, brushing the question aside. "We left everything on the pitch for the fans today and I think it's safe to say they did the same for us. The crowd was incredible."

The reporter had given her a come-on-give-me-something bob of her blonde curls, which Alex ignored. If she'd hopped the fence to kiss a boy, no one would have noticed.

But no. In her post-win elation, she'd been delirious enough to think it was a grand idea to hoist herself over the railing and kiss the wife—no matter they were divorcing—of the monster running for president. The woman who had all of England abuzz with her media-frenzied blood feud with her father—one of the most prominent businessmen in London.

But whatever. In truth, she didn't care. *So kiss me*, Catharine had told her. So kiss her she did. And, despite the momentousness of her current World Cup achievement, *kiss her again* was all she really wanted to do.

Temporarily lost in her booze soaked reflection while her teammates danced and drank and reveled in celebration, Alex felt two arms close around her, swooping her into a firm embrace and dragging her out of her reverie.

To her astonishment she found Izzy Atwood, the US head coach, a woman who had been tougher on her, both mentally and physically, than any other coach in her career—a curt, straightforward, uncomplimentary woman who had constantly reminded Alex her place on the team was as stable as a mudslide—looking down at her with unconcealed affection from beneath her champagne soaked bangs plastered to her forehead, glitter and confetti garnishing her hair.

"*You*, kid," she clutched Alex's shoulders in her iron grip and gave them a shake, emphasizing each word, "have made me proud. Made your whole damn country proud." Her keen gray eyes radiated a sincerity Alex had previously never experienced from the stalwart Welshwoman. "You've been the best risk I've taken in a long time, Alex. I hope you realize that."

Hearing the stoic, ruthless woman validate her performance, acknowledging the work she'd put in and the battles she'd overcome, brought an unanticipated wave of emotion funneling to the surface, pent up from the four-week rollercoaster they'd traveled throughout the tournament. And, for Alex, a much lengthier seesaw of turbulence.

Alex swallowed back tears—tears encompassing the entire gamut of emotion: elation, frustration, relief, joy, and the inevitable let down of it all coming to a close—and allowed reality to settle in. It was over and they'd achieved this unbelievable, incredible, beautiful thing. Atwood's words eased away the sting of the controversial win and returned some of the pride Alex wanted to feel in the accomplishment. The idea that, maybe even without Ashby's imbecilic intentional foul, they'd deserved the win. They'd *earned* the win.

With a broad smile revealing a speckling of glitter that had worked its way onto Atwood's teeth, the gruff woman pulled her into another hug. "Next stop, a gold in Melbourne! What do you say?"

Untrusting of her voice, Alex only nodded. The Olympics, little more than a year away. Hosted, ironically, by none other than Australia. No team had ever won a World Cup and then clinched an Olympic gold the following year. It was a feat left unclaimed. One more goal to set their sights on.

There was a jarring pop, followed by screams of laughter above the pounding bass blaring from the playlist on Molly Rodrigues' phone, and before Alex's self-preservation could kick in to alert her to close her eyes, she was struck full in the face by a blast of foaming champagne, shielded little by Atwood, also falling victim to the assault.

"*USA, USA, USA*," an exceedingly intoxicated Jill Thompson cheered, spinning the fizzing bottle around like a water cannon. The typically poised, somewhat haughty, always composed forward turned the bottle to her lips, chugging until she choked, her blonde hair falling over the beer goggles sitting haphazardly on her face. "*USA*," the last chant came out in a garble of unintelligible gurgling before she twerked her way across the slippery floor to find her next target, snagging a fresh bottle along the way.

"If we don't take gold for soccer, we can definitely medal in shotgunning champagne!" Alex shouted over the music to her coach, wiping at her face with her jersey.

Atwood smiled. "You're Americans. You like to one-up everything!" She gave Alex one last clap on her shoulder before moving on through the room, happier than Alex had ever seen her.

Eyes still stinging with alcohol, Alex tried to blink the surrounding area into focus, looking for Halsey. She was hoping to talk her into going in search of Catharine and Clancy. She wanted to see Catharine before they headed for the hotel. The team had an early flight back to the States in the morning, where they would start a two-week tour of media obligations and Stateside celebrations beginning with a ticker-tape parade in New York, and Alex wasn't sure when she'd actually get to see her again. As much as she wanted to party with her squad, she wanted to see Catharine even more.

Spotting the goalkeeper across the room in the full throng of a dance-off with their assistant coach, Trent McGuire, Alex headed in her friend's direction. But before she reached the circle of girls cheering Halsey on, Alex felt the buzz of her cell phone inside the pocket of her track pants. She glanced at the screen. Regina Schaff, the manager of *Kickstar*. Without hesitation, Alex sent the call to voicemail. Whatever Regina and HEG had to say—be it firing her for her celebratory kiss, or congratulating her on the World Cup win—it could wait.

Scrolling her texts, she checked once more to see if Catharine had responded. The message she'd sent as soon as she got to the dressing room remained undelivered, which either meant the service in the stadium was too overloaded to send the text or Catharine's phone was dead.

Before she could dwell on it, her attention was jerked in another direction as the song flipped to a remix of *We Are The Champions* and Alex found Erin Halsey abandoning Trent to launch into her arms, nearly knocking her to the ground with the half a head and thirty plus pounds she had over her.

"Buuuuudddddy!" She twanged, her Mississippi drawl exaggerated with alcohol. "Waited for you forrrrrrrrrever to finish with the press! You need a drink!"

She did. But first. "Do you think we can find Clancy and Catharine? Before we head to the hotel?"

Halsey took a step back, her face skewed in disbelief. "Dude. We're celebrating. I'm not going in search of my aunt when there's free alcohol to be had by the gallon. I'll see her when we get home. Trust me—she doesn't want to see what goes on at that rooftop party tonight. That ain't for the faint of heart. Besides," she nudged Alex with a broad shoulder, "I've no doubt Clancy left forever ago. Game's been over for more than an hour. Press conference had you locked down while the rest of us are a six pack deep."

Alex had forgotten about the party Atwood promised them at their hotel if they finished the tournament victorious. They could bring their dates, if they wanted. But it would be a cold day in hell before Alex asked Catharine to come to that disaster. It wasn't like going to the college bar in Portland...

Halsey smirked at her fallen face. "My girl, they don't allow conjugal visits on team-time, anyhow." She winked, snagging a beer from Jill Thompson's hand as she strut by, and took a long swig. "Give it up—right now it's time to par-tay!!" She finished the bottle and tossed it into the growing pyramid of debris beside the makeshift bar, before dragging Alex into the conga line that had formed, despite its blatantly off-beat cadence to the Queen classic.

Alex reluctantly joined the line behind the keeper, trying to decide how she could make a stealthy exit. Catharine didn't even know she was flying out in the morning. They hadn't had a chance to talk about a timeline or plans for after the game. But with the press commitments and victory tour waiting for the team back in the States, followed by the second half of the NWSL season, God only knew when they would see each other again. Especially with Catharine's ongoing lawsuit confining her to London. It could be weeks. Months, more likely. And at the moment, even five more minutes seemed too long after all the time they'd spent apart.

But as they snaked their second lap around the room, stepping on each other's heels and swaying to the awkward beat, Alex knew Halsey was right. The game had ended over an hour ago. Catharine would be off to her apartment in Bermondsey and Alex's squad was never going to allow her to sneak out without fanfare.

On the third pass around the lockers, Abby Sawyer spotted Alex and scrambled from the line to slip between her and Halsey, passing back her half drank beer, the rim smeared with her plum lipstick.

"Suuuugar," she sang through her unremitting smile, shaking her hips to the music, "we just won the World Cup. World Fucking Cup, do you hear me?!"

Resigning herself to a night of burning off steam with her friends, Alex laughed and accepted the bottle as they tripped over one another in the ridiculous dance line. She took a sip, allowing a smile to turn her lips.

Sawyer was right.

They'd won the World Cup. The *World-Fucking-Cup*.

Tonight was a celebration.

It would just be that much better if she could find a way to see Catharine.

Chapter Two

"Well?" The cocky young woman from Tyneside set her hand on the low railing, the tail end of a serpent tattoo spiraling across her wrist and disappearing down her index finger. "Shall we go see the girls?"

Catharine scrutinized their surroundings. When Sam Huntley—a former football legend, according to Clancy—had boasted she could get them to the US team's dressing room, Catharine had mistakenly presumed she meant in a legal manner, by way of a respectable route. A poor assumption, she was learning quickly. She hadn't envisioned darting through a vacated press box to get to a nonpublic janitorial alley, slipping down two flights of poorly lit backstairs, and coming out in the bowels of the stadium in an area not heavily patrolled by security.

"A little stroll to the tunnel and we're golden," the cheeky footballer pitched her angular chin in the direction of an opening in the dark scaffolding a few dozen meters past the other side of the low construction barricade.

Clancy's scowl was resolute behind the waterfall of perspiration streaming from her forehead, her red, white, and blue face paint oozing down her neck, darkening the collar of her *Halsey* goal-keeping jersey.

"You want me to hop a fence and make a run for the tunnel?" the woman panted, incredulous. "You're out of your mind, Sam Huntley. When you said you could get us back to the lockers, this wasn't what I envisioned."

The Geordie shrugged. "I *can* get you back to the dressing room —we just have to do it my way." She twirled an impatient finger. "It's not like it's a bloody ten foot wall. The fence is barely waist high. One step and we're on our way."

"Says the athlete. I'm a fat, old lady—"

"Yeah, yeah, and I've got one leg. C'mon, now, up and over."

Clancy didn't budge. "And if I do squeeze through to make it to the tunnel—what then? You think I ain't got the sense God gave a piss ant. When we get caught down here—"

"I've got enough clout here to keep us from getting booked, trust me." Sam flashed a grin and glanced at Catharine. "And if I'm wrong, I'll wager Mrs. Cleveland has enough quid to spring us from the pen—am I right?"

Catharine listened to the exchange, trying to decide how much further she was willing to let this play out. It was no longer shocking Alex had ended up high and plastered in a Wapping park in the middle of the night after an evening out with this character. However, the fence *was* only waist high and the entrance to the tunnel wasn't far off. And if Sam Huntley had even half the illustrious career Clancy had described to her, she did have to carry a certain amount of sway with the stadium personnel, which would hopefully be taken into consideration if they were caught where they didn't belong.

On the other hand, wouldn't the media just be delighted to run a story about the illegal escapades of their current favorite scapegoat? *Fallen Businesswoman Arrested on Trespassing in Attempt to Reach Her Controversial Lover.* If that wasn't what tabloids were made of…

She decided it was worth the risk. Clancy had said the girls were scheduled on an early morning flight and she was determined to see Alex before she disappeared to the States again. With her phone dead, she had no other way to reach her, and was at the mercy of Sam's back alley shenanigans.

Placing a hand on the barricade, Catharine swung herself up and over to the other side, grateful to be in jeans and trainers. A skirt and heels would have complicated the situation. As her feet found purchase on the dusty concrete, the disturbing sensation of a sticky residue settled across her face as she plowed headfirst through a downed cobweb. She bit back a grunt of disgust, allowing herself a virtual pat on the back for managing not to flinch as she plucked the tacky filament from her hair and skin, before turning to find a twisted smirk plastered across Sam Huntley's face, her dark eyes shining.

"Took one for the team there, Cleveland. Short straw, going first." With an easy grace Sam hopped over the wall with nothing but her knuckles making contact. It was evident, regardless the loss of her leg, the younger woman still kept herself in the form of an athlete. "I see it a little more, now—Grey's infatuation with you. You're not quite the pompous toff you make out to be."

Catharine ignored her and looked to Clancy, who had taken a retreating step toward the stairs. "No. No! You're both off your rockers." She looked over her shoulder in the direction they had come. "I love Erin, but I'll love her just as much back in Mississippi come offseason."

"Suit yourself," Sam shrugged, taking a further step into the shadows.

"It was a pleasure, Catharine," Clancy extended her hand over the wall, her handshake clammy with perspiration. "I hope very much to see you at a Sirens' game this fall."

"You can count on it."

"If you're not sitting in some London prison after running wild with this one, I suppose."

Voices in the adjacent tunnel cut their farewell short and soon after Catharine found herself following Sam Huntley along a wall of scaffolding as she navigated her way to a section she deemed more suitable for their surreptitious arrival into the halls leading to the dressing rooms.

Pushing open a door with her shoulder, Sam passed into a narrow corridor, dimly lit with work lights, but with the promise of impending civilization. "See, nothing to it," she held the door for Catharine, "you're a real bobby dazzler, Cleveland. Nowhere near the gammer I took you for."

"The dressing rooms, Miss Huntley?" Catharine said pointedly, disregarding the insult. She had little more than a decade on the brazen girl. Hardly what would qualify her as a *gammer*.

"Just Huntley. Or Hunt. You can save the posh titles for your easy street friends."

Catharine's response was dampened by a sudden grunting, thudding sound coming from around the corner of the vacant hall, followed by the muffled tone of angry voices. Australian voices.

Without a word, Sam rounded the corner, swift despite her uneven gait, and as she disappeared Catharine heard her call out a warning. "Hey! What gives! You dafty wankers!"

If climbing through the abyss of backstairs and labyrinth of alleys in the heart of Wembley Stadium hadn't been on Catharine's agenda to reach the US dressing room, stumbling into a three-versus-one melee of vexed footballers had never crossed her mind. But as she turned the corner, she found her mettlesome guide bounding into the fray of a fight, grabbing at the hair of a muscular blonde who Catharine recognized as the Matildas' goalkeeper.

"Howay man! Get off her!" Huntley yanked the taller woman backward, away from a crouching figure against the wall, but the keeper rammed her elbow behind her, catching Huntley in the face and sending her stumbling. Two other women had their hands on the cowering shadow, trying to drag her to her feet.

"Get the fuck off me!" It was an American, Catharine realized, though it took a moment to place the voice, the face hidden behind the curtain of blonde hair that had been wrestled from its ponytail during the scuffle. Huntley, shaking off the blow to her nose, grabbed again for the goalkeeper, but before she could find leverage on the girl who outweighed her by at least two stones, a new arrival approached from the opposite direction, immediately muscling her way between the three Australians and American.

"You fucking bogans!"

Catharine recognized the newcomer at once. *Amelia Walker.*

With Huntley's help, the pair broke up the tussle, and Catharine watched from the short distance down the hall as the Matildas' captain slammed her goalkeeper against the wall, pinning her to the rough surface with a strong arm across her chest. "Are you a bloody imbecile?!"

"She cost us the fucking match—"

"She's going to cost you a lot more than that in a minute, you fucking galah!" Livid, Amelia shoved her toward the door where her other two teammates were slinking their way down the adjacent wall. "Get to the dressing room. Now!"

"It'd be just like you to defend the bloody Yanks! Fucking dobber, mate—"

While the keeper and captain cussed at one another, threatening to come to blows, the girl on the ground rose and staggered further into the darkness, suddenly finding herself face-to-face with Catharine. Despite her disheveled hair and bleeding nose, Catharine recognized the US defender, Monica Ashby, as soon as she turned her face in her direction.

"Oh!" The startled girl faltered, her hand flying self-consciously to her face, wiping at the blood trickling down her upper lip.

Catharine forced aside the awkwardness between them and reached to touch her elbow. "Is there anything I can do to help?"

Tears sprung at once to the wide blue eyes, followed immediately with a wave of anger fueled by humiliation. "No!" Monica jerked her arm away. "Don't touch me!" She dragged her forearm across her eyes, her lower lip quivering, before shooting a glance toward Sam Huntley and Amelia Walker, standing a dozen feet away. The other three girls were gone. "Get away from me, all of you!" Stumbling backward over a shop broom, she darted down the hall, her voice choked with tears. A garbled threat was hurled at Amelia as she passed the Australian, and then she was gone, a heavy door slamming in the distance.

"Well," Huntley broke the silence that had settled between the three of them, her voice riddled with amusement, "nothing like having a barney after a match to keep with tradition." She slapped Amelia's hip. "Seems your gals are taking the loss hard, what?"

Amelia didn't return her smile. "All losses are taken hard, Hunt. Don't be a gronk."

"Just making convo, marra."

"What are you two doing down here?" Amelia was staring at Catharine but the question was meant for Sam.

"Working our way to the dressers. Ginnel was locked up tight, so thought we'd take a detour."

"You're looking for Grey, I imagine?" She continued to stare at Catharine, who hadn't moved from the end of the corridor.

"I am." Catharine regretted her unintended frost-laden tone. She and the Australian had left on amicable terms in San Francisco, but the unexpected encounter had thrown her off balance.

"Her squad just loaded the bus for their hotel. Might still be able to catch them," she gestured with her thumb over her shoulder, "no doubt they're waiting for that dero, Ashby."

Catharine masked her disappointment with a shrug. "Another time, then."

"I see no introductions are needed here." Huntley leaned against the wall with a smirk. "Not with the mutual friend you both share."

"Can it, Huntley." Amelia shot her a glare.

"What?" Huntley feigned innocence. "Small world, isn't it?" She pushed herself off the wall, trying to hide a grimace as she shifted her weight to her bionic leg. "I have an idea—let's grab a pint! I reckon the three of us have earned one!"

This time Catharine did not hesitate. "Thank you, but no. This is where I'll call it an evening."

"C'mon, Cleveland—you said yourself you couldn't reach your driver with your mobile dead and all. You don't want to be up in that crowd alone. Come have a pint. I know a canny pub just down the road—it's off the beaten path. You can charge your phone and I'll get you back to your car safely. Or to the hotel to see your girl. Whichever you prefer. But a pint's in order, either way."

Amelia appeared equally disinterested in the suggestion, but from somewhere beyond the door a cheer went up followed by a chorus of *USA* sung at the top of the lungs of rowdy passers by, and with a half shrug she nodded toward Catharine. "All right, why the hell not? A coldie never hurt anything. First round, my shout, Mrs. Cleveland. In honor of *your girl's* win."

Huntley's smile broadened. "There's the radgie Walker I know. Bitter 'til the end." She stepped to the door and held it open, looking at Catharine. "Well, Cleveland?"

Catharine didn't move.

The last thing she wanted to do was go to a pub with Amelia Walker and Sam Huntley. But at the same time, the Geordie was right—she wouldn't be able to get a hold of Malcolm until her mobile was charged. And she didn't really care to find herself alone amongst the horde of inebriated football fans swarming the stadium above them.

"Fine. One pint." She stepped through the door Huntley held. A beer with an unashamed reprobate and her girlfriend's ex-lover was no doubt on the lower end of the scale of questionable decisions she'd made in recent history. What was the point of playing it safe now?

Besides, a pint was sounding better with every passing minute.

Chapter Three

The bus was loaded. Or rather not the bus, but the people on it—though the bus was brimming at capacity. Alex wasn't sure she'd ever seen such an assorted variation of levels of drunkenness.

There was tipsy. Izzy Atwood was a shining example of this gradation. Shoulders bobbing to the music, upbeat attitude, broad smile concreted to her face for no rhyme or reason. Just happy.

Next advancement: sloshed. Bevvied, Catharine called this. Munted, Amelia would say. Sawyer'd always liked the term gassed; which she, and the majority of their team, currently were. Dancing, jubilant off-tone singing, loss of articles of clothing and the sudden need to twerk and vine their bodies up against one another—regardless of sexual orientation—grinding against the seats, the champagne bottles, the bus windows… the alarmed, but forgiving bus driver. Glassy-eyed, red-faced, foulmouthed, and loving every hell-raising second of life. This was definitely the bulk of the squad.

And lastly, at the pinnacle of the tier—the blitzed. Trolleyed, to Catharine. Maggot, Amelia would confirm. Shitfaced, Erin Halsey would have enunciated. That was, if Erin Halsey's brain was ever clear enough to enunciate again. Three sheets to the wind, drunk as a lord, under the table, wrecked—whatever a person wanted to call it, the US goalkeeper was so deep in her cups she would have put Jack Sparrow to shame. Verging on one drink shy of a blackout, Alex persistently tried to persuade the keeper to take in some water as she raucously joined in on the "we got four stars on our shirts" song the girls had improvised to the tune of *We Got the Whole World in Our Hands*. But Halsey kept forgetting the lyrics three words into the seven word verse. She and Jill Thompson were neck and neck for securing the award for most tanked on the team—which, at six a.m. the following morning, would also likely win the prize for most-miserable-flight-across-the-Atlantic. If that was a prize one wanted to win.

Alex had a conversant sympathy for both women in the hours to come. And the days after. Neither were big drinkers, both were adherent rule followers, and though they themselves might not remember their heroic celebration, the dozens of cell phone videos flooding onto Insta and TikTok and Twitter—not to mention the footage captured by the press on their way to and from the bus—certainly would. Coming from a place of recent experience, Alex held great empathy for her friends.

But whatever. They'd *won the World Cup!* Live it up, ladies. The Olympics were a short fourteen months away.

Alex slung Halsey's arm over her shoulder, and with the help of Sawyer, safely got her off the bus and to the sidewalk, all while she vigorously sang "we got four… we got four…" By the time they were into the lobby the exuberant lyrics had faded.

In the elevator, Alex leaned against the cool steel and closed her eyes, thanking God she'd had that nightmare of a shitshow after the pub with Sam Huntley when they'd first arrived in London. Otherwise it may have been her in Halsey's position, and she already didn't love flying—so crossing the Atlantic on a colossal hangover would have been a cataclysmic failure.

And, if not for Huntley and her push for poor decisions, Alex never would have drunk dialed Catharine. They'd still not be speaking. She'd still be drowning in self-pity.

Which reminded Alex… Sam Huntley's name had popped up on her screen when they were disembarking the bus, but she'd been too busy lugging Halsey down the stairs to swipe open the text.

As the elevator flew to the top floor of the Hilton Wembley where half the team was already beginning wave two of their Night One celebration, Alex retrieved her phone and tapped into her messages. Five texts, all from the English footballer.

—*swell match, Grey. Ran into a friend of yours.*

An image followed, taken on the sly, a candid of Catharine sitting in a booth, a drink in her hand, her eyes turned up to a bar room TV.

Alex smacked her head against the elevator wall as she jerked to attention, swiping to the next text.

Fuck.

—oh, another friend, too. Check out that shiner.

There was Amelia, walking toward the camera, three pints in one hand and flipping Huntley the bird with the other.

Why did it look like she was in the same pub? The same TV in the background? Three beers in hand?

And why the hell was Catharine there with them?

The last text read:

—cheers, man! We'll take good care of her, honest. <a winking emoji> Steer clear of the absinthe, ya lightweight! Xoxo <a kissing emoji>

The door to the elevator sprung open and the crowded box flooded onto the rooftop, greeted by the blast of Macklemore thumping from the hammering subwoofers.

—What the hell are you

Alex's fingers flew across the keyboard, but her response was interrupted as Sawyer dragged her through the closing door where she narrowly missed being sent back to the first floor to pick up the next round of partygoers.

"Come on, lover girl," Sawyer chided, snagging a pair of long-neck bottles from a passing server, "you can text your lady love later!"

"I'm not—it's not—" Alex started to explain, but stopped, unable to think straight. The booming chorus of *Can't Hold Us* wasn't helping her train of thought.

"Drink up, buttercup!" Sawyer shoved a Newcastle brown into her hand as Alex gave a surveying sweep of the rooftop. More tinsel, more confetti, more balloons that spelled out USA. And dozens and dozens of dancing people she didn't know. Friends of friends of friends. Cousins twice removed. On the dance floor. Along the railings. Atop the bar counter. On a double take, she realized it was Salty, Shelly Altman, and Trent McGuire on the bar top—doing the Chicken Dance.

Alex took a sip of the beer. Only her second of the night. But then downed the bottle. They'd just won the World Cup, after all. Four stars on their shirts.

And Sam Huntley and Amelia Walker were sitting in a pub with Catharine Cleveland.

"Keep an eye on her, Sawyer!" she had to shout over the music, pushing her friend toward Halsey, who was eyeing the bar top dancers with a clear intention to join them. "I'll be right back!"

Finding the emergency exit staircase, Alex let the door slam behind her, the music plummeting to a muffled reverberation thumping through her bones.

—What the hell are you doing, Huntley?!

She finished the text and hit send.

Chapter Four

"It's a bonny shot, at least, Cleveland. I see the cover of *Time Magazine* or *Tatler* in your future."

Sam Huntley was kicked back on the wooden bench of the pub booth, her futuristic leg draped over the corner of the table, effectively blockading Catharine against the wall. Amelia sat across from them, her blackening eye beginning to match the color of her drink.

"I doubt magazine covers are new to Mrs. Cleveland," the Australian offered in a lukewarm tone that was beginning to lighten with her second round.

"Ah, right," Huntley appraised Catharine. "I keep forgetting you're a proper mazer. Sitting here, you could almost pass as normal, despite reeking of capital." She swiped her pinky into the foam of her lager, watching it drip back into her glass. "Well, and having the ability to make Victoria Beckham look like a seven— when we all know she should never dip below a solid nine and a half. Other than that, marra, you're practically a regular bird."

"I believe that's Huntley for your-head-isn't-stuffed-as-far-up-your-arse-as-the-headlines-would-have-you-think," Amelia translated, the emerald of her one good eye reflecting the dim glow of the dusty overhead TV.

The back alley alehouse was all but empty, its deserted tables still strewn with debris from patrons who'd departed after the match. Catharine had found the vacancy a tide of good fortune, given *BT Sport's* World Cup footage had spent as much time focusing on her interaction with Alex as it had any actual highlights from the championship.

Over and over she'd looked up to see the image of Alex, dangling off the wall by her elbows, the pair of them in mirrored *Grey* jerseys, sharing a kiss.

She wasn't ignorant. She'd known, even in the moment, that it would cause a stir. It was the exact footage the cameras had been waiting for. But at the time, she hadn't really cared. And to her surprise, despite staring at herself on international primetime for the past half an hour, she found the sentiment still held.

She didn't regret it.

Even if it meant Gordon Liebermann was uttering every Be-rakah his lips could mutter, thanking God he was no longer re-sponsible as her lead counselor. Even if Carlton was doing a two-step, kicking up his heels in celebration that his wife had just gifted him with a flagrant display of immoral behavior—the justification for divorce in the middle of his presidential campaign. And even if her father used the photo—*hundreds* of photos—to fuel his fire as he burned down another corner of her empire—she would do it all over again.

She loved Alex. She no longer cared if the entire world knew.

Which, based off the relentless clip of her kiss on loop, the *entire* world knew.

"So, Grey's back to the States in the morning, and you're stuck here in London?" Huntley gave a low whistle, shaking her head. "That's some piss poor luck—her jetting off, the two of you with-out a single night of horizontal refreshment. Can't say I could do the long distance thing myself." She winked at Catharine. "Hope you've been brushing up on your sexting."

Across the table Amelia put away the rest of her beer and slammed the empty glass back to her coaster, the dull thud draw-ing a taunting smirk from the meddling northerner.

"Too soon, Walker? Never knew you to be the sentimental type. Love 'em and leave 'em's always been your motto. Didn't really see you getting hung up on this Shakespearean love triangle shite. Besides—Grey just knocked you off the podium. Laws of football demand you hate her at least a little bit."

"Do you ever shut the fuck up, Hunt?"

"Just taking the piss out of you, marra. Don't get your knickers in a twist." She held up three tattooed fingers toward the barman. "Time to get you mortal. No better remedy after a loss like that."

"No," Amelia waved off the beer, "I'm flying home in the morn-ing. Haven't seen my oldies in a minute." Her gaze turned judgmental as she slid it to Catharine. "Anything I should warn my old man about when it comes to his livelihood?"

In the chaos of the evening, Catharine had forgotten Amelia's father worked for *WorldCargo*. That his job was on the line along with thousands of others.

"I am doing everything in my power to keep things afloat. I wish I could give you a better answer."

"I imagine you're much like a cat, Mrs. Cleveland. You'll land on your feet either way. It's everyone else that's going to be left floundering." The frostiness had returned, Amelia's green eyes unblinking above the contrived smile she'd forced in place.

And how could Catharine blame her? She was right to worry about her father's career. Right to point out the blatant disparity. It didn't matter how hard Catharine had worked, or whether she'd dedicated her life to the company—if in the end she was unsuccessful at saving her job, her life of privilege had given her the ability to build a safety net; to allow her to fail without losing everything. Men like Dave Walker had not been born into that appanage, regardless the sweat of their brow. And there were thousands more just like him, waiting to see which way the tide swayed.

"If it comes to a situation in the Port of Melbourne, have your father contact me directly. I have connections in the industry. I can help him find—"

Amelia cut her off. "Thank you, but we're not your charity case, Mrs. Cleveland."

"Cheery convo, this!" Huntley raised her glass. "Think of it this way, Walker—you made more quid losing the World Cup than Cleveland here pulled in on her last month's paycheck. That's a hell of a feat, given the zeroes I imagine she usually rakes in."

Catharine was relieved to hear Amelia laugh at the Tyneside girl's endless raillery. There was something so abysmally straightforward, so candidly unfiltered about Sam Huntley, it rendered her persistent provocation effectually harmless in the long run.

"You're a real bastard, Hunt. As much now as you ever were on the pitch." The side of Amelia's mouth turned up in a smile, before she winced at the effort. The purple of her eye had spread along her temple, the swelling from brow to cheek.

Catharine couldn't fathom the steel it had taken to take a hit like that—to be stapled on the field—and return to the match. And then to sit here, putting on a front of indifference, as if she hadn't just lost her life's dream.

She'd garnered Catharine's admiration, if for nothing more than that. Her grit. Her resolve. Her fortitude. She was inspiring to her teammates. A leader through and through. It was apparent now, behind her caustic sarcasm, behind her unreserved contempt, what Alex would see in her. How they had fit.

But she and Alex fit, too. Of that Catharine was certain. No amount of admiration for the Australian would sway her mind on that. It hadn't been their fault the world had been against them.

And it was time to make up for that.

Redirecting her thoughts to the present, Catharine listened as Amelia and Sam's conversation deviated to the upcoming Olympics, and the probability of which twelve teams would qualify to compete. On the TV above them the sports station had resumed its cycle of the World Cup coverage, highlighting the missed Australian PK, Alex's winning goal, the post-match press conference, and, yet again, the bloody photo of her and Alex.

She was tired of looking at them on the screen, knowing Alex was only a few minutes away. Knowing in a matter of hours she'd be across the Atlantic, with no telling how long it would be before they saw one another again. Knowing nothing of what might happen in between.

"Sam," she interrupted a burgeoning argument about the fate of a coach for Arsenal FC. She couldn't sit in the pub another minute. Not when there was another option—prudent or otherwise.

"Hunt," the Geordie corrected over the top of her amber lager.

Catharine disregarded the monicker. "If I take you up on your offer to get to the Hilton Wembley, is it going to involve a fire escape and a life insurance policy, or does your professed *clout* grant you access to a front entrance and a legal lift?"

The woman's dark eyes brightened with a challenge as she set down her beer and cracked her knuckles. "Oh, I don't need to be on the cover of *Vogue* to stroll through those doors. This is my bag. My people. My environs." She laced her fingers behind her head, kicking back further in her seat. "There's no red tape for Sam Huntley—of that I can assure you."

Across from her Amelia rolled her eyes.

Catharine optioned not to mention the trek through the underground of Wembley to get to the dressing rooms. "Shall we head over then?"

Sam's smile grew brazen. "I like your style, Cleveland. Months on the down-low, then bam—here you are: PDAs on international telly, wearing your girl's name on your shirt, crashing an afterparty. I can't wait to see what's next." She chucked her square chin at Amelia. "Doubt you're up to storm a do, eh, marra?"

"Buckley's chance of that. I'll spit the dummy if I see that gronk Ashby again." Her monovision shifted to Catharine. "Give Grey my regards. She played a top-notch match tonight." Her former draftiness was absent as she held a hand out to Catharine. "And I hope you give your old man hell, Mrs. Cleveland."

Chapter Five

"Oh, my dour love, if only you could see your face." Sawyer pressed Alex's cheeks between her hands, her lavender eyeshadow sparkling in the flashing disco light roving the rooftop bar. She'd found Sam Huntley's series of texts hilarious, and taken great pleasure in ribbing Alex about her distress. "Relax. What's the worst that could happen?"

"It's Sam Huntley… you tell me."

"Something tells me Catharine Cleveland isn't going to find herself swayed by debauchery and lawlessness as easily as some people in present company." She winked, kissing Alex's forehead, leaving behind her signature plum lipstick in its wake.

Alex would have liked to have found a more convincing scowl, but even Sam Huntley's baiting texts weren't enough to dampen the buzz of exhilaration flowing through her veins. High off her teammates' excitement, adrenaline up from the celebration under-way, and a tipsy vibe beginning to take its hold, her frustrations were quickly fading. Whatever Huntley was up to, she knew Catharine would call her. Fill her in on whatever bizarre situation had brought them all together.

"Touché," she tugged on one of Sawyer's perfectly spiraled ringlets falling across her golden ochre eyes, wondering how her friend could always manage runway-perfect makeup in the time it took to dress and shower in the lockers. Alex considered herself lucky when she'd been able to scrub all the grime of the pitch off her elbows and wrangled her wet hair into something that didn't require a ball cap.

"Now," Sawyer continued, shifting her attention across the terrace where a number of their teammates had gathered, cheering boisterously in the direction of the tiki-style bar, "if you get a video of your woman looking like *that*, it might be cause for concern."

Salty, who'd joined the realm of *blitzed* with a growing number of others, was sprawled across the bar top clad only in Daisy Dukes and a sports bra, with half a dozen tequila shooters spread evenly along her tan, lean frame. Jill Thompson and Molly Rodrigues stood at the ready, waiting on a whistle from Trent McGuire, before bolting forward, their hands clasped behind their backs as they raced to see who could down the most shots off their teammate. It ended in a tie—three-and-three—before the two collided, tumbling to the floor in a heap of laughter.

"Sweet Jesus," Sawyer whistled through her teeth, raising an eyebrow, "it's going to be a fun flight in the morning. I'd usually say if we can't beat them, we should join them, but…"

Alex gave an adamant shake of her head. "Been there. Done that. Hard pass this round. Beer'll do me fine."

"In that case," Sawyer snagged a couple of browns from a passing server, clinking a bottle to the gold medal hanging around Alex's neck, and then to her own, "cheers to us."

As the crowd grew denser and the music louder, clothing began to turn into an optional accessory the heavier the barkeep poured. Though—as Halsey loudly proclaimed during the brief silence of a music track change—no tits had made an appearance yet, so the night was still young.

"So," Alex leaned close to Sawyer's ear from beside one of the balloon-wrapped columns supporting the open air veranda dangled with lights, "at what point do we reel her in?"

She gestured toward Halsey, who'd found her second—third? fourth?—wind, and was presently sharing a smoke with Shelly Altman, while calling for the DJ to play the Macarena. World-Cup-Win-Halsey was a far cry from Awkward-Girl-From-Mississippi-Halsey, and Alex imagined, as her roommate, she was going to be in for a long night.

Before Sawyer could answer, Alex's phone buzzed, and she yanked it from her pocket anticipating it to be Catharine. It wasn't. To her disappointment, Regina Schaff's name popped up once again on her caller ID.

"Shit." She flashed the screen toward Sawyer. "Third time she's called me tonight."

"No messages?"

"Just to call her back at my earliest convenience." Alex hit decline. "Doesn't really sound like a congrats call, does it?"

"Well," Sawyer leaned over the balcony overlooking Wembley Stadium, only a few hundred yards away. The lights were still on, creating an arched globe over the soaring stadium walls, and the parking lot remained full of tailgating merrymakers who weren't ready to let the evening end. "Can't say you haven't really gone out of your way not to blow their conservative, Bible-thumping, narrow little minds, can you? I mean, in eighteen months you've given them a wildcard run for their money. They thought they hired Shirley Temple in cleats and instead you offered up Marilyn Monroe on JFK's lap."

"You're a real rock of support—"

"Truth stings, darling. And you damn well know I support the ever-loving shit out of your chaotic, precious life. I wouldn't have you any other way. But I'm just saying—you've Billie Jean King-ed them, given them #Amex, inadvertently chased off their star international player, rollercoastered on and off and on the National team, gotten yourself tangled up in a hot bed of high press presidential election bullshit, and come off the World Cup win guns-a-blazing by very publicly making it clear *Amex* might not be a thing, but *Greyland* is a definite."

"What the fuck is Greyland?"

"Pop on Twitter and you'll find out. Better than Cathlex, I suppose. Though the irony there would have been superb."

Alex finished the beer she'd been dallying with for the last half hour. "So definitely not a congratulations call?"

Sawyer toyed with the long black curl framing her narrow face. "Who cares, really? After tonight you'll have *Nike, Under Armour, Adidas* kicking down your door. *Kickstar* dropping you might be the best news you could hope for."

"Says the gal locked into a multi-year, pretty-penny contract with *Puma*." Alex tugged on the medal around Sawyer's neck, the riposte in good humor. She'd been over the moon for her friend a month earlier when she'd landed one of the highest dollar endorsement contracts in women's sports history. Long overdue for a player of Sawyer's talent and experience, but a progressive step forward all the same.

"Don't worry—if everything falls apart, I can score you a pair of free cleats." Sawyer winked.

Alex rolled her eyes, resting her shoulder against Sawyer's, taking a breath to soak in the evening. "You know," she said after a moment, watching as two members of their physio team tried to convince Izzy Atwood to shotgun a Guinness, "if you had told me two summers ago I would move to California, make the National team, win a World Cup, and somehow become the poster girl for closeted Southern gays everywhere, I would have laughed in your face."

"Well, the Southern Sapphic poster girl was hardly a surprise—the rest, however…" Sawyer stuck her tongue out and Alex flicked a wad of the beer label she'd been peeling, landing a lucky shot in her mouth.

"Oh, damn you!" Sawyer spit, laughing, but her attention was swiftly diverted over Alex's shoulder in the direction of the elevators. "Well, Lord have mercy."

Before Alex could turn around, the unmistakable accent of Sam Huntley cut through the treble of Avicii's *Wake Me Up*, drawing heads from around the roof top, despite the rough and rowdy mood pulsating from the patio.

"Hey hey hey, my canny marras! Time to set-a-had this hacky rage!"

Alex spun from her place by the pillar to find Huntley striding across the dance floor, a cigar in one hand and bottle of whiskey in the other, her round face lit with a shit-eating grin as she headed straight for her and Sawyer. "How goes, man?"

"Proof they let anyone up in this joint," said Sawyer, but whatever greeting the two women exchanged was lost on Alex as she realized Catharine was working her way through the crowd just a few paces behind, her eyes finding Alex's with a subtle smile.

Promptly forgetting the existence of everyone else on the rooftop, Alex bolted forward, but hadn't made it two steps before she found herself abruptly propelled backward. "Yo," Sam had a hold of her collar, "mates before dates, man. Or for you yanks, pals before gals—dudes before prudes? Whatever you'd rather." She lifted her chin, her smile crooked across her handsome face. "You look a touch better than the last time I saw you. And one star loftier."

"Thanks. You, too," Alex replied lamely, uncaring about her blunder as she shook herself free of Sam's hold and intercepted Catharine. She stopped a step short, uncertain how to greet her, settling for a whispered "hi."

Catharine's smile was slow, the blue of her eyes reflecting the overhead string of lights hanging above the dance floor. With her calm, unflappable confidence, she reached forward to take both of Alex's hands, and leaned to kiss her cheek. "Hi yourself." Her lips lingered against Alex's ear, and the world shifted on its axis as Alex's heart doubled in time to the Diplo remix.

"I tried to call you."

"I hope you don't mind me showing up uninvited."

"Oh, she doesn't mind," Huntley countered, crowding in beside them, exhaling a long puff of smoke from her cigar directly into Alex's face. "Pretty certain the only thing ol' Grey here minds is an early morning flight and a roommate on curfew. Doesn't leave much time for tashing on, does it?" She flicked the end of her claro, the light breeze swirling the ash to the floor. "Just remember, Cleveland, when she flies out for the States tomorrow, I'll still be here." She winked, smacking Alex on her back.

"An offer I'll have to keep in mind," Catharine returned, and Alex could swear even Sam Huntley blushed as the recipient of Catharine's alluring smile.

"So," Catharine suppressed a sigh as Huntley moved off with Sawyer, allotting the two of them a modicum of privacy away from the crowded dance floor. "New York tomorrow?"

Alex looked down at their interlocked fingers, trying to remember the last time she'd felt that touch—had held those hands. How many agonizing, impossible, unconquerable hurdles had risen up between them, promising they'd never share a moment like this again? Yet here they were, together. But by tomorrow morning, they'd be half the world apart.

Sam Huntley wasn't wrong. At present, she'd have traded the shiny new star above her crest to be afforded a single self-governed night in London—to wake up in the morning in Catharine's arms.

With the anticipation of the game over, the tournament complete, the adrenaline of four weeks of strung nerves and high emotions beginning to wane, Alex longed for a repose of quiet. Of privacy. Of peace. But that was not something readily to be had. Not with the obligations that followed after the World Cup win. Not in the middle of the NWSL season.

"No rest for the wicked." She looked up, savoring the press of Catharine's fingers against her palms. Would it be so bad, she wondered, to kiss her, here on the rooftop bar? She'd just kissed her in front of the entire world. Half of her teammates were half-clad, shimmying up to boyfriends, girlfriends, strangers, hotel staff... No one paid any of them attention. They didn't have to think twice. But already Alex could feel the eyes turned in their direction. Feel the inquisitive stares. Catharine Cleveland was not the kind of woman who entered a room unnoticed.

And Alex didn't want to kiss her like that, with everybody watching. Not this time.

"How do you do it?" she asked, settling for stroking her thumbs along the inside of Catharine's wrists, inhaling the subtlety of the familiar perfume. "Pretend like you don't know everyone is watching you?"

"Are they?" Catharine didn't take her eyes from Alex. "It's difficult to notice when the only person I care about is standing right in front of me."

The buzz of three beers was nothing compared to the intoxication of standing beneath the steady blue gaze, reveling in the unabashed way Catharine reached to brush her cheek, sweeping back a loose strand of hair. The simplicity of the touch cleared Alex's mind of all the things she meant to ask her—how she'd ended up with Sam Huntley? Why Amelia had been there? Now, her thoughts consisted only of when they would see each other again. How soon and where?

"I have to leave in the morning." It felt more like a prison sentence than a victory tour.

"I know." Catharine toyed with the ribbon holding the gold medal around her neck.

"You have to stay in London?"

"For a little while."

"But you'll come back? No matter the outcome?" She needed to hear her say it. To promise, regardless what happened with her business. With her father. With Carlton and the election. She needed to hear her say she'd return.

"I'll come back."

Catharine's eyes were on her lips, her hand slipping around to the back of her neck. She would kiss her, Alex was certain. Kiss her despite the audience of onlookers, indifferent to the frenzy of the rooftop party and the chaotic atmosphere. And suddenly there was nothing more Alex wanted—privacy be damned.

Drawing Catharine closer, she moved to lean against the pillar, but immediately lunged forward in response to a violent explosion piercing the air.

The balloons, she realized, only half comprehensibly, her fight or flight mode kicked in high gear. She'd leaned back against the balloons…

In spite of the pounding bass strumming through the speakers, the pop had been loud enough to draw the entirety of the attention from the dance floor. If Alex's feeling of being watched had been a figment of her imagination, there was now no question that was no longer the case.

A shrill catcall went up from somewhere across the rooftop, followed by a handful of playful jeers.

"Get it, Grey!"

"Hubba-hubba!"

Before Alex was allotted the time to be embarrassed, she found herself suddenly separated from Catharine by the lumbering, stumbling form of Erin Halsey.

"Yeah, mama!" The goalkeeper pried her way between the pair, slinging an arm over both their shoulders. Through the aroma of smoke and whiskey, Alex detected a faint smell of ammonia, which she feared indicated her friend's night was officially over, and the half sentient Mississippi girl was on track to rue the day she was born.

"Thur'playin' yer'song, 'ollywood."

Through the mumbled slur of words, Alex briefly tuned in to acknowledge the Rihanna hit, *This Is What You Came For*, blaring in the background.

"An' e'erybdy's watch-in' 'er," Halsey attempted to keep along with the lyrics, stridently off-key, swaying between the two of them, "but shez lookin'at yoo-oo-oo, yoo-oo-ooo!" She jabbed a finger at Alex's chest, her warped smile teetering on the verge of incoherence. "Yer a'lucky girl! B'cuz P'rtl'nd's hot! An' shez only lookin'a'you!"

"Ohhh kay," Alex shifted her weight underneath her friend's arm, hoisting her up straighter, worried she was going to slip to the floor. "And that's our cue." She looked over the careening goalkeeper's shoulder, offering Catharine a smile laced with a grimace. "Think I'll put this one to bed." She looked for Sawyer, but instead found only Sam Huntley, where she'd been taking a shot with a blonde in a miniskirt.

Recognizing Alex's silent plea, Huntley strode over and pressed the half empty whiskey bottle into Catharine's hand before looping an arm around Halsey's waist, relieving Catharine of the burden. "Right, time for your scratcha," she quipped, more to Alex than the keeper, as they began a shuffling gait through the crowd. "Ah, and a hose down," she added, once the four of them were closed in the elevator, her nose crinkling at the unpleasant smell.

Between unintelligible rambling and a feeble protest to not leave the party, Sam and Alex managed to drag Halsey into the shared hotel room, depositing her directly into the shower.

"Your mate," Sam said, backing toward the door. "Clean up's all on you. I'll just be grabbing a nightcap with your lady."

Twenty minutes later, Alex, Sam, and Catharine wrangled Halsey—fresh in her Teenage Mutant Ninja Turtle pajamas—into her bed amongst disjointed mutterings pertaining to stars above her crest, bangers and mash, and her distaste for the color blue.

"Stay with me here, pet," Sam slapped her cheeks, ordering Halsey to open her mouth. From out of nowhere she materialized a handful of ibuprofen and a couple of Tums, depositing them beneath the keeper's tongue, before pressing a glass of water to her lips and ordering her to drink.

Momentarily resurfacing from her stupor, Halsey's wide russet eyes swept across the hotel room, settling on Catharine, who was watching in muted amusement from the foot of the bed.

"Portland?" The keeper was startled. "Y'r not s'pposed t'be 'n my dreams. I don't think Grey'd like that." She took another sip of water, oblivious to Sam beside her, before her eyes landed on Alex. "Oh, hey, Grey. You're both'ere. Weird. Not m'thing." Her loopy smile swayed with her vision, and it seemed she was giving in to unconsciousness, but as she reeled toward her pillow, she caught sight of Sam and recoiled. "Oh, *hell no!*" she annunciated very clearly, slammed flat against the headboard. "Get out of my nightmare, Sam Huntley! You're nothing but trouble!"

"Best thing anyone's said to me all night," Sam shrugged, undisturbed, forcing one last sip of water down Halsey's throat. "I'm leaving you my bottle of Jack. You'll need it in the morning. Don't say I never gave you anything."

Before she'd finished the sentence, Halsey was out, her mouth open, her breathing heavy, the reptilian beak of Donatello peeking out from her pajamas beneath the cover.

Sam set the glass on the nightstand and stood. "Can't say I'll envy you in the morning, Grey. Rough flight ahead with this one. Positively mortal." She shook her head. "Can't really blame her. Hell of a keeper. Hell of a match." Rubbing the place above her knee, a wistfulness crossed her expression, replaced just as quickly by her insolent smile. "Well, looks like you two might get lucky—she'd sleep through a nuclear war at this rate. I'll leave you to it." She stuck her hand out at Alex. "I'll admit, you're not the muppet I thought you'd be, Grey. If you ever get bored pissing around in the States, give me a shout. I know the gals at OL would be happy to give a Yank a run for her money."

Alex shook her calloused hand. "I'll consider it, thanks."

Huntley tipped an imaginary hat at Catharine. "Remember, Cleveland—when you get tired of little Miss Vanilla—you've got my number." Still grinning, she gestured at the bottle clutched in Catharine's hand, looking over at Alex as she strode to the door. "One shot when she first wakes, one before you board the plane, one mid-flight. Keep her drunk and you won't have to deal with the hangover. Win win for everyone."

And then she was gone, the only sound remaining Halsey's discordant breathing.

"Wow." Alex stared at the door, feeling as if she'd been clotheslined. She gathered herself from the last half hour—or last several thousand hours—of mayhem, before finally turning to look at Catharine.

"What a night."

Catharine set the bottle on Halsey's nightstand, then crossed to join Alex in the middle of the room. "What a night," she agreed, her eyes bright with humor. "Miss Vanilla?" Her hand went to

Alex's cheek, brushing along her jaw, sliding up into her hair. "Is that so?"

Alone at last—well, almost alone—Alex inhaled the nearness of her, grateful for the brief intimacy they'd been afforded. For the first time in what felt like an eternity, there were no eyes on them. No cameras. No comments. The moment was only their own. She closed her eyes, leaning her forehead against Catharine's, unable to come up with a quip, to tease in return. She could think of nothing beyond the fingers in her hair, the subtle heat warming her face as they soaked in one another. It would be such an impossibly short freeze frame in time, but she wanted to commit it to memory, to take with her as their lives once again drew them apart—for how long, and with what new challenges they would face, neither could know.

A few feet away Halsey coughed, flipping to her side with a moan, and flung the comforter over her head, taking the bottle of Jack and her glass of water off the nightstand. Alex was slow to step apart from Catharine, but the interruption was enough to trespass upon their private meditation. The things she wanted weren't to be had in this setting. Weren't to be had tonight at all.

Repressing a sigh, she brought her fingers to the sleeve of the white jersey Catharine wore, the number eleven emblazoned across the front. "You look good in my shirt."

Whatever jesting response had risen to Catharine's lips was curtailed by boisterous, bawdy laughter filling the hall, followed by another round of *We Got Four Stars On Our Shirts* belted from a cacophony of voices working their way to their own rooms, calling it a night.

"Four a.m. bus, ladies!" A voice louder than the laughter hollered above the chant, a harsh pounding raining down on each door along the corridor. "Four a.m. and no excuses!" It was the deep tenor of Mallory Bell, their admin coordinator and team babysitter, by all curses of the job.

"Twenty-five years out of university and still being forced to slink out of the halls by the resident monitor." Catharine's cerulean eyes danced, her fingers brushing through Alex's hair before she leaned forward and kissed her—lightly, chastely, an option better for them both—before taking a step back, her hands falling to her sides. "You'll call me when you land?"

Alex didn't want to think about calling her tomorrow from across an entire ocean—not when she was here, right now, tangible and within reach. Not when her lips lingered so close she could taste the maltiness of her ale. Smell the citrus of her skin. Tomorrow, when she called her from JFK, this chapter of the summer would be closed. This chapter of her life. The good, the bad, the monumental and devastating. So much in such a short time.

But so much more was to come. She only wished it would begin with Catharine Cleveland by her side.

But they would get there. For once, Alex believed it. Catharine would come back. No matter what happened, they would be together. Catharine had promised. And for the first time, Alex could see the clarity of their future together without haze.

It was the only thought that made the following morning's flight bearable as Alex watched the sun rise over the eastern Atlantic as the United Kingdom disappeared thirty thousand feet below.

Chapter Six

The crisp autumn evening blew in an unwelcome downpour, drenching Catharine's blazer and leaving her hair dripping by the time she stepped into the foyer of the downtown Canary Wharf hotel. She was early, the barrister from *Crown Bridge Chambers* not expected to meet with her in the chic cocktail lounge for another half an hour.

She'd left her Bermondsey flat without a coat, too distracted by her phone call with Gordon Liebermann to consider the weather. He'd rung early in the morning, dialing her from his wife's mobile. "I'm sorry, Mrs. Cleveland," he'd begun the call, his tone more clipped and detached than usual. "All my correspondence has been curtailed. Any future communication will need to go through your counsel directly to my office or I'll be facing a malpractice suit."

His office. The one sharing the floor with her executive suite in San Francisco. Exactly the place she should have been, conducting her own business, overseeing her own staff, leading the company she'd dedicated the better part of her life to.

She wasn't surprised by his admission. She'd known it was coming. People could only stick their necks out so far until they had to decide to save their own skin. Self-preservation was human nature, after all, but it still hurt all the same.

"I understand, Gordon." She'd been grateful her voice remained impassive, unrevealing. "I will move forward on my own, then."

"I'm truly sorry."

"Don't be." She imagined she'd been little successful at stifling the bitterness she felt. Twenty years they'd worked together, and now, when she needed him most—when her entire life's work was on the line—he was the one hired to fight against her. And she still had the pleasure of paying his retainer. The irony of it all…

But it wasn't his fault. He hadn't been the one to put her in this position. "Erev tov, Mr. Liebermann."

She'd hung up the phone and immediately dialed Elle Kirkland, a Queen's Counsel barrister who worked out of the prestigious *Crown Bridge Chambers*. A woman Catharine had elected to be the most qualified individual to replace the Wrightman Firm, after they'd proven to be as worthless as a glass hammer. She'd spoken to Ms. Kirkland a handful of times over the past two weeks, but hadn't pulled the trigger on making anything official. But it was time. Elle Kirkland had the reputation of being cutthroat. A bulldog of a barrister. A woman willing to do whatever it took to win her clients' cases.

Exactly what Catharine needed.

"You picked a charming evening to stop mucking around."

Still prying off her wet suit jacket, Catharine turned in the lobby to find a woman approaching her, shaking out an umbrella. She was sharply dressed in a pencil skirt and tailored blazer, befitting of her profession, but Catharine found herself thrown by the cardinal red of her stiletto heels matching the flaming copper of her hair. She was near Catharine's age, plus or minus a couple years.

"Ms. Kirkland?" The query was only a formality. Catharine recognized her forthright tone from their interactions over the phone.

The woman hummed past her, motioning she should follow. Without pausing for the maître d', she brushed into the crowded dining room and headed for an empty table beside the window. A moment later a server appeared with a highball and bottle of seltzer water.

"Catharine?" The barrister looked at her expectantly as the server lingered for her order.

"Tea, thank you."

"You'll want something stronger for the direction this evening is about to embark." The woman tossed her red hair over her shoulder and slid her glass toward Catharine, motioning for the waiter to bring them another. "Now tell me," she said without pause, leaning her elbows atop the table, "have you come ready for a proper fight, or have you pointlessly dragged me into this miserable weather for nothing?"

They'd discussed her options at length over the phone. Elle Kirkland felt strongly that continuing to attempt to reach middle ground with Benjamin Brooks was a fruitless affair. All previous efforts of reconciliation had been met with irrational demands and ludicrous buy-out offers at less than half the value of her stock. It was time to move to the next measure: suing for oppression of a minority shareholder. A task, Elle had informed her, that would likely be impossible to prove, but a necessary advancement all the same. They needed to rattle the cage. To poke the bear. She wanted Colonel Benjamin Brooks off the rails. Intent to provoke him into deliberate action to make the company fail—and then use the irrefutable proof he'd gone out of his way to founder the corporation to nail him in a suit for violation against their shareholder agreement. All which Elle hoped to achieve by hitting him with a series of less significant litigation.

It was complicated and messy and against every one of Catharine's natural inclinations. She wanted desperately to triage the arterial hemorrhaging of numbers that continued to decline with her father in command. It drubbed her to her core to watch as the corporation floundered, knowing it was all just a stunt to force her to surrender. Her father didn't want Brooks Corp to capsize any more than she did. It was in his blood as much as it was in hers. But he was proving his willingness to risk everything in order to close her out—and they'd entered a game of chicken she wasn't certain either of them could win.

But if anyone could beat him at it, she'd come to decide it would be Elle Kirkland. The woman hadn't fought her way into the center ring of London's most distinguished set of barristers to lay down when a battle turned bloody. She was qualified to stand toe-to-toe with Gordon Liebermann, whether Catharine liked the scarlet of her six-inch heels or not.

"I'm ready to fight."

"Are you?" The woman leaned back in her chair, crossing one long leg over the other, and regarded her beneath the thickness of her painted lashes. She was skeptical in her assessment, her crimson lips pressed in consideration. "Are you certain you are aware of what that might entail?"

"I like to think I make few decisions without being fully informed."

"Ha." Elle reached for the highball sitting in front of Catharine, no longer waiting for the server to return with another. "If I had a penny for every time I heard that, it would be me living on the milk and honey, instead of trudging through a downpour to cater to every flush client's whim." She sipped the whiskey before returning it to Catharine. "If we swing and miss, it's my duty to be certain you understand your father could push for dissolution."

Catharine stared at her through practiced impassivity, knowing the woman was hoping for a reaction. Not to the mention of dissolution, but to the brazen disregard of her station. A reaction Catharine would not grant her.

"As I said, I rarely make decisions unless I am acquainted with all possible outcomes."

"And in this understanding of consequences have you decided what you will do if we fall flat on our faces?"

"It is a decision I will make if and when the time comes."

The barrister steepled her fingers, the ruby-red of her manicured nails accenting her hair. "Fifty-one percent at market value is not a nominal expenditure, even for someone of your silk-stocking status, Catharine. No doubt you realize that."

Catharine said nothing, deeming an answer unwarranted. The woman was right. Fifty-one percent of Brooks Corp. was unattainable. Even if she stockpiled everything, liquified her assets, turned her investments to cash, she wasn't sure it would be enough to purchase her father's stock at face value if it came to a forced buyout. And even if it was, there was no guarantee she would be able to keep the corporation afloat after the last six months of turmoil that had shaken it from its foundation. Not with how much revenue they had lost. Not while Carlton was holding up divorce proceedings while trying to lay claim to her capital. It was a risk she knew would be imbecilic to take. But it was not a decision she would commit to today. Not while there were still avenues to explore.

"Well then," said Elle in response to her silence, "let's string the bastard up. Hold his feet to the fire." She offered a purely rapacious smile, the glint in her caramel eyes unapologetic. "I'll draw up the paperwork and you can pay off my mortgage."

Outside the Canary Wharf Station, Catharine called Alex. It was late in New Jersey, where Alex had arrived two days earlier, but she'd asked for Catharine to call her after she met with the barrister. The rain had stopped, driving the pedestrians back to the street on a busy Friday night, the lifting cloud cover leaving the temperature arctic.

Leaning on the railing overlooking Middle Dock, Catharine wrapped her arms around herself and pinned her mobile to her ear with her shoulder. The sidewalks were glistening with the freshly fallen rain, mirroring the water, reflecting the lights of the towering high-rises sprouting up along the wharf.

"I was just thinking about you." Alex's voice was warm, welcoming compared to the damp frigidity of the night.

"Were you? Good thoughts, I hope?"

"The best thoughts."

Catharine closed her eyes. It was coming on three months since she'd last seen Alex after the World Cup. What was she still doing in London? She had an overwhelming desire to hop on a plane. She could be in Newark by morning. Watch Alex's match tomorrow night. Tell her father to get stuffed and walk away from everything.

"How was the lawyer?" Alex interrupted her thoughts, bringing her back to reality.

"Not what I expected." She thought about Elle's terse manner and brazen comments. The slit in her skirt that rose above mid-thigh. The ridiculousness of her open-toed stilettos on a night suited for sensibility. "Rude. Cocky."

"Aggressive?"

"Barbarous, I imagine."

"Perfect." Alex smiled across the Atlantic. "Just what we ordered."

We. The two simple letters brought a breath of life to Catharine. The feeling she wasn't entirely alone.

There was laughter somewhere on Alex's end in the background. Catharine opened her eyes and watched as a boat skirted along the glossy water. "How's Jersey?"

"Cold! But beautiful. I dragged Halsey to the city to take a run in Central Park this evening and then our subway line had a malfunction and it took us more than three hours to get back

across the Hudson. We just walked in the door a few minutes ago."
Alex hushed someone, then resumed the conversation. "Last game
of regular season tomorrow."

Pulling her hands out of her damp suit coat, Catharine rubbed
them briskly together, trying to return some warmth back into her
fingertips. Her underground left in four minutes, but she knew, as
soon as she stepped into the station, she would lose the call.

"A win by four goals puts the Sirens in second place—granting
you home turf advantage for the semifinals. A win by less than
four seeds you for third. A draw—fourth. And a loss—*not* going to
happen, by the way—finishes the season no lower than fifth. All
outcomes leading to the playoffs."

Alex laughed. "Someone's been paying attention."

"I wouldn't miss a minute of it." Catharine adjusted the phone
in the crook of her shoulder. "I hope you know that, Alex."

"I do." Her answer was sincere and immediate. With each
passing day, Catharine worried she'd begin to resent her. To question their ability to make things work. But Alex had been nothing
but understanding. Encouraging. Gracious in her acceptance that
Catharine was doing everything she could, as quickly as the law
allowed. And for that, Catharine was wholeheartedly grateful. It
wasn't easy for either of them, but having Alex's support made the
mess of her life tremendously more tolerable.

The notification on her watch indicated the *Jubilee Line* was
arriving. She tapped it closed. Another train would follow shortly
after. "Have you had any word from *Kickstar*?"

"No. I'm still scheduled for the Utah photoshoot, as far as I
know."

Alex's new agent had queried the company about an early
termination of her contract. They'd expected the endorsement to
drop her after the World Cup, given the public display against the
grain of their so-called *family values*. But now Alex was worth too
much money, and cash was king in business—trumping their self-
proclaimed morals.

Still, Alex wanted out. *Nike* had approached her, along with
Under Armour. Both brands offering to fully support her without
clause or condition retaining to her personal life.

In another time, in another place, Catharine would have made
Samson Hargrove a buy out offer, but in her current position it was

out of the question. An uncomfortable realization that had forced her to accept the verity of her situation.

A rowdy bunch of young men in suits brushed past Catharine on the walkway, jocular and tipsy from their night on the town. One, with his tie askew and dress shirt half buttoned, turned around to give her a whistle, walking backward as he held up his thumb and pinky to his ear in an imaginary mobile. "You can call me, baby. Anytime!" His mates laughed, dragging him along, and Catharine angled her body back toward the water.

"Where are you?"

"Canary Wharf Station."

"You took the tube?" Alex laughed. "With Malcolm?"

"No. I came by myself."

"Catharine!"

"I'm fine. I don't need a babysitter for every appointment."

"It's not safe right now!"

Malcolm had been of similar opinion, put off by her recent insistence at taking liberties to go places on her own. But she wanted to feel some sense of normalcy. Some form of independence. The threats she received were mostly insubstantial. Blustering busybodies and disgruntled employees making their anger at Brooks Corp. known. It wasn't like she was in the States, where Carlton's fanbase had her name on a voodoo doll in every backwoods town.

Alex's thoughts must have swayed the same direction. "I still can't believe if we get to the semifinals, we'll have to play in DC. Just my luck during an election year."

It was the closest they'd gotten to talking about Carlton. About acknowledging his win over the summer at the National Convention, and his continued rise in polls as they moved into autumn. It was the one subject Catharine didn't want to discuss. Not with Alex. Or Nathalie. Not with anyone. She didn't care if it seemed like she was simply burying her head in the sand.

Part of her was. She refused to accept he'd made his party's ticket. That in six short weeks his presidential bid could actually become a reality. If she didn't lend it oxygen, she could continue to pretend it was all part of the same lingering bad dream.

In any case, come November, it would be decided one way or another. For better or for worse. At least for her it was no longer until death did they part. That was affirmed.

She'd thought his advisors would hustle him to settle out of court. To be done with their divorce proceedings by the time the election rolled around. Instead, he'd driven them straight into a deadlock, reneging on every agreement they had made. He wanted more than she was willing to offer. Unreasonable requests she couldn't financially withstand. And he'd made it clear he was willing to go to trial to try and strip her of everything she owned.

It was just one more temptation to let everything sink. To brush her hands and walk away and be done with the whole damn thing.

But she still had the employees to think of. There were still people counting on her.

And now she had someone willing to fight in her corner. It was possible, with Elle Kirkland, she'd found the champion she needed to get her back in the ring.

"DC… Florida… Timbuktu… it doesn't matter." Catharine made light. "We all know that trophy is coming home with the California team."

"Ha—don't count those eggs before they hatch. We still have a long road ahead."

"Are you guys talking about the championship?!" Catharine could hear the exasperation of Erin Halsey's Mississippi drawl in the background. Alex shushed her but a second later there was a scuffling sound and then the keeper's blaring voice came on the line."What are you trying to do, jinx us, Portland?!"

"Hello, Erin."

"God. I always forget how much that English accent does me in." She tsked. "Still—you know the rules by now. No talking future matches. No matter how sexy you sound."

"Halsey—!" Alex's voice was muffled.

"No, your bright idea cost me three hours of my evening—now you can make up for it by letting me talk to your girlfriend for a while—"

There was another tussle, interspersed with laughter, and then finally Alex returned to the line. "Sorry. Some people, I swear!"

Catharine smiled. "Don't be." She tucked the phone back in the crook of her shoulder and crossed her arms to try and ward off the growing chill. Her watch was notifying her she'd missed the second train. "I'll be cheering for you tomorrow."

"Will you be able to watch?"

"Every second."

"If I score, it'll be for you."

"Oh, gross," Halsey shouted in the background. "Get a room."

Catharine laughed. "Tell her as long as she's not in it, that's a deal."

"I heard that, Portland!"

Alex was quiet for a beat. "I miss you."

"I miss you, too."

"Offseason is right around the corner."

"I'm counting down the days. But first things first—"

"Don't even say it," Alex laughed. "Erin's going to pop a vein."

"Call me after the game?"

"Always."

They hung up and Catharine shook out her stiff limbs as she headed toward the entry of the station. She'd have to wait for the next late night underground.

Chapter Seven

Halsey dropped her iPad onto the breakfast table, hauling her six-foot frame into the chair beside Alex, upsetting her half-eaten bowl of oatmeal. It was Sunday, the morning after their two-nil win against Kryptonite FC in New Jersey. The Sirens had come in third place in the league, solidifying their second consecutive postseason push for a championship title. They'd head into the quarterfinals a week from Wednesday, and as a reward for their efforts, had been granted a week of rest. A reprieve Alex would have gladly welcomed, if she hadn't been scheduled for a three-day commitment in Utah for a Kickstar photoshoot.

"Dude." Halsey jammed a finger at her iPad, drawing Alex's attention to the screen. "I swear, you're like the heel of Achilles when it comes to Ashby."

Alex wasn't sure she wanted to look.

She'd intentionally woken early, beating the rest of her teammates to the self-serve breakfast bar. Sore, tired, and nursing turf burn across her shoulder, she'd hoped to find a peaceful morning alone. Halsey, however—brimming with giddiness—had other plans.

"What now?" asked Alex. She hardly wanted to know.

Last night, at the final whistle, Caleb had orchestrated the Sirens' visiting supporters' section to play a fanfare on the drums and horn, while he stood on the sidewall with a sign that read "Monica Ashby, it's my *goal* to *score* your hand in marriage."

The crowd had ooed and awed—despite his pathetic puns—when Caleb dropped to one knee on the field, soaking up the television cameras turned in his direction. Monica had gone all out for an Oscar-winning performance as she feigned shock at his proposal, jogging over to meet him and throwing herself in his arms.

"They've planned it for three weeks," Rodrigues had scoffed as she, Alex, and Halsey headed for the tunnels. "I heard her and Valerie going on about it in the weight room. They wanted as much television coverage as they could get and decided since this game was aired on *CBS* it would be the best bet for prime time."

Impatient, Halsey shoved the iPad toward Alex, sloshing it through the spilled oatmeal. "She can't win for losing when it comes to you."

Alex glanced at the screen. There, on *The Athletic*, was her photo. She'd scored the first goal of the night, and, in an impromptu goal celebration, run to the sidelines to face one of the TV cameras and held her hands up in the shape of a heart, lipping *I miss you* into the lens. She'd known, even as she did it, that the action would get some publicity, but she hadn't really cared. It was no secret she and Catharine had established themselves as a couple—and it was even less of a secret that they'd spent the last three months apart while Catharine was in London. The news was fascinated with Catharine's battle for her company and Carlton was never quiet on his disgust for his soon-to-be-ex-wife for long. The headlines were daily.

But she hadn't realized, by making the simple gesture, she'd be stealing the limelight from Monica and Caleb. As Halsey swiped through the article of their win against Jersey, she saw her name pop up numerous places, even noting the word Cleveland in the match recap, but there was no mention of Ashby. Or the proposal.

"It's like that on every headline. 'Sirens win big in Jersey and Alex Grey sends adorable message to her overseas girlfriend,' to paraphrase. Only *SheBallz* even picked up on Ashby's engagement —running a thumbnail photo at the bottom of the story—Caleb on his knees. Right where he belongs." Halsey smirked. "Your photo, of course, is the feature."

"Wonderful." Alex mopped up her oatmeal with a paper napkin. "One more thing for her to hate me over."

"You should retweet his proposal video from your birthday with the caption: *Second Time's A Charm*."

"Shut the hell up."

"Can you imagine?" Halsey snagged the napkin from Alex and wiped off her iPad. "Her head would literally explode."

"You guys talking about Ass-by?" Molly Rodrigues dropped into the seat opposite Alex, holding a plate of butter covering the hint of a waffle. "Bree said she's absolutely fuming." The defender bumped her with a tatted forearm. "The evil thunder-stealer strikes again."

"*Hollywood! Hollywood!*" Halsey pumped sotto voce in a mock chant.

"Will you both shut up? I scored a goal. I celebrated it by throwing a heart at the camera. End of story. I didn't even know they had anything planned."

"It was just epic timing. The whole world is in love with the idea of you and Catharine Cleveland. You finally gave them something to talk about and now #Greyland is on the rise again."

Despite Halsey's blithe amusement at Alex's unintentional trumping of Monica's publicity stunt, Alex was less enthused. She hadn't meant for it to be a big thing. She'd only wanted to send Catharine a message. To let her know, no matter how far apart they were, she was constantly on her mind. And, when she'd spoken to her after the game last night—albeit briefly, since it had been two a.m. in London—she'd been glad she had. Catharine had sounded so genuinely touched by the gesture. There'd been nothing but sheer joy in her voice when she answered the call. When she'd told her she received her message. That she missed her, too.

Alex didn't want the media to ruin that.

"Speaking of the devil," Molly's eyes veered toward the breakfast bar where Monica Ashby had just arrived, taking an unusual amount of time to select a banana. It was obvious she was delaying, hoping more of their teammates would turn up so she didn't have to decide between sitting with the two new rookies who'd been signed over the summer, or awkwardly avoiding their trio at the table in the center of the hall.

"Did you see she started a Vlog?" whispered Halsey, safely beneath the Barry Manilow muzak filtering through the room. "*Ashby on the Eighteen, Life as a Professional Soccer Player.*"

"Should have been called *How to Shorten Your Shelf Life as a Professional Soccer Player*, the way she's going." Molly leaned conspiratorially closer. "I'm really hoping the next episode will be titled: *Marrying Alex Grey's Sloppy Seconds.*"

Halsey laughed, too loudly, and Alex watched as Monica stiffened, still sorting through the fruit. Even if she couldn't hear them, she'd know the laughter was directed at her, and Alex didn't want any part of it.

"You guys... *quit*." She meant it. "I don't want any drama."

"It's Ass-by. There's always drama."

Alex bumped Molly's shin beneath the table. "Yeah, and it's all fun and games until it's at your expense."

After what felt like forever, Monica selected her banana and opted to skirt out the door, leaving the room more tolerable. The two rookie girls were slowly shoveling cereal into their mouths, half asleep, while a handful of other hotel guests had filtered in, waiting on the waffle maker.

"Do you think Atwood's going to call her to camp?" Halsey asked no one in particular.

With the Olympic year quickly approaching, they'd have a mid-winter training camp, followed by a handful of friendlies, and then the *SheBelieves Cup* in mid-spring. Based on that tournament, Izzy Atwood would have the impossible headache of whittling down the Melbourne Olympic roster to eighteen. Fortunately, this time around, in Alex's present place in her career, she felt she had a high probability to be chosen to represent the States in the late Summer Games. Unfortunately, she imagined Monica did, too.

"She's still our best center back."

"Yeah," said Molly through a mouthful of waffle, "but she hasn't got the balls to show her face in Melbourne. Doubt she wants her face punched in by Walker a second time."

"What?" Both Alex and Halsey echoed the question.

"You guys live in a clam shell or something? Monica got her ass kicked after the match. That's why she never turned up at the after party. No doubt she was licking her wounds back in her hotel room, too embarrassed to acknowledge she'd been called out."

"By Walker?" Alex didn't believe that. It didn't sound like Amelia. But then again, she had hit Caleb...

"She told Kylie an Australian ambushed her in the tunnel. So, I mean, put two and two together." She grinned. "I'm really hoping she does one of those "The Things We Have in Common" Vlog episodes for her and Caleb... one of the questions can be: What traumatic experience brought you both closer together? And the answer can be: we both had our noses broken by the same Australian."

Alex rolled her eyes. It still didn't sound like Amelia. But it wasn't like she was in a position to text her and ask. She hadn't talked to her since the World Cup. And despite everything, her friendship was still sorely missing in Alex's life.

As more of their groggy teammates rolled into the breakfast hall, the conversation drifted toward the upcoming postseason and likeliness of what two teams would make it to the finals. Naturally, they felt the Sirens would go all the way. Even with their third place finish in regular season standings—two spots down from their inaugural year—they felt strong going into the quarterfinals. Even if they were without their best player.

The only thing Alex was apprehensive about was knowing the semifinals would be held in DC, given the Tyrants second place finish had earned them a guaranteed home game. She didn't relish the idea of being anywhere near the hotbed of the political arena while Carlton Cleveland was still in the race. Especially after the World Cup win, where the otherwise soccer-indifferent United States had suddenly become fully engrossed in the women's game. This year's NWSL Championship was expected to draw a massive number of viewers—more than the previous two postseasons combined. And Alex was finding herself—along with the twenty-two other members of her World Cup squad—recognized by the average Joe more often than not. *Hey, aren't you...?* The girl who kissed Carlton Cleveland's wife on international television? *Yep, hi.*

Alex's phone rang, pulling her out of the conversation with Halsey and Rodrigues. Unexpectedly, it was Nathalie Comtois.

"Hey," she answered, apprehensive.

"Alex, salut! I have a proposition for you."

Chapter Eight

"What do you mean by late?" There was an edge to Nathalie's voice Catharine hadn't anticipated. It wasn't like her to care.

"I don't know, Nat. A couple hours? I'm not sure. I'm sorry, I know it's last minute, but she wants to present the suit before we call Liebermann in the morning."

"You've known I was coming for a week, Cate."

"A couple hours alone in my flat won't kill you!" Catharine glanced at her watch, standing outside the underground station. It was just after five. She had to be in Canary Wharf by six to meet Elle and even if she made the next train, she was cutting it close to running tardy. Something she didn't imagine the peppery barrister would easily pardon. "Have you even retrieved your bag yet? I can have Malcolm pick you up—"

"No! I'm perfectly capable of getting to Bermondsey." Nathalie was still cross. "I guess I'll find supper out on my own and you can ring me when you're available."

"Nat." Catharine sighed, growing frustrated with her friend's vexation. It wasn't like she was out galavanting around London. She was preparing to throw a lawsuit at her father that was bound to blow up in her face. Her meeting with Elle Kirkland was merely to orient her with the minefield she was treading. "Look—I didn't think you'd mind. You usually sleep half the day when you fly in, anyhow. I didn't know Elle was going to want to meet this late on a Sunday, but she got the paperwork finalized and wants to present it to Brooks Corp.'s legal counsel first thing in the morning. I couldn't tell her no—she's gone out of her way to get the ball rolling."

"Oh, well in that case, by all means. We wouldn't want to inconvenience Elle Kirkland. No doubt it's been a strenuous journey for her to take the lift from her sky rise office and meander across the street to whatever swanky restaurant you're meeting in. Nothing as simple as a twelve hour flight in coach with a pack of pretzels and half a can of coke to sustain oneself on. It's fine, really, Catharine." Nathalie pulled out her heavy artillery—she never called her *Catharine.*

"Come to Canary Wharf. Meet us for dinner."

Catharine made the offer with the certainty she'd decline. The last thing Nathalie would want to do was sit through an evening of legal jargon. "We're just going to comb through the documents and discuss possible outcomes. Come have a drink, hold my hand— talk me over this ledge I'm about to jump off."

"Well." Nathalie was silent for a beat on the other line and Catharine paced in front of the entrance to the underground station, waiting for Nathalie to assure her she'd be perfectly satisfied making herself at home back in Shad Thames. "If you insist."

No.

That was a hundred percent not what she wanted. In fact, it was entirely disastrous. Elle Kirkland and Nathalie Comtois would blend together as seamlessly as Matisse and Rembrandt.

Nathalie continued. "What's the dress code?"

"I—" This was her opportunity to remedy her blunder. Assure her it was ritzy. No slacks. Nathalie wouldn't want to have to change. To be forced to dress for the occasion. Not after a long flight. "It's—"

"It doesn't matter. Text me the address. I'll look it up. You'd better hurry. You don't want to keep the dragon waiting."

"Nat—"

The line was dead. Catharine stared at the home screen on her phone. She'd been played perfectly. Nathalie had gotten exactly what she wanted. Her dear, conniving, meddling friend. No doubt she wanted to size Elle up for herself. See if she was as Catharine had described—brutal, brash, opinionated.

Everything Catharine wanted in her legal counsel. And everything she didn't want in the presence of her similarly supercilious best friend.

She sighed, sent over the address for the restaurant, and took the escalator stairs two-by-two in an attempt to make the next train.

The restaurant turned out to be far more posh than Catharine anticipated. Waterfront along South Dock, the only saving grace was that Elle agreed to a table on the patio which ran adjacent to the paverstone sidewalk riddled with businessmen and tourists meandering along the waterway. It gave the setting a more laid-back air, unlike the ramrod formality dictated by its interior. At least on the patio, if Nathalie wasn't properly attired, it wouldn't be so glaringly obvious. Of the Frenchwoman's numerous pet peeves, being underdressed in a social setting was amongst her least favorite.

"I'm not in the habit of having extraneous company join my clients during a business meeting," Elle told Catharine when she mentioned Nathalie might drop in. "I find it distracting and futile. But," the unreserved woman shrugged in concession after instructing the waiter to bring them a pair of Macallans on the rocks, "we're on your penny, Catharine. So I suppose do what you will."

What she *would* was not have someone ruin her whisky with ice cubes, but she held her tongue. Elle Kirkland was impertinent. Presumptuous. Patronizing. But she was a woman playing in a man's world and it was something Catharine admired about her. Something she understood. Her uncouth social graces and dismissal of proprieties was irrelevant when it came to her merits. Brilliant, consummately educated, au courant, and cosmopolitan.

As the evening commenced—Elle pouring over page after page of legal outlines pertaining to the case against her father—Catharine began to have hopes she and Nathalie might get on. At least peacefully enough to glide through the night without a nuclear Armageddon.

Hell, from what Catharine gathered, Elle was single—and there was something about her energy that denoted men might not be her only type. Perhaps...

She abolished the thought immediately. That was the last thing she needed—Nathalie Comtois and Elle Kirkland teamed up together.

It was on this detour Catharine's thoughts had deviated when a shadow crossed over the candlelight of the table, darkening the document Elle was elucidating, one of her manicured nails—today, a blazing coral to match the vibrant peach of her heels—pausing in annoyance at the disturbance.

"Another round of Macallans," said the barrister without looking up, her fingertip tapping the empty glass on the coaster. "Then leave us, please—no further interruptions until we call."

"I'd gladly oblige, but I'm not certain the staff will allow me to pass through the bar again dressed the way I am."

The voice was so unexpected, so offsetting to the scene, even when Catharine looked up, her gaze fully sweeping the figure before them, it took her a moment to respond. A moment to trust her eyes. And then she was out of her chair, uncaring about the commotion it made dragging across the polished concrete, and enfolding the arrival in her arms.

"Oh my God! Alex!" She breathed in the startling nearness of her, the warmth of her cheek against her lips, aware of the eyes of the diners turned their way at the astonished interjection, but without a single consideration for the queries. Even Elle Kirkland's tut of disapproval wasn't enough to dampen her delight. "How...?"

"A good surprise, I hope?"

"The best. The very best." Still off kilter, but beginning to regain some sense of propriety, Catharine withdrew half a step, her hands still clutching Alex's forearms. She was afraid, if she let go, it would all prove to be the runnings away of her imagination. "Aren't you supposed to be in Utah?"

"I am. I—*was*. I... rescheduled."

Catharine didn't imagine rescheduling *Kickstar's* fall catalog photoshoot was a simple matter of changing dates, but she didn't ask. It wasn't the time or place.

"And Nathalie?" She looked around. "Have you come together?"

"No Nathalie, I'm afraid. Just me."

"Just you." Catharine was unable to curb her smile, even as she turned toward Elle and regarded the unmistakable display of annoyance radiating off her arched brows.

"Now that that's over, shall we get back to business?"

Catharine ignored the barrister's effrontery. "Alex, this is Ms. Kirkland. She is handling my litigation with Brooks Corp." Her hand still lingering on Alex's arm, she reached across to an empty table and drew a third chair to their setting for two. "Elle, this is

Alex Grey. My—" she hesitated. She'd never introduced Alex before. Not in this way. It caught her off guard.

"I'm aware of Miss Grey," Elle broke in curtly, casting an indifferent glance in Alex's direction. "How do you do." The greeting was flat, disinterested, and her attention was just as quickly back to Catharine. "Now, if this touching reunion has reached its completion, could we perhaps continue?"

With the subtlety of an amused smile shared between them, Alex took up the added chair, and Catharine attempted to return her focus to the discussion of dilatory procedural tactics and blatant interference mismanagement employed by her father. But Elle may as well have been reciting a translation of the Iliad in Biblical Hebrew. Catharine's only center of concentration was on the warmth of the fingers pressing hers when she found Alex's hand beneath the table, and the intoxication of breathing in her unexpected presence. They'd talked about Alex flying out for a week after the postseason—still weeks away—never once had she expected her to turn up any sooner.

But for all Catharine's focal derailment, Elle had no such trouble, barreling on ahead, determined to finalize the proposal.

"As we discussed the other night, he's given us a fair amount of ammunition, but we have to provoke him to the next level. Make him take a clear step over the edge. I want there to be no question as to his path of vengefulness, rather than sagacity. Does that make sense?"

Catharine had tuned back in just in time to catch the tail end of the question.

"Yes."

"*Catharine.*" There was admonishment in the word. "I hope you're taking this seriously." Elle's eyes skimmed pointedly to Alex, who she—not without reason—clearly felt was a distraction. "I need your focus here."

"It makes sense."

She knew Elle was simply being thorough. She wanted her to understand the magnitude of repercussions avalanching their direction once they embarked on this path of legal action. She'd read the paperwork the barrister had sent over line for line the night before. She knew the corporation was going to flail in the fray, listing in the fight. Jobs would be lost. Exportations halted.

Contracts withdrawn. This was going to cost her far more than capital. It was going to cost her integrity. Peace of mind. Families would be hurt in the loss of employment. Lives changed. Catharine had gone from tiptoeing around her father, protecting her employees with everything she had, to now being the one to willingly throw down the gauntlet, baiting him to compromise as many jobs as she could in an effort to show blatant mismanagement and acts of violation against their shareholder agreement. Those people would be on her conscience. Whatever happened to them—she would be the one to blame.

She just didn't know any other way. As Elle had told her the night before, she couldn't sit around on her thumbs and hem and haw while simply hoping to keep an even keel. Holes had already staved the hull. Continuing to do nothing was the surest way to sink the ship. She had to take action. And she wasn't going to go down without a fight.

But she didn't want to talk about it anymore. They'd exhausted all the possible avenues. She trusted Elle to lead her in the right direction. And now the only thing she wanted to do was end the meeting and find herself alone with Alex. Find out how long they had. Hours? Days? A week? The Sirens would have their first postseason match the following Wednesday, so it wouldn't be longer than that.

Alex squeezed her hand and Catharine realized the table had gone silent. Elle was looking at her expectantly. A question had been asked.

"I'm sorry?"

"You know," Elle's amber eyes narrowed, glinting in the candlelight of the centerpiece, her hair glowing a hue of crimson to match her incensed tone, "I didn't earn my silks, nor build my reputation as one of the most formidable barristers in all of Great Britain, in order to waste my time sitting third-wheel in your heartwarming reunion. Perhaps, Catharine, you and Miss Grey would like to take a hiatus and you and I can reconvene on some later date when preserving your tumbling empire is of more importance?"

Catharine opened her mouth, prepared to snap an offense, unable to imagine Gordon Liebermann speaking to her in such a manner. But then she imagined Elle Kirkland handling Liebermann with the same striking indelicacy, and held her tongue. This was why she'd hired her. She'd not retained her for her charm.

"If it's okay," said Alex, without any sign of affront, "I've been sitting for the last ten hours. I wouldn't mind stretching my legs." She stood, not allowing Catharine the time to oppose her leaving. "Why don't you finish your meeting and text me as soon as you're done?"

"A footballer with sensibility," said Elle, nodding in curt approval. "What a rare combination."

If Alex took offense to the backhanded remark, she didn't show it. Instead she smiled at Elle with an acquiescing tilt of her head, and bent to kiss Catharine's cheek. "Don't rush on my account," she said cheerfully, and then, with her lips lingering against her ear, whispered, "but I promise I can think of a better way to spend the evening than discussing legalese."

Catharine missed whatever dismissive comment Elle tossed at Alex's departure, busying herself with a sip of the watered down whiskey. She was certain her cheeks had colored, but if Elle noticed, she gave no indication, instead returning at once to their discussion, tapping a coral nail to another file folder.

"Now, he doesn't possess drag-along rights, so that will work in our favor…"

Resigned to finish the meeting, Catharine stared at the document, trying to pretend her attention hadn't just followed Alex out the door.

Chapter Nine

Skirting along the Canary Wharf docks, where gulls dipped and dove into the still October water, Alex continued south on the peninsula. She had no destination in mind, but welcomed the walk after spending half the day strapped into a seat beside a neighbor who never got the memo armrests were meant to share.

Her duffle—consisting only of a change of clothes, her running shoes, and a paperback she'd grabbed in the Newark airport—bounced against her hip as she jogged across East Ferry Road toward a sign indicating an upcoming park. She felt as if she were seeing London for the first time, even after having spent the better part of July viewing England's capital through a bus window. But that had been different. That had been work. Soccer. Goals. Pressure. This was just—life.

She regretted interrupting Catharine's business meeting. Not only because she'd irritated Elle Kirkland—who was every bit as brusque and dogmatic as she'd been made out to be—but because she truly didn't want to distract Catharine. Not with the things at stake. Not knowing how much stress Catharine was under.

For days she'd been second-guessing herself on the phone to Alex, trying to make the right decisions. It was the reason Alex had hesitated coming when Nathalie called and made the suggestion. She hadn't cared that she'd have to call *Kickstar* and make up an excuse to put off her trip to Utah, but showing up in London, unannounced and uninvited, was a different situation. She hadn't been sure the unexpected visit would be fair to Catharine.

Which was exactly Nathalie's selling point.

Catharine needed her. She was going through one of the most difficult times in her life. Having Alex there to support her would be good for her heart.

"She needs what you can offer her, ma poupée," the French woman had persisted, all innuendos intended, "far more than she needs me. Trust me on this, Alex." So trust her, Alex had. And within thirty minutes of the call she'd postponed *Kickstar*, sent her travel gear home with Halsey, and redirected her departing flight from Newark to land in Heathrow.

And, judging by Catharine's reaction to her arrival, she'd made the right call. Even if she had disrupted the business meeting and turned herself into Public Enemy Number One in the eyes of Catharine's fire-breathing counsel. It had been worth it.

Taking the stairs two-by-two to the park rolling out below the roadway—an impressive amount of greenery, given she was in the middle of the densely populated business district—Alex felt none of the fatigue she should have after crossing the Atlantic. She was wound too tight with the simple knowledge she was in the same city as Catharine. That—after nearly eleven months since the worst day of her life the past Christmas Eve—they would have more than a few minutes together. As she skirted the last steps of the stone staircase, she could think of nothing more than the sensation of Catharine's cheek against her lips.

Reaching the walkway separating the grass fields and sports complex from a neighboring wooded area with a marker that read *Mudchute Park and Farm*, Alex slowed her steps to watch an assorted group of girls kick a ball back and forth along the mediocrely kept pitch. They were unevenly matched, seven-versus-eight, shouting and laughing and heckling one another as they lobbed the ball across the grass.

A long-haired brunette, more talented than the rest, outpaced a pair of midfielders before driving a pass to a waiting attacker beside the far post. The play was offsides, but it didn't matter, because the forward missed the trajectory of the header and bounced the ball away from the net, where it rolled past the end line to land at Alex's feet.

"Oh, c'mon, Freya," the brunette groaned, followed by various utterances of disappointment from the rest of her squad. "You botch every cross!"

The forward, Freya, kept her eyes on her cleats as she shuffled to retrieve the ball.

With a flick of her toe Alex bumped the ball into the air, bouncing it from her knee to her chest and back to her foot, before gently lobbing it into the girl's waiting hands. Clumsy, still feeling the effects of her teammates' disappointment, she dropped the ball and had to chase it back across the end line.

The midfielder who'd made the cross sauntered over with all the arrogance of a newly anointed teen.

"Ya dunce," she threw at Freya, before snatching the ball from her arms and turning her attention toward Alex. In a ostentatious display of what she no doubt felt was unparalleled skill, the girl juggled the ball from foot to foot, finishing with a heel flick to catch it nonchalantly behind her back.

"You play?" she asked Alex with the shrug of a bony shoulder. "We're short one."

Alex was going to decline—her jeans and Vans incompatible for running up and down the ill-maintained grass—but her absurdly over-competitive drive found her mirroring the girl's flippant shrug.

"Sure. Why not." Alex pulled out her cell and dropped Catharine a pin of her location, then tossed the phone in her bag. She considered changing into her running shoes, but forwent the effort, reminding herself they were just teenagers playing pickup, for God's sake.

"You any good? If so, you're on our team," said another girl who had jogged to the end line. "Otherwise you can be with Freya."

"She ain't going to be any good, she's a coffin dodger—keep her on your side, Lily." This was from a sloop-shouldered, round-faced girl with acne-covered cheeks.

"Well?" The brown-haired midfielder, Lily, bounced the ball impatiently on the grass. "Do you know how to play proper or not?"

Alex schooled her twenty-eight-year-old-self to chill out—they were only kids—as her first instinct was to tell the kid who'd called her a coffin dodger to fuck off.

She gestured for the ball. "Let's go. I'll take Freya's team." She glanced at the girl who'd missed the header who was regarding her shyly from behind a veil of mis-chopped bangs. "From the goal kick, then?" The girl nodded uncertainly and Alex jogged past Lily, popping the ball from her arms and tossing it to the keeper.

They played for about fifteen minutes, Alex tucking into the midfield, taking care to pass to her least talented teammates and go easy on the defense. The game was mostly a series of stops and restarts while the two teams hacked the ball up and down the pitch and out of play for throw-ins. The girl who'd called her a coffin dodger—Olivia was her name—was aggressive and late with her tackles and threw her brawnier weight around, careless with her fouls and challenges. By the third time she'd come in for a fifty-fifty ball and found Alex's shin instead, Alex abandoned her attempt at fair play tactics, megging the girl and leaving her standing by center circle while she split a pair of center backs and arched a perfectly weighted ball from outside the eighteen directly into the far corner of the net.

"Mint!" A red-haired midfielder—all knees and elbows—fist pumped the air in triumph, rushing over to pat Alex's back. "What a screamer!"

"Bet you can't do that again," grumbled Olivia, trodding up with heavy steps to reset.

A slender girl with intricate cornrows shot Olivia a disdainful look. "Fiver says she can. You don't know who she is."

Alex realized her new champion was actually a boy—the only boy amongst the group of hormonal teenage girls—delicately-featured and tenor-toned, his voice not yet having gone through puberty. She could tell from his side-eye he knew who she was. It was a look she'd grown accustomed to in airport terminals and super market aisles, jogging trails and restaurants.

The admonishment rallied Olivia's interest, her eyes narrowing, disappearing into slits below her acne festered brow. "Oh yeah? Who is she then?"

The boy jutted out his angular chin. "Alex Grey."

Olivia's eyes snapped to Alex. "The American? Nah, you're full of shit." She shook her head. "My dad says she's a doughnut bumper. She don't look like one. Too pretty."

"Shut the hell up, Olivia. Mia's mum's gay." They all looked over at a tall, gangly girl who suddenly shrunk a half foot into the uneven turf.

"Yeah, but her mum looks like one of them carpet munchers." She jerked her nonexistent chin at Alex. "She doesn't."

"Who cares what she is," Lily, the leader of the pack, spat, annoyed. She'd softened to Alex over the course of play, recognizing she was no longer the most skilled player on the team. "Are you really Alex Grey?"

Alex gave a wave of her hand, a little staggered by the turn in conversation. She'd forgotten how ruthless teenagers could be. "Every day since birth."

There was a surge of excitement, followed by a rapid-fire round of questions intended to prove her identity, and then the predicted request for photos. Alex obliged, even for Olivia, who felt the need to tell her she'd been rooting for the Aussies. "Least they know it's football," she goaded, even while smiling for the camera.

"You're a tool, 'Liv," said Lily, tossing back her cell phone. "They call it soccer in Australia."

Alex ignored the argument between the teens and unzipped her bag to see if Catharine had called. There were no notifications, so she went back to play for a while, which turned to Alex answering questions about footwork and showing individual players what they could work on to improve their skills.

It was in the middle of showing Mia-with-the-gay-mom how to strip the boy, Anthony, off the ball—which unfortunately took little effort—that Alex realized Catharine was watching from the touchline. She was leaning up against a light post that had come on at sunset to illuminate the field, her silhouette cast in shadow.

Distracted, Alex lost the challenge to Mia, and her teammates all cheered, while Alex offered her a pat on the back and a rushed *well done* before jogging off the grass.

There were a few more requests for photos, but Alex waved them off—been there, done that—and wished them well on their game. By the time she reached Catharine the play had resumed behind her and the kids were back to harassing one another, arguing who would take a free kick.

"What is the saying? You can take the girl away from football, but not football away from the girl?"

Alex wiped a forearm across her brow, realizing her shirt was damp with sweat and her jeans speckled in mud and grass—an acute contrast to Catharine's pressed formal business attire.

"Sorry," she smiled, embarrassed she was still trying to catch her breath. "I think I got a little carried away."

"I'm not sure which of us had it worse—me with Elle Kirkland or you in a melee with a group of teenagers?"

Alex laughed. "I think you win—I'll stick with the kids." Slinging her bag over her shoulder, she fell into step beside Catharine, following her as she lead to a bridle path that climbed away from the sports park and up into a canopy of trees, before letting out on a well-maintained trail winding between paddocks of a farm. *Mudchute Equestrian Centre* read a sign along the side of the path, the letters barely distinguishable in the settling darkness.

In their silence, Alex became acutely aware of their privacy— their aloneness—with nothing but a small herd of llamas and horses grazing in the distance to share their company. The former tightness returned, a heightened sense of nervous anticipation as they walked along the white rail fence, so close together their hips were nearly brushing.

"I can't believe you're really here," said Catharine suddenly, stopping in front of one of the horse paddocks, catching Alex's hand.

"I'm sorry I interrupted your meeting."

"It was the best interruption I could have asked for."

"I'm not sure your attorney would agree."

Catharine smiled, the contour of her magnificent cheekbones lifting in her silhouette. "Fortunately I'm not paying her for her opinion on my dinner dates." The playful temerity of her voice died off as she slid her hand up Alex's arm, drawing her forward by her elbow, intent to close the space between them. And then all at once the months of hurting, of aching, of uncertainty and anguish, flooded to the surface, then abruptly disappeared as Catharine's lips met hers.

If there was such a thing as the proverbial *coming home*—of finding your way after having been violently shifted off course, floating adrift through wayward waters until at last a current stronger than your errant wanderings funnels you back where you belong—it was this. This moment. This familiarity. This demanding needfulness that matched her own.

Found.

And then lost again—lost in the efficacy of yearning, the headiness of being unable to distinguish where her mouth ended and Catharine's began. The outlying knowledge that this fervency, these shared seconds of unabashed, unrestrained desire were only the beginning.

Tempted by the dark, by the seclusion of their current situation, Alex forced herself to grapple for a foothold on reality. Reminding herself—even as her fingers sought skin from beneath the hem of Catharine's tailored blouse——where they were. That this quaint park in the middle of the city was not the place to take this too far —not when they were just a few hundred feet from the sporting fields just down the slope, concealed only by trees and dusk darkened greenery.

Catharine—her hands in Alex's hair, her own breathing as erratic as the discordant strumming of Alex's heart—must have had similar considerations, as Alex felt a half strangled laugh escape Catharine's mouth, and the reluctant withdrawal as Catharine dropped her hands to her shoulders, slowly, delicately separating their lips.

"I think I'd better not add defending me against a charge of outraging public decency to Ms. Kirkland's laundry list of tasks we'll be taking to court."

"Where's your sense of adventure?" Alex teased, struggling to catch her own breath.

In the paddock behind them an ambling shape shifted through the shadows, approaching the ranch rail fencing, and a long neck stretched forward over the top board, making a lazy inquiry to the evening visitors.

"Well, hello," said Catharine, reaching to stroke the velvet nose of the friendly horse, who was joined immediately by another. "This is exactly what I'm talking about. We've a pair of stalking voyeurs."

Alex laughed, piecing herself back together as she offered the back of her hand to be sniffed by a whiskered muzzle. "I can't believe there's a riding centre in the middle of the city."

"I think you'll find we do love our parks here in England." Catharine stroked the broad forehead. "My first riding lessons were taken at this farm, in fact. My mum drove me twice a week to ride a fat pony named Polka."

Alex's thoughts diverted, trying to picture Catharine as a child. Trying to imagine her carefree, without the weight of responsibilities surrounding her now. And then she realized there had probably never been a time like that in Catharine's life. She had probably never been given opportunity to simply be a kid. The expectations of her had never been less than what they were. It wasn't like an after-school soccer program or parks and rec dance class to fill the Friday nights. For a child of her station it was simply what was expected. A hobby at which she must excel.

"Did you enjoy riding?" she asked, all the same.

Catharine's attention remained on the horses. "I did, actually." It seemed a revelation to herself. "I rode all through university, but I was never a great equestrian. Not like my mother. She was good at sports—very athletic. Accomplished at horses, tennis, fencing, sailing—anything she picked up." She slipped her hand into Alex's, resuming their walk. "You'd like her."

"Have you heard from her?" A couple months earlier Catharine had said she was going to try and contact her. To reach out not only to seek her aid in attempting to sway Colonel Brooks' mind when it came to the business, but also in an effort to reconnect the relationship they'd lost. But she'd not mentioned it again and Alex hadn't asked. She'd never been forthcoming on discussion of her family.

"No." There was no elaboration on if her inquiries had been ignored or if she'd never tried. "So tell me," she said, turning the conversation, "how did you and Nathalie ever manage to pull this off without me suspecting a thing?"

Hip to hip, they strolled through the park, passing the barns and arena, their steps turning onto a long asphalt drive that wound through another series of paddocks and treelined barrier until it let out on the roadway running adjacent to the train station. The Sunday night crowd was thin, the platforms sparsely habited with commuters and locals making their way home for the evening.

They'd talked easily about Nathalie, and Elle, and Alex's impromptu visit allotting them the four days they'd have together, but as the underground let out on the south side of the river and they began an unhurried walk toward Catharine's home in Shad Thames, Alex found herself growing quiet. An unexpected timorousness had worked its way into her nerves, not too dissimilar from the uncertain anticipation she'd found on the drive to Half Moon Bay a year and a half earlier.

Things had changed, of course, since that drive along the coast. She'd known Catharine so little then, and known herself even less. Now, she knew Catharine well, despite their time apart, and had found herself in the meantime.

But it didn't change her shallowing breath as they stepped into the private elevator, or the tingling sensation that met her skin as their hands brushed exiting on the top floor of Catharine's penthouse.

The home was different than she'd remembered it. Brighter. More open. They'd come out on the master suite landing, the spacious bedroom unfolding into north-facing walls of glass, Tower Bridge brightly lit little more than a hundred feet in the distance.

As Catharine went to her dresser to drop her purse and phone, Alex stepped onto the balcony. The night held none of the chill expected of an October evening in England and despite her whirling mind, she found the view mesmerizing. The snaking river, the historic docks, the magnificence of the city skyline—all headlined by the beauty of the bridge. It was so different in this context. So different from the only other time she'd been on that balcony, after her mishap with Sam Huntley. She'd left that day, certain she'd lost Catharine forever. Certain to never find herself in this position again.

Steps sounded on the travertine, but Alex didn't turn. Instead she welcomed the arms that slid around her, leaning back into Catharine, savoring the warmth of the embrace. She could feel the rapid heartbeat drumming through Catharine's chest, aware of the subtle stiltedness to her breath. The simple knowledge Catharine shared in some of Alex's trepidation was soothing to her nerves.

"It's beautiful," said Alex, referring to the view.

"You are." The words were smiled into the nape of her neck as Catharine brushed her hair aside, her lips hovering against her ear.

Alex's immediate reaction was to laugh, to self-deprecate, but Catharine silenced her with a gentle fingertip pressed against her lips.

"You are," she repeated, her hands moving over the slope of her shoulders. "Beautiful," she continued, caressing a path down her breasts, "thoughtful," her palms glided along the flat of her stomach, "brilliant," they stopped at the button on her jeans. "Talented. Considerate. Witty. Clever. Shall I continue?"

Alex's body stilled, strung taut as a violin, though she was unable to keep herself from smiling at the double entendre. "I wouldn't stop you," she offered coyly, leaning further into Catharine's embrace.

This was what she'd been missing.

It was so much more than just the physical reaction. More than just the mouth that found every contour of her neck, setting her synapses on fire, or the free hand that ventured up her shirt, working deft fingers beneath the smooth charmeuse material of her bra. More than the hand that unfastened her jeans, trailing an excruciatingly slow, tortuous path to find her, to wake her, to rouse her, making her entire body shudder. It was more than the breath which was stolen from her as she struggled to keep her legs from buckling, forced to reach forward and hold herself up against the railing.

It was all of that—but it was so much more. It was the way she looked at her when Alex turned in her arms, the depth the blue eyes saw. The need. The mutual want. The understanding. She saw so much of her—all of her—things Alex wasn't even sure she wanted to share.

The physical need of her was intense, irrefutable, almost paralyzing, but the emotional want was of a similar extreme. Just as powerful. Just as raw.

When it became too much, when Alex could stand it no longer—when weakness flooded through her, her body aching, not just to be touched, but to respond in kind—she disentangled herself from Catharine, breathless, urgent as she caught her hands and pulled her with stumbling steps through the balcony doors, the glass reflecting the forgotten lights of London in the background.

Well after the sounds of the late night traffic had dwindled, the lights fading into little more than a glow on the horizon—when their bodies were spent and slack from tension, their clothing discarded in a trail across the polished wooden floor, the luxurious sateen sheets twisted between them—they lay together, limbs intertwined, the quiet broken only by the shallow whisper of their breathing.

Alex's fingers drew a lazy pattern from the crest of Catharine's hips, up along her ribcage, tracing the outline of her breasts. Wondering, already, how she would drag herself onto a plane in a short ninety-six hours. No, she looked at the face of the clock on the wall. Ninety-three hours. She calculated how many days it would be until the official end of postseason—should the Sirens make it to the championship. Twenty-one days. She worked out the math. Five hundred four hours. Plus an eight hour flight if she left directly after the match. Five hundred twelve hours. More than thirty thousand minutes. Almost two million seconds.

"Sagacious."

The word drew her from her arithmetic, and she caught Catharine's eye in question.

"You didn't let me finish earlier." Catharine arched the subtlety of a brow, rolling onto her side, propped up on an elbow.

Alex told herself not to stare. Then cast away the self-admonishment. She could stare all she wanted. Put to memory every curve, every feature, every perfect detail.

"I think you finished," she challenged with a smile, rolling on her own side to press against the length of her. "More than once, if I recall."

"Cheeky," Catharine countered, continuing with her list. "Enchanting. Captivating. Surprising. Scintillating."

Alex laughed. "What even is scintillating?"

"Similar to effulgent, but with more chatoyancy."

"You're teasing me."

"Never." Catharine smiled, and Alex felt one of her hands work its way along her thigh as the other slipped to the back of her neck, drawing her forward. "You'll know when I'm teasing you."

Alex closed her eyes, trying not to count the hours.

Chapter Ten

Elle Kirkland's harrying tone struck the solace of the morning like a diminished chord in the middle of a consonant harmony.

"You sound half asleep. Why are you whispering?"

Catharine crossed the back of her hand over her eyes, squinting into the early light sinking through the east-facing wall of glass. Judging by the sun, it wasn't more than six-thirty in the morning.

She rolled away from Alex, trying not to wake her. "Is everything all right?"

"I've had a thought on the Service of Process. Is now a bad time?"

Catharine could hear Elle tapping her pen against her desk on the other end of the line. Impatient. Judgmental. As always.

"No." She sat up, her voice still hushed. Alex remained asleep beside her. "It's fine. Give me a moment."

"Long night?"

It was difficult to differentiate the woman's teasing from her disapproval. Not that Catharine cared either way. But she couldn't fault her for doing her job. It was Catharine who had abruptly ended their meeting the night before after Alex's unexpected arrival. She'd tried to keep her mind on business, trying to focus on what Elle was telling her, but half an hour after Alex had disappeared down the wharf, she'd told Elle they'd need to adjourn for the evening.

She'd meant to reconvene at the barrister's office later this morning, as they'd planned. She hadn't expected a sunrise phone call.

Sweeping her hair into a loose pony tail, she pulled on her dressing gown and padded silently across the floor to slip onto the balcony. It was brisk, the weather having turned from the warmth the previous day.

"I'm sorry," her volume normalized as the glass door clicked shut behind her, "please continue."

The woman tutted and Catharine could practically feel the roll of her eyes. "Well, as we were discussing last night—before your libido took your brain hostage—we want him acting without thinking. We want his immediate knee-jerk reaction. So in the middle of the night, while you were... doing whatever you were doing... I had a change in plans—I want to draw the charges out. Hit him with one suit at a time. Make him feel like it is an on-slaught of impending, never-ending litigation. Starting with the sexual orientation discrimination. Then the wrongful termination filing. Followed by the complaint for retaliatory action. Then," she continued without pausing, "we wait for him to make the next move—hoping he'll take the bait to allow us to charge him with breaking the binds of the Shareholder Agreement. It may not win your job back, but it will certainly up the ante."

Catharine didn't relish the upcoming legal campaign. She'd initially refused the idea of allowing Elle to sue for anything pertaining to discrimination based on sexual orientation. She hadn't wanted to expose her life—or Alex's—to the onslaught of media that would follow. She'd wanted to keep her private life private.

But that ship had sailed. And now she needed every ounce of help she could muster to try and win this battle.

Fortunately, Alex had sounded unconcerned when she'd men-tioned it to her the previous week on a phone call. She'd simply told Catharine to do whatever she needed to do. She would sup-port her whatever route she took.

But at what point the cost superseded the value, Catharine wasn't certain.

"All right," she said, leaning against the railing overlooking the Thames. The morning was gray and the river was swathed in fog, the towers of the bridge visible in only a dew laden silhouette. "Whatever you think is the best course of action."

"I would never suggest anything but the best course of action," Elle returned loftily. "Now—can you be at the office at nine, or has your young paramour turned your attentions elsewhere?"

Catharine stifled a sigh, reminding herself Elle Kirkland was the right choice to go up against Gordon Liebermann. Not only the right choice, but one of the only choices. There had not been endless London litigators willing to take on Benjamin Brooks. They were intimidated by him, undesiring to draw his ire. But Elle had shown no hesitation at crossing swords with Catharine's father. It garnered her a touch of leeway in her audacious lack of decorum. "All right. Nine."

She hung up and stepped back into the suite. Alex had shifted, rolling onto her back in Catharine's absence, but her face was still slack with sleep. Catharine watched her—the dark, sweeping lashes, tanned skin, the hint of dimples dormant in her cheeks—and memories of the previous night cycled on repeat.

Catharine had worried, on their walk from the train station toward her flat, that an awkwardness might arise. They'd been apart longer than they'd ever been together, and their relationship had been fragile from the start. It would be natural for some hesitation to take place. Some reservation to creep in. But to her surprise, Alex had shown nothing of her former uncertainty. Rather, she was bold, decisive, confident in ways she'd never been. She left no room for apprehension. She knew what she wanted— and knew what she wanted to offer in return. It had been startling, yet intoxicating—alluring—slowly getting to know a person all over again. A person who had grown. Evolved. Who had once felt fragmentary, but now seemed complete.

An evolution Catharine imagined she had Amelia Walker to thank—a concept she wasn't currently willing to entertain.

Across the room, Alex's eyelids fluttered—perhaps in an unconscious response to being held under observation—and Catharine fought the urge to return to her bed. To blow off her commitments. To wrap herself in Alex once more.

Her body carried a welcome ache in the wake of their evening. Her lips felt bruised from kisses she'd never wanted to end. Her muscles taxed. The entirety of her awakened, heightened and alive.

As she headed for the shower, she could smell Alex, even now, the scent of her branded on her skin. The subtle combination of shea butter and ivory soap, combined with an aroma that was just distinctly Alex—fresh, the outdoors, as if someone could bottle sunshine and the wind.

Catharine took a last glance at her, before stepping into the en suite, reluctant to start her day. She'd have forfeited her fortune to spend the little time they had together. To wake, hours from now, by her side.

Discarding the dressing gown on the doorknob, the thought crossed her mind that perhaps she had given her fortune for the right to lie beside her. Their relationship had cost her everything. And she would do it over, again and again, even if she'd known the outcome in the end. Brooks Corp., Carlton, her father… She would change nothing. Not if lead back to where they were this morning.

Lost in these thoughts, standing in the cool stream of water, movement over her shoulder caught her eye.

Alex—dazed with sleep, her dark hair tussled—stood at the entrance to the shower, Catharine's dressing gown wrapped around her.

"Good morning." Catharine caught her eye in the reflection of the silver faucet before turning to face her.

A slow smile touched Alex's lips as her eyes swept across her from head to toe, and Catharine—no matter how ridiculous the notion—found herself grappling against an impulse of modesty. It was not as if there was any part of her Alex hadn't seen. That she hadn't shared. Yet in the brilliant glow of the morning sun flooding through the skylight, she couldn't help but appreciate the gossamer curtain of water between them.

"Good morning." Alex leaned against the flush wall of granite, continuing to watch her. "You're up early."

"The misfortune of a meeting at *Crown Bridge Chambers* at nine, I'm afraid."

"Some things never change." Alex's tone was playful as she pushed her lean frame upright and slackened the tie loosely draped around her waist. "I still wake to find you running out the door. What is the saying? You can take the girl from her work, but can't take the work from the girl?"

"In my defense, I did think it was Nathalie I'd be running out on this morning."

"Well, in that case," said Alex, shrugging off the dressing gown and tossing it carelessly to the vanity counter, "perhaps I'll have better luck finding a way to convince you to delay?"

For whatever reticence Catharine contended, Alex showed no sign of sharing in her timidity. And why should she? Michelangelo himself could not have sculpted a more pristine reflection of physical perfection. Lithe, graceful, at the height of fitness and with the fountain of youth still lending Alex its gift of flawless transcendence, there was not a single consideration for which she should have been self-conscious. Unlike Catharine, who—though not so self-critical to think she'd lost all her allure—was beginning to feel the slow march of age. In the fine lines that threatened when she laughed. The crease that deepened when she smiled. The sprinkling of gray hairs that dared to make an unwelcome appearance at her temples.

Her apprehensions were forgotten, however, as Alex approached. "It depends," she said, matching the sultriness of her tone, "on if the reward is greater than the wrath of Elle Kirkland."

"A steep challenge, but I think I'm up to the task." Alex smiled. "Only one good way to find out." She stepped into the overhead stream, but immediately recoiled as the chill of the water took her by surprise. "Jesus!" She stumbled backward, half laughing, half gasping. "What are you, a monster? What kind of person willingly takes a cold shower!?"

Amused, Catharine reached behind her, turning up the dial to a more reasonable temperature. "A vampire, perhaps?"

"Hmm," Alex disagreed, "I was thinking more along the lines of Dorian Gray."

"Ah. Less bloodsucking. More soulless. I'll take it."

"Well, that, and—" Alex reached forward, testing the water, before stepping close to Catharine, water rivulets trickling down her face. "Eternally beautiful."

"You're only saying that in case it does, indeed, turn out that I'm a cold-blooded monster. Flattery will get you nowhere, Miss Grey."

"On the contrary," Alex touched a finger to her lips, tracing it down her neck, along the curve of her collarbone, teasing a hardening nipple, until she came to rest her splayed palm against her abdomen. "It's only flattery when it isn't true. However," she offered a waggish smile, her fingertips gliding further south, past her navel, skimming only the faintest touch across her skin as the steam from the water rose around them, "even if it weren't true— which, it is—but even if it weren't, I'd still wager flattery will get me plenty of places." She knelt, slowly, deliberately, retracing the path of her fingers with her mouth, awakening every fiber of Catharine's body.

For a moment, Catharine found her attention swayed by the awareness of a tattoo she'd not seen in the darkness of the previous evening. Along her left ribcage, inked in black, was the very simple outline of a compass with the words *Big Picture* written in the center. It was small, crisp, unobtrusive. Little different than the soccer ball she had on her hip. But this one was new since Catharine had last seen her, and the words, unremarkable on their own, were familiar. She'd heard them more than once in postmatch interviews—it was a common phrase spoken by Amelia Walker. "The best players step on the field and always have their mind on the big picture."

A permanent reminder of the time they'd had apart. Of the person who'd been there for Alex through her darkest hours.

Catharine tried not to let it bother her. Tried not to dwell on it. They were just words, after all. A saying in sports—in life in general. *Always look at the big picture.* Advice she would do well to remember herself.

And as quickly as her thoughts had been sidelined, her attention was turned again—turned to the hands that teased her with the brush of fingertips, the preface of a prelude as Alex kissed a trail across her hip, commanding Catharine's body to forget everything but the present moment, water pooling down her skin.

She hadn't known, hadn't realized—in all the time they'd been apart—to what extent she'd missed the intimacy they'd shared. How much she craved it. Not only in the physical reaction—the awakening of her desire—but the emotional connection; the shared closeness, the allied confidence and growing familiarity.

Oblivious to the time, or to her impending meeting downtown in Elle Kirkland's high-rise fifty-second floor office, or to the pruning of fingertips and tangling of hair, Catharine lost herself in the sheltered world contained behind the vitreous shower walls. To arched backs and racing hearts. Limbs weakened by fervor. Breath stains on water-streaked glass. The cool press of granite.

Breathless.

Uninhibited.

Rhapsodic.

It was a quarter after eight when Catharine tugged trousers over her damp skin, her hair still dripping down the navy blouse she'd struggled into in her hurry. She could feel Alex's eyes on her as she sat cross-legged on the furthest end of the vanity sink top, a towel draped casually over her shoulders, the rest of her unclad.

Even in her rush, Catharine found her gaze straying to catch Alex's in the reflection of the mirror, unable to hide her smile. "You've made me late."

"I'd wager it was worth it."

Catharine gave a feigned huff, steeped in pseudo-indifference, as she finished fastening a pearl earring and debated on taking the time to apply a layer of basic makeup. In truth, she wasn't sure how she was going to manage to sit in front of Elle and her associates, listening to their endless monotony of litigation recommendations, while pretending her mind was anywhere other than reliving every detail of their morning. As if her entire body wasn't humming. As if the taste of Alex didn't linger on her tongue. The sound of her staggered breath wasn't caught in her ear. As if she couldn't still feel the tremble of their bodies clasped together.

Forgoing the makeup, she took a last look in the mirror, resigned to meet Elle as-is. She was a mess. Hair wet. Ruddy-faced from the heat of the shower. Her pantsuit clinging to her damp skin. Her gaze flicked to where Alex sat watching her, the towel dropped to her waist. Even sitting as she was, cross-legged, her elbows on her knees, bent at an angle that would have given any woman pause, she looked ridiculously faultless. The lean muscles of her stomach flat, her breasts shapely, yet petite, suited to her athletic body, the well-knit slope of her shoulders half-hidden by the length of her wet hair, currently black as the underside of a raven's wing.

"You're nervous," Alex observed as Catharine drew near, intent to kiss her goodbye.

Catharine realized she was—there was a tightness in her body, a fidgeting in her hands. She didn't relish the morning in the barristers' chambers, knowing, whatever came of this meeting, her father's wrath would be soon to follow.

"I am." She rallied a rueful smile. "I much prefer running the meetings, than finding myself the subject of them."

"Is there anything I can do for you?"

"More than flying across the world to spend what precious few days off you have with me?"

"I'd do anything for you."

Catharine's smile broadened, her tone teasing. "Anything?"

"Well," Alex countered, her eyes shining, "I guess there are a few restrictions I should put in place. For instance, if you want me to carry out a hit on your father, I'm afraid I must decline. My scores came back lower than average when it came to assassinations and I'd likely botch the job. But," she stretched out her legs, casually slipping off the counter, securing the towel around her waist, "if you want me to fake an injury that will keep me out of postseason and force me to stay here with you in London, with the promise that we never have to get dressed or leave the bedroom, it's definitely something open to negotiation."

"Don't tempt me on the latter," Catharine ran the tip of her finger across Alex's bare stomach, watching goosebumps follow in its path. She leaned in to kiss her. "I happen to be a very good negotiator."

Behind them her phone vibrated on the counter. It had to be close to eight-thirty. The tube was going to be a nightmare.

"You'd better go," Alex whispered into her mouth, sighing against her. "Elle Kirkland already thinks I'm a bad influence."

"To hell with Elle Kirkland." Catharine kissed her once more, before reluctantly pulling away. "All right." She smoothed her blouse and slipped her suit jacket off the hanger, checking her reflection in the mirror once more. It was time to get the morning over with.

"You look beautiful," Alex called after her as she disappeared out the door.

"You look a fright." Elle Kirkland minced no words after the meeting was over and they'd reached an agreement to proceed the way Elle felt was best. As the last of her team of solicitors cleared the threshold, leaving her and Catharine alone in the boardroom with nothing but empty coffee cups and a sprawling conference table, the woman pulled off her tailored blazer and flung it over her chair. "Hair in a pony tail. Sans makeup. A pantsuit that would give Rachel Maddow a thrill. I see you've taken the sexual orientation discrimination to heart."

"I wasn't aware this morning's dissertation required a red carpet walk."

"No, but when one of the most fashionable businesswomen in London shows up looking like they fell out of bed, crawled into the shower, and threw on the first thing they could find in their wardrobe, it doesn't really go unnoticed."

Catharine busied herself with putting away her reading glasses and organizing her file folders in the hopes that Elle couldn't see how close she'd come to the truth. "Well, if I'm ever looking for advice on haute couture, I'll be certain to ring you."

This earned her a rich laugh as the barrister stretched her back like a cat before hoisting herself to sit on the edge of the solid oak table far more nimbly than her skyscraping heels should have permitted. "For fashion guidance, I charge double." She clicked her heels together. "So what do you and your lovesick pup have planned for tomorrow?"

"Alex is *not* a lovesick pup."

Disregarding the edge to Catharine's tone, the woman offered an indifferent shrug. "Languishing lass? Besotted bint?"

"Careful, Ms. Kirkland—"

"Oh, please, don't *Ms. Kirkland* me. For the unforeseeable future, I'm about to be the best mate you've ever had. You'd better get your mind wrapped around that."

"As this so-called 'best mate,' you'd do best to learn quickly where my tolerance for impertinence ends. Alex is off limits."

"I see." The smug smile didn't leave her cocksure lips. "So Catharine Cleveland has a backbone after all. I've been waiting for it to show itself. I guess all it took was a good shag to rouse your fighting spirit."

Catharine was unamused at the barrister's game. She was willing to put up with the woman's constant criticism and cheeky remarks when it came to herself, but she wasn't about to allow Alex to be dragged into it. "If you don't mind, Ms. Kir—*Elle*," she corrected, carefully, "I would like to leave my personal life out of this."

"Au contraire," Elle singsonged, slipping from the table to stroll across the room, pulling a bottle of whisky from a well-stocked liquor cart. "Your personal life is completely at my disposal. It's what got you into this." Dropping an ice sphere into each glass from an insulated canister, she poured a measured finger into the pair. "It's what—if the Gods of the London Commercial Court are willing—will get you out of it."

"I'm sorry?"

"The High Court of Public Opinion, Catharine. We need the people on your side. You don't want to turn into an Elon Musk right now—with the entire world hoping to watch a giant fall. We need you to be David—the poor, martyred lesbian do-good, unfairly outcast by her father. And Colonel Brooks, of course—Goliath. The tyrant. The homophobic monster. The misogynist willing to destroy a kingdom just for the pleasure to watch it burn."

"I'm not entirely sure I see how that varies from the truth." Catharine accepted the whisky, annoyed by the unpleasant clink the ice made against the glass.

"Convenient, isn't it?" Elle touched the glass to Catharine's, then tipped it back, finishing the drink in a single swallow, before blotting her cherry-colored lips with the palm of her hand. "Wouldn't have mattered either way—we can paint you in whatever light is most flattering, but in this case, there isn't much to sell. I simply need you to drop that curtain and reveal yourself." Her amber eyes glinted with the burn of the liquor. "All puns intended, of course."

"I'm still not following."

"You're going to need to put yourself out there—loud and proud. You're shagging America's sweetheart, for God's sake—use that to your advantage. Be seen—speak out!"

Catharine turned the glass around in her fingers, the condensation dripping onto the polished planks of the boardroom floor. "Alex and I—we aren't, either of us, very open people. I am not interested in using our relationship as a pawn to garner public appeal."

"It's not such a matter of what you're interested in, as it is a matter of what is necessary. If all this works—if we coax your father over the ledge and get him to purposely sabotage the corporation, you're going to take a drastic hit when it comes to your image. As the workforce totters and jobs are sacrificed, they'll be looking for someone to blame, and you're the easiest target. No one cares about Colonel Benjamin A. Brooks. He's never been in the limelight. But show me a household in the US or Europe that doesn't know the name Catharine Cleveland right now—between that delightful, charming, fuck-of-a-dolt you call your husband, and your very blatant same-sex PDA at one of the world's most televised sporting events, combined with an eleven-figure company threatening to go under... and you aren't exactly flying under the radar."

"What exactly are you wanting?" Catharine took a sip of the whisky, the burn muted by the dissolving ice.

"I'll have my team work out a couple photo ops. But first things first, back to my original question—what are you doing tomorrow?"

"I've no idea. Preferably nothing. Spending the day with Alex."

"Oh, bollocks—what way is that to celebrate your birthday?"

Catharine stiffened, the second sip of the drink halted en route to her mouth. Birthdays weren't something she celebrated. They never had been, not even as a child. They were just another day. Another year older. Nothing would change tomorrow beyond the simple mathematical variation of going from forty-three to forty-four.

"How do you know that?" It was a stupid question; one she regretted as soon as it was uttered. Elle had access to an infinite amount of her personal information. Her birthday would be a simple no-brainer. A glance at her file.

"Please, give me some credit. My job is to know everything about you. Now, surely, you and your—what is it I'm allowed to call her? Inamorata? Lorette? Delilah?"

"She's my girlfriend."

"Pish—so mundane. Boring. Simple. You're the type that give us Englishwomen so drab a reputation." She flicked a manicured hand in dismissal. "To each their own. Anyhow—surely you and your *girlfriend* have some form of plans. After all, she flew halfway across the globe to be here. You can't spend all of your time in the bedroom."

"Can't we?"

Elle smiled. "Ah, there is a sense of humor in you yet."

"What gave you the indication I was kidding?" Catharine raised a brow, her expression deadpan.

"Well, your blush, for one thing. No hiding behind the paleness of that Anglo-Saxon skin. At least not when you venture out sans-foundation. But regardless, to a more acute point: you're no spring chicken. I don't care how hot your little leman—excuse me, *girl-friend*—is. No possibility you're going to withstand a marathon tangled in those sheets days on end."

If Catharine hadn't been flushing prior, she was certain she was now. She hadn't planned on a treatise of her sex life following the legal discourse of the morning.

"Have you any point to this?" She hid behind another sip of the watered-down whisky.

"Certainly. I want you to go see your mother."

A searing sensation blazed down her throat as the single malt took the wrong pipe down. With her eyes watering through a fit of coughing, Catharine managed to narrowly avoid tripping over the leg of her chair as she turned to set the offending glass on the table.

"Pardon me," she managed, once the burning had subsided, tears streaming down her cheeks. "I seem to have misheard you."

"God, how aggravating it must be with that highbrow breeding and beat-in propriety to live by such a standard of manners. Don't you ever just wish you could tell someone to fuck off, Catharine? Look them straight in the eye and toss a glass of whisky in their face? Instead, you muddle by, day-to-day, with your 'beg your pardons' and 'if you don't minds,' standing there on your own dime while I get a rise out of rattling your cage." There was a lack of the habitual amusement in the woman's taunting as she poured herself another round. "I mean, no wonder your father and husband have learned to walk all over you. You haven't even got the mettle to tell me you don't prefer ice in your drink. What kind of life is that, I wonder?"

"You don't know a thing about me," Catharine said after a long moment once she was certain she had control of the quiver that threatened her voice. Whatever rise Elle intended to gain from her display, she refused to give.

"I don't need to. I've represented dozens of your kind. You're all the same. Too polite. Too accommodating. Too afraid to push the boundaries of your safe little box. Unwilling to step on toes. To get your hands dirty. Well, let me tell you this, Catharine—that's not how it's going to work from here on out. It's time to give tit for tat. Shed some blood. And we're going to start this game of chess by you going to visit your mother."

Chapter Eleven

Alex cussed beneath her breath as boiling water spilled down her fingers, the kettle lid sliding askew in her rush to fill the to-go tumblers.

She was nervous. Nathalie had warned her any mention of Catharine's birthday would be met with opposition. That it was best to let the day pass without acknowledgement. It was simply how it had always been. How it would always be. She'd been surprised Alex even knew the date—it was not something Catharine readily made available.

Alex had not elaborated, leaving the Frenchwoman's inquiry to mystery—though the truth was unexciting. She'd seen the date on her driver's license when Catharine had been carded that first night in Portland. It hadn't been something she'd intended to commit to memory. At the time, she'd never imagined two years later she'd be waking in London in the enigmatic Englishwoman's riverfront penthouse, nude and languid in her bed. That the woman who'd jotted her number on a ticket stub would shake the foundation of her entire world. That in such short time she'd become the cause of Alex's greatest heartaches and also the nucleus to her happiness.

No, she'd known none of that—but perhaps fate, or providence, or simple premonition had leant its prophecy, for the date had stuck in her mind. And regardless the warning from the person who knew Catharine best, she'd decided to go ahead with her plan.

With the two tumblers in hand, a banana for them both, and an internal prayer she wasn't making a mistake, Alex took care to silence her footsteps as she turned up the stairs toward the master bedroom. She'd been careful not to wake Catharine when she'd risen before the sun several hours earlier, determined to complete the finishing touches on the day's itinerary without it ever being known she was gone. When she'd gotten back to the apartment, she'd peeked in and been pleased to find Catharine still sleeping, giving her time to make their tea and change from her running clothes, but now, as she approached the suite entrance, she could hear the rise and fall of the soft English lilt muffled through the door.

"I haven't solidified anything."

Alex eased open the door to find Catharine standing in front of the balcony windows, a t-shirt pulled on, lounge pants hanging low on her hips, her attention on a phone call as she impatiently tapped her bare foot against the glass. She listened for a moment before responding tersely.

"Because I'm still not comfortable with the idea, to be honest. I made that clear yesterday."

Another short silence.

"Yes, I did. And I will. But it won't be this minute."

There was a longer silence as Alex crossed into the bedroom, allowing the door to close behind her with a resounding click, wanting to make her presence known.

With a glance over her shoulder, Catharine caught her eye, offering a stiff smile. "Listen—I'll make the call, as I said I would. But I won't make promises beyond that. Now, I'm sorry, but I have to go."

Whatever the caller said on the other end of the line made her laugh, losing some of her rigid agitation, and Alex felt her shoulders slacken in relief when Catharine fired back, "wouldn't you like to know," her tone teasing as she disconnected the call.

"Well," she waved a hand to dismiss the conversation, tossing her phone on the bed, and smiled, this time without the former strain. "You were up early." She eyed the mugs in her hand. "And busy, I see. Cuppas to-go, even. Is this a two-tea kind of morning for you, or were you anticipating company?"

"I'd be lying if I said I didn't have my heart set on company." Alex bit her bottom lip, anxious how Catharine would receive her request. Nathalie had been adamant. "I thought we might..." she shifted, tucking the insulated mugs under one arm, wondering if she should tell her now, or if it would go better if she coaxed her from the apartment under false pretenses.

She opted for honesty.

"It's your birthday—"

"Alex—" the tone held an instant rebuke, and regardless how gentle, it made Alex's heart sink. "I don't want to celebrate my birthday, and I promise you, I don't mean that in some form of doublespeak. It's not a day I enjoy, and damn Nathalie for—"

"Nathalie had nothing to do with it," Alex cut her off, with no intent other than to defend Nathalie, but instead the words came out sharp, her frustration building in her concern that her plan would go wrong, coupled with annoyance that Catharine assumed Nathalie was behind any of it. "She warned me, actually, not even to mention it. But," looking down at the fruit in her hand, Alex suddenly wished she'd left it in the kitchen. It was one thing to take a scolding while holding tea. It felt another to be clutching a pair of bananas. "There's something I wanted to do for you, and I hope you'll stay open-minded enough to give me a chance. If you hate it, we can abort the plan and go on with our day—and I promise I won't bring it up again."

Catharine was quiet and Alex could feel her measuring her response, before exhaling an ill-concealed sigh, followed by the ghost of a smile. "Do for me?" The perfect arch of an eyebrow lifted, her tone turning teasing. "I would say I'm intrigued, however—I must admit—the bananas have given me pause."

"Oh—" Alex took another glance at the fruit, feeling an unwelcome heat rise up her cheeks, already warm from the exertion of her morning run. "No—I mean, I didn't—they're just—breakfast."

"So it's safe to assume breakfast in bed is not what you had in mind?"

"Well," despite her flush, Alex returned her suggestive smile, "my plans are flexible—we could start there, if you'd prefer. Though, I'd had after-dinner plans scripted into the program."

"Sans fruit?"

"Where's your sense of adventure—declining with your ascending age?" Alex quipped, stepping back to avoid the swat of Catharine's hand as she drew closer.

"What an impertinent mouth." Catharine feigned indignation.

"I'm certain that's not the word you used for it last night."

"Mind your *elders*, Miss Grey." Catching Alex's forearm, she leaned in to kiss the groove where her jaw met her ear. "And this morning? What exactly does that entail?" She grazed a slow knuckle down Alex's body, taking full advantage of the incapacity of her tea-and-banana filled hands.

"Kiss me like that again, and I'll have no choice but to alter the agenda. And then you might never find out."

"You realize I'm unaccustomed to being made to decide between one thing or another. Not when both are within my means."

"All the more joy I'll receive," said Alex, extricating herself from Catharine's hold, "in forcing you to choose."

"Fine," Catharine gave an affected gesture of disgruntled acquiescence. "We'll stick to your program. But be forewarned, Alex—if you mean to force me into acknowledging this day, I expect you to do it right. I'll be holding you to your 'after dinner' plans."

"I'm counting on it," Alex smiled. "Now get dressed. We're going on a quest."

Stepping off the elevator, Alex steered their steps away from Shad Thames and through the narrow alley that led to a stone staircase descending to the river bank. To her relief, she'd gauged the tides right, and the water was still out, leaving the shore dry.

"Okay," she stopped at the bottom step, pulling a card from her back pocket, and handed it up to Catharine, who'd paused a few steps above her. She was nervous, uncertain how Catharine would respond, momentarily second-guessing the idea. She might find it childish—silly... But it was too late to change anything now. She was committed. "Your first clue."

"Clue?" Curious, Catharine took the card, turning it over. A short riddle was written on the back.

Not too far from right here
Is a structure that was once a pier
If you have a look around
You'll find your next hint on the ground

Catharine read the card twice before looking up, perplexed. "What is this?" Alex was relieved to see she was entertained.

"You're going to have to suffer through my atrocious poetry to find out. I apologize in advance for my lack of skill in rhyming. It only gets worse from here."

"Is it a game?"

"In a way, yes."

Catharine read the card again, then took a quick glance along the riverbank. "So I just search along the shore?"

"You tell me. It's your clue. I'll follow wherever you go."

"I hope you planned for a lot of walking today. I'm bound to lead you astray."

"I can think of nothing I'd enjoy more."

Without another word, Catharine bypassed Alex on the staircase and stepped onto the rocky bank. A half dozen yards down, beside the rotting steel of the original Butler's Wharf Pier, she bent to collect a card that had been tucked into a dry bit of driftwood, raising it to wave at Alex, clearly pleased with her success.

She returned to the staircase, her eyes alight with the challenge. "How did you do this? When?"

"Magic."

The card still unread, Catharine leaned forward and kissed Alex, unconcerned with the half dozen tourists milling around the wall above them, their cameras turned toward Tower Bridge. "I don't deserve you."

Breathing in the chaste brush of her lips, Alex was certain the seven miles she'd covered on foot, along with the half dozen train changes and one pre-dawn bus ride had been worth every step.

Catharine read the next card aloud.

A stone cetacean can be found
In a fountain, small and round
If you search like you should
Your next clue lies beneath a seat of wood

"Cetacean...? Not crustacean?" Catharine tapped the card against her lower lip, deliberating. "That falls into the marine mammal category, yes?"

Alex gave no answer, her only thoughts on how it should be illegal for one single person to look so exquisite—to be so perfectly stunning—dressed in jeans and a t-shirt, her hair pulled back in a loose ponytail. So different than the woman of pencil skirts and tailored suits. Pearls, updos, stockings, and heels. It would be impossible to determine which of the two she was in love with most.

"Oh!" Catharine interrupted her thoughts, grabbing her hand. "I think I know!"

A short walk across the bridge, Catharine located her third clue beneath a wooden bench feet away from the famous *Girl with a Dolphin* fountain. She was undeniably delighted, her dazzling smile never leaving her lips. As the day went on and they traversed the city—across Westminster, down to Canary Wharf, up to Hyde Park, back to the Maritime Museum, zigzagging along the Thames to the London Eye and Big Ben—Alex wished she'd had time to hide a dozen more cards. That the day would go on forever.

After a clue led them on a train ride to Wembley Stadium, Catharine tracked down the eleventh card taped on the bottom of a lamppost outside a pub regaled for serving "the best fish n' chips in London Town." They paused for lunch and a pint, squeezed into a corner booth where Catharine reached lazily across the table and stole Alex's chips, one by one.

"You went to a lot of effort," she said over the rim of her lager. "And I almost mucked it up for you this morning by being obstinate."

"It was worth the gamble." Alex caught the thieving fingers that reached for her plate, enfolding them in her own. It still felt inconceivable—that she could touch this woman at her leisure. Hold her hand in public without the necessity of secrecy. That she was hers. They were each other's. "I knew you might not go along."

"And I never would have known what I threw away. All your hard work and time."

Alex squeezed her hand. "But you didn't. So it doesn't matter."

"Where did you come up with this idea?"

"My mom." Alex eased her hand from Catharine's to pick up her pint, still more than half full. "She used to hide my presents—birthdays, Easter, Christmas—and make me hunt for them through riddles. I loved it more than the gifts themselves." Taking a sip of her ale, she offered a rueful smile. "She, of course, was eloquent and clever—which, as you have clearly learned today, I am not. But it's the thought that counts, right?"

Catharine shook her head, the sapphire of her eyes warm. "Don't sell yourself so short," she tapped Alex's foot with her shoe beneath the booth in gentle rebuke, before sitting back against the fading upholstery. "Do you look like her, your mum?"

Alex considered the question, recalling the last image of her mom that came to mind. Dark hair, brown eyes flecked the color of a viridian sea, tan, slender, laughing. In her memory her mother was smiling, looking out over the Carolina sunset, holding Alex's hand. She could still feel the warmth of the late summer sun as it faded into nightfall. Smell the lavender notes of her mother's perfume. They'd gotten ice cream on the pier and watched the pelicans crashing into the water in search of their dinner. The next day her mom had flown with her father to a work trip in Alaska. By that evening they'd crashed into the Blying Sound.

Alex caught the outline of her reflection in the glass Catharine was holding. She'd not given it much thought as she'd grown older, though when she'd been a child she'd wanted nothing more than to be her exact replica. Through her juvenile rose-colored glasses she'd been certain her mother was the most beautiful woman in the world.

"Yes." It felt good, she realized—how much they looked alike. That so much of her mother could be seen in her own likeness. "I guess I do."

"She must have been positively radiant."

Alex laughed. "You might be biased."

Catharine tsked. "I like to think myself something of a connoisseur of beauty. Are you questioning my impeccably good taste, Miss Grey?"

"I'm questioning your motives."

"Oh?" Catharine rested her chin on her hand, the smile in her eyes glinting. "And tell me, what are my motives?"

Alex shrugged, struggling to maintain her casual facade of indifference without cracking a smile. "Get me drunk. Court me with your convincing flattery. Offer to share a cab. Then invite me upstairs."

"Hmm—a plausible scenario. But you've forgotten one small detail." Catharine gestured at the stack of note cards piled at the end of the table. "You're the one currently wooing me with words."

Alex feigned a grimace of guilt. "Well, you're onto my game. I thought it might be a more surefire thing than asking you around for dinner and a movie."

"Isn't that what your generation calls Netflix and Chill?"

Alex laughed, cringing. "God, I don't know why it is so appalling, hearing that come from your lips."

"Perhaps it is my—what did you call it?—*Advanced* age?"

"*Ascending* age," Alex corrected, hiding behind her hands. "You're never going to forgive me for that, are you?"

"It will take some effort to earn back my pardon."

With a long draw, Alex finished her beer and set the glass down with a punctuating clink. "In that case—up and at 'em, Mrs. Cl—" she wavered on the word. It didn't feel right anymore. It never had. She'd heard Catharine refer to herself as Ms. Brooks in travel. A few of the newspapers had adopted the moniker since her split with Carlton. Alex wasn't certain it was entirely suiting, but it was better than the alternative. "Ms. Brooks," she tested, pushing to her feet. "Let's get this challenge over with so I can explore avenues to exonerate myself."

"Oh, I have a few ideas," Catharine returned, her smile artful, but as she stood, her expression shifted, as if her thoughts had run across something unpleasant. Distasteful. She gathered the cards and said nothing as they worked their way to the sidewalk, sliding her finger beneath the envelope to break the seal on the latest clue. But instead of pulling it out, she paused outside the door and looked at Alex.

"There is something I'd like to ask of you, Alex."

The words roused a quiver of anxiety. It was the discomfort with which she said them. The flatness of her tone. Gone was all the teasing. All the playful repartee. Alex wasn't sure what to make of it.

"But I need you to know," Catharine continued, her fingers fiddling with the stack of note cards, "you are under no obligation to say yes. If the idea is at all disconcerting, please, know that—"

"Catharine," Alex cut her off, her pulse pounding, "what is it?"

"I need—I'd *like*," she corrected, as if rehearsed, "to go see my mother. I know our time is short together, and I completely understand if you'd rather I wait until you are back to Oakland, but I'd love for you to come, if—"

"Of course I'll go with you!" Alex felt as if a band had snapped around her chest, allowing her to breathe again.

Catharine continued to thumb through the stack of cards, uneasy. "I'm not even certain I can arrange it all in time, but..." Her voice trailed off.

Alex had answered so quickly, she hadn't given full thought to the situation. Catharine hadn't seen her mother in... she didn't even know when. And now, with everything going on with Brooks Corp., she realized how monumental this was for Catharine. How difficult. It didn't feel like the kind of conversation that should be held on a sidewalk while a red London Transport double-decker lumbered by.

"And your father—?"

"—is in Liverpool."

"Have you spoken to her?"

"I've—we've exchanged emails. Nothing has been decided. I wanted to talk to you first. I'll call her this evening. She'll be in Henley this time of year."

"And she'll... see you?" Alex didn't know how to better phrase the question, but Catharine seemed unperturbed.

"Yes, I think so. She's asked to see me for years."

That was news to Alex. She knew they'd drifted apart, but she'd thought it had been mutual. She hadn't realized it was Catharine who'd closed her out.

The timing seemed odd—with everything going on—that she'd want to see her now. But Alex didn't say as much. She didn't want to risk dissuading her. If her mother could be of any help in the turmoil between her and her father—if she could offer any guidance to calm the impending storm—the visit would be worthwhile.

"We would go tomorrow?" It was her last full day in London. Less than forty-three hours remaining. She pushed the thought aside.

"Yes."

Alex had a dozen more questions, but Catharine's attention returned to the riddle on the note card, the conversation dismissed with a flippant wave of her hand.

"Enough of that. Back to more important things." She smiled, and though the action was rigid, by the time she'd pulled the card from the envelope and read the rhyme aloud, her expression had softened and her merriment returned.

> *Our first date in London was a wreck*
> *I think you'd like to've rung my neck*
> *Not my proudest moment, this*
> *Where you found me: quite amiss*

She laughed before she'd ever reached the end of the riddle, tucking the card back in with the others. "Well, perhaps not your proudest moment—I'll warrant that—but if it hadn't have happened, I don't imagine we'd be where we are now. So I suppose I have Sam Huntley to thank." She slung an arm around Alex's shoulders as they walked toward the train station, their hips brushing stride for stride, and Alex let all talk of Henley-on-Thames and Catharine's mother slip into abeyance.

An hour later they turned off Wapping High Street into Hermitage Riverside Memorial Garden where Alex had definitely lived out one of the worst nights of her life. Worst *and* best. Catharine was right. That night had brought them back together. Had been a turning point in Alex's life.

Tucked into the sculpture of the dove was the twelfth clue.

> *A final card you must define*
> *Across the river and to floor nine*
> *If all goes off without a hitch*
> *You'll find it in a comfortable niche*

Catharine pronounced niche *neesh*, as was customary of British English, and Alex rolled her eyes.

"What? It's a derivative of the French word, *nicher*. That's how it's pronounced!"

"Humor me and my inferior American linguistic deficiencies just this once, will you? You're ruining my rhyme."

"Just once? As in, I'll never be asked to humor you again? Forever?"

"You are impossible." But Alex liked that word, *forever*. It meant longer than this. More than this.

Catharine caught her hand, dovetailing their fingers, pulling her into her embrace.

Never in her wildest dreams had Alex imagined three months after her drunken night with Sam Huntley, she would stand in the same spot she'd called Catharine from in hysterics and tears, kissing her in public, as if they hadn't a care in the world. That they would continue kissing as a boisterous group of school children jostled by, backpacks swinging as an older boy whistled a catcall. And that Catharine's only response would be to laugh, before reluctantly extracting herself from Alex's arms.

As they strolled hand-in-hand across the bridge toward Shad Thames, a woman a few years younger than Alex—wearing an Arsenal jersey—rubbernecked as she past. Twenty feet later she reappeared, falling into step beside them.

"You're Alex Grey!" It wasn't a question. She waved her cellphone at Alex. "I'm a huge fan! Could I get a—?" her eyes flicked to Catharine, "—oh my God, it's really true!"

Alex could feel the tension in Catharine's hand as they slowed their steps at the interruption, but to her surprise, Catharine appeared amused, rather than irritated.

"What gave it away?" Catharine's tone was droll. "Surely not the photo of us kissing at the World Cup on the cover of *ESPNW*? Nor could it have been my soon-to-be-ex-husband's constant campaign talking points about how his wife has trespassed onto the devil's path and his country needs to be returned to Jesus? It must have been something more drastic? More blatant? Oh—like, strolling home on a Tuesday night, completely unassuming and unostentatious?"

"I—" the woman glanced between them, realizing Catharine was razzing her for the obviousness of her observation. "I'm sorry —I just meant—you're really a thing. My wife has been obsessed with Greyland. She thinks you are the most perfect couple. She's never going to believe me when I tell her I ran into you. Is there any chance you'd...?" She held up her phone again.

Alex opened her mouth to politely decline, but Catharine beat her to it with a shrug of agreement. They stood for a photo—one by themselves, the other with the Arsenal fan stretching her arm out for a selfie—and then they were on their way, Catharine never having released her hold on Alex's hand.

"I can't believe you agreed to that." Alex side-eyed her when they were another hundred feet down the bridge.

"I'm sorry. I should have asked you—"

"No, I'm fine—I go through that all the time. I just mean—I didn't think you'd be okay with that—with me."

"She would have taken a photo either way, so we may as well have it on our own terms—at least that way it gives me the opportunity to pick my more flattering side," she teased.

"As if you have a 'more flattering' side," Alex scoffed. "There's not an angle that wouldn't suit you."

As they reached the staircase leading down to Shad Thames, Catharine paused to look over the low footbridge wall, the building encompassing her apartment less than a hundred feet away. The weather was crisp, the air cooling considerably as the sun sank below the city skyline, and the pedestrian traffic was sparse. They had the moment to themselves—the culmination to the perfect day.

"Thank you." Catharine rested her elbows on the railing, the glare of the sun off the water catching the outline of her flaxen hair, setting it aglow. "For this. For today. For everything you've done for me. For coming here. For being you."

Alex leaned against her, relishing the feel of their hands intwined.

Forty-one hours. How was she ever going to drag herself onto that plane? Return to life as she'd known it. Life without waking with Catharine by her side. She never wanted this day to end.

"There's no place I'd rather be. No one I'd rather be with."

When they stepped off the elevator onto the ninth floor of the riverside apartment, Alex hung back a couple steps as Catharine found the final envelope, marked #13, sitting on the balcony table beside a palm-sized package wrapped in brown paper.

Unrushed, Catharine took her time pouring them both a lowball, before settling at the table to pick up the card.

Alex found herself anxious. She hadn't known what to get Catharine. What did you get the person who had everything? Who needed nothing? So she'd put her effort into the day, instead, and come up with only a token gift at the end—something she worried Catharine might find corny, when it came down to it.

"I'm afraid it's all been a build up for something really insignificant, honestly." She toyed with her glass, turning it around and around, never lifting it to her lips. "I didn't know what else to do for you."

Catharine ran a finger beneath the flap of the envelope, her eyes lifting to Alex. "There's not a gift in the world more significant than what you've done for me today, Alex." She looked down at the card. The cover was of a 1942 classic wooden ketch—a nearly perfect replica of *L'lune Alouette*, Catharine's yacht birthed back in San Francisco Bay. On the inside was Alex's imperfect handwriting that simply read *Happy Birthday, Catharine. All my love, Alex.* She'd wanted to write "I love you," but had vacillated on the expression. She loved her. She knew Catharine knew she loved her. She'd told her so standing in the doorway of her elevator the night after the semifinals in July. Yet still she struggled to say it. Even in a card.

Catharine ran her thumb over the words before returning to the cover to study the sketch. "It's beautiful. The very likeness."

"Believe it or not, classic wooden ketches aren't overly popular on cards," Alex smiled. It had taken a deep web search through Etsy to come up with it, but it had been worth it.

Catharine lifted the edge of tape that held the package together, her fingers working in their meticulous fashion. Inside she uncovered a small white box, lifting off the top to reveal a silver charm, smaller than a quarter. It was a Sunfish sailboat, intricately detailed to include the facsimile fish decal on the head of the sail. Picking it up, she examined it closely, turning it over in her hand to where it was engraved in small print on the backside of the sail: *love, Alex.*

"You don't have to wear it," Alex broke the silence. "It's just a charm. For your keyring or a purse strap or something. I know its not—"

"Alex." Catharine reached across the table, pressing her hand, quieting her. "It couldn't be more perfect."

"I didn't know what else—"

"This entire day was perfect." She touched the tiny sailboat, unfolding the necklace that was hidden beneath the cotton of the box, "*this* is perfect. I love it." She clasped it around her neck.

"A good birthday, then?"

"The very best."

Leaning back in her chair, relieved at the outcome of the day, Alex felt like Catharine truly meant it. "Then I will consider it a success."

"However," Catharine smiled at her over the rim of her glass, "I believe you promised me two parts to this celebration."

"Ah." Alex finally took a sip of her drink, trying not to wince as it blazed its way down her esophagus. Who in their right mind actually enjoyed drinking hard alcohol straight? "I seem to remember something about that. Sans fruit, yes?"

Catharine gave a casual shrug. "Oh, I don't know." She ran a languorous finger along the rim of her glass. "Strawberries and pomegranates have always had their time and place."

"Pomegranates?" Alex laughed. "I think that might require a trip to the market."

"Well… it is my birthday after all."

Alex knew she was teasing. But she also knew Catharine needed to call her mother. She'd seen her discreetly check her phone over the course of the afternoon, and knew, no matter how much she was enjoying the evening, the phone call was weighing on her. A short run to the market would give her the privacy she needed.

"In that case—it might just be your lucky day—it happens to be pomegranate season." Alex stood, stretching, and knew she was right when Catharine made no effort to stop her. She paused at the glass door of the balcony, turning back, appreciating the perfection of Catharine's silhouette against the dying rays of daylight. "However, Ms. Brooks—after this, I expect full exoneration from my earlier transgression."

She was rewarded with a brilliant smile. The kind that made her breath hitch and sent her pulse catapulting.

"I don't know—in my ascending age, I've perhaps developed a touch of senility. I imagine you'll have to seek my pardon more than once to receive complete absolution."

Alex held her unwavering gaze. "You should know by now— I'm always up for a challenge."

"I'm counting on it."

As she jogged along the cobblestone street that ran the distance of Shad Thames toward the market, Alex couldn't decide what had been better—winning the World Cup or spending an uninterrupted day with Catharine.

Chapter Twelve

Catharine's heart felt like it was galloping away from her. She watched as the familiar streets—remarkably unchanged from when she'd last seen them a quarter of a century earlier—rolled by out the window, unfolding the quaint beauty of the riverside town.

It thrived as a tourist destination. Antique shops, bookstores, cafes dotting the twelfth century plaza with its ancient stone structures and white, blue and red pendant flags criss-crossing the rooftops of market centre and the town square.

From Alex's expression, she could tell the town was charming. She tried to imagine what it would be like to see it for the first time. The beauty of St. Mary's Church, with its historic bell tower and earth-tone stained glass windows, the majestic architecture of its archways and doors. Or the rolling expanse of parkland stretching out across the river, the water colored with scullers out for an afternoon row.

To Catharine, it felt only small; suffocating, even after all the years. It had been a place she'd never intended to return to, an echo of her past she never cared to relive. It had once held a thousand happy memories of her time with Nathalie—matinees at Kenton, clandestine kisses in cobblestone alleys, hand-in-hand strolls through high-walled gardens, nights that knew nothing more than youthful ignorance fueled by desire. But those memories had long been abandoned, erased by the final haunting hours at Honour Stone Manor.

Expressionless, she watched as they passed the old theatre, heading east on New Street before curving onto Thameside. A short drive over White Hill bridge and they'd be a breath away from her childhood home.

Though *home* it had never been.

"Malcolm." She broke the silence she'd fallen into since arriving in Oxfordshire, drawing the attention of both the Scotsman, who glanced at her in the rearview mirror, and Alex, who'd been watching out the window beside her. "Pull over, please."

There was a rowers' pub—Power 10—along the waterfront, popular amongst the locals, but less frequented by tourists, who preferred the more eye-catching eateries with broad front windows and clever names. At least that was how it had been two dozen years ago. By the look of the shuttered windows and peeling varnish on the wood slate door, not much had changed.

She checked her watch for the hundredth time. They were early. More than an hour early. Her mother wouldn't mind. She'd been excessively accommodating—from Catharine's first email, to her last minute phone call the night before—treating the self-proposed visit as if it weren't entirely out of the blue. The conversation had been brief; terse on Catharine's end, tentative on her mother's.

Yes, she would be pleased to see her. Yes, it was acceptable to bring Miss Grey. And that had been the end of it. No mention of her father. Of Brooks Corp. Of the palpable animus that hung in the air. Just an agreement on a time, followed by an awkward farewell.

Now, as she debated on stepping out of the car as it came to a stop in front of the pub, Catharine was certain she'd made a horrible error. She'd allowed Elle to talk her into this, knowing the barrister was hoping a visit with her mother would lead to a heartwarming reunion. That they could glean some form of assistance from Emily Brooks in dealing with the colonel. And no matter how many times Catharine tried to explain to Elle that wasn't how it worked in her family, the woman had been unrelenting. So she'd finally given in.

"Let's get a drink, shall we?" Without waiting for an answer from Alex, Catharine tugged open the door handle, pausing only long enough to meet Malcolm's eye in the mirror. "Thirty minutes."

He nodded. He'd been without any of his jocular banter, well aware of the irascibility of her mood. It was amongst his finest qualities—his ability to read a room, and Catharine was glad she'd decided to have him drive them. Public transportation was one thing whilst she was in the city, but Honour Stone was different.

Even with her father two hundred miles away, Malcolm's nearness was a comfort. And, if she was honest with herself, she knew—no matter how much she wished to deny it—she wanted her mother's approval. To prove her success. Her status. That she was still one of them. Whatever that meant. Whoever *they* were. She hated herself for it. But it was true all the same.

"Are you doing okay?" Alex settled into a booth beneath a plaque boasting George II had once drank a pint in that spot.

Catharine's lips turned up while her eyes didn't crinkle. It was lunacy to have dragged Alex out here, wasting their last day together.

"Alex is likable," Elle had insisted. "Endear her to your mother. Trust me on this, Catharine. I know what I am doing."

Elle, perhaps, knew what she was doing. But Catharine did not. With each passing minute she had to fight not to return to her car, return to the city, and call the whole thing off. But she'd been tilting at windmills for months, without coming any closer to a resolution.

So she forced herself to keep her seat and turned her eyes to the drink menu.

"I'm—I'll be fine." It was more reassurance for herself than anything else. "I just need a cup of courage. It's been a long time."

Alex reached beneath the table and found her hand, ceasing the fretful drumming of her fingers against her thigh. "Maybe you'll be pleasantly surprised. She's probably just as nervous as you are."

Guilt wound its way around Catharine's conscience. Alex had been so supportive of the venture. So genuinely pleased she wanted to see her mother. Catharine hadn't the heart to tell her the visit hadn't been of her own volition. That she'd been strong-armed by the barrister with an ulterior motive.

Browsing the top shelf cognacs—a benefit of Henley's affluent populace—Catharine looked up to order a double *Paradis* as the barman arrived with two glasses of Hennessy.

"Lad in the cap bought you a pair."

Catharine glanced in the direction of the man indicated, seated at the bar, wearing a flannel and newsboy hat, his sinewy frame unmistakable of the rowers throughout town. She shook her head.

"Thank you, but we're not interested." It was a pet peeve of hers, men sending unsolicited rounds. "A double of your *Paradis*, and—?" she looked up for Alex's order, finding the man in the flannel had approached their table, his hat twisting in his hands.

"Cate?"

The name sent a reverberation through her body, too familiar and too reminiscent of memories in this town. With his hat off and hair swept away from his forehead, she had a better look at his face. Beneath the peppered gray at his temples and sun-wrought wrinkles creasing the corners of his eyes, she recognized the chestnut gaze and arch smirk of the boy she'd once known.

"I thought it was you." His smile spread with his certainty. "You don't look any different. More beautiful, perhaps, if it is even possible."

"Geoff." Catharine didn't know what else to say. The son of her father's foreman when she'd been in university. They'd been an inseparable triad of friendship—her, Nathalie, and Geoff. It was with him her father had assumed she was having an affair—him who he'd expected to find in her bed that morning. Or perhaps that had only been his hope. Anyone but Nathalie.

"I'd wondered about you over the years. And then, well," his smile turned sheepish, "I saw in the papers—this summer, of course…" He gave Alex a little gesture of acknowledgement before looking back at Catharine. "I also saw the Colonel had…" His hat twisted another revolution in his calloused fingers. "Anyhow—I guess, just—I'm sorry, Cate—about… everything you're going through… you've gone through."

It was she who should be apologizing. After everything had fallen apart—after her world had burned down—her father had fired Geoff Mills, his father, and his uncle—out of sheer spite. Simply because Geoff had befriended the wrong girl. Because he had held his friends' secrets close to his vest. Twenty years the older Mills had worked for the Brooks family. Twenty years of loyalty—snuffed out.

"Geoff, I—" What could she say? What did it matter now? Too much time had passed. She motioned toward the seat beside her. "Will you sit? Join us, please."

"Honest, I don't mean to disturb. I only wanted to say hello— that you look well. Took a gamble Hennessy might still be your drink after all these years." He nodded at the glasses the barkeep had left behind.

Catharine assured him he was no disturbance, and after an introduction to Alex, of whom he proclaimed himself a fan, he perched at the end of the table, filling Catharine in on the highlights of the past twenty-plus years. Married. Two kids—the youngest heading to university this year. He asked, with an apologetic glance at Alex, about Nathalie, and told Catharine the summers the three of them had spent together were some of the best days of his life.

After a few minutes of chat between Geoff and Alex about football teams Catharine had never heard of—and Geoff's enthusiasm for a Welsh club that was getting promoted to a different tier the following season—he rose to bid his farewell. It had felt uncannily familiar—the three of them, sitting there—only now it was Alex instead of Nathalie, and they were no longer children, spinning up dreams for a future they knew nothing about.

Leaning over to give Catharine a hug, Geoff set a card on the table and told Catharine if she was ever in town again, to give him a ring. "Give your mother my best, will you? Mrs. Brooks was always good to our family. Even my father, who won't tolerate the name Benjamin Brooks in his presence, thinks kindly of your mum." Then with a tip of his hat to Alex, and a wink to Catharine, he was gone, and it was time to leave for Honour Stone.

The stone arch loomed above the entrance, the iron gates already open in their unwelcome snare. Catharine reminded herself to breathe as they drove through the winding woodlands, bare from the autumn freeze, but which would be covered in bluebells come spring. Absently she wished Alex could have seen the drive in the magnificence of summer, when the juneberries and paperbark maples canopied the drive. When the lake was surrounded by the deep purples and pure whites of the snake's head fritillary, and when the dog violets and corncockle grew rampant through the brush and bramble covering the parkland hills.

And then the manor came into view and all thoughts of the beauty of the estate slipped from her mind.

It was the same as it had always been. Colossal. Frigid. Imperious. Surrounded by endless acres of manicured lawns, its steep gables and ornate arches struck at Catharine like the dull edges of a cockspur thorn. Alex could not hide her marvelment beside her.

Catharine had known the part of her that loved architecture would admire the elaborately carved columns and excessively detailed turrets, the mullioned windows and openwork parapets that symmetrically framed the facade.

"Wow." The word was wonder and disbelief and apprehension all in a single breath. "I guess I was expecting something more like your home in South Carolina."

"Just as hollow, just as heartless. Only on a grander, senescent scale." Catharine failed to smile. "Brick and stucco and plaster. Nothing more."

"Your mother stays here?" Alex took another glance at the expanse of rolling hills and woodlands, gardens and lawns. "Alone?"

"She has the staff. Undoubtedly she still spends most of her time in the city. When winter hits in earnest, they'll have this closed."

"You were raised here? This was your home?"

"Part of the year." Catharine did not elaborate. Be it Henley-on-Thames. London. Geneva. Saint-Jean-Cap-Ferrat. Zürich. Barcelona. Singapore. None of them felt like home. She'd not told Alex this was where her life had collapsed with Nathalie. It would have done nothing to sooth either of their nerves.

A valet appeared but Malcolm beat him to their door.

"Ms. Brooks." He waited for instruction as they gained their feet. She stifled an involuntary smile at the overprotective Scotsman. She was *his* mistress. *His* duty. With his excessive propriety, he was making that abundantly clear.

The valet cleared his throat. "Mrs. Cleveland." His eyes shifted to Alex, but no further acknowledgment was expressed. "Mrs. Brooks is taking tea on the north veranda."

It was strange, to not know the faces. To not know the staff. To know every inch of a place so intimately, yet feel like she didn't know it at all.

With an imperceptible nod toward Malcolm, dismissing his service, Catharine reached for Alex's hand. She could feel the valet's stare as he ushered them toward the entrance. Feel his disapproval. But she didn't care. She'd asked Alex here. She would not allow her to feel like an outsider. Like she was anything other than what she was—the person Catharine loved.

Approaching the staircase to the double entry doors, she paused a step to gather herself. The last time she'd gone up those steps she'd skipped them two-by-two with Nathalie at her side. The last time she'd come down them she had been dragged by her father, alone.

"This way, please."

Her jaw tightened. She knew the bloody way.

Finding it difficult to breathe as they stepped through the archway, Alex squeezed her hand. No doubt she could feel the odd beat of her heart as it skipped against her chest, and was aware of the rigidity of her fingers. Had she been on her own, she wasn't sure she would have had the courage to continue. Two dozen strides back through the front door to her waiting car and she could be on her way.

Instead she followed the draconian form of the silent valet down the familiar hall and through the east wing sitting room until he stepped aside to hold open the door to the north veranda. And there, for the first time in twenty-four years, Catharine laid eyes on her mother.

Chapter Thirteen

The woman who extended her hand toward Alex wasn't what she'd been expecting. She wasn't an older version of Catharine—a woman with the same tall, poised, willowy frame—fair featured, sophisticated, aloof. Born for the cover of magazines. Excessively elegant. Extraordinarily striking.

She was none of that. Petite in stature, squarely built, broad shouldered, with hair the color of dark copper, she looked no more related to Catharine than Alex herself. She was an attractive woman, her features round and smooth, with a fullness to her that gave her a classical allure. There was nothing of Catharine's high cheekbones and prominent angles, nor the cerulean blue eyes so skilled at concealing the thoughts behind them. Instead her gaze was comprised of a rich caramel, direct and candid, close-set and round. When she smiled, however, it was all Catharine—slow, confident, and genuine. She looked younger than she probably was, though the velvety skin of her handshake was soft with age.

"How do you do, Miss Grey." Her voice harbored a pleasing warmth beneath the custom of formality. Alex was immediately compelled to like her. "Welcome to Honour Stone."

She had risen to greet Catharine first—a moment of palpable tension present as they stood a few feet apart on the terrace, uncertain how to proceed. Alex wished she could have given them a moment of privacy. That she could have disappeared as Emily Brooks soaked in the sight of her daughter, her forthright gaze taking in all the changes over all the years. She couldn't imagine what it would feel like to see her own mother now—to see her through the eyes of a woman, no longer a child.

It was Emily who finally stepped forward with an intent to hug her daughter, but Catharine put out her hand instead, forcing an uncomfortable handshake.

"Catharine." The older woman's voice had wavered faintly as she held onto her daughter's hand longer than necessary.

"Hello, mum." Catharine had then turned to Alex, wasting no time in her businesslike introductions. "Please meet Miss Grey. Alex, my mother, Mrs. Brooks."

Now, with her hand still in the older woman's grasp, Alex mustered a smile and prayed, for the umpteenth time since arriving, that she would manage not to say anything stupid or make matters worse for Catharine than they already were.

"It's a pleasure, Mrs. Brooks."

"Emily, please."

Emily invited them to sit and a woman in a navy skirt suit appeared with tea as Catharine and her mother stumbled through a halting exchange of innocuous conversation relating to the drive from London and turn in the weather as it edged toward winter. The small talk sounded so unnatural, so foreign on Catharine's lips, Alex could feel the edginess radiating off her as they sat side by side on a garden settee, Catharine's arms crossed guardedly over her lap. Alex could tell by the rigidity of her hands that she was consciously disallowing herself to fidget. She would have reached for her hand, or touched her arm—anything to try and sooth the obvious discomfort—but she didn't dare.

"I'm glad you called, Catharine," Emily Brooks said once the tea was served and they were alone again, moving the conversation away from the trivial. "I would like to speak plainly, if you will allow it?"

Catharine stared at her, saying nothing.

"This drivel between you and your father—"

"Mother—"

"No, let me finish." Emily had the commanding tone of a parent —the reminder that they were in her home, that here, Catharine did not hold the authority to which she was accustomed—that she was in her mother's domain, and limited on her jurisdiction. She respectfully quieted as Emily continued. "This drivel between you and your father has stolen from me my greatest joy, my dearest love, my world. I have spent a quarter of a century grieving the loss of my only child—a loss felt as heavily as if I had lost you to death." She held up a steady hand when Catharine lurched forward, her elbows landing on her knees, her mouth twisting with angry words begging to fly off the tip of her tongue. "I will remind you, Catharine, you are in my house, as my guest, and as such I will ask you to hear me to completion. When I have finished, you will be permitted to say everything you wish to say."

Once more, to Alex's surprise, Catharine retreated. This time, however, her fingers won their battle with her nerves, and an agitated drumming commenced against her knee.

"And am I to blame?" Emily proceeded, undaunted. "Yes. I blame no one more than myself. As a mother it was my duty to never lose you to my life—to allow nothing to come between us, no matter what it took. I did not do that. I did not protect you as I should have, and even later, when all was said and done, I allowed the distance to grow, the divide to widen, until the time came when it became too great, too insurmountable to repair. You stopped calling, I stopped reaching out. I lived in a life where I was no longer permitted to speak your name—as if you had never existed at all. And I accepted it. I did nothing. I said nothing. Because it was the easier road to travel." She paused, the bourbon brown of her eyes becoming unreadable, and Alex realized her openness had faded, and she'd donned an impenetrable mask as easily as one slipped on a glove. She had more in common with her daughter than Alex had first surmised.

Yet still, her gaze remained anchored and her eyes unblinking, her focus solely on Catharine.

"I have loved you, Catharine, from the moment they laid you in my arms, and there has not been a day I have not loved you since. I have failed at showing it, and let me be clear—I do not expect your forgiveness, nor your understanding, nor would I ask for it. But before you leave here today, I will have you know this: whatever choices you have made in your life, whatever path you decide to take—I will always respect that, Catharine. I will always support you, even if only from afar. Your happiness is all I have ever wanted. Twenty-four years ago I wish I had stood up and told you that then—I wish I had encouraged you to follow your heart and leave this life you did not ask to be born into behind you. But I was afraid. I was afraid of your father, but more than that, I was afraid I would lose you." A dry, brittle laugh broke her warm voice, and Alex winced at the sound. "How ironic it is when I look back on things now. I lost more of you by not letting you go than I ever would have had I encouraged you to set yourself free."

She was silent then, her oration complete, her expression stolid yet serene, the acceptance of a condemned woman awaiting her sentencing. Alex realized Emily Brooks harbored no hope of a reconciliation. She'd wished only to say her piece—to be granted her final words before being cut off completely. The only signs of her discomfort apparent in the sheen of sweat that glistened on her finely wrinkled brow and the steady throbbing at her temples. Her hands remained folded in her lap, her tea grown cold beside her.

More than ever, Alex wished she could vanish. This wasn't a conversation for her. This was a moment they ought to have alone with no third party intrusion. But neither woman seemed disconcerted by her presence. Instead, after a silence that extended far too long, Catharine reached over and took her hand, though it was an action done abstractedly.

"I don't know what you wish me to say." Her voice was level, but Alex could feel the pounding pulse that ran through her fingertips.

"I don't expect you to say anything, Catharine. It was just something I needed you to hear." The impassiveness was wearing from her expression. "And I want you to know that I am happy for you. That I am happy for you both." She said these last words directly to Alex, her sincerity convincing.

It was disconcerting, watching Catharine process her emotions. Watching her absorb everything her mom had said, watching it pass through all the hurt, the anger, the betrayal, and—somewhere buried beneath it all—the love she still felt for the woman who had once held such a significant place in her life. The woman she had shut out, written-off, and now regarded as little more than a stranger. Someone—she told Alex the night before as they were laying in bed, Catharine having one of her rare moments of transparency—who had been dead to her for so long, she'd sometimes forgotten she still existed.

All of this Catharine managed to appraise with a degree of stoicism, a detachment Alex knew she raised in self-preservation, unwilling to risk the chance of getting hurt.

"Thank you. It is good to hear you say that." She squeezed Alex's hand. "We are happy." Her tone remained guarded.

With unfortunate timing, the woman in the skirt suit returned to check the status of the tea and cakes, lingering longer than necessary as she gathered the tray and kettle. Her pale eyes drifted toward Catharine more than once, her intrigue evident.

"Carmen," Emily's voice carried a warning as she inquired about the status of the kitchen and requested a fresh brew, effectively sending her on her way.

As the woman disappeared through the French doors, Catharine stood, the interruption giving her time to gather herself, and walked to the edge of the veranda to look out over the rose garden.

"Do you remember," asked Emily tentatively, keeping to her seat across from Alex, her eyes fastened to her daughter's rigid back, "the year the groundskeeper misplanted the summer roses—when that rogue red bush bloomed amongst the whites? You couldn't have been more than six, but you found it positively maddening, and spent all day digging up the wayward shrub and transplanting it to the proper row."

"Yes," Catharine turned, the sapphire of her eyes flashing, her body tenser, even, than before. "I remember. I had soil under my nails when I came to tea—and father... well."

It was impossible to miss the older woman's sinking disappointment, regardless her attempt to distract herself with the sudden urgent adjustment of her scarf. Her hands fumbled with the cream cashmere knotted about her neck, her eyes diverted to the polished stone of the veranda floor.

"I'm sorry," Catharine exhaled, repentant, but Emily shook her head.

"No. You should not be the one who is sorry." She stood abruptly. "Please forgive me a moment, I must step inside." Her eyes drifted to Alex, where she rallied a smile identical to one she'd seen Catharine wear dozens of times when the truth of her feelings was forcibly tucked aside. "I hope you will stay for dinner?" Her gaze returned to Catharine.

"Thank you, but it is a long drive back to the city."

"Of course. I understand." Emily turned away from them. "Perhaps you would care to show Miss Grey the arboretum? It is, of course, more lovely in the summer, but the winter blooms do hold their charm." She didn't wait for an answer before disappearing indoors.

When the doors had swung closed and the only sound remaining on the veranda was the distant trickle of the marble water fountain, Alex rose to join Catharine at the low alabaster balustrade. They stood a few moments, both keeping their own counsel, before Catharine slipped her arm through Alex's, leading her toward a central staircase that let down to a walking path forking out to the various ponds and gardens.

Several minutes into the walk they stepped through an arched trellis covered in vines and came to a stop on a narrow footbridge. Beneath them a stream flowed atop smooth rock, surrounded by reeds and wild river grass. The manor, though less than a quarter mile in the distance, felt smaller behind them, and Catharine seemed to breathe a little easier out of its shadow.

"I'm sorry I put you through this." She leaned against the moss covered stone that made up the railing. "I don't know why I thought this would be easier."

"I'm glad to be here with you." Despite the discomfiture of the afternoon, Alex meant it. She'd been given another glimpse of Catharine's life. A glance at her upbringing. Never in her wildest imagination had she prepared herself for Honour Stone. For the enormity of it. The formality of it. The inconceivable grandeur overshadowing its undercurrent of austerity. It belonged to a world outside the realm of her comprehension, peeling back one more layer of Catharine's indecipherable ambiguity.

And Emily Brooks, at the center of it all, was an unexpected warmth in the heart of a home that felt as brittle as a museum. Despite the tension running between her and Catharine, the hurts built up over the course of a lifetime, Alex felt the woman was sincere in her regrets. Honest in her apology.

Alex settled beside Catharine on the railing as silence resumed, Catharine's idle fingers brushing across the carpet of moss, her thoughts once again turned inward.

"Do you think," she asked after a few minutes, "I should have said yes to dinner?"

Alex thought about the deflation in Emily Brooks' shoulders when Catharine declined the invitation. The faltered breath when she excused herself from the veranda. It wasn't her place to sway Catharine one way or another, but she couldn't help but feel for her mother. "If you are comfortable with the idea," she said carefully, "I think your mother would be delighted."

"I don't know if I will ever see her again." Catharine stared at the running water. "I guess I just… I don't know. It is harder than I thought it would be to say goodbye."

"At least it is a choice you get to make." Alex hadn't meant it as a rebuke, nor had she intended it in any regard to her own mother, but from the quick glance Catharine gave her, she knew that was how it had been taken.

"I'm sorry. That was thoughtless."

"I didn't mean it like that."

"Nevertheless, you are right. I am fortunate for the choice." She exhaled a long breath. "She seemed… earnest? What she said— about being happy for us?"

It was clear Catharine wanted to believe her mother. That she wanted to be given permission to let down her guard. To find forgiveness where she'd previously offered none. To find a reason to stay.

"I think she meant every word about wanting to see you happy." Alex slipped her hand into Catharine's, distracting it from the dissection of the moss. "Let's stay for dinner, Catharine. We're already out here."

"Your flight—"

"—is approaching too quickly, no matter where we are. A couple more hours won't change anything."

"You just don't want to suffer through my cooking again." It was the first genuine smile to touch Catharine's lips since they'd crossed into Oxfordshire.

"Transferring take-out from a to-go box to a plate isn't cooking, so don't flatter yourself."

Catharine gave a hapless laugh and Alex squeezed her hand, bringing it to her lips. Even if the laugh was strained, she was glad to hear it.

"You know, I've never had anyone bring me home to meet their mom before. I'm taking it as a sign you mean for this to be more than just a long weekend?"

"Don't get ahead of yourself, Miss Grey. We haven't even made it through dinner."

Before Alex could find a smart-ass response, Catharine leaned over and kissed her. Slow, unrushed, her lips brushing between Alex's own. It wasn't a kiss that wanted more, her breathing remaining measured and calm. It wasn't *I want you*—it was neither the place nor time—but was instead *I need you*. A sentiment equally powerful, equally thrilling, quickening Alex's pulse all the same.

"Thank you," Catharine whispered at last, drawing away only far enough to kiss Alex's forehead. "For coming here with me."

Alex wanted to tell her she was the one who was thankful—for being allowed behind one more wall, for being given one more piece of Catharine she never thought she'd be offered—but decided enough had been said, and was instead content to stroll hand-in-hand back toward the manor.

After an uneventful meal in which Catharine and Emily slowly warmed to one another, Alex sat in an overstuffed armchair in what Catharine called the *Yellow Room*, listening to the elder Brooks' give a surprisingly educated opinion on the World Cup and the state of women's football.

"It is outlandish—the disparity in prize money—between the men's and women's tournaments. Not to mention the absurdly low pay at the women's professional club level."

"I had never known you to have a keen interest in football," Catharine cut in from across the room, where she'd reappeared after using the restroom. She crossed the room with her graceful stride, coming to sit on the arm of the chair Alex was occupying.

"Catharine, you were not raised in a barn. Sit properly," Emily mildly rebuked, waving her off the armchair. To Alex's amusement, Catharine complied, moving to the adjacent settee, as Emily gave an unflustered shrug and swirled her drink in hand, resuming the conversation. "And anyhow—I hadn't, until reason arose this summer." She touched her glass to her lips, sipping slowly, her eyes holding Catharine's in a dare. It was a look Alex had come to know well—another trait she'd passed on to her daughter. When Catharine said nothing, the corners of Emily's lips twitched as she returned to her discussion with Alex.

"Have you considered, Alex"—the formalities had lessened over the after-dinner brandy—"coming to play for the Women's Super

League here in England? I understand that is what many Americans do to better learn the European style."

Alex had considered it. With *Kickstar* on the rocks and her contract expiring at the end of the season with the Sirens, she was uncertain what the future would hold. Sam Huntley had texted her a handful of times, informing her several European clubs were actively seeking to fill the nine spot—and she was certain Alex would be a top candidate—if she was interested.

But Alex wasn't ready to make that change, with so many other things undetermined. And after seven seasons in the NWSL, she felt an underlying loyalty to the league, even with all of its problems.

She said none of that, however.

"It would be a consideration after my contract is up in Oakland."

"Well, wouldn't that be a suiting situation?" Emily glanced at her daughter. "It would certainly be a shorter distance than the breadth of the Atlantic."

"My time here in England will be limited," Catharine said curtly. After an awkward interval, her eyes catching Alex's with a hint of an apology for dampening the convivial nature of the conversation, she added, "besides, Alex is going to have her hands full with the summer Olympics in Australia."

"Ah, yes," Emily took her daughter's peace offering, "if I understand correctly, no nation has ever won the World Cup and Olympics back to back?"

After the topic of football was exhausted, Catharine and Emily fell into a cautious, yet amicable discussion about the state of UK politics that had the country in an uproar. Unfamiliar with the situation, and relieved that Catharine was thawing to her mother's charm, Alex excused herself from the discourse and rose to examine the decor of the room. Unlike the rest of the manor, the Yellow Room was bright, welcoming, with a cheery air. Alex imagined it was the room Emily Brooks spent the majority of her time in—meticulously decorated with a personal flair. The art was colorful—paintings in pastels, sculptures in polychrome, florals bursting with vibrant hues atop fastidiously polished antique furnishings.

On the mantle were a half dozen paintings—signed E. Brooks in each right hand corner—expertly portrayed in watercolor. There was a landscape of Beachy Head, a snow covered rendition of Honour Stone in winter, the Henley Bridge, the London cityscape, a lighthouse in a storm, and an artful execution of a small, colorful sailboat. It was this last one Alex paused to look at, the image known to her well. It was an abstract rendering of the photo that sat on Catharine's desk back in San Francisco—the one Alex had commissioned into a painting the Christmas prior. The one Carlton had desecrated, shred-by-shred, sitting at her kitchen table. Two faceless figures cast in shadow—Catharine and her mother. It was the only depiction of Catharine on display. The only indication a child had ever existed in the Brooks' household.

From her place by the mantle, Alex noticed Emily had moved to sit on the ottoman in front of the cream settee, where Catharine sat perched on the edge of her seat, unwilling to get comfortable. The small talk had tapered off and a silence had come over the room, disturbed only by the hushed howl of the wind that had risen outside the manor.

In the glass reflection of what Alex suspected was an original Cézanne, she watched as Emily leaned forward on the footstool, reaching to touch the Sunfish pendant hanging at Catharine's throat. "This is beautiful. Do you still sail?"

"Not as much as I would like." Catharine sat back, out of reach, the necklace slipping from Emily's time-worn fingertips. But at her mother's unmistakable wince of hurt, she softened. "But yes, I do." She touched the Sunfish, worrying it like a talisman. "It's actually how I met Alex."

"Oh?" The inquisitive honey-colored eyes shifted to Alex across the room. "You are a sailor, Alex?"

"I—" Alex hesitated.

"No," Catharine interposed, "she swims."

The low, dark brows—so unlike her daughter's—lifted in question.

"I tried to drown myself off Daufuskie and Alex happened to be there." Catharine turned her gaze from the fire, catching the look of horror on the older woman's face, and quickly elaborated. "Not like that, Mother. It was an accident."

"I see." Emily regathered her thoughts. "I'm glad to hear you still enjoy the water. I haven't been sailing in… Well, I don't sail anymore."

"Pity. You loved it so."

"It was the company, my dear, not the sailing."

Catharine had intended to reply. Alex had watched her exquisite mouth open in response, a slow, unforced smile turning the corners of her lips—but whatever words had arisen were abruptly lost as Emily Brooks' face shifted in front of her. Shock. Disbelief. Fear. The brown eyes had lifted over her daughter's shoulder, focused on the open door of the sitting room. Her mouth clamped shut, her gentle eyes widening, as Alex turned to determine the source of her astonishment.

It became immediately clear why Catharine did not resemble her mother. Why her tall, elegant, lithesome form had taken nothing after the compact sturdiness of the woman sitting in front of her. There was no longer question where she got her flaxen hair. Her pale skin. Her extraordinary beauty and consummate grace.

Her features belonged to her father.

The man filling the doorframe stood ramrod straight, his height impressive, his fair hair silver with age. He was almost uncannily handsome, despite his advanced years, his face chiseled with all the same striking lines and angles as his daughter. But more than anything, it was his eyes that mirrored Catharine's. Wide-set, deep, alarmingly blue beneath his intelligent brow. And behind them, a cold austerity Alex had glimpsed from time to time in Catharine.

The room fell agonizingly silent.

In Alex's position by the mantle, out of direct line of sight from the door, the man hadn't noticed her. His attention was entirely on Catharine, who—other than the whiteness of her knuckles as her fingers pressed into her knee—remained remarkably calm, her gaze unwavering, her face inscrutable.

Alex quit breathing. Unblinking, willing herself invisible, she stared at the ticking of Colonel Benjamin Brooks' jaw just below his earlobe.

"What is this, Emily?" he asked his wife, never taking his eyes from Catharine.

Chapter Fourteen

In her professional life, Catharine prided herself on her ability to think on her feet. She could stand at the head of a boardroom table, navigating every twist and turn thrown at her. Her ability to outmaneuver, circumvent, checkmate, and negotiate came naturally. Rarely was she caught unprepared, uncertain how to continue.

This was an exception.

Staring at her father in the doorsill, Catharine's body failed to process the basic commands her mind tried to deliver. *Get up. Walk out.* The two directives repeated over and over. But nothing functioned. Nothing complied.

A distressful sensation of déjà vu flooded through her. She was twenty years old again, caught in flagrante delicto, with no place to run.

"What is this, Emily?" he repeated the question, still standing, suit and tie, briefcase in hand, halfway through the threshold. The sound of his voice was like a slap across the face. His stare frigid. Acerbic. Hateful. It snapped Catharine out of her torpor.

He'd yet to see Alex, she realized, forcing herself not to glance in her direction. She needed to come up with a course of action. A plan to get them out of there. But she was having trouble thinking straight beneath the weight of his brewing outrage.

Eyes flashing to her mother, her first consideration was that she'd been set up. That her mother had sold her out, hoping her father could bully her into submission—force her to sign away her ownership in Brooks Corp. But one look at Emily Brooks said otherwise. The natural warmth of her cheeks had gone ashen, her breath stilling beneath the satin of her blouse. She was stunned by his appearance. And unquestionably horrified.

Still looming in the doorway, her father dropped his briefcase, the brass corners clattering against the century–old wood floor, causing Catharine to flinch involuntarily.

"What game are you playing?"

The words were quiet, measured, but the tightness in his jaw gave him away. The quiver in his fingertips. Catharine knew the look. She knew his anger was simmering, beginning to boil; that it was pressing at his seams. Across the room she could feel Alex's eyes on her, asking what to do. But she didn't have an answer. Her thoughts were spinning a hundred miles an hour. She could hardly think at all.

She forced herself to stand. She was not a child. He did not hold the power over her he'd once had. Still, her legs felt unstable as she faced him.

"There is no game. I came to see my mother." She wasn't sure where the steadiness of her voice came from, given her pulse was thrashing against her breast, but she was grateful for it. The rational side of her brain knew he couldn't touch her. She was no longer a child. He was just an old, bitter man whose last stronghold of power was being used to tear her world apart. But the unreasonable side of her wanted to grab Alex's hand and bolt for the door. To push past him into the hall. To run until Honour Stone was nothing more than a pile of stone and mortar an infinite number of miles behind her.

"It was my invitation, Benjamin." Her mother, also risen, took several steps forward to intercept him. "You were in Liverpool and I wanted to see my daughter."

"Yes, Liverpool—until I was summoned to London by my counsel." A look passed between them, a challenge which Emily finally conceded, her eyes dropping to the hand-knotted silk rug lining the floor. Catharine couldn't focus, her attention drawn only to the realization that nothing had changed over all the years. Her mother still bowed to his every whim, cowed to submission.

Colonel Brooks laughed, a dry, serrated sound—disbelieving of the situation—and returned his gaze to Catharine. She could feel the intensity of his disgust—his loathing—seeping into her; a slow-acting poison she'd failed to find an antidote for through all the years.

"Of all the things you are, I never took idiocy to be one of them." His voice was flat, quiet, no more than a whisper. The calm before the storm. That was how it always was with him—flat seas before a hurricane. As a child, it had made the impending explosion all the more terrifying. As an adult—Catharine was disappointed to discover—the effect remained the same.

"I should have known better. You've never ceased to disappoint me." He smiled, cold, malicious, waiting for Catharine to look away, but she resisted the temptation, unwilling to allow herself to stoop to weakness.

"Tell me—did you think demanding a pen-and-ink signature in London would keep me in the city so you could have your tête-à-tête without me? Were you so daft to not even realize I was up north—where I would still be, if not for your meddling?"

It took a moment for Catharine to process what he was saying. She had known nothing of a request for an in-person signature. That would have come from Elle. Elle, who had known the only reason Catharine had agreed to meet with her mother was because her father was half the country away, attending business at the container terminal in Liverpool. It was a trip he'd made like clockwork every month since she'd been a child. It was the only account he'd maintained a hands-on presence in since the handover of control to Catharine fifteen years prior. Never once had she known him to cut the trip off early.

All of which she'd told to Elle when agreeing to come to Henley. There had been no mention of requesting her father's audience in London. If there had been, she never would have come, knowing he would never stay a night in the city when he was less than forty-five minutes from his preferred country home.

"Have you nothing to say—" he began, but his sentence was cut short as he took a step into the room and caught sight of Alex from his peripheral. Visibly stunned, his mouth fell open as the deep-set wrinkles above his brow furrowed. "Who—?"

The blue of his gaze whipped across the room, first to his wife, then back to Alex, before settling decidedly on Catharine. With the slow dawning of understanding his rigid posture grew even more austere, his stare turning glacial. Catharine wasn't certain if he was more outraged at being caught unaware, or at the actual comprehension of the situation.

"You would dare... bring her... to disrespect me..." The words were halting, faulty, spit from his mouth in contemptuous seething, his focus swinging turbulently between Catharine and her mother. "In my house! In *my* house!"

The kettle had boiled over, his anger erupting from the core. This was the man she knew. The man she'd hidden from under her bed and behind closed curtains as a child. The man who'd berated her, belittled her, and made her feel unworthy of the simple air she breathed no matter how hard she strived to please him. The man who could laugh with his colleagues, charm his competitors, smile at his adversaries. Magnetic and brimming with charisma in the public eye when the occasion suited him, yet made Catharine's life a living hell behind locked doors. The man she'd wanted to escape so desperately she'd thought it better to give up everything— *everyone*—to marry a stranger and move halfway around the world, rather than live in his proximity.

"Benjamin—" her mother's tone was delicate, the word lost to his uproar.

"Get out!" He took a staggered step toward Catharine, his pale face crimson, the dilation of his pupils rendering his blue eyes black. "Both of you—get the hell out!"

Out was all Catharine wanted. Her, Alex—*out*. To the car. *Away.* Yet she found she could not move. Through the pounding in her heart, she could only stare back at him, stricken with panic, transfixed by memories of a man who'd haunted her even in his absence, whose shadow she had lived under, despite the distance and years. She tried to summon Catharine Cleveland—a woman who'd grown to fear almost nothing—who'd learned to take life on the chin, rolling with the punches. A woman who'd stood toe-to-toe with business tycoons and political giants and rarely found her back against the ropes. The woman who'd had the courage to divorce her husband in the middle of a presidential election. The woman who'd finally been brave enough to embrace who she was, no longer hiding from her happiness.

But in the moment that person was missing. She could only find Cate Brooks, a twenty year-old child, incapacitated with fear beneath the weight of her father's wrath.

"Now!" In his rage he booted the vintage coffee table in front of him, upending her mother's beloved Venus Italica, sending the Canova sculpture clattering to the sitting room floor.

"Benjamin! Enough, please!" Emily stepped over the fallen marble, putting herself between her husband and Catharine. As a child, her mother had interceded as best she could when her father's frustration with Catharine grew excessive—when she'd spilt her dinner or interrupted a phone conference or run too quickly down the hall. His anger had exhibited itself in little more than verbal threats back then—accentuated by curses and flung dinnerware and slammed doors. Her mother—young, raised to be obedient—would attempt to assuage his temper with calm reasoning, furtively offering Catharine a gentle look of reassurance while picking up shattered bone china from the floor. It wasn't until later, when Catharine was a teenager, that her father's unfounded resentment for his daughter became more virulent—a slap for an imperfect exam, a backhand for speaking out of turn—but by then, the colonel's variable rage had become a taboo subject the two women of the Brooks' household left unacknowledged. Her mother did not get between her father and his anger, and Catharine learned to hide the repercussions of his fury with a stroke of foundation in her vanity mirror.

So it was unexpected to see her try and step up now, after all these years. Unexpected and undesired. The time for white knights was long past. The girl who'd needed her mother's protection had given up hope of a champion decades ago.

"Don't bother," she said to her mother, motioning for Alex—who'd taken the interlude to step a wide berth around Benjamin Brooks and come up beside her—to follow her out the door. She didn't care that their coats were in the cloakroom as she hurried down the familiar hall. Coats were replaceable. She only wanted an escape. To leave this place forever.

As they reached the main foyer she heard her mother's fast, light footsteps closing in behind them. And somewhere behind her, the militant, unforgiving cadence of her father.

"Catharine—wait!"

The doors were heavy and her fingers were shaking, but she didn't look behind her until she'd found herself on the landing, the comfort of Malcolm standing by the car just a dozen yards away.

No doubt he'd seen the colonel arrive—but decorum dictated he remain outside unless invited—though she little doubted he'd have turned up in the hall to check on her if he'd been made to wait much longer—decorum be damned.

At Catharine's rushed appearance, he started up the stairs three at a time, but stopped midway when he realized they weren't alone.

"Catharine, please, just wait." Her mother was out the door behind her. "Benjamin," she turned at her husband's arrival, "this is madness! Can we not just talk? She's our daughter, for God's—"

She reached an entreating hand to grasp his arm, but in his outrage he flung her away, catching her off balance, causing her to stumble on the top stair.

For the flash of a second the colonel appeared stunned—regretful—at the sight of his wife on the ground, but the remorse was vanished when Alex lunged to Emily's side, dropping to her knees, beating Malcolm to help her to her feet.

Catharine watched—the events transpiring too quickly for reaction—as her father took a step toward Alex, his intent unknown, but before he'd managed a second step, Malcolm was between them, unflinching behind the colonel's venomous glare.

"You like lampin'on women, do you? Care to have a-go at someone your own size?" Not nearly as tall as her father, but half his age, with all the athleticism of a cat, Catharine knew the hotheaded Scot would more than welcome the opportunity to return tit-for-tat. His loyalty to her, coupled with his innate sense of chivalry, was begging to put the colonel in his place—but Catharine couldn't afford that.

"Malcolm." Her tone held just enough warning, just enough command to garner the Scotsman's attention. "See Miss Grey to the car, please."

For a long second he hesitated, his expression insolent as his gaze swept between Catharine and her father, and then to Alex, where she'd helped Emily gain her feet. The older woman appeared dazed, but unharmed, her hand still resting on Alex's forearm.

"Catharine," Alex shook her head, "we can't just—"

"They'll sort it out, same as they always have." She hated that her tone was so cold. So unfeeling. But how could she explain this was how it was? This was how it would always be.

"Catharine—!"

"Malcolm!" She looked for aid from the Scot, the request turning to a demand. "To the car, please!"

Her mother whispered something to Alex, a reassuring pat on her arm, and without looking at Catharine, Alex pushed past her on the landing, following Malcolm to the waiting car.

Affording herself one last look at her mother—wondering what had ever made her think coming here would fix anything? Wondering if this would be the last time she would see her?—Catharine turned to follow them down the stairs.

"That's it." She could hear her father's smile. Hear the triumph in his voice. The certainty he'd won. "Take your dog. Take your slag. Run away, like you always have—"

Catharine turned. Her fear of him had dissipated, replaced only with depthless hatred.

"If I were a better person," she said, ascending to the top of the stairs to confront him, stepping so close she had to tilt her face back to meet his eye, "I'd feel sorry for you. That a man of your wealth, your education, your upbringing, is still so pitifully insecure. You hide behind your insults, grasping for power—but all you are is all you've ever been—a low-class bastard suited in gentlemen's clothing."

She didn't know what compelled her to say it when she could have just walked away. When she knew piquing his lividity would accomplish nothing—would help no one. Part of it, she knew, was simple pride—simple satisfaction. She'd never been in a place before to speak a word to him of opposition. That she'd endured twenty years of his insults, his abuse, his threats and hostility, without a single push of resistance. That she had done everything he ever asked, and still it had never been sufficient.

Or maybe she'd wanted to push his buttons. To strike at him the way he'd always come at her—taking care to hit the most sensitive places. For him, she knew, his power was everything. He enjoyed the fear, the control he held over those he found beneath him. His father had instilled in him a self-doubt that he'd never be enough. No matter his successes. The same he'd tried to do to her—the only difference was, she'd learned her worth, she knew her value, and he was left where he'd always been—cutting other people down to hoist himself above their level.

Whatever the reason, she couldn't feign surprise at his reaction. She couldn't pretend, after twenty-five years, that she hadn't imagined he would still be blind enough with rage to hit her. She knew him better than that. She knew no thought of pending lawsuits or coming trials would sway him from the immediate gratification of retaliation.

The blow was unremarkable. She'd been standing too close for him to have any real power, to make any forceful impact. His knuckles glanced her cheek, the only actual sting from his signet ring as it grazed across her skin. She didn't flinch. She hardly blinked. Just stared at him, wondering how she'd ever allowed herself to care about his opinion. To crave his respect. To want his approval. But the thoughts were cut short as Malcolm came racing up the stairs. She never saw him coming until he'd grabbed her father by his collar, slamming him face first to the ground, his knee in his back and his fist wrapped in the thick silver hair as he pressed his cheek to the dew dampened marble.

"Calm down, you fucking fanny," Malcolm growled as her father cussed and threatened and struggled in his hold. "I told you already, if you want to go belting on ladies, you're going to have to start with me." He looked up at Catharine, already on the defense, aware she'd not approve. "You can't just expect me to let him go thumping on you!"

Get up was all she could think. *Get off of him!*

Benjamin Brooks had just struck her—in front of three witnesses! Even if the damage had been minor, it was still an assault. Something they could use in court, should the need arise. But now, with her man kneeling atop her father's back—*fuck!*

"Of course not," she consented as calmly as she could manage, not wishing to allow her father to realize she felt her man had taken it a step too far. "I'm certain the colonel has received the message. Thank you, Malcolm. Now if you please." She motioned for him to rise.

The Scot's blonde brows knitted, suspicious of her approval, but without further question he casually sprang to his feet, as her father scrambled to his knees.

"That will be all."

Slowly, keen on her father's reaction, he started down the steps, but when the colonel made no further move toward Catharine, she could hear Malcolm's footsteps retreat toward the car.

On his knees, Benjamin Brooks raised a hand to his cheek, brushing off the fine pebbles and dirt imprinted to his skin. When he was finished he lifted his eyes, guarded and unrevealing. "You made a mistake, coming here."

"No." Catharine stared down at him through her impassive gaze, so similar to his own. Unconsciously she touched her chin, the bite of his ring still present. "We're even, then. An eye for an eye. But listen to me very carefully—" her eyes flicked to her mother, half a dozen feet away, silent once again. Doing nothing. "If you ever try to lay a hand on me again, I swear to you—"

He laughed. "You swear to me what? You'll… have me thrown in jail? How long do you think that charge would stick? I own half the police in London."

"Prison's the last thing you need worry about. I promise you that."

His smile broadened. "Are you threatening me?"

"No," the word hung in the silence, flat, heavy. His smile faltered and she knew, for once, he was listening. She was no longer the child he'd terrified and beaten into submission. If he wanted a fight, she was ready to prove herself a worthy adversary. "I don't make threats." Resisting a final glance at her mother, she turned and walked down the steps of Honour Stone to her waiting car.

"You set me up!"

The car headlights illuminated the towering iron gates of Honour Stone as they pulled onto the familiar road that wound through the surrounding parklands. Catharine knew she should have waited to make the call. Waited until she'd calmed down. Until she had privacy. But she was too irate. Too disbelieving to think clearly. Her fingers were shaking even as Elle answered on the second ring, her patronizing laugh grating.

"Well, good evening to you, too."

"Enough with the games! You orchestrated the whole thing!"

"That's a weighty accusation."

"Are you denying it?" Catharine felt out of breath as she stared out the window, the town of Henley glowing in the distance.

"No." The flat, unapologetic answer from the barrister was unsurprising. "Let's cut the bullshit, shall we? I told you from the start—I do what I need to do. I wanted him off the rails, and by your tone, I take it I got what I was looking for."

"This is not what we agreed on! You have no idea what you've just done."

The barrister scoffed. "Oh, I think I do. Don't be such a martyr, Catharine—you need to see the bigger picture."

The bigger picture. The words infuriated Catharine, her mind flying to Alex's fucking tattoo, settling there for half a second before returning to the imbecilic, meddling woman on the other end of the line.

"How dare you…" Dare she what? Prove Catharine to be a fool? She should have known this was all a set-up. She should have known Elle Kirkland had not sent her to Honour Stone to try and win the favor of her mother. The woman was a shark. A win-at-all-cost prizefighter. Catharine had just been too distracted to see the writing on the wall. Too idiotic. Too gullible.

"Listen," the woman sighed a long, audible exhale, the word dripping with condescension, "I'm sorry if I put you in a spot. I knew you wouldn't agree to it otherwise. But I promise you, this will work to our advantage. Come by my office tomorrow, fill me in on the detail, and we'll plot out our next advancement."

Plot out their next advancement. As if this was a game of *Risk*. As if her life wasn't held in the balance.

"You can't just—"

"Ten a.m. would be acceptable. Now if you'll excuse me, I'm about to step into the theatre."

The call went dead and Catharine dropped her mobile into her lap, disbelieving of the entire situation.

On the seat beside her she could feel Alex's unblinking stare through the dark, the albatross of her anger unmistakable, but neither of them broke the silence as the car turned onto the dual carriageway carrying them east toward London.

Maidenhead. Slough. Turnoff signs for Heathrow. An unnecessary reminder that Alex would be leaving in a handful of remaining hours.

"So we only went because of your lawyer?" Alex finally said once Malcolm had dropped them at her flat, the two of them pressed into the private lift.

"No." Catharine punched the button for her suite on the top floor harder than she intended. "It's true, she asked me to go. But I went because I wanted to." She hesitated, knowing all Alex could see now was the setup—Elle's ulterior motive. "I asked you to join me because I wanted you to meet my mother."

Alex's laugh was cynical, as grating as the gears that dragged the lift along its pulleys hidden deep within the nineteenth century building. "I'm sure that was the least of your considerations."

"Alex—"

"Don't patronize me, please. You treat me as if I were a child."

"That is not my intention—"

"You had me ushered to the car!"

"I wanted to get you away from him!"

"I'm not the one you should have been worried about! I think I can hold my own against an old man." The lift settled to a stop as the door slid open and Alex stepped into the suite, her back remaining to Catharine. "We shouldn't have left her there."

Catharine allowed herself the time to take in a slow breath before responding, already knowing Alex would not accept her answer.

"There was nothing else we could do."

"You didn't even ask her if she was okay!"

"She was fine." The words came out clipped as she stepped past Alex into the room, her agitation mounting at her resentfulness of the entire disaster of an evening. She'd known better than to think she could ever go to Honour Stone without drama following her through its hellish halls. "They'll get on as they always have—by morning, it'll be as if nothing ever happened."

"You don't know that for certain."

She didn't—but in all the years Catharine had lived under her father's rule, she'd never seen him so much as lift a finger toward her mother. That wasn't the relationship they had. He'd discounted her, degraded her, cut her down with endless vitriol throughout their marriage—but the vilest side of his anger he'd reserved only for Catharine.

But she couldn't explain that to Alex, because she didn't understand it herself. She never had. It was just the way it was. The way it had always been.

"Just let it go, Alex. It's not your concern."

Alex stared at her in disbelief. "You don't even care?"

"It has nothing to do with caring and everything to do with reality."

"Catharine, she's your mother, for God's sake—!"

"That does not make her my responsibility!" Catharine threw open the balcony doors, welcoming the blast of autumn air fanning her burning cheeks. It was a truth she didn't feel she had to defend—just because a person had birthed another did not leave the latter in unconditional indebtedness. Her mother had abandoned her when she needed her most. When she'd needed her support. Her love. Her advocacy. All Alex saw was a woman seeking forgiveness for regrets long overdue. It was a start— Catharine had appreciated her effort—but it was only one brief moment in time in a long and marred history.

"How can you be so cold?"

"Alex," Catharine turned, exasperated, "there are things in my world you will never understand. Please do not presume to think you know my feelings."

Before she'd even finished the sentence she knew it was the wrong thing to say. The unjust thing to say. None of this was Alex's fault. She'd asked her here. She'd put her in this situation. She was taking her frustration out on the one person who didn't deserve it. But the words were out and couldn't be unsaid, and she knew from the look on Alex's face she'd struck a nerve she hadn't meant to uncover.

"I'm sorry," she closed her eyes, taking a deep breath, hoping to find a remedy to undo the hurt she'd committed. "That isn't how I meant it—"

"It's okay." Alex cut her off, looking away, receding inward. "I got the gist." She laughed, a sound that held no mirth, and turned her back to Catharine. "It's been a long week—we're both tired. I think I'll shower and go to bed early, if you don't mind? Tomorrow's going to be a long day." Without waiting for a response, she crossed to the ensuite, and Catharine dropped onto the balcony settee, feeling the weight of the evening.

Chapter Fifteen

The booing had begun to grate on Alex's overstrung nerves.

Exhausted, her taxed muscles burning, adrenaline was the only thing keeping her legs moving up and down the Capitol Tyrants' field. The DC Stadium was packed, the fans eager to watch their team take down the Sirens, who'd beaten the Texas Bluebells in the quarterfinals four days earlier. They'd come out in droves, hoping to cheer the Tyrants on to a win to move on to the championship the following weekend. But the odds were looking less and less in their favor.

In the third minute of the game, Alex had opened the scoring with a back heel strike, giving the Sirens an early lead and allowing the Oakland team to set the pace to control the match.

The booing, however, had started prior to her goal. The moment she stepped on the field for warmups, she'd heard a handful of catcalls and jeers from the DC supporters' section. She'd been expecting it. The two times the teams had met during regular season, she'd been greeted with the same welcome. The Tyrants' fans were unforgiving of her preseason collision with Bethany Hayes', resulting in the rookie's shattered leg and Alex's red card expulsion.

"Ignore it," her coach, Rodney Collins had told her.

"It's a badge of honor," Halsey'd assured her.

"Fuck them," Molly Rodrigues had flashed the heckling stands the hand symbol for rock n' roll—which had a very different connotation in Portugal.

And for the most part, Alex had. But after her second goal just moments before the end of the first half—the score two-zero, Sirens —the jeers had spread from the hardcore supporters' section to the fans in the regular seats of the stadium, the boos growing louder and more distracting.

A pattern, to Alex's annoyance, that had carried over into the second half.

As the minutes ticked away, the clock growing closer to ninety—the reality of the end of the Tyrants' postseason efforts looming—the rowdy fans trash-talked and whistled, hollering taunts each time she made a run down the pitch. It was hard not to glance at the stands. To not let it get under her skin.

"Tell you what," Jill Thompson whispered as they jogged to take a corner in the seventy-eighth minute, "let's really give 'em something to cry about." Adjusting her blue headband to hold back her mane of golden hair, she bobbed her chin toward the far post, raising a dark blonde eyebrow with a smirk. "I know that big ol' head of yours is dying for a hat-trick."

"They'd stone me," Alex laughed, waving her off as she headed for her place in the box. But as the ball sailed in—a gift from Jill's left foot airmailed directly to Alex's forehead—she knew as soon as she left the ground she was going to bury it in the net.

The stadium erupted, the boos magnifying, but Alex no longer heard them. *Three goals*—her fourth career hat-trick—and a few minutes later when the whistle blew, signifying the end of the semifinal, the Sirens were heading to their second consecutive championship match.

"Fucking girl on fire," Rodrigues body slammed Alex into a bear hug, swinging her in a full circle before dropping her to the grass. "You are one bad ass bitch!"

"Listen to 'em—they love ya!" Halsey teased, waving an arm in an arch around the stadium, the DC fans' jeering beginning to subdue with their loss. The goalkeeper grinned and waved, her already-huge hands amplified by her gloves, giving her a comedic aspect. "You're making pals all over the Capitol!"

"DC's favorite daughter," Rodrigues hip-checked her on the way to the tunnel.

Alex rolled her eyes. "Thanks for the buzz kill."

"Gotta keep that ego in check somehow." Halsey draped an arm over her shoulders, ruffling her hair. "I mean, who else in this league can say their love life single-handedly doubled the amount of primetime viewers for women's postseason football? That's a feat even a semifinal hat-trick can't outshine."

"Oh, shut up," Alex poked her in the ribs. "I think the World Cup win had a little more to do with it."

"Bullshit," Halsey coughed into her hands.

Her teammates had gleefully been giving Alex hell ever since the photo of her and Catharine taken by the fan on Tower Bridge had surfaced a few days earlier on social media. The photo itself wouldn't have made much of a wave in her life. After the attention they'd received for the *Kiss Seen 'Round the World Cup*—as Halsey'd dubbed it—it was hardly remarkable. The remarkable part had been Carlton Cleveland's response to it when a reporter brought up the image during a pre-rally press conference two days earlier. The man had queried the GOP nominee about the status of his divorce, asking if it bothered Carlton that his wife had clearly moved on—'in a different direction.' The senator had reiterated his longstanding response to the matter, citing *Deuteronomy 24:1*: "If a man marries a woman, but she becomes displeasing to him because he finds some indecency in her, he may write her a certificate of divorce, hand it to her, and send her from his house."

This time, however, he'd felt the need to cherry pick the tail end of Hebrews *13:4*, closing with "for God will judge the sexually immoral and adulterous."

The attack had lit a fuse that extended well beyond the women's soccer fans, once again dragging Alex's name into the mainstream media. The response had been split amongst those appalled by his blatant homophobia he so proudly placed on a pedestal, and the ultra conservatives praising him for his "willingness" to bravely combat the immoral agenda by the "woke" left crying for equality. At least those were the words Alex had tried to tune out from Monica Ashby as she'd read a headline aloud at the hotel breakfast hall the previous morning. It was a favorite of hers—making sure to point out Alex's most unfavorable critics in the news and on social networks.

Ironically, between the circulating photo of Alex and Catharine, and the senator's disgruntled response, the buzz had cast a spotlight on the semifinal match between the Tyrants and the Sirens, and the networks had estimated a record number of viewers compared to the previous year—anticipating an even greater snowball effect for the final the following weekend.

A win for women's sports. A loss for Alex's cherished private life.

"The league should really put you on salary for advertising," Halsey continued to tease as they toweled off from the showers and pulled on street clothes, the locker room buzzing with the win. "I swear, every damn thing you do makes the headlines."

"Whether I want it to or not," Alex huffed, indignant, zipping up her backpack. "Trust me, I'd be okay if I never made another headline."

"Yeah," Halsey drawled out the word, the corner of her mouth twisted in a wry grin, "something tells me that ain't gonna happen. Not the way you're going."

Alex didn't ask if she was referring to her on-pitch success or off-the-field drama. The former she didn't mind. The latter was more likely. At least now, with a solid postseason performance under her belt, the media might be inclined to talk more about her game day achievements than obsessing over her love life.

She should have known that was never going to happen.

It was a quarter past one when Halsey came charging into their shared hotel room, grappling for the unfamiliar light switch on the textured wall. Alex had declined the outing to the local sports bar with her teammates, preferring to skip whatever welcome downtown DC had in store for her, opting instead for some R&R in the hotel.

She'd intended to take advantage of the privacy to call Catharine, but the game had ended late and by the time the van dropped her off it was almost midnight. Four a.m. in London. Too late to call.

A relief she'd tried not to admit to herself.

Things had been left awkwardly between them. Regardless that they'd talked or texted every day since she'd arrived home, the strain of their departure had lingered.

Catharine had driven her to the airport. The two of them had hardly spoken since the night before, Alex feigning sleep by the time Catharine came to bed that night, and Catharine up before dawn the following morning. Alex had woken to the muffled simmer of an animated conversation in French on the balcony, Catharine presumably relaying the events of the previous evening to Nathalie. Her tone was clipped, irritated, and though she'd curbed her agitation by the time she settled into the driver's seat, the first minutes of the drive had passed in silence.

"About last night," Catharine had finally said, waiting at a stoplight, her eyes on the car ahead of them. She'd taken a deep breath, her fingers loosening their death grip on the steering wheel. "I'm sorry. I didn't—"

A car honked behind them, drawing Catharine's attention to the light that had changed in her state of distraction. With the words left hanging, the apology unfinished, Catharine pressed hard on the gas, speeding up the onramp to merge into the weekday traffic. Signs for Heathrow rolled by, one after another—a deflating acknowledgement their time together was coming to an end. An end difficult enough without the added stress of the discomfort between them.

In an effort to assuage the uneasiness, Alex had turned her gaze out the window and brushed away the interrupted apology with a noncommittal flick of her hand.

"It's fine, really." And though it wasn't, she'd said it with finality, and Catharine, in her reticent, taciturn way—her invisible battlements still risen from the events of the previous evening—had accepted the statement at face value, withdrawing the subject indefinitely. A few minutes later she'd turned the conversation to Alex's coming games, and expressed—with genuine regret—how sorry she was she couldn't be there. Honour Stone had been swept under the carpet, and Alex had boarded a plane to the States with the bitterness of an unfinished conversation still weighing between them.

An agitation that still hadn't wholly dissipated.

"Dude!" Halsey found the light switch, upending a vase of fake flowers in her wake, but making no effort to gather them as she threw herself onto the foot of Alex's bed. "Safe bet to say you haven't been on Twitter?"

Alex, blinking at the intrusion and unwelcome shift from sleep to blinding light, pulled the covers over her head. "Whatever it is, I don't want to know."

Halsey ignored her. "I'll start with the good news. You've gained at least a half million followers. Probably double that by morning. Your name is trending. The finals next week are going to be blazing!"

Alex groaned against the duvet. No part of that was good news. She wasn't naive enough to cling to the hope that any of this had to do with her hat-trick against DC.

"The, uh—less good part…" Halsey left a pregnant pause until Alex dared to peek out from hiding.

"What is it?"

Her friend's freckled cheeks were flushed, her expression positively giddy. Part of her was enjoying this—which made Alex all the more wary.

"Carlton Cleveland went on a rant about you tonight on Twitter." The goalkeeper's eyebrows arched in what would have been a comical expression, if Alex's stomach hadn't felt like it had fallen to the floor.

"What?"

"Like… a tirade of bizarre tweets," she started to scroll her phone, "he starts off with a shoutout to the Tyrants on 'a game well played' but then goes on…" she scrolled enthusiastically, "here! *Congrads*—that's seriously how he spelled it—*to the Oakland Sirens on advancing to the championships. The girls*—girls, barf," she added to her running commentary, "*played well. But tell me…*" more scrolling until she got to a second tweet, "*I can't be the only one tired of watching Alex Grey hog the ball. Someone apparently didn't learn the Golden Rule in kindergarden*—again, that's how he spelled it—*that there is no I in team.*" Halsey looked up to make sure Alex was listening, her eyes gleaming.

"Please tell me you are fucking with me." Alex pushed herself into a sitting position. The man was running for president, for God's sake. It was two weeks out from the election. He couldn't be so imbecilic to post nonsense like that on a public platform while trying to earn the respect of the country. That kind of thing simply wasn't done.

"Oh, I couldn't make this shit up, dude. It gets worse."

Alex let her head fall back against the headboard. Carlton Cleveland had tens of millions of followers on Twitter. He'd devised himself into the political equivalent of a rockstar, the Southern Baptist come to save the country from ruination. Outspoken, politically insensitive, tactless and offensive—the leader of a cult of citizens who fancied themselves an army, waiting with bated breath for every absurd thought that fell from his slack-jawed mouth.

Up until now, she'd managed to deflect his offhanded remarks to the media without any real damage. His focus had been primarily on his wife, and Alex had been little more than a civilian casualty caught in the crossfires of the war he waged with Catharine. But this was different. This was personal. Zeroed-in.

"You are the biggest shit magnet, Grey. God love you."

If God loved her, he'd have made Mark Zuckerberg and Jack Dorsey interested in medicine instead of media.

"Just give me the CliffsNotes," Alex pushed Halsey's phone aside. No need to have the play-by-play. She already felt like she was going to be sick.

Disgruntled by Alex's disinterest in her detailed chronicles, Halsey hugged her legs to her chest and propped her chin on her knees. "Fine. Basically he popped off on a tirade of bizarre, somewhat illegible nonsense—claiming you cause turbulence everywhere you go and that you were chased out of South Carolina for not being a team player and that you never should have been permitted to wear the Stars and Stripes." Halsey laughed, as if any of this was funny. "I guess he's too stupid to realize you were a national hero at the World Cup this summer. Anyhow," she steepled her fingers, thinking. "Oh—last thing he said was something about you being an Agent Provocateur—spell check must have helped him with that one—and tagged his 'good buddy,'" she made air quotes around the term, "Sampson Hargrove, and told him the best thing he could do was throw your endorsement with *"Kickstart"* to the wind. Such a good pal and he can't even get the company name right." Halsey shrugged. "Consensus is he was drunk and the Tweets will be deleted by morning. But don't worry —I have screenshots of all of them, just in case we need them." She glanced at her phone. "Yeah, man—look at that—you're at 4.2 million followers and climbing. He kicked the hornet's nest with this one."

Never one for perceived social graces, Halsey only suddenly seemed to realize how still Alex had grown. How nauseous she was feeling.

"Look—before you panic—Rage has already issued a strongly worded rebuttal about his claim you were chased off the team. In fact, Marty went so far as to say you were the best player the club has ever had the honor to sign and that they were heartbroken to see you leave. Something I take offense to, really," Halsey teased, swatting at Alex to try and rouse a smile. "I mean, hello…what was I, chopped liver?"

Alex didn't smile. She didn't even breathe.

"Okay, listen—all kidding aside—the guy is just a jackass. You can't take it to heart. All he did tonight was make himself look like a looney tune. The soccer community is going to bat for you big time. Everyone is, really. It's only the tin-foil-hat-brigade that's lapping up his retweets. The rest of the planet can see what a clown he is. For all we know, you may have just singlehandedly saved the American people from four years of living hell under his presidency." Stretching out a foot, she poked Alex's leg with the toe of her Converse. "Everyone loves you, Alex. Minus a few DC fans tonight." She winked.

"Sampson Hargrove doesn't."

"So what?" Halsey rolled her broad shoulders. "You've been hoping they'd drop you for months. Maybe Hargrove will take his *buddy's* advice and release you. They'd be doing you a favor and you know it."

That wasn't the point. This was her job. Her livelihood. Her *life*.

Alex flung off the duvet and leapt to her feet. She couldn't sit still, but felt equally immobilized. Incapable of thinking. Grabbing her phone from the nightstand, she flicked through the silenced banners. The little red number above *Twitter* showed 100+ notifications. There were more than a dozen text messages from friends congratulating her on the win, and more recent ones with screenshots and links to various social media outlets. She ignored them all and pulled up her missed calls. One from Marty Bales, the coach of Rage FC, and six from Catharine.

So she'd already seen.

Kicking her bare feet into Halsey's too-big slides carelessly discarded in front of the TV, she grabbed her room key off the nightstand and turned for the door.

"Alex—come on. Where are you going?" Halsey rocked to her feet. "The dude's a certified bastard. You can't let him get to you."

Easy to say, when she wasn't the one subjected to the front running presidential nominee's retweets.

"I just need to walk a little."

"It's like thirty degrees outside." Halsey motioned at her shorts and sleeping tank. "You'll freeze to death."

Given the way her night was going, the prospect didn't seem the worst of her options. "I'll be fine."

The goalkeeper's warning about the cold hadn't been invalid, however, and ten minutes later Alex found herself sitting on the edge of the hotel's hot tub, her feet dangling in the steaming water, her racing mind savoring the darkness of the closed aquatic room, the only sound the slow gurgle of the pool's filter.

Condensation built on her blackened phone screen, the smell of chemicals and chlorine thick through the humidity.

Resigned, she swiped open her contacts and selected "favorites," punching the number at the top of the screen.

Catharine's voice filled the quiet on the first ring.

"Hey." The English lilt was tentative. Apologetic. Condoling. So much said in one small syllable.

"Hey."

"I saw."

"Yeah."

"I'm so sorry, Alex."

"Well, I guess if I look on the bright side, it made getting booed at the game tonight seem like small change. Everything in perspective, right?" She regretted the barbed edge to her voice, but couldn't curb it.

Catharine failed at hiding her sigh. "Is there anything I can do for you?"

Return to the States.

Come to her championship game next weekend.

Be there when she woke up in the morning.

Those all sounded like viable options. But none of them were feasible, and despite her mood, Alex wasn't spiteful enough to dangle her want of things Catharine couldn't give her.

"No." She trailed her fingers through the hot water. Her knees were scabbed from the turf of the DC field. A bruise was darkening on her thigh from a knock she'd taken earlier in the week during training. The outline of KT tape remnants turned sticky in the chlorinated water. She suddenly felt thoroughly exhausted. Her body as tired as her mind. "I just wanted you to know I'm okay. Really, I am."

A brief silence hung between the line.

"You were outstanding tonight," Catharine finally offered.

"You watched?"

"Alex." The word held a subtle reprimand. "Of course I watched. Don't be ridiculous."

"It was just late your time. Next week the game will be earlier."

"I'll be watching."

Again, Alex wanted to ask her to fly out. To come, even if just for the night. To be there.

But she didn't. She knew Catharine had a preliminary hearing at the end of the week. The beginning of what would undoubtedly be a miserable few months to come. With both her fight for her business and Carlton's election looming, a soccer game couldn't hold a candle to Catharine's mounting list of concerns.

"Well," Alex said instead, skimming her pruned toes across the surface of the water, "I have an early flight tomorrow." Her team was flying straight to South Carolina, where the championship would be played the following weekend. Tomorrow, Rage FC squared up against the Portland Warriors—the winner of that match destined to face the Sirens for the final. And despite the Warriors being heavy favorites, Alex had a feeling her old team was going to pull off the win. With the chance to play a championship game in their home stadium, the South Carolina squad would be on fire—and even with the semifinal match hosted in front of the Portland home crowd, Alex doubted the Soccer City team stood a chance.

"You'll call me when you land?"

"Yes."

"I miss you, Alex."

Alex stared at the chlorine crusted concrete. "I miss you, too," she said quietly, before forcing herself to stand, the chill of the air cold against her wet shins.

"I'm sorry, again… About…"

"I know." Alex slipped back into Halsey's slides. "Goodnight, Catharine."

She stood for a few minutes in the dark, staring at her illuminated screen. Her phone vibrated, the endless notifications piling. Decisively, she held her thumb to the small blue Twitter icon, waiting for the *edit* option, and then clicked the *x*, confirming *delete*. Then followed suit with Facebook. Instagram. TikTok.

Slipping her phone back into her pocket she headed for the elevators. Carlton Cleveland could kiss her ass. This time next week the South Carolina senator could tweet to his heart's content about how Alex Grey stole the win from his home state's team.

Chapter Sixteen

"Hello, darling."

The insipid drawl raised the hair on the back of Catharine's neck, tensing every muscle in her body. From across the hall she could see Elle watching her through the lightly frosted glass of her office, the door open just enough to make privy her conversation. She turned her back to the room as Carlton continued.

"My apologies for not returning your call sooner. Perhaps you've not noticed, but I've been somewhat busy." She could hear the smugness of his smile, could imagine him sitting at his desk with his heels kicked up over a stack of papers, an Arturo Fuente cigar dangling from his stubby fingertips. "Now tell me, to what do I owe the honor?"

"You know why I called."

"To tell me you've missed me, darling? To throw yourself at my feet in light of the knowledge I'm soon to become the most power-ful man in the world?" he laughed. "Fret not, my dear—ask nicely and I'll take you back. I've always loved the sight of you on your knees."

"Go to hell, Carlton." Her words were shaky, his name stilted on her tongue. In the months she'd not spoken to him she'd almost forgotten how much she loathed the sound of his voice. How inciting the condescension of his laughter.

"It's such a turn on when you talk dirty."

"Fuck you!"

Again, he laughed. Loud. Bold. Grating. "That could be arranged, I assure you. Shall we schedule a date? Say, Inauguration Day? Bent over the desk in the Oval Office? I've always fantasized that's how I'd begin my reign."

Catharine's fingers shook in her rage. She had to slow her breath. Calm her mind. She hadn't called to enter a pissing match. To stoop to his level.

"What is it going to take," she said instead, "for you to leave her alone?" She'd speak his own language: buy-offs, bribery, hush-money. Whatever it would take to turn Alex from his sights.

"You think you can buy me, Catharine?" Complacency was replaced with anger looming behind its glacial tide. "You think you can pull out your checkbook? Manage me like you've always done? You've forgotten who the fuck you're dealing with if you think you can control me now!"

It was laughable, him thinking he didn't have a price. They both knew it. Carlton had been bought and sold his entire career. He was a politician. Ever open to the highest bidder.

"You want to play your games, Carlton—play them with me. Leave her out of it. What is it you want?"

"Beyond the enjoyment of watching your total demise?" he scoffed, but she could hear him thinking. Calculating. He was many things, but a man to miss an opportunity was not one of them. He'd have had a price in mind before he ever returned her call. "What's she worth to you, your little toy? An eight figure check? Your house on the bay? No..." he clucked his tongue. "I saw the photo of you, you sick, besotted fool. She's got you tripping over yourself—hook, line, and sinker."

"You have fifteen seconds before I hang up this call. What's your price, Carlton?"

"There she is—my charming, hardball wife. You always think you hold the court—"

"Ten."

"It must drive you absolutely insane, losing control. Watching your kingdom crumble—"

"Five."

"Fine," he caved. "Twenty-six percent."

Catharine laughed. The request was ridiculous, even for him.

"You know that can't happen. Even if I wanted to."

"And would you want to? If you could?" His voice was slick, oily. "Is she worth that to you?"

"It doesn't matter. It's irrelevant." They both knew that. The stock in Brooks Corp. was nonnegotiable. It belonged to her trust, of which he held no control, a design implemented by her father. It was the one thing Colonel Brooks had protected in her marriage. His beloved corporation. Brooks Corp. would never belong to anyone but a Brooks. Even if Carlton fought her for it, he would never win.

"You would." The thickness in his chuckle made her skin crawl. "Look at you, my wicked Aphrodite with your fabled heart of stone. Your Achilles' Heel has been found. You'd sign it away, wouldn't you? Controlling interest in your shares just to keep her head between your legs."

"We're finished with this conversation, Carlton, if you've no reasonable negotiation—"

"How infuriating it must be—the indomitable Catharine Cleveland—forgive me, *Brooks*, is it?—unable to buy her way to what she wants? You were so certain, my dear, that I'd cave to whatever proposal you came to offer… that you could manipulate me, as you always have. But what figure, what sum, could possibly be better than watching you suffer? More satisfying than knowing you are powerless to get everything you want. I want to see you destroyed, Catharine. I want to sit back and watch while you lose every Goddamn thing you've ever had—"

She hung up. Hung up before she could hear him laugh again. Before the threats she wanted to make could fall from her mouth.

The insolent, arrogant bastard! The worst part—he was right. He held the upper hand. For what could she do? What offer could she make that would mean more to him than knowing he'd slipped beneath her skin? That he'd found a way to get back at her through Alex. She'd given herself away by calling him, by trying to negotiate. She'd been a fool and played right into his hand.

"Going that well, is it?"

Catharine startled at the voice, her mobile slipping to the floor.

In her stilettos and skintight pencil skirt, Elle Kirkland bent to retrieve the dropped device, settling it into Catharine's palm. "Divorce is a bitch, isn't it?"

Catharine ignored her, stepping into the barrister's corner office overlooking the Thames. This was her third meeting at *Crown Bridge Chambers* over the past two weeks, and though they hadn't readdressed the subject, she was still livid about the woman's meddling at Honour Stone. She wasn't willing to forgive her yet, and the last thing she intended to do was discuss with her the tumultuous dissolution of her marriage.

Unperturbed, Elle settled a hip against the corner of her executive desk as Catharine took a chair, uninvited.

"It seems you got what you wanted." Catharine set a stack of envelopes atop the desk, pushing them toward the barrister.

Elle's lips lifted into a willful smile. "I usually do."

Unamused, Catharine motioned toward the pile. "He's done it. Guangzhou, Rotterdam, Cape Town, Long Beach, Melbourne. Layoffs en masse. Nearly eight thousand jobs. It will be staggering."

"The financial hit was expected."

"I meant for the families. The loss of work before the holidays. It's disastrous."

"It's what we wanted."

"*Needed,*" Catharine said firmly. "None of this is *wanted.*"

"Semantics," Elle shrugged, picking up the first envelope and flicking it open with a blood red nail. "Ah—fan mail," she laughed, reading the messily scrawled letter aloud. *"Watch your back you peacocking bush biter. You're going to get yours! I'll fuck you til you're dead."* Elevating a perfectly penciled brow, she glanced at the Melbourne postmark. "Charming. The Australians certainly know how to woo a lady." She picked up the next one, a thick card stock elegantly scripted in hiragana. "A disgruntled Chinese employee, I presume?"

"*Japanese.* The gist of which says 'the bread you have stolen from our mouths should be shoved down your throat until you cannot breathe.' It also mentions shoving it other places."

"I see." Elle fanned the stack of death threats and hate mail. "Well, don't take it to heart. Hazard of the job for women like us, I'm afraid. I get a few a week, depending on my caseload and whose feelings I've stomped on lately." Her rosewood stained lips flickered. "Almost all from men with their big bravados and uncouth mouths. They're all talk. It's the articulate, no-nonsense ones I watch out for. They usually come from women—and women can mean business."

Catharine didn't care about the threats and hate mail. It was the employees she was worried about. The dockworkers. Longshore-men. Freight handlers. Stevedores. Cargo crews. Those that were counting on a paycheck. Those who now saw her as a villain—the person responsible for their loss of income. As the Wall Street Journal had reported it, Catharine was to blame for the turmoil within the corporation—a greedy socialite who selfishly refused to accept a ten digit buyout, persisting instead with a baseless lawsuit that would be stonewalled in the courts of London, leaving the workers to suffer in her tantrum. Lazy, biased reporting she could do nothing about. Carlton held the conservative paper in his back pocket, and the publication was eager to print anything that turned her into a monster. The kind of woman who would abandon her husband in the middle of his presidential campaign. Who would allow the blue-collar workers to bleed just out of greed.

And the people believed it. They needed somewhere to point a finger.

"How much longer do we let this hemorrhage?"

"A round of quarterlies. Maybe two. Let the financials slip and prove intentional negligence against minority share—"

"That's January—"

"June, more likely—"

"This cannot continue until June—"

"Catharine." The staccato word was frustratingly condescending. "You agreed we were in this for the long haul. I can't squeeze butter out of a cow, but if you give me enough time, I'll churn up something. You need to be patient in the meantime."

Patience wasn't the problem. Catharine could be patient. She was in a privileged position where time was not of dire essence. It was the workforce that made up the foundation of *WorldCargo* that did not have the luxury of waiting months on end. Eight months was detrimental.

"What about his settlement offer?" She stared at the smooth surface of the barrister's cherrywood desk, not daring to meet her eyes.

"What about it?" The question held a lethal edge.

"I could take it under the promise that he'd reopen—"

"He's offering half the value of what the stock is worth! No, Catharine! This is exactly what he is preying on! Your sensitivity is your weakness. It is how he intends to win. He knows you are soft. He knows you are a sympathizer for the people and he'll use it to his full advantage." Elle tapped her desk with the silver tip of her ink pen. "Let me ask you this: do you really believe he will run the corporation better than you have? Do you believe the employees will benefit from your absence in the long run?"

Catharine stared at the stack of letters wishing her misfortune, wishing her misery, wishing her death. These people loathed her, and for good reason.

And yet still, she believed firmly in her answer—the corporation would not benefit in her absence. Nor would the people.

"No."

"Then bear with me, Catharine." Elle pulled out a bottle of Mortlach and poured them both a jigger. "Don't get me wrong," she said, sliding a glass across the table, "I don't want you to settle because my paycheck benefits tremendously the longer we roll this thing out. But, believe it or not, I'm not an entirely selfish tosser—I like to win the good fight. And this is a good one. Women like us weren't meant to be pushed around. And I don't like conceding to those bastards who think they can crush us beneath their heel. We're better than that." She tipped back the scotch. "But enough about that." She glanced at her watch. "Almost time for the big match, isn't it?"

Catharine was thrown by the turn in conversation. "Alex's?"

Elle paused in the middle of her second pour. "Are there other footballers I don't know about? Are you entertaining Arsenal's starting XI in your boudoir?"

At Catharine's sullen eye roll, Elle smiled, resuming her task and her banter. "I imagine one young superstar is hard enough to hold on to at the moment. I'm surprised your American will still speak to you after the latest antics by your husband."

Catharine set the scotch to her lips to hide her annoyance. It was just one more subject that didn't belong within the walls of this office. And verging too close to the truth to be comfortable.

Today was Alex's championship match in South Carolina. Her final game of the season. Catharine should have been there. A simple flight, even if just for one night—eight hours and she could have been there to support her.

But Alex hadn't asked her to come and Catharine hadn't felt merited to show up without an invitation. Not after the last three weeks of upheaval. The cataclysm of Honour Stone. The maelstrom Carlton had brewed on Twitter. Life in general as Catharine was beginning to know it.

If she went, she worried it would turn attention away from the game. With the election around the corner, the media had become unrelenting. She didn't want to turn the match into a spectacle. Or cause any additional undue criticism for Alex. If Alex had wanted her there, she would have said so.

In Catharine's silence, Elle took another sip of scotch and swirled her ice sphere. "Look on the bright side—it's been brilliant for women's football. All that media. All that coverage. Would be a fabulous time to invest in the game, come to think about it. Ratings are elevated. Interest is piqued. Nothing like a scandal to draw an audience." She finished her glass. "So—where are we watching?"

"We?"

"Well, you can't very well go home and watch it by yourself in the lonely luxury of your empty penthouse. That's not how football was meant to be enjoyed. Come," she slapped her desk with the flat of her palm, her gaudy gold bangles rattling on her wrist, "we're going to Brigadiers. It's not far from yours and you won't find better Indian cuisine in the city. Not to mention the array of whiskies."

Catherine swept up the pile of scattered letters, intent to decline, but paused, staring at the strokes of the beautifully scripted kana. What good was there in going home to sit in her quiet flat? She'd pour herself another whisky, watch Alex on her flat screen, and stare at the outside world through her walls of glass.

Company sounded bearable. Almost held an appeal. She needed a distraction. Even if it was in the form of the overbearing barrister and her intolerable lack of tact.

It was better than watching the game alone.

"It won't start until after ten. Are you certain they'll play the US match?"

Elle waved a derisive hand. "They will if I tell them to. No one says no to me."

Ignoring a *reserved* card perched in the middle of the table, Elle settled into a booth in front of the upscale barroom's largest flat screen. There was a brief innuendo-packed conversation with a server half her age, in which the young man's eyes were primarily glued to the barrister's impressive cleavage, and then Elle was left in charge of the TV's remote.

Despite jeers from fellow patrons invested in the last minutes of a men's Liverpool vs. Manchester United football match, Elle flipped through the channels until she landed on the coverage leading to the American championship.

"Here we are." She dropped the remote into her Birkin bag and hung the clutch on the hook beneath the table, flashing a *get-stuffed* smile toward the most vocal protestor at the end of the bar top. "What'll you have, Catharine? Since you're buying, might I suggest the Aberlour A'Bunadh? A positively dear single malt from the Highlands." Without waiting for Catharine's approval, she raised two fingers toward the bartender, who nodded and pulled a pair of glasses onto the counter.

It turned out Elle Kirkland was a fervent fan of football. As the clock ticked toward kickoff, the footage cutting back and forth from the starting XI for both Rage and Sirens, to highlights from the recent matches played in the WSL—England's professional league—Elle rattled off standings and statistics, combined with an unapologetic opinion on player performance and managing style.

Within minutes, Catharine was forced to admit she was little more than a novice when it came to understanding the game.

Elle tsked her disapproval. "I played all the way through university until I began my Bar course. I would have gone pro if there'd been any money in it at the time. Back then, the salaries were almost nothing and footballers weren't prone to catch the interest of billionaires muddling through a midlife crisis."

Catharine fixed a cold gaze on the barrister. "I'm hardly going through a midlife crisis." But her tone was without any real warning, as she'd begun to grow accustomed to the endless barrage of taunting from the meddling woman, and found no real annoyance at her teasing. "At least not as far as Alex is concerned." When it came to the rest of her life, *crisis* didn't account for the half of it.

Her attention flicked to the tv, where a clip was being shown of the previous weekend's match between Arsenal and Chelsea. Amelia Walker sat in the press box for the post-match commentary. In the replay, a reporter was asking her how she felt after the loss in their home stadium against their longstanding rival team.

"No loss is ever taken lightly," the familiar Australian voice asserted, her shaggy blonde hair hanging in her dirt streaked face, her Arsenal jersey sticking to her boyish figure. "But it's early in the season and we have to stay focused on the big picture. Our possession, passing accuracy, shots on frame…"

The big picture. Those words were forever going to nettle her.

Catharine tuned the rest of the interview out, turning her eyes back to find Elle silently analyzing her. She didn't doubt the woman was well aware of the history between Alex and Amelia. Anyone who could name the third string goalkeepers for every team in a league five thousand miles across the sea would be up-to-date on the rumors following the athletes.

To her credit—or perhaps it was due to her sensibility as a barrister—she did not comment on Amelia's presence on the screen. She may have enjoyed toeing the line when it came to subjects that riled Catharine, but she knew well enough when not to step across it. For that, Catharine was grateful.

"So tell me," Elle diverted, leaning back and folding her hands behind her head, her auburn hair hanging loose over her shoulders, "if you weren't a fan of footie, how exactly does a straight, married, English businesswoman fall into a relationship with a footballer from California?"

"Carolina."

"Hmm?"

"Alex is from South Carolina."

"You're deflecting."

She was. She shrugged. "It's a long story."

On the TV the US national anthem wrapped up and the two captains—Erin Halsey for Sirens and Abby Sawyer for Rage—shook hands, before the teams spread across the field. Catharine's eyes fixed on Alex. Her dark hair was pulled into her habitual high bun, her lips disappearing in a tight line, her expression serious. Catharine loved the intensity she radiated. Her determination and focus. If the Sirens won tonight, she and Erin Halsey would make history as the first NWSL players to win a championship with two different teams. But Catharine knew the championship more to Alex than just record breaking and statistics. With all the attention Carlton had dumped on her, anything other than a win would make her entire season feel like a failure. Regardless that she'd had one of the best seasons of her career.

"Earth to lover girl," Elle snapped her fingers, drawing Catharine's attention. "You can lech over your starlet later. As I was saying—ninety minutes seems like a fair amount of time to render a synopsis."

"I want to watch the game."

Abby Sawyer drilled the ball down the pitch and the NWSL championship match was underway.

As the game took off at a measured pace, dictated by Rage's counter press—explained by Elle—Catharine found herself coaxed to divulge the basic summary of how she and Alex had arrived in their relationship. The day in Daufuskie. The game in Portland. Fate sending Alex to play in Northern California. Where it had gone from there.

"So one little near-death experience and you flipped teams faster than a Birmingham City fan on relegation night. I imagine you mustn't exactly have had sparks flying in your marriage for you to survive drowning and suddenly decide, 'I'm going to pursue a female footballer'?" Elle laughed, amused at herself. "I mean, don't get me wrong—if you were going to slide down that slippery slope, I can't fault you for choosing her." She bobbed her chin toward the TV where Alex was on screen, faceplanting into the grass from a hard clip from behind. Elle continued, blissfully unaware of Catharine's anxiety as she waited to be certain no injury had been acquired. "She's winning to look at—in an All-American sort of way. Top-notch baller, no question."

Alex climbed to her feet, no worse for wear, and the game resumed with a free kick.

"Great arse, I'll add."

Catharine pinned Elle with a look, to which the woman only laughed, flinging her fiery hair over her shoulder.

"What? You can't fault me for noticing. The two of you do make a striking pair. No doubt one day they'll make a movie out of your tumultuous love affair. It'd be a blockbuster."

"It'd be a better film if one of the protagonists wasn't watching her corporation founder while her workforce was hung out to dry."

"As Tolstoy once said, 'the two most powerful warriors are patience and having a little damn faith in the expertise of your barrister.'"

Catharine couldn't help but laugh. "And all these years I thought the quote was 'patience and time.'"

"Bollocks. It was definitely the former." Elle nodded toward the TV. "Corner for the Sirens."

The cross arched near the far post, but was headed away, and the match resumed a back and forth turn over in the midfield. Elle rattled on about tactics and her anticipated substitutions as the minutes ticked by, the game nearing ninety minutes without a score.

"Now," sang Elle, her voice growing husky as she neared the end of her third round, "if it's still a draw at the whistle—"

"Both teams play two fifteen minute segments of extra time."

"Well, look at you," Elle's Cupid's bow lips turned up at the corners, the effects of the whisky glinting in her amber eyes. "And you claim to know nothing about footfall."

"I said I didn't know the intricate details, I didn't say I was an utter ignoramus."

Elle's smile grew. "Growing irascible in the final minutes of the match, are we?"

It was true, Catharine could feel her tension mounting with every passing minute the Sirens didn't score. She refused to entertain the thought of what would happen if they didn't win. What it would do to Alex. How she would feel.

What Carlton might do…

The whistle blew and the match moved into extra time, Catharine's anxiety increasing with each run down the pitch.

"Excuse me, Mrs. Cleveland?"

Catharine turned toward the voice as an unfamiliar hand was placed on her arm. A young man in thick, round-rimmed glasses stood at the edge of their table, assessing her with an inquisitive stare.

"You are Catharine Cleveland, aren't you?"

She'd been taken too off-guard to deny it, and responded with a curt nod.

"Grand!" He had a boyish grin. "I thought as much. Seen you on the telly." He eyed the trio of Elle's empty glasses and Catharine's half-full first round. "What're you ladies having? I'll buy you a pair."

"You couldn't afford it," Elle dismissed him with no hint of apology, bored at his intrusion.

A shout went up around the bar and Catharine returned her focus to the TV, only to have her heart pummel to the floor. The South Carolina players were surrounding Abby Sawyer, whooping and swinging her into the melee of a team embrace. Elle's eyes never left the screen. "Don't fret. It'll be called back—the play was offsides."

The young man—fixtured beside them—disagreed. "Nonsense. That'll stand."

At this Elle did at last bless him with her attention. "Care to wager on it?"

Behind his thick glass lenses, the man's eyes lit with the challenge. "Fiver says it's clean."

"A fiver? Don't insult me. Go back to your uni mates."

"A century, then?"

On the pitch the official held a hand to her ear, waiting for the external review.

"Tell you what," Elle leaned back, crossing her stockinged legs, and regarded the man with a baleful smile. "If the goal stands, my friend here will buy the bar a round. If it's ruled offsides—which it will be—you'll fuck off without another word and leave us alone."

Catharine's eyes snapped from the referee to the barrister, appalled at her brazen gamble. This was no low-end bar with watered down whisky and wage-earning workers who'd be satisfied with weak ale.

Elle cut her protest short with a wave of her hand.

"Untwist your knickers. She was offsides by a mile."

A moment later the official turned to the crowd, the review complete, and made the shape of a box with his hands, before blowing his whistle and raising an arm in the air. Catharine didn't have to ask for the action to be translated—the Carolina players went wild, the home crowd on their feet, waving their scarves in elation. The goal had stood.

"Sod it," Elle hissed, slapping the table with her bangled arm. "Bollocks call!"

"Lads!" The man clapped his hands together, drawing attention over the din. "The gracious Mrs. Cleveland is buying the room a round in celebration of the Carolina goal!"

Catharine's protests that that was positively *not* the reason for the round was lost over cheers from several dozen patrons crammed between the bar top and tables, who'd now taken an interest in the American women's match.

"You're a sport, Catharine." The man ran his fingers across the stubble on his chin, grinning like a Cheshire Cat. "Nothing like the cold-hearted bitch I've read about in the papers." Pulling out his phone, he pointed it in her and Elle's direction. "Smile, ladies, will you? A little keepsake for the evening? A remembrance of our lovely benefactress."

"Piss off," Elle snarled, but not before he'd snapped his photo, then sauntered away to where the bartender was pouring shots for the crowd.

"What an arrogant, impertinent little—oh! Yes! Yes!" Elle gestured wildly at the TV, before slamming her palms against the table, "yes! Yes! Bloody pearler, that!"

Catharine looked up just in time to see Jill Thompson—a winger for the Sirens—head a stunner into the back of the net.

"Balance is restored!" Elle flashed a cheeky smile, remaining unapologetic for her earlier blunder. "Don't look so cross. What's a couple grand when your girl's team is back in the match?"

Catharine could think of no reply that would keep her decorum intact.

Instead she watched the minutes toil by as the bar grew rowdier, every one of her nerves standing on edge. A text came through from Nathalie.

—Ç'est de la folie!

Catharine didn't reply. It *was* madness. She'd never imagined an evening where Alex didn't win. That had never been a consideration. But the second half of extra time was dwindling to an end, and the championship game was moving toward a shootout.

"Well, if this isn't exciting," Elle hummed, helping herself to Catharine's unfinished drink.

"Alex hates PKs."

"Because she's too much in her head. Tremendous goalscorer, but an overthinker—it's written all over her face."

There was no defense to that. As the cameras panned in on Alex and Molly Rodrigues walking toward center circle after the whistle blew on extra time, Catharine could plainly read the nerves on Alex's face. The entire game she'd been tight, careful, clearly second guessing herself. The stress of the external noise in her life had gotten to her—external noise Catharine couldn't help but feel like she had brought about.

South Carolina won both coin tosses, putting the shootout at their end of the field, and giving them choice of going first.

Abby Sawyer, irrefutably one of the best PK-takers in the league, calmly stepped to the spot. Without preamble, Catharine watched as the lean, lithe figure of Alex's best friend took a decisive jog forward, eyes up, a smile on her face, and drilled the ball into the far corner of the net. Erin Halsey had guessed correctly and lunged to full extension, but with the speed and placement on Sawyer's ball, she'd never stood a chance.

"Beautiful," Elle gave an appreciative whistle. "Conviction. No indecision. A woman after my own heart."

"I'm pretty certain she's available," Catharine said dryly, unsmiling, her hands clenched on her knees. She liked Abby Sawyer, but at the moment she would have traded a sizable number of shares to have seen her shoot wide.

"Well then," Elle dashed a look through the veil of her curled lashes, "perhaps an introduction is in order?"

Catharine cast her a sideways glance. If there had been any question as to Elle's tendencies, she'd just made them clear.

"She's far too good for you, trust me."

Elle laughed, unperturbed, and refocused on the match.

Sawyer's goal was answered by one from the Sirens, followed by another round where both goalkeepers were on the losing end. On Rage's third round, Erin Halsey made a spectacular dive, finding the ball with nothing but gloved fingertips, and tipped the ball over the net. Catharine forgot herself, pummeling her fists onto the table, and jumped to her feet.

"Yes!" She remained standing as one of the younger Sirens' midfielders overshot into the stands. "Damn it!"

"She's going to have a rough night," Elle shook her head. "Even if they win, she'll be kicking herself for that one for a long time. Rookie mistake."

Catharine continued standing as the fourth round commenced, another success for Rage, followed by the unmistakable form of Molly Rodrigues as she strode toward the spot.

With a flex of her heavily tattooed arms stretched out behind her, Molly rolled her shoulders, jumped a couple times in place, and ran for the ball, sinking it with perfect precision in the upper left corner of the goal. The keeper for Rage remained flat-footed in the center of the frame, having been thrown off by the immense speed of the ball.

"Miserable deal for the keepers," Elle lamented, sharing a moment of sympathy for the towering blonde goalkeeper who shook out her lanky limbs like a soaked cat. "It's all about who can psyche out who—with the disadvantage always going toward the keeper. Their only hope is to get inside a kicker's head—to capitalize on the pressure each player is feeling, knowing the fate of the game is in their hands."

As Rage's fifth player scored, Catharine tuned out Elle, waiting without breathing to see what player would be chosen to take the Sirens' final shot. If this goal was missed, the game was over, the win going to Rage.

An audible sigh of relief escaped her lips when Jill Thompson jogged from the center circle.

"Phenomenal player, Thompson," Elle said, watching as the confident golden-haired veteran adjusted her blue headband, then calmly approached the ball and launched it into an unreachable corner of Carolina's net. "Hasn't missed a PK in…" Elle racked her brain, "hmm—might have missed one her second year with the Bluebells. Hundred percent conversion rate with the national team. It'll be a sad day when she retires."

Catharine didn't care about Jill's retirement. Or conversion rates. Or Elle's trivial recollection of arbitrary stats. She only cared about what happened next—five shots taken by each team, level at four-to-four.

"Now what?" Did they go another round of five?

"What happened to the football guru?" Elle teased, then recanted at Catharine's irritable stare. "Now we have a proper dilemma —sudden death." Her eyes gleamed with the drama of it all. "The first player to miss after the other team has scored loses the match. Brutal, but Sod's law in sports, m'dear."

A sixth player from South Carolina stepped to the spot and bested Halsey before Monica Ashby trotted from the center circle to answer the Rage. She had a cocky smirk on her face Catharine had come to loathe, and took her time getting across the pitch, sashaying with a slow, deliberate trot. There was no doubt she knew all eyes were on her, and wanted every moment of individual airtime that could be acquired.

Spending a length of time fixing a perfectly laced shoe, she straightened, smiled brilliantly toward the cameras, and darted forward, abruptly changing her cadence as she took a shuffle step before reaching the ball. The Carolina keeper tipped left at the feint and Ashby rolled a slow ball right, twirling around and shooting her fists in the air.

"Cheap," Elle rolled her eyes, putting back the rest of Catharine's drink. "Never cared for a stutter-step myself."

Ashby skipped back to her teammates, high-fiving players on either side of Alex. Catharine contemplated what sort of bribery could convince HEG to trade the little bitch to a different team. Or perhaps just bench her indefinitely.

The seventh shot from Carolina was converted and Catharine's heart rate doubled as Alex jogged toward the box.

"She looks stiff," Elle commented over the howling din of the bar. The patrons were merrily enjoying their rounds and the lout with the round-rimmed glasses caught Catharine's eye, a smirk on his thin lips, and toasted her in a silent salute. Catharine sharply turned her attention back to the TV.

Alex's face was unreadable, her jaw clenched as she set the ball and took several steps backward.

The American commentator was rambling on about Alex making the short list for MVP, and how she'd finished regular season as the runner-up for the Golden Boot—second only to Amelia Walker, who had played little more than half the NWSL season.

"Yes," agreed the English pundit, "but it's no secret Alex Grey has an aversion to PKs. Incontestably not her strong suit."

Catharine's skin was crawling.

The whistle blew and Alex paused—too long, it felt, compared to her teammates—before taking a last look at the keeper, who was waving her arms and jumping up and down on her line. Then, with a single breath, she ran forward and booted the ball with her favored left foot. Still standing, Catharine watched as the goal-keeper guessed correctly, diving left as the ball flew across the turf. But the shot was wide, bending quickly, and the ball sailed a foot outside the net. The camera panned to Alex, staring emptily in the direction of the ball, before covering her face with her hands and sinking to her knees on the grass. A wide angle appeared, showing the Rage keeper racing past Alex with her arms pumping above her head, diving into the mass huddle of her teammates who greeted her with a frenzy of hugs and screams of celebration. Rage FC had won the championship on Alex's missed kick.

"Rotten luck," Elle was saying, clever enough not to remark on all the ways Alex's kick had gone wrong, but Catharine wasn't listening. She just stared at the screen, watching faces she knew alight in jubilance while others sunk in despair.

Rachel Parsons and Sylvia Santos—both former teammates of Alex's who Catharine had met at the bar in Portland—raced around the grass, collecting flowers thrown from the stands. Erin Halsey, who habitually had a smile on her freckled face, trudged downtrodden toward the tunnel, fighting back tears. Rodney Collins, the coach of the Sirens, quietly gathered his jacket from the bench. Marty Bales, head coach of the Carolina Rage, shrieked a mock disapproval as five gallons of Gatorade was dumped over her head.

And there was Alex, still kneeling on the ground.

Catharine felt physically ill.

She should have been there. She *needed* to be there.

"Win some, lose some," she managed, her voice tight, as she pulled out her wallet to settle the bill. She refused to allow Elle to see how much this hurt. "Always next year."

"Perhaps," Elle shrugged, unable to hide her indifference to the loss. "Shall we drown away our sorrows with another round?"

Catharine tapped her card against the mobile kiosk without looking at the bill. On the TV behind the bar, the cameras zoomed in on Abby Sawyer, who had left her celebrating teammates, and knelt next to Alex, one hand on Alex's cheek, the other clutching her hand.

She'd been right about what she said earlier. Abby Sawyer was far too good for Elle Kirkland. She was truly a gem.

Signing the electronic receipt, Catharine turned from the booth and wove her way toward the front door.

Chapter Seventeen

Several compassionate hands reached out to touch Alex's arm or brush her shoulder as she slumped down the aisle, the last team-mate to board the bus.

Her red-rimmed eyes were hidden behind dark sunglasses, despite the late night hour, and her hoodie was zipped all the way to her chin in an attempt to block out the world around her. To her relief, she'd made it out of the post-match press conference and into the tunnel before breaking down in tears, but now, for every well-meaning word of support, every glance of understanding, every kind-intentioned touch, she wanted to tell the sympathizer to fuck off. To leave her alone. To let her disappear.

Her teammates meant to be comforting. To show her they didn't blame her. To assign no fault, knowing any one of them could easily be in her shoes. Alex knew that. She herself had offered seasons of consoling words to players who'd spectacularly blundered, but she'd never been on the receiving end of that sympathy —not to this extent—and the view from the trench of anguish she'd stumbled into was very different than the top.

Carlton Cleveland had gotten in her head. All game she'd battled to keep her mind dialed in, to maintain her focus where it belonged, but when the match had come to a shootout, he may as well have been standing on the pitch with her; an audible devil in her ear.

Twenty-four hours earlier Alex had walked into the training room to hear several of her younger teammates talking about the bastard's latest post on Twitter.

Tomorrow I guess we'll see if Alex Gray is the hero her Commifornia fans keep bragging about.

Bree Decker had been reading the thread out loud, annoyed by the hashtag—#heroesdontkickballs—his followers had tacked onto the retweets, which was currently trending on Twitter.

As soon as she saw Alex, the young forward had dropped her phone, her face turning white, and bolted for the door.

"The jackass can't even spell your name right," she'd offered in lame apology, before disappearing into the showers.

Alex had tried to put it from her mind, but no amount of meditation, of focused breathing, or relaxation techniques had left the words off the pitch the next night. When she'd finally stepped to the spot to take her shot, all she could think about was what would happen if she missed? What would he say next? Then she'd struck the ball too high on her laces and let everybody down.

Her teammates. Her coaches. Her sponsors. Her friends.

She'd given away the match.

Even if her teammates didn't hate her, she hated herself.

"Are you going to be okay tonight?"

Jill Thompson either neglected to notice or chose to ignore her *leave-me-the-fuck-alone* vibes. As the bus pulled out of the familiar South Carolina stadium parking lot, America's Golden-Girl-of-Soccer moved back two rows to drop onto the empty seat beside Alex.

"Alone, I mean?" she persisted, when Alex offered nothing more than a nod, burrowing deeper into her sweatshirt.

Halsey—Alex's assigned roommate—had left straight from the game to fly home to Mississippi with her aunt. Alex had initially been disappointed she wouldn't have any time to catch up with Clancy, but with the way things turned out, it was a relief to know she'd have the hotel room to herself.

"I'm good." She cleared her throat, trying to cover the rawness of her voice still thick with tears threatening to reappear. "I just want to crawl under the covers and lay low for a while."

"That's fair. Tonight's going to hurt." Jill set a hand on her knee and gave it a squeeze. She wasn't the warm and coddling type. All business on the pitch, no nonsense in the locker, full focus on the training field. It was one of the things Alex admired most about her. One of the reasons she made such a stalwart captain for the National Team. Full of candor, sugarcoating nothing, the players could always count on Jill for her honesty.

"We all have bad games, Alex—to varying degrees. Tonight wasn't your night. And it's your right to lock yourself away, drown your sorrows with tears and misery, indulge in self-pity for a while —and then, come morning, snap out of the bullshit, get dressed, slink down to breakfast, and remind yourself you're one of the best God damn strikers this league has ever seen. One bad showing doesn't make a rotten season—just as one loudmouth critic doesn't speak for the rest of the world. It's your job to remember that. Do you know what I mean?"

Alex nodded obediently.

"Good." Jill gave a curt nod and moved back to her seat.

As the bus pulled under the mildew-stained veranda in front of their hotel, Alex's phone vibrated. She glanced at it, expecting it to be Catharine. She'd called earlier while she was still in the recovery room, but Alex hadn't answered. She hadn't wanted to talk while she was surrounded by her teammates. Not while she was still struggling to just take one breath after another. She needed to be alone for a while, to be given the chance to cry—unabated, without feeling the strain of self-consciousness. To find a way to piece herself back together and gather her emotions. She'd return the call as soon as she was sure she could get through a conversation without crumbling into a sobbing mess of heartbreak.

But the call wasn't from Catharine. It was Matt Jacobs, her agent. At eleven p.m. on a Saturday night.

The drumming in Alex's head crescendoed as she sent the call to voicemail. Matt would want to talk shop, to come up with a statement after her farcical showing in the championship. Damage control for her sponsors. Something to appease the fans. She liked Matt, but his mind translated everything to dollar signs. It wasn't something she could deal with tonight.

Turning the deadbolt on her fourth floor twin room, Alex tossed her game bag on Halsey's empty bed. She left the lights off, shuffling through the cramped space by the glow of pulsing LED lamps filtering up from the parking lot. Her entire body hurt. Getting through ninety minutes of a high intensity game was strenuous in its own merit, but adding thirty minutes of extra time, followed by the emotional stress of a shootout, was nothing short of exhausting.

But it wasn't her aching muscles or screaming joints that held her attention. She could focus only on the crushing disappointment—the nauseating knowledge—that every one of her teammates would go to bed tonight knowing she'd failed them.

Shoes still on and fully dressed, Alex dropped onto the top of her comforter and stared at the ceiling and cried.

Sometime later, caught between drowsiness and unconsciousness, a knock stirred her from her stupor. She blinked at the blurry numbers on her watch—it was half after midnight. It was likely to be Rodney Collins. He was known to check in on his players when they were feeling the weight of a less-than-stellar showing. Alex closed her eyes, willing him away, but the knock came again.

Resigned, she unfurled her stiff body and sulked to the door, fumbling with the lock in the dark.

It wasn't Rodney.

The illumination of the light in the hall cast a shadow on the figure leaning against her door frame, but Alex would have known the silhouette anywhere.

"Oey," the jumbled word fell out of her mouth, a mangled cross between *oh* and *hey*.

"Thought you might be in here feeling sorry for yourself." Amelia Walker ran a hand through her familiar shock of blonde hair—darker than when Alex had last seen her, a telltale sign of the absence of the California sun. A silence passed as they stared at one another, before Amelia cocked her head and flicked her green eyes—ever-present with their habitual impertinence—over Alex's shoulder into the room.

"May I?"

"Um," Alex paused, then opened the door wider to allow her to pass, "sure, yeah."

Flipping on a light, Amelia surveyed the bland surroundings before taking a seat on Halsey's bed. "I was a little worried about you," she said, watching as Alex took up station beside the window.

"So you just hopped on a plane and took a supersonic flight across the Atlantic to do a check-in?"

"Don't flatter yourself. I reserve all supersonic efforts for my opponents on the pitch."

"Well, aren't we?" asked Alex, before she could stop herself. "Opponents?"

Amelia's fair brow lifted. "That's a loaded question. Way to come out swinging."

If Alex hadn't known her so well, she would have been fooled by the lazy smile and blasé manner, meant to cast an air of indifference. But beneath her cool exterior, she could tell the Australian was uncharacteristically nervous, trying to gauge Alex's response to her unsolicited visit.

"You know," Alex said, sliding to perch against the windowsill, trying to turn the conversation in a safer direction, "if you were concerned, a text would have sufficed."

"A text didn't feel like enough."

Enough for what, she wanted to ask? For six months of silence? For running away without a word? For giving Alex no say in the matter—no ability to try and salvage the friendship they'd self-destructed?

She stuck with the present, determined to leave the past in the past.

"It's been a rough night, but I'll be okay, if that's what you were wondering."

Amelia nodded appraisingly. "You look like hell."

"Thanks."

"For the record—I didn't know they were going to drop you."

Alex's eyes flashed up in an expression Amelia misconstrued for something other than what it was—confusion.

"I swear I only found out when I saw the Tweet." She ran her fingers through her messy hair. "I hope you believe me—if I'd known, I would have told them to shove the latest *Kickstar* commercial up their arse."

"What Tweet?" Alex finally managed, aware of an uncomfortable tingling sensation spreading through her limbs as her pulse rate escalated.

"The one from—" Amelia stopped abruptly, realization dawning. "You didn't know." Her shoulders deflated.

"Know what?"

"Listen, Alex—"

Shoving off the windowsill, Alex planted herself in front of Amelia, holding out a demanding hand. "Show me the Tweet."

"Alex—"

"Cut the crap, Amelia—show me the fucking Tweet."

"They should have called you," Amelia sighed, reluctantly allowing Alex to snatch away her phone.

Without thinking, Alex pinned in the familiar six digit passcode and scrolled until she found the blue social media icon. Twice her shaking fingers miscued the letters before she managed to search for mentions of HEG.

The first thread to pop up was from *SheBallz*, posted at 9:13 PM —just minutes after the final whistle.

1/ A spokesman for Hargrove Entertainment Group has confirmed the dropped Kickstar endorsement of US National Team soccer star, Alex Grey.

2/ The severance of ties comes immediately after the NWSL Championship, in which Grey's missed kick in the penalty shootout subsequently ended the match.

3/ The dismissal comes at no surprise after last week's comments from presidential nominee, Carlton Cleveland, called for Sampson Hargrove to end the endorsement of the Kickstar athlete.

4/ Rumor has it tension has been high between the global entertainment giant and Sirens FC starter since..."

Alex stopped reading and slumped to sit on the bed. "Fuck."

"I'm sorry, mate."

If she'd bothered to listen to the message from her agent, she probably wouldn't have been caught so unaware.

Her mind spun, trying to wrap itself around the information.

At least this meant she wouldn't have to do the rescheduled photoshoot she'd been dreading next week in Utah.

Alex took a long, slow breath, determined not to cry. She refused to shed a single tear over that bigoted bastard, Hargrove.

"I don't even know why I'm upset. Three months ago my agent was begging them for an early release from my contract. I guess it's just..." she trailed off.

"Getting blindsided?" Amelia's chapped lips disappeared into a line. "Nothing like kicking a dog when it's down."

"Yeah." Alex exhaled. "I take it you saw the game?"

"I did. Well, the parts of it I could see when that bogan ex of yours wasn't standing and waving his sign that read *Ashby's going to be an Anderson: t-minus 37 days.*"

"He didn't really have a sign that said that!"

"I assure you he did."

"God." Alex's face twisted in disgust, making Amelia smile.

"See—there are worse things than missing the game-deciding penalty in a championship match. You could be marrying a drongo like that."

"When you put it that way…" Alex tried to find a smile of her own, but was unsuccessful, the night still weighing too heavy to find levity.

Amelia was quick to read the direction of her thoughts.

"You know, Grey—even Bradman made a duck. It happens. You can't take sole responsibility for the result of the match—there were ten other players on that pitch for a hundred and twenty minutes. Trying to put it all on your shoulders is bold—even for you."

"You would," Alex challenged, earning another crooked smile.

"Fair dinkum. Though I did read somewhere recently that there is no I in team."

Alex finally laughed, feeling a release of relief break free in her chest, like the first breath after being under water.

She'd forgotten how much she missed her. Her cockiness. Her bizarre sayings. The infuriating way she could shrug off anything.

Alex had been blessed with extraordinary friends—Sawyer, Halsey, Rodrigues—but her friendship with Amelia had been different. Amelia had gotten her. Seen through her. Known when to push, and when to give her space. And the loss of that, after the demise of their relationship, had left a sting that hadn't gone away.

Catching the small glimpse of that—the easiness that had existed between them—suddenly made Alex wary. She didn't want to hurt again. She didn't want to hope for something unattainable to hold onto.

Handing Amelia her phone, Alex stood, returning to the window.

"So what brings you here?" she asked, grateful for the even keel of her voice.

"I told you. I was worried about you. I wanted to make sure you weren't drawing yourself a toaster bath."

"Jesus, Amelia."

"Well, you can be dramatic."

"Why are you *here*, instead of back in London, preparing for your match next weekend against Liverpool?"

Amelia's lips flickered. "Keeping track of my schedule, are you, Grey?"

"Don't flatter yourself," Alex recycled the phrase, but unlike Amelia, she had no defense to combat it. She *had* kept up with her schedule. She knew Arsenal was sitting in first place. She knew they'd lost to Chelsea the previous weekend.

The Australian hiked a casual shoulder. "I had a commercial shoot with *Kickstar*."

"In South Carolina?"

"Chicago."

"Ah." Alex folded her arms. "Long layover in Charleston?"

"Nah. Flew in deliberate. Had a mate with a big match this weekend."

"I see." Alex mimicked her perfunctory tone. "Came to support Ashby, then?"

"Shut up, Grey," Amelia drawled out of the side of her smile. "You know I was here for Halsey."

Alex's face involuntarily shifted and Amelia rolled her eyes. "Don't be such a galah. Yes, I came to watch you."

"Why now?" It came out more accusatory than Alex had meant it, but the question still stood. If Amelia had wanted to mend their friendship, she could have started after the World Cup. But she hadn't. Neither of them had reached out. They'd had no contact between them. So why the change of heart?

"Because I needed to talk to you."

Alex's wariness returned. "About?"

"We need to put to rest any awkwardness between us."

She said it so simply. Like it was that easy. Like they could shake hands and begin again.

"Why now?" Alex repeated, no longer trying to hide her growing anger.

Amelia stared at her, unblinking. "Because HEG called in my loan. They want me back here by preseason."

Alex looked away, trying to cover the sucker punch she felt. "Just like that, huh? You show up, we shake hands—pretend like nothing ever happened?"

"If we can, yeah."

Out of the corner of her eye, Alex saw Amelia shrug. It was infuriating.

"Why not have Arsenal buy out your contract? You never wanted to be here in the first place."

"Because HEG wouldn't sell it. And I've agreed to an extension."

"Why?!" Alex turned back, incredulous.

"Because they offered me a lot of money. And right now, I need it."

The venom of her last words struck Alex full in the face. She knew WorldCargo had closed down their terminals in the Port of Melbourne. She'd read the articles about the thousands of jobs that had been displaced. And she hadn't forgotten for a moment what Carlton Cleveland had said about Amelia's father, Dave Walker. About his bad investments. His debt. His fragile mental health.

Amelia'd long been helping support her family. And now, with the loss of jobs in Melbourne, she'd be carrying them all by herself.

"I heard. I'm sorry."

"I don't need your sympathy, Alex. I just need to know that we can play together."

Alex was quiet. Somewhere down the hall a door slammed. A drunk teammate returning after drowning their sorrows. Or one who couldn't sleep—heading out for a midnight run.

"We're both professionals." It seemed the safest response.

"We are," Amelia agreed, "but I don't want it to be like that. We were friends, Grey."

"We *were*," Alex snapped, unable to stop herself. "Until we weren't. Until it was something different. Until you walked away without a word!"

"That was self-preservation," Amelia leveled, unapologetically. "I didn't want to get hurt."

"You're the one who left!"

"Right! Because only a masochist would hang around for someone who's in love with someone else!"

Alex laughed, disbelieving. "Oh please, don't pretend you were in love with me. You made it clear that was never going to happen from the get-go. I mean, Jesus—you went so far as to invent a nonexistent girlfriend so you didn't have to commit to anything!"

"Are you really this fucking daft, Alex?!" Amelia unfurled herself from the bed, her body radiating with fury. She took a step toward the door, then paused, drawing a deep breath, and turned back to the room. "I stuck with that story because I knew I was just your pastime. Your dalliance until you sorted things. And I don't blame you for that—you never led me to believe otherwise. You were honest; I was not. And I fucked myself in the meantime."

"Why—" Alex took a shaky breath. "Why didn't you just tell me?"

"Because I knew who you were—who you *are*. You would have hung around out of loyalty. And I didn't want that." Amelia softened, her shoulders relaxing with a long exhale. "Look, Alex—it's in the past. I took the time I needed to get my head on straight. I'm good. You're good. I just came here to make sure we were on the same page. To make sure we could play together."

She was all business once again, her anger gone, her pragmatic practicality returned.

Alex tried to match her composure, knowing the pounding pulse at her temple probably gave her away.

"Yeah. Of course." She shrugged. "Like I said—we're both professionals. We're friends. It'll be great to have you on the team again."

"Okay." Amelia nodded, a slow, wry smile resuming. "Good. Because it's obvious you need me if you ever want to win a championship."

"Says the girl who lost to Chelsea last weekend."

"So you *are* stalking me?"

"*Please*. A five-two loss makes all the headlines."

Amelia flipped her the bird, still smiling. "Would have been five-nil without me." She shifted, glancing at her watch. "Well—I'll leave you to your wallowing. You fly out in the morning?"

"Yeah. You?"

"Not 'til Tuesday. Going to enjoy a little Carolina sunshine."

"Nice." The return to small talk felt shallow.

Alex stayed by the window and Amelia stepped toward the door.

"Cheers, then. Looks like I'll see you in the spring."

"Good luck at Liverpool next weekend."

Amelia waved over her shoulder. "I make my own luck," she called, then closed the door behind her.

After Amelia had gone, Alex stared absently out the window, trying to get a grip on her feelings. From the blistering disappointment of the lost championship, to the unexpected midnight visit, she really wasn't sure how to process everything.

Her mind wanted to hang on the loss of the game. Her failure. Her mistakes. But her heart was stuck on the hurt hidden behind Amelia's anger. On the things she'd said without ever really saying them.

Alex had never meant to hurt her. She'd never thought she could. Amelia had always been so adverse to sentiment—to revealing any feelings. And somehow Alex had fucked it all up, and never seen past her own self-centered need.

Her phone chimed on the dresser and Alex dragged herself across the room to check her notifications. Three missed calls—one each from Halsey and Sawyer—and an earlier one from Catharine.

Her teammates would have seen the latest from HEG and would be worried about her. But she couldn't bring herself to hit redial. To rehash it all again. Instead she shot off a group text between the three of them, acknowledging she'd seen the news, and promised she was okay and would talk to them both in the morning.

Then she pulled off her shoes, climbed under the covers, and called Catharine. All of a sudden she needed to hear her voice. To ask her if it would be all right if she upped the date of her plans to fly to London. Now that she didn't have to worry about the *Kickstar* catalogue, her schedule was free for the better part of offseason. And after their strained communication of the past few weeks, she was anxious to put the awkwardness behind them.

The call went straight to voicemail.

She checked the time in the UK—shortly after 6 AM—and tried again. Catharine was guaranteed to be up already. But the call was once again directed to her inbox. There'd been no message from her earlier call and she'd sent no texts. Despite knowing it was ridiculous and petty, Alex felt a twinge of bitterness at her unavailability. At her minimal effort to reach out to her on a night nearing the top of the list of Worst Nights of Her Life.

Alex turned off the light and tossed and turned. Her body hurt. Her head hurt. Her mind wouldn't turn off. She worried what Carlton Cleveland would say next—with the loss of the game and her departure from *Kickstar*, she'd given him plenty of fuel for the fire.

Unable to sleep, she picked her phone up and decisively re-downloaded Twitter. The anxiety of not knowing was becoming more crippling than actually reading the hateful threads about her. She'd rather know than not—at least that's what she convinced herself.

She'd rather have a heads up than get caught off guard, like she had with *Kickstar*.

Surfing the feed, she quickly found the tightness in her chest dissipating as she realized Carlton Cleveland hadn't said anything new about her. There were thousands of threads about the game— which Alex made sure to steer clear of—but no new mentions from the GOP frontrunner.

Her first win of the night.

Alex scrolled aimlessly, her eyes growing heavy, and was about to shut her phone down when a Tweet refreshed at the top of her notifications. @*Sportsguru678* had posted a photo with the caption, "I Just Got Catharine Cleveland to Buy All the Boys A Bottle." It had surfaced on Alex's feed from the *keyword alert* she'd set for Catharine's name some months earlier.

Alex clicked on the image.

The photo enlarged to reveal a douchie-looking guy in John Lennon glasses, standing in a swanky bar, smirking in a selfie. Behind him he was pointing at a booth containing Catharine and Elle Kirkland. There were a cluster of empty glasses in front of them, their attention held in intense conversation.

Alex checked the time stamp. Five hours earlier. Sometime in the middle of her match.

Swiping out of the app, Alex dropped her phone on the night-stand.

Had Catharine seriously set up a business meeting on the night of her championship final?

Given the number of empty glasses on their table, it was no wonder her phone was going straight to voicemail.

Another fifteen minutes passed as Alex stared at the shadows on the popcorn ceiling. She thought about texting Sawyer. Asking if she'd want to hang out for a few days, maybe rent a place on Seabrook Island? The thought of flying home alone to Oakland in the morning became more and more depressing. Halsey was on her way to Mississippi. Molly was leaving for Lisbon.

Alex swiped open her phone, her fingers hovering over Sawyer's number. Sawyer would be high with the win of the night, while Alex was at her lowest. It wasn't fair to ask her to absorb Alex's heartache when she deserved a weekend of celebration.

Deliberating a few more minutes, Alex scrolled to a different contact. One she had long removed from her list of favorites.

—Hey. I'm thinking about staying over in SC for an extra night or two. Might catch up with Sawyer. Want to grab a drink tomorrow? It's my first night as a free woman.

Alex hit send before she could talk herself out of it, then reread the text, panicked, and quickly sent a second one.

—(free from HEG, I mean)

The three dots appeared, then disappeared, before reappearing again. Finally a text returned from Amelia.

—ok. sure. where?

Alex didn't know. She hadn't thought this through. She just knew she didn't want to get on that plane headed for Oakland tomorrow morning. She quickly keyed in bars south of the French Quarter.

—Blondie's near The Battery? 1?

—ok. see ya.

Chapter Eighteen

After eleven hours crammed into the last row of the economy cabin—seated directly ahead of the toilets—Catharine raised the window shade to glimpse the Pacific Ocean for the first time in half a year. The Boeing 777 dipped its wing in preparation to circle around toward the San Francisco airport, which elevated the curiosity of the active toddler sitting beside her. The child, who'd been awake since they'd left the ground at Heathrow, craned his body over the armrest, trying to get a better look. Catharine stared at his sticky fingers and chocolate stained corners of his pudgy lips, before casting a glance at his mother, whose attention was glued to a movie on her iPhone.

The decision to fly to San Francisco had been last minute. It had been after one a.m. when she left Elle at Brigadiers, and by the time she got to her flat in Bermondsey she'd made the decision to catch the first available flight in the morning. It would put her in California by midday Sunday, and though she could stay only one night—her presence was required at a *motion to dismiss* hearing first thing Tuesday morning—the turn around trip was worth it. She needed to be there for Alex. To support her after her game.

When she'd arrived at the ticket window, the predawn flight had been nearly sold out and a ticket in coach had been her only option, which Catharine had gladly accepted simply to get on the plane. Accustomed to First Class and private charter, she'd not entirely comprehended the cramped conditions of the economy seating, nor the proximity to the toilets that flushed all flight long. Nor had she anticipated sitting beside a three year old hyped up on sugar, fidgeting endlessly with a soiled stuffed dragon, while his mother dozed with her headphones on.

Over the course of the hours, Catharine had opened his pretzels, spread cheese on his crackers, mopped up spilled juice, and woken his mother when he needed to use the loo.

Now, as the plane circled west, the child sniffed and wiped his nose with the back of his hand, before unclipping his seatbelt and perching onto his knees. Crumbs tumbled down his t-shirt, clinging to the cartoon emblazoned across his chest that resembled a smiling hunk of yellow cheese wearing trousers.

"Water!" he informed Catharine, pointing at the bay.

Following his gaze, Catharine scanned the breadth of the approaching city, sweeping over the hills and skyline, and familiar beauty of the magnificent California coast. She tried not to allow her eyes to linger on the soaring silhouette of Bridgeview Tower, where her staff carried on without her, and instead turned her focus to the aerial image of Marina Green, and the rows of sailboats with their masts rising up out of the low lying fog.

She missed this place. She missed her home. Her friends.

Brooks Corp. had consumed her life. For as long as she could remember it had held hostage over her attention, occupying her thoughts, dictating her actions, controlling her every move. It had become her sense of purpose, synonymous with her success as a person, and ultimately how she viewed her self-worth. Without it, she felt lost.

Permitting herself another glance at the gleaming office tower, she decided on an ultimatum.

She would give Elle Kirkland until June. Eight more months to fight this battle, and then she was through. If this was not finished, if things were not settled, she had to move forward. To accept that her life may need to take a different direction, veering from the script she had planned.

It was the best she could do.

The landing gear dropped and the plane rumbled, diverting the boy's attention from the water and springing tears to his dark eyes. His lower lip quivered.

Intent to avoid an imminent meltdown, Catharine pointed out the window.

"Do you see that?" In the distance lay the Golden Gate Bridge, the brilliance of its red towers glistening through the clouds.

The boy stared at her, distracted. Despite playing nursemaid over the Atlantic, Catharine had spoken to him little, beyond simple reassurance during turbulence. She had no experience with children. No knowledge of what to say; what he would understand.

The engines whirred as the plane slowed for descent and his lip trembled again.

"That bridge is almost a hundred years old," she found herself saying, hoping to keep his mind off the landing. "At the time it was built it was the longest suspension bridge in the world—making it an immediate international sensation."

Settling back in his seat as the plane leveled, he allowed her to clip him in as the seatbelt light chimed on. Catharine kept talking.

"It was initially estimated to cost a hundred million US dollars to bring it to completion, which would be over 1.5 billion dollars in today's economy. However, the chief engineer did not have only a brilliant mind for design, but was also a mathematical finance tactician, who managed to construct the bridge on a thirty-five million dollar bond with four million in financing. A truly modern act of ingenuity."

Catharine turned from the window to find the toddler gaping up at her, the dark pool of his eyes curious beneath Cheetos-crusted eyelashes. As the wing flaps deployed, he forgot about the unfamiliar sounds of the landing and reached forward, touching the necklace hanging at her throat.

"Boat." He smiled, toying with the charm. "I like."

Catharine credited herself for her slow extrication from his gummy grip as she withdrew from his reach, turning his attention to his half-eaten bag of pretzels and the comfort of his weathered dragon.

As the wheels touched down on the San Francisco tarmac, she could feel the weight of the charm resting against her skin. She liked it, too, she thought, closing her eyes as the plane decelerated, maneuvering toward the terminal to connect to the jet bridge. And she couldn't wait to see the giver of the gift again. No matter how briefly.

Chapter Nineteen

Lacy bras and gossamer thongs dangled from the ceiling, forcing Alex to duck and weave her way through the crowd to the bar top.

"Cheers," Amelia greeted her over the reverberating strains of Usher, tipping her long neck bottle in a salute thick with sarcasm. "You're late."

Alex glanced at her watch. "It's 1:02."

"Exactly." Amelia took a sip of her Newcastle as a waitress in Daisy Dukes and thigh-highs squeezed needlessly between them on her way behind the counter. "So," Amelia whispered, giving Alex a once-over, "is this your incognito, I'm-Not-Famous costume?"

Alex was still wearing her sunglasses, despite the dim environment, and had her hair down, the brim of her ball cap pulled low over her brow. The bar was busier than she'd expected for a Sunday afternoon. Beach-goers in bikini-tops and flip flops crowded around beer-stained tables, while locals bellied up to the horseshoe bar, shooting shit with the bartenders.

No one paid them any attention—aside from the waitress who seemed to have her eye on Amelia—and Alex felt a little silly, but kept the shades on all the same.

"I mean, I can see why you might not want anyone to recognize you in such a..." the Australian arched a brow in an exaggerated gesture as her green eyes swept their surroundings, "...unique establishment."

There were dollar bills plastered across the walls, inked with caricatures of celebrities and politicians. Toothpicks carrying tiny American flags adorned pineapples floating in cheap daiquiris. Tucked in between the pinball machine and jukebox—original from the fifties—a bubblegum-style vending machine promised popcorn and condoms for a quarter.

Alex grimaced. "It's not exactly what I'd imagined."

"Oh, c'mon, Grey—you can't convince me this isn't an old haunt of yours. I bet this was a favorite hangout with the girls after a match." She winked, hooking a finger through the strap of the silk bra hanging from the ceiling above them and flicked it toward Alex. "You ever leave any souvenirs here during your wild college days?"

"You know me," Alex deadpanned, "I definitely got a little crazy."

Amelia's smile was amused. "Liar, liar, pants on fire. I'd bet a stack that goody-two-shoes-collegiate-Alex never set foot in any bar, let alone a dive bar. You'd have been way too conchy."

Loathe to admit she was right, Alex rolled her eyes and snatched Amelia's beer from her hand, helping herself to a sip. "Will you just pay your tab so we can get out of here?"

"Panties on the walls got your knickers in a knot?"

"Hardly—but any place claiming PBR on draft is *the beer of champions* isn't a place I want to be caught dead in."

Amelia stole her beer back. "Since when did you become a connoisseur of fine brews? All that posh company you're keeping is rubbing off on you." There was no malice in her teasing, however, as she slid off the stool. "Speaking of company—are we waiting for Sawyer?"

"No." Alex's gaze diverted away from the lingerie decor and onto a nude cartoon of Mrs. Potato Head hanging above a framed copy of the Declaration of Independence.

Alex had known she'd ask, so she'd prepared a white lie: Sawyer already had other plans and wouldn't be able to join them. A truth unless dissected. There was no doubt Sawyer *was* busy. Doing what, Alex wasn't certain—she hadn't called her—but whatever it was, she wouldn't be coming.

"Is that because she woke up feeling rougher than a badger's foreskin after partying like a rockstar? Or because you didn't ask her?"

Alex opened her mouth to stumble through her story, but shut it again, knowing Amelia would see right through her. Even now—months and miles wedged between their friendship—she was certain Amelia could read her thoughts. Both the ones spoken and those left unsaid.

"I didn't ask her," Alex confessed, shifting her gaze to a particularly graphic sketch on a dollar bill of an alien with her legs wrapped around the face of George Washington. She continued with the first half of the truth, "I didn't want to dampen her mood or dull her victory."

"Ah, so I'm the lucky one who gets to absorb your morning-after disappointment. Ace." Amelia's smile was wry. "C'mon, then… let's go, Eeyore." She slapped down a twenty. "You owe me a beer."

Alex appreciated that Amelia didn't press her. That she probably suspected the second half of the truth, but was satisfied to leave it undisclosed. Alex wanted to spend time with Amelia without diversion. She wanted to know if they could repair their friendship. To see if things could go back to the way they were. Before they'd fucked things up. Before they'd made things complicated.

"Hey, hun!" A voice heavy on the twang waylaid their exit.

They both turned. It was the cocktail waitress, holding up the twenty.

"Need me to check you out?"

From the head-to-toe sweeping glance the woman gave Amelia, the exchange had nothing to do with making change.

"I, uh—" Amelia's lips twisted into an uneven smile, "thank you, but, I'm afraid it's time for us to do the Harry."

The waitress gave a coquettish tilt of her head, stuffing the twenty into the pocket protruding from her hemline. Up close, Alex realized she was younger than the lines around her mouth indicated, her voice husky from years of smoking.

"I'm a big fan of yours—seen you in those commercials." The words were sung as if it were a secret between them.

"Fair dinkum?" Amelia shot Alex a glance, her expression rich with amusement. "I'd've wagered London to a brick on you not being much of a sporting fan."

Popping her chewing gum, the waitress leaned her elbows on the counter, promoting her expansive cleavage. "I've no idea what you just said—but you're sure cute saying it. I'd let you talk to me like that all night long, sugarplum." She gave Amelia another pointed inspection. "I'm fixin' to get off here in a minute."

Alex had to force herself not to roll her eyes. Amelia was laying her accent on thicker, exercising liberal use of her absurd colloquialisms, entertaining herself.

"As hard as it is to resist such a bonzer offer, I'm afraid my mate here would be mad as a cut snake if I just left her hanging."

The waitress shot Alex a glance beneath her glue-on lashes, before deeming her inconsequential. "She doesn't look much like your type."

"And you don't look like hers," Alex snapped, annoyed, catching hold of the sleeve of Amelia's hoodie. "Party's over."

Amelia offered the woman a surrendering wave, allowing Alex to drag her to the front door, smothering her laughter.

"C'mon, Grey! I had a real chance there."

"Of what? Catching crabs?"

Amelia was still laughing. "Jealous?"

"Of you? Psh. Please!"

Amelia smacked the bill of her hat, shoving it over Alex's eyes. "You're just salty because she didn't call *you* sugarplum."

Alex fixed her hat and resettled her sunglasses. "Trust me—if you want me to go back in there and get her number for you, I will."

"Yeah, nah. I'll save her for a later date. I'd rather spend the night with you."

They'd fallen into step on the sidewalk, ambling away from the shady bar with no determined destination, but Amelia drew up short at the tension that sprouted between them.

"I didn't mean it like that, Grey."

"I know." Alex responded too quickly.

"To be clear—I know you didn't ask me out tonight for a shag. I'm aware people can be friends without fucking."

"I know," Alex said again, her embarrassment evident.

"Grouse. Glad that's settled then." Amelia resumed walking. "So where are we off to? What fine establishment in this city is going to allow you to drink away your sorrows without living in terror someone is going to resume #Amex on their Twitter feed?"

Alex swiped open her phone, her fingers poised above the keyboard, contemplating what to search for. Where could they go, in all reality, where between the pair of them, they wouldn't draw attention? Her face had become a hotbed of contention in the

South with Carlton's obsessive attention directed at her career, and Amelia was one of the most recognizable female athletes in the world.

Last night, amidst the misery of the loss, she'd not given adequate consideration to the situation.

"How's the room service at your hotel?"

Amelia shrugged. "Probably crook, but HEG's footing the bill, so you won't find me whinging."

Alex flicked to her call log, checking her messages. There were none. Catharine still hadn't returned her calls. When she'd tried her again this morning, it had continued to go straight to voicemail. Tonight, if she couldn't reach her, she'd decided she would call the office of Elle Kirkland. She wasn't sure what to say, but it seemed like the only place she knew to start.

She shoved her phone in her pocket. "Well, better than the vending machine and twist-top bottles of zinfandel at my place."

"Horseshit," Amelia flicked her heel mid-step, almost succeeding in taking Alex's feet out from under her. "You're just trying to keep me from going back to take ol' sugarplum up on her offer."

"Hardly—like I said, if you want to catch the clap from little miss Daisy Dukes, that's your business. I just want to get out of buying you a round."

Amelia laughed, snatching Alex's *Giants* cap off her head and tugging it on backward over her unruly mess of ash blonde hair. For the first time since the ball had left her foot in the shootout the night before, Alex felt a breath of tension abate from her shoulders. She had missed this. This friendship. This easiness. The freedom to be no one but herself.

Falling into familiar step with Amelia's swift stride, they turned toward the French Quarter.

An hour later Alex sat crosslegged on the floor of a suite in The Charleston Place, sipping a vodka soda while she browsed a room service menu rivaling the haute cuisine of a Gordon Ramsey restaurant.

"I see now why HEG's been putting us up in La Quintas and Best Westerns—they had to save their pennies to wine and dine you this weekend." She scanned the list of a la carte steaks. "Who the hell pays $76 for a sirloin?"

"The company that *really* wanted me to sign an extension." Amelia flopped down beside her. "Let's face it—I'm worth it."

"Your heightened sense of humility is mind boggling," Alex razzed her.

"Honesty is not arrogance." Plucking the menu from Alex's hands, she gave it a once over. "Anyhow, you're one to talk. I imagine gourmet dining has become part of your regular repertoire."

Alex wasn't sure if Amelia was referring to her post-World Cup rise to stardom, or if she was still harboring some hint of resentment toward her relationship with Catharine. Either way, she played it safe, and avoided the latter.

"Well, as of last night it looks like I'm back to the dollar menu."

"Fuck *Kickstar. Nike* will scoop you up. Whatever they offered you in the summer—don't sign until they double it."

"Yeah, because completely bombing the championship definitely gives me leverage to negotiate—I'm sure *Nike* will be pounding down my door." She forced a laugh. "We can't all be Amelia Walker." When she looked at Amelia, however, she was surprised to find her regarding her with absolute seriousness.

"You know, two years ago I was willing to write-off your insecurities as a result of adjustment to transition. You'd been traded to a new team, in a new state, without a single cap under your belt. I figured you just needed to find your stride—to reaffirm your self-value. But now, mate—I'm beginning to think you might just be daft."

"Wow. Thanks for that."

"I mean it, Grey. I don't get you." Amelia tipped back the remainder of the whiskey she'd poured herself. "You've been named one of the top five footballers in the world by FIFA. You've just come off an absolutely brilliant season. Your performance this summer was the stuff dreams are made of. There wasn't a better player in the tournament."

Alex waited for her to follow with the punchline—her customary *well, except for me, of course*—but it didn't come. Risking a glance in her peripheral, she found Amelia still unsmiling, staring at her with an intensity verging on the cusp of anger.

"Yet here you sit, indulging in the ludicrous notion that a single substandard second under pressure can wipe away the entirety of your success in a winning year. It's bullshit. I know it. And I know you know it, too."

"It's been less than twenty-four hours. Get off my back."

"You don't deserve any coddling—what you need is a bloody backbone. Toughen up, Alex—stand a little taller. Find some of that confidence you love to hassle me about."

"I'm not you—!"

"No—you're Alex Fucking Grey—stop comparing yourself to everybody else!"

Alex's response was cut off by the vibration of her phone, clattering where it sat on the tile floor between them. Catharine's face appeared on the call screen. A smiling photo from her birthday. How had that been only a few weeks earlier?

"You'd better get that." Amelia shoved to her feet, crossing from the living room to the wet bar.

The phone vibrated twice more before Alex answered, composing her thoughts as she raised it to her ear.

"Catharine?" A momentary terror gripped her that it would be somebody else. Someone to tell her something terrible had happened. That's why she hadn't called.

"Hey!"

Relief seeped through her. It was Catharine. The English lilt greeted her warmly. She sounded cheerful. Far more cheerful than Alex felt. "Are you home yet?"

"I—no." Alex was thrown by the question. "I stayed over in Charleston. I needed a few days to regroup."

The other end of the line was silent so long Alex thought she'd lost the call. She'd expected Catharine to ask about her game. To show some sense of understanding about how much last night had hurt. She hadn't realized it until then, but it was Catharine's opinion that mattered most to her—not the thousands of armchair critics on Twitter, or the talking heads on the media, or even her teammates and coaching staff. It was Catharine she needed to hear from. Her support and reassurance that she sought.

She needed more than silence.

"Catharine?"

"Yes, sorry. I…" She was out of sorts, the lightness drained from her voice.

"Is everything all right?" Alex's earlier dread threatened to resurface.

"It's just… it's been a long day." The laugh that followed was dry, her sigh evident. "Forgive me, I should be asking you the same. How are you doing? My heart broke for you last night."

"I'm okay." The response was automatic; she didn't feel okay at all. "I wish you could have been there."

It took another long moment for Catharine to respond. "I would have liked to have been. I wasn't honestly certain my presence would help."

Alex stared at the fraying laces on her Vans. It stung—to feel so separate. Their lives pages apart.

Being with you always helps she wanted to say. "It's fine, really. I promise you didn't miss much," was instead what came out of her mouth.

"Will you come to see me when you are finished in Utah?"

It was Alex's turn for silence. She was stunned Catharine didn't know *Kickstar* had fired her. That her jackass husband had successfully convinced Sampson Hargrove to terminate her endorsement, magnifying her already miserable night of humiliation. It seemed impossible she'd not have seen the news. It was blasted across the internet—the sports sites taking as much interest in the drama as they had over the actual championship. Schadenfreude at its finest. The brutality of human nature to kick a dog when it was down.

Alex thought about the photo of Elle and Catharine—their rounds of empty glasses at the swanky downtown bar. Again she couldn't help but wonder if Catharine had actually watched any of the match—or if she'd been too preoccupied with the barrister to take notice of the game at all?

She looked up to see Amelia leaning against the door frame and decided not to mention the severance of her contract. It didn't feel like the time or the place.

"I'll call you when I get to Oakland, okay?"

"Alex." The word hung on the line and Alex waited, but Catharine just exhaled. She sounded tired. In the background there were voices from a different conversation. It would be evening in England. Wherever Catharine was, she wasn't home.

"Please do. I want to see you."

"I will. Me, too," she said, self-conscious under Amelia's scrutinization. "Goodnight, Catharine."

Hanging up, Alex got to her feet and brushed past Amelia to the wet bar. She was angry and she didn't even know at what. At herself. At Catharine. At the rift that refused to narrow between them. At Carlton. At the penalty kick. At the cork of the Grey Goose bottle that refused to pop off.

"That seems to be going well."

Alex spun around. "If you have something to say, then say it."

Amelia was unfazed by her outburst. "It just goes back to what I was saying earlier. Football, your personal life… it's all the same. You've got no resolve. No conviction. You just lay down like a trod on doormat."

"You have no idea what you're—"

"Do you know you've looked at that phone a hundred times since you got here? You've been waiting for her call. And you didn't even have the guts to admit that you're upset. To tell her how you're feeling."

"Oh, and you're suddenly the expert on how I feel?"

She'd meant to throw it as a slight, but the words fell flat, dying off as Amelia stepped too close in front of her. Alex was still holding the vodka bottle, having lost the battle with its stopper, and her hands were shaking in anger and adrenaline.

"I think I am, actually." Amelia took the bottle from her hands, setting it on the counter behind them. "I think I can read you pretty well. Better than anybody else."

Alex was too aware of the shallowness of her own breath. Too aware of her closeness. Of the familiarity and comfort it evoked.

She knew Amelia was going to kiss her. She knew it before she shut her eyes. Before the warmth of her lips ever reached her. And she knew she wasn't going to move, even though her mind demanded she step away.

She just stood there.

And then Amelia's lips were on hers and her thoughts collided in a spiderweb of contrasting directions.

Catharine's silence. The taste of Tennessee Honey from Amelia's mouth. Carlton Cleveland's barrage of attacks. The teammates she'd let down.

She needed the non-stop carousel of thoughts to quiet. To forget everything that hurt for a while.

This felt easy. Familiar. The welcome path of least resistance. A sirens call while everything else in her life was falling apart.

But it wasn't what she wanted.

Amelia was right. Somewhere down the line she'd allowed her appraisal of self-worth to become dependent on winning. She'd fallen into the trap of an unattainable drive for perfection, and without it, she felt like nothing.

But Amelia had been wrong about one thing. Of every uncertainty Alex faced, there was one aspect of her life in which she was unconditionally unwavering: she wanted no one other than Catharine. Of that there was no doubt.

Alex stepped back so hard she upset the bottle of Grey Goose on the counter, pushing Amelia away with both hands.

"*Don't.* I can't."

Amelia smiled—her slow, clever, infuriating smile. "No?"

"No. I—" Alex stopped. She was going to say she was sorry, but the truth was—she wasn't. And she was tired of apologizing for failing to meet expectations set by everybody else. Ones she'd never set for herself. She shook her head. "No," she repeated, and left it at that.

"I was hoping you'd say that."

Alex's emotions spun on a tilt-a-whirl. "What the fuck, Amelia?"

"Look at you—you found your backbone after all."

"Jesus." Alex slumped against the counter, trying to steady her hammering heart.

"Let's be honest," Amelia reached behind the bar and selected the bottle of Tennessee Honey, working the cork off with one hand. "You can't pretend there isn't still something between us—that you weren't standing there contemplating allowing this to go some place else—"

"It doesn't matter! I can't. I *won't*—"

"And *there* is the first sighting of the elusive pair of balls you seemed to have lost." Amelia lifted two wine glasses from the rack hanging over the bar top and poured each a measure of whiskey. "I had to make sure we could still play together. That we could maybe even still be friends."

"And that was your way of finding out? By just fucking with me?" Alex snatched one of the glasses off the bar.

"Oh, no, mate—don't be stupid—I was more than willing if you were." She winked, clinking her glass to Alex's, and then abruptly shed some of her brazen demeanor. "I needed to hear it from you —and now I have. And I promise you, Alex—I won't do that again."

Her genuineness deflated some of Alex's anger, despite her having just picked at a wound that had taken months to heal. She had to admit there was relief in having addressed it, offering a reassurance for them both.

"You're really impossible, you know." Alex set the whiskey to her lips. "And exasperating. And cocky."

"Were you peeping in on my meeting with Sampson Hargrove? I feel like I just had this same conversation with him." Amelia's smile returned. "Except I think he used the words 'presumptuous' and 'rebarbative.' I had to look up the latter. Gotta hand it to the old man—it fit me to a tee."

"You really met with Hargrove himself?" Alex had never even seen Sampson Hargrove in person.

Amelia shrugged. "It was a large sum of money, what can I say?"

"Does that mean—" Alex hesitated. She wasn't sure if it was a subject she wanted to broach. But they were already here. Already kicking through doors that had meant to be permanently closed. Why not fling another one open? "Does that mean your family will be okay? After…"

"After your girlfriend chose her pride over her people? After my dad gave thirty years to a company that's leaving him flat?"

Alex didn't argue Catharine's principles. She didn't defend the reasons Catharine had not sold out. Amelia wouldn't understand them—they'd just go 'round and 'round.

Her face must have betrayed her regret in even asking, because Amelia softened and repressed a sigh. "It's all good, Alex. Don't make me feel like I just kicked a puppy." She leaned against the counter and swirled the whiskey in her glass. "I wasn't honest yesterday. I don't *need* this contract. I've been one of the fortunate few to make enough money in this profession to the point where none of my family actually need to work another day. Football's given me that. HEG's offer was just too good to refuse—and though I hate to admit it, I look forward to coming back." She bumped Alex's leg with her toe. "There happens to be this team who I think has a pretty decent shot at a championship... there's just one single x-factor that they lack."

"Which—let me guess," Alex's eye roll was diminished beneath her inability to hide her smile, "just happens to be you?"

Amelia's blonde brows arched over the rim of her whiskey. "Naturally."

As the night drew on, the tension eased between them, until— half a bottle of whiskey and a pair of ridiculously priced ribeyes later—it eventually felt like nothing had ever changed. They lounged in the luxury suite catching the end of the Liverpool match, and argued about which was worse—man buns on the pitch or skinny jeans on the technical staff.

When the local news flicked on and the anchors switched to talk of the presidential race, Amelia turned the TV off.

"It's incredible to think that bastard's made it this far." She slid off the sofa to join Alex, where she was stretched out on the floor. "How's your—" she tabled whatever distasteful term she intended to use, "how's Catharine taking it all?"

Alex was surprised Amelia'd broached the subject again. It was such a taboo topic between them.

"Not great. She doesn't really talk about it. But I know she's worried."

"The whole country should be worried." Amelia tipped her head back and stared at the ceiling. "When do you head to London?"

"I'm not sure."

"You know you should have been on a flight there this morning."

Alex made a dismissive gesture and Amelia turned to look at her. "It kills me to say this—but you really need to cut her some slack."

"What do you mean?" Alex glanced over. Amelia was a little drunk and Alex didn't feel far behind her.

"It's obvious you're upset she wasn't at your game—but knowing you the way I do, I'd wager you didn't even ask her to come. So honestly, Alex—give her a break. From the outside looking in, it's obvious the woman is arse-over-tits smitten with you." Tucking her hands behind her head, Amelia returned her attention to the ceiling. "I have to admit, it was a jolt this summer when I saw her sitting in the stands wearing your name on her back. It sent me for a loop for a minute. And for a while I wasn't sure what was worse —waking up the next morning and knowing I'd lost my fifth—and likely last—chance at the World Cup, or going online to see that damn photo of the two of you plastered across every sport head-line in the world. And before you think I'm saying that in search of sympathy—I'm not. I'm saying it because I think her actions have made it loud and clear just how much she supports you—and how much she loves you. Divorcing her husband, jeopardizing her career, potentially losing her company—I don't think you can ask for much more than that."

Alex closed her eyes. "I know." She *did* know. She didn't ques-tion any of that. She just wanted things to get easier. She wanted a sense of peace. A sense of security. Without all the turmoil that followed them around.

"I guess I just…" She was quiet for a moment, before opening her eyes to join in staring at the ceiling. "I want things to be normal. For life to quiet down."

Beside her she could feel Amelia smile.

"Like I said: you're Alex Fucking Grey. Good luck with that."

Chapter Twenty

Hostile drops of water pelted the glass walls of the sunroom extending over the bank of the river, the towers of the bridge blurry through the curtain of rainfall. It was a fitting start to the dreary morning—as if even the climate knew the world was about to fall apart.

Catharine didn't rise from where she sat staring at the hazy lights of the city when footsteps sounded on the stairs. Nor did she leave her place of brooding meditation when she heard the kettle click on. It wasn't until BBC began to drone in the background that she resigned herself to her feet and made her way to the sitting room.

Nathalie perched on the edge of the coffee table, a steaming cup hovering in front of her lips, her eyes glued to the TV above the glass-encased fireplace. When she saw Catharine she had the decency to look guilty, moving off the table to settle on the settee.

"I didn't realize you were up."

Catharine had never made it to bed. Her mind had been unwilling to shut off.

"Must you start with that so early?" Her eyes swept the room for the remote. Carlton's smug face appeared on the screen, an image from the night before at his eve-of-election rally in Charleston. The mere sight of him turned her stomach. It was mind-boggling to realize this time tomorrow the fate of the next US presidency would be decided. And Catharine had grown increasingly certain she wouldn't care for the outcome.

Locating the remote, she punched mute. "The polling stations haven't even opened yet."

Nathalie was undeterred. "*FiveThirtyEight* is showing Bennett with an advantage in Ohio. If the state were to flip, *AP* is reporting —"

"Nat!" Catharine didn't have the patience for this. Byron Bennett—trailing Carlton in all major polls by a sizable margin—didn't stand a chance at Ohio. Not with Connie Graves as his running mate. Not after the New York senator had called Cincinnati a slum and referred to Ohio as a "flyover-state" during a spat in congress six years earlier. Those soundbites were being played on loop—as if any good Buckeye had forgotten.

But it didn't matter. Even if common sense suddenly seized the voters of Ohio, the outcome at the end of the day looked bleak. Carlton had been clever. He'd made himself the champion of the working class, the good-old-boy to the corporate suits, the equal to the elite. The people swallowed his rubbish, devouring it as gospel. They truly believed he'd build the castle he'd sold them in the sky.

And for those who couldn't wrap their head around the tainted list of accusations following Carlton wherever he went, they had Bill Sherwood.

It had been clever, Catharine had to admit—seducing the former vice-president to run on his ticket. It was an unprecedented move, asking a man to be willing to table his ego and shoulder the burden of second-in-command—again. But Sherwood had gone for it, and the peculiar match had won Carlton exactly what he needed—the votes out of his reach.

Bill was quiet. Upstanding. Devout in his religion. Popular amongst the Sunday Morning Sermon crowd. A West Point graduate and hero to his home state of Pennsylvania, with sixteen grandchildren to show for his scandal-free thirty-six year marriage. If a man like Sherwood could stand tall beside Carlton Cleveland—surely the vulgar, abusive, womanizing grandstander couldn't be as monstrous as he seemed.

On the muted screen *BBC* was showing a recent tweet from Carlton, briefly capturing her interest.

Tomorrow the people are going to reclaim their power! Tomorrow they are going to rise up and return our beautiful country back to the hands of God! Tomorrow they are—

Catharine stopped reading. She didn't care about his drivel. She only cared that it wasn't about Alex. A seemingly ridiculous concern, given the man was only hours away from the first votes being cast for the presidential election. Any conventional candidate's attention would be exclusively focused on reiterating campaign promises and wooing undecided voters—but Carlton had proven himself anything but conventional. The entirety of his campaign had been a three-ring circus from start to finish. He'd developed a new breed of American politics—a glimpse of a party to come that did not fit the current mold. Undignified. Uncontrolled. Without moral compass or compassion. He'd taken the concept behind smear campaigns to a whole new level, attacking not only his political opponents and adversaries, but setting his sights on high-profile celebrities, tech tycoons, global conglomerates—anyone who dared a critical word.

How his handlers allowed it—the insanities of his posts—Catharine couldn't comprehend. But his followers loved it. They loved the smell of blood in the water, enjoying the frenzy of feeding off his ruthless attacks, tearing apart his detractors, boycotting brands, badmouthing any name he sicced them on.

And caught in his crossfire had been Alex. Not from any wrongdoing on her part—she'd declined time and again to make any comment against him—but out of personal spite and the pettiness of his growing vendetta toward Catharine.

His latest attack had come after Alex's loss in South Carolina.

Catharine had received a call from Elle the night she returned from her futile trip to California.

"It baffles me how a woman with your inclination toward mathematical brilliance ever tolerated marriage to an imbecile without basic comprehension of elementary statistics. Have you seen your husband's latest revilement of bullshit?"

She hadn't.

Elle texted a screen shot. Carlton had gone on a rant about Alex's end-of-year stats with the Sirens, comparing her numbers to women who'd played every minute of the club league season—taking no account for the fact that she'd missed matches on injury, suspension, and six entire weeks over the World Cup summer. The comparisons weren't the same, but when the figures were listed side-by-side as he'd presented them, it made Alex look substandard. Whatever junior aid had drummed up the data had done a success job at deliberately misconstruing facts.

His final tweet read: *I mean, she even lost the top score award to that Australian girl (boy? Hard to tell on that one, they let anyone play on*

*women's teams these days) who left the league midseason. Maybe Alex
Gray isn't as good as she thinks she is?*

The barrister had carried on about how the tirade had backfired
on him—referring to Amelia Walker as a boy had crossed a line for
some of his more moderate-leaning followers—but Catharine's
mind drifted from the conversation until Elle mentioned Alex's
dismissal from *Kickstar*.

She'd been certain she'd misheard her. Alex would have said
something.

Excusing herself from the phone call, Catharine had immediately gone online, wading through a half dozen news articles all
ending with the same conclusion: the night of the NWSL championship, Alex Grey had been fired from the HEG subsidiary company, *Kickstar*, shortly after Carlton Cleveland had called on Sampson
Hargrove to dismiss her.

And Alex had said nothing.

Nor did she say anything when she called Catharine to let her
know she'd made it safely back to Oakland.

It wasn't until the next day when the subject was finally
broached between them. Alex had called after midnight, apologizing for the middle-of-the-night interruption, but said she'd been
too excited to wait until morning.

Nike had reached out to her, requesting an in-person meeting at
their NYC headquarters. She glossed over her termination from
Kickstar, as if it hadn't mattered, focusing only on what the upcoming dialogue with the sports apparel baron might bring.

"They've asked to meet on Monday," she'd added, after the
initial elation of her news bearing had waned. "I'm really sorry."

Catharine knew what that meant. She wouldn't make it to
London before the election, as they had planned.

"I could ask to push it back?" Alex offered, her enthusiasm
fading.

"Don't be ridiculous."

Catharine wouldn't hear of it. She'd assured Alex she'd be
perfectly fine, and as much as she looked forward to seeing her,
there was nothing more important than her meeting with *Nike*.

And she'd meant every word of it. She knew exactly how much
this meant to Alex—what it could mean for her career—and
wouldn't allow her to jeopardize it for anything.

Which meant when Nathalie called, insisting she fly in for the week, refusing to allow Catharine to go through the election alone, Catharine had cautiously agreed.

She'd been worried Nathalie's obsession with the election would drive her crazy.

A concern presently proving to be valid.

"I don't want to do this all day." Catharine buried the remote beneath the morning paper and turned to face her friend. "It is what it is, and no amount of fretting over it is going to change anything."

"I don't know how you can be so calm," Nathalie snapped, shoving to her feet to pace the Wenge wood flooring. "After all he's done, how can you not care that he might win? That he might get away with everything?"

Catharine's glance turned dangerous and Nathalie immediately hid behind a long sip from her cup, aware she'd overstepped.

"I'm sorry," she muttered, trying to pretend she hadn't just scorched her lips. "I know you care. I just..." She offloaded the offending mug onto the coffee table, her attention returning to the television. "I can't believe this is happening."

Catharine shared the sentiment. She'd sat up all night staring at walls. Her bedroom wall. The shower wall. The glass walls of her sitting room. Nowhere she migrated offered any better peace of mind. The parts of her that refused to believe it would ever come to this felt numb. By tomorrow morning she doubted the mercy of the numbness would supersede the dread closing in.

"Ça va aller," Catharine said, trying to reassure herself, as much as Nathalie, that everything would be fine.

She tried to take it as a good omen that her phone chimed just then—a text from Alex. But as soon as she swiped into the message, the optimism for the *good* portion of the omen fled.

"Let me guess," Nathalie's tone was dry as she read Catharine's expression from across the room, "another delay?"

Yesterday Alex's negotiations had wrapped up early. The counteroffer Alex's agent presented to *Nike* had been accepted without revision—an offer beyond her wildest expectations. She'd called to say she'd booked a last minute flight to London—a surprise Catharine had readily welcomed. But already her first flight had been canceled and the next one twice delayed, leaving her arrival time uncertain.

"It's not her fault the East Coast has been hit by a blizzard."

"N'importe quoi."

"What's gotten into you?" Catharine asked the question already knowing the answer. Nathalie had been irascible on the subject of Alex ever since Catharine had shown up at her theatre the previous week and been forced to explain her unexpected presence in San Francisco. Forced to explain her spur-of-the-moment trip had been for nothing.

Nathalie retrieved her cooling coffee but didn't take a sip. "Do you think she actually has any intention of coming, or is she just making excuses—?"

"Jesus, Nathalie. She can't control the FAA."

"You didn't even tell her you flew all the way to—"

"And I'm not going to! We've been over this. She isn't clairvoyant—she had no way of knowing I was coming—and there is no point in making her feel worse about that weekend than she already does. Case closed! I don't know what your issue is lately. You liked Alex—"

"I *like* Alex," Nathalie corrected, defensive, "but I'm your best friend, and it's my right to worry about you."

The turn of the conversation did nothing to settle Catharine's nerves. "Worry about me how?"

"I'm worried you're going to get your heart broken. *Again.*"

"Why?" Catharine's temper was kindling. "Because she took an extra couple of days to recover after a humiliating loss to the end of her season? Or because she had to meet with a company offering to salvage her endorsement profile after Carlton has spent the last few months trying to tank her career? Or is it because she hasn't figured out a way to harness the weather under her control?"

"It's more than any of that and you know it."

Catharine wasn't certain if she was angry because the tables had turned and Nathalie was the one currently remaining levelheaded and rational, or if it was because her friend was planting concerns where they didn't belong. Or at least where she hoped they didn't belong.

Her pride demanded she acknowledge neither, and hold to her present course of repudiation. "You're being ridiculous."

"And you're being willfully naive—which isn't like you."

Catharine spun on her heel to face Nathalie, but said nothing. Was she being willfully naive?

"Look, Cate," returning to the settee, Nathalie resumed with unusual caution. "I'm just worried you might have more invested in this relationship than Alex. And before you go off on me," she held up an adamant finger in anticipated defense, "understand I'm not saying I don't think she wants this—because I think she does. I'm just worried she may not be thick-skinned enough—that she may be too sensitive—to withstand the storm that's holding you in its eye. Not everyone has your innate ability to persevere—they shouldn't have to—but when it comes to your life, I'm afraid it's requisite. And I don't want to see you hurt."

Catharine remained quiet. She didn't want to have this fight.

In the reflection of the glass wall overlooking the Thames, the silent footage from the TV showed prediction polls across the United States. Seven ostensibly impartial surveys—all but one of them forecasting Carlton to take an early lead.

Nathalie followed her gaze and reached beneath the newspaper to retrieve the remote, intent to turn it off, but Catharine dismissed her. "Just leave it. I'm going back upstairs." She wanted to hide away from it all. Lock herself in her room until it all was over. Or maybe forever—whichever came first.

Three steps up the suspended glass staircase, her phone vibrated, and Catharine paused.

Another text from Alex. She'd found a flight leaving Washington DC that would put her in around seven p.m. at Heathrow, providing there were no further delays.

Catharine read the text again. *A flight in DC.* It was a long way from JFK to Dulles International.

Before she could respond, her phone buzzed a second time.

> *I already rented a car and I'm on my way. I'll text you before I board. I can't wait to see you. Everything is going to be okay. xoxo*

Catharine stared at those last four letters—xoxo.

It was the middle of the night in New York. Storms were pummeling the East Coast from every direction. Dulles was at least a four-and-a-half hour drive from Queens. And to make matters worse, Catharine was well aware of Alex's fear of flying. Despite spending hundreds of hours in the air each year, Alex was a nervous traveler, who hated taking off in pristine conditions—let alone wind and snow.

It wasn't a superficial effort. Alex was doing everything she could.

Catharine leaned against the ironwork bannister, feeling like she could catch her first full breath in days. Realizing Nathalie wasn't the only one who'd begun to have her doubts.

But Nathalie was wrong.

It was true, Alex *was* sensitive. But sensitivity wasn't a weakness. It was what made her who she was. Thoughtful. Conscientious. Empathetic. And she'd used that sensitivity to strengthen her resilience, weathering as much, or more than Catharine, and still not given up.

Catharine read the text a final time. *Everything is going to be okay.* And despite the low hum of the TV that had resumed in the sitting room, where an election analyst was doubling down on his prediction for Carlton's early lead, Catharine could almost believe it. As long as they had each other, it would be okay.

Darkness had long set when the intercom sang out its three-note chime, signifying a call from the street level. It was shortly after seven-thirty.

Catharine double checked her watch. It was too early to be Alex, nor would it have made sense for her to ring the bell, given Malcolm had gone to pick her up at the airport. It was the compromise they'd come to after Alex insisted she would take the train and Catharine had wanted to pick her up herself. Alex had been resolute in her refusal for Catharine to come out this late, on this night, in the foul weather. So Malcolm had provided an agreeable medium.

At the sound of the bell, Nathalie had gotten up from where she'd been lounging on the settee, her MacBook propped open on her lap, covertly trying to follow the election news while making a pretense of reading through a script she was considering directing in the spring season.

"It's a woman," she said from the hallway, looking into the video intercom. "Shoulder-length hair. Full makeup. If I were to guess, I'd say maybe a Garavani blazer. She's quite attractive, in a Claire Dearing-meets-Joan Holloway sort of way. It looks like she's —"

Catharine stepped between Nathalie and the intercom, interrupting her friend's running commentary as she pressed the call button, anxious to find out what exactly had brought Elle Kirkland to her door at this time of night.

"Elle! Is something wrong?"

The woman stared straight into the camera with her expressive brows raised, her hair meticulously in place, despite the sheet of rain pummeling onto the street behind her.

"Aside from the concerning reality that a majority of voting-age citizens of the United States are about to prove themselves halfwits —no. Buzz me up. I'd prefer not to take my dying breaths being made to wait on your doorstep in this frigid weather."

Catharine hit the button allowing Elle access to the private lift, then turned quickly into the sitting room, inspecting the area to see if anything was out of place.

"Who—?" Nathalie trailed behind her.

"—my barrister." Catharine picked up two cold cups of coffee and the remnants of an almond biscotti Nathalie had abandoned on various end tables and collected a half finished page of sudoku her friend had doodled on from *The Times*. "Kitchen, please," she pressed the debris into Nathalie's arms.

"What is she doing here?"

"I've no idea."

"Does she make many house calls?"

"Nat, the dishes!" Catharine gestured toward the kitchen. "Please."

By the time the lift dinged its arrival, Catharine had worked through half a dozen polite excuses to send the woman away. Tonight was not the night for business. It was only midafternoon in the US and already she'd found herself struggling not to refresh real-time state-to-state voting results on her phone every time she stepped out of the room. She'd promised herself she wouldn't do this. That she wouldn't allow the outcome of the day to affect her. But she'd been failing miserably ever since the first voting stations opened on the East Coast.

"Catharine," Elle alighted the lift as if it were perfectly natural to waltz into the Shad Thames penthouse without invitation, "the extravagance of this place is spectacular. I should have asked to see it before I took your case. I would have doubled my rate." Without waiting for a response she strutted to the glass wall overlooking the river and regarded the view, before turning and placing two bottles of liquor on the nearest table. "I've come bearing gifts. A bottle of Macallan for tonight," she tapped the golden top on the whisky, "and, for your stuffy kind that frown on drinking scotch in the morning, but pretend cognac is the solution before noon—a bottle of Hennessy. Methinks you're bound to need it tomorrow."

Lifting her gaze to survey the remainder of the floor, her attention fell on Nathalie, who'd been watching from the threshold of the hallway.

"Hello," Elle said, her head tilting in question, as if she weren't the one who had intruded. "Elle Kirkland, QC. And you are?"

"Nathalie."

The single word resonated from the hardwood floor to the high-beamed ceilings, filling the room with enough friction to light a bonfire as the two women sized-up one another.

This was entirely *not* what Catharine needed.

"Well, *Nathalie*," Elle mimicked the thickness of the French accent Nathalie had poured onto her name, "I hope I have not interrupted anything?"

"Tous les avocats font-ils des visites à domicile?" *Did all barristers make house calls*, Nathalie asked, the question intended for Catharine as she strolled to claim her place at the center of the room.

"When the necessity arises on rare occasion," responded the barrister, turning her attention to the bottle of Macallan, artfully utilizing her fuchsia nails to delicately break the seal on the collar. "Or," the withdrawn cork made a resounding pop, "when the paycheck warrants the inconvenience. In this case both conditions apply." She offered Nathalie a favorable smile—a smile Catharine imagined was reserved most often for the judges of the High Court

—and switched to flawless French, asking Nathalie if they should allow the bottle to breathe while she gave her a tour of the house.

Nathalie, thrown by a woman as brash and brazen as herself, glanced at Catharine, but looked away before Catharine could silently communicate her promise of absolute retaliation if she took Elle Kirkland up on her inquiry for a tour. Catharine had little doubt the shape of the barrister's lean calves in her stiletto heels, along with Nathalie's unwavering inclination to never back down from a challenge, played equal parts in her acceptance of the request.

"Allons-nous commencer par la cuisine?"

"The kitchen is always the perfect place to start," Elle agreed, stepping aside to allow Nathalie to pass. "Après vous."

Catharine's hope for a quiet evening had officially come to an end.

Chapter Twenty-One

"And they say chivalry is dead," Alex teased, squeezing along the brick wall of the narrow stairwell. The Scotsman was fighting to hide his labored breathing as he carried her suitcase, backpack, and duffle—along with her purse slung around his neck. They'd been forced to take the stairs after the elevator doors had malfunctioned on the street landing. "I could have carried my own luggage, you know."

Malcolm's side eye was ineffective beneath his good humored smirk.

"Fine time to say so now, Miss Grey—I notice ya weren't boasting about it seven flights ago." He winked, the two of them knowing perfectly well Alex had offered multiple times to carry her own bags, and tipped his chin toward the door. "Now, if you dinnae mind putting your wee muscles to use…"

Burdened with only the umbrella he'd grudgingly allowed her to carry, she grabbed the handle of the heavy fire door leading into the vestibule.

"I don't know if my *wee* muscles can handle such a task," she said, razzing him as she dragged open the door with exaggerated effort.

"Ah, getting lippy, to boot." He brushed past her with feigned disdain as he navigated his cumbersome cargo. "No matter—Ms. Brooks will have you set straight in short order."

"Psh," Alex scoffed, snagging the keycard from his overloaded hands, and swiped them through the second door leading into Catharine's apartment. How refreshing it was to hear Catharine referred to as anything other than Cleveland. To hear her maiden name so naturally on someone else's lips. There had been so much talk of her in the news lately, it was as if her identity had become synonymous with Carlton's. *Cleveland* this, *Cleveland* that.

She was certain, after the build up to this election, she'd be okay if she never heard the word *Cleveland* again. Not as if that would ever happen.

Shouldering through the doorway, the pair stumbled over luggage and the raised threshold, and in Alex's efforts to make way for Malcolm, she inadvertently bumped the lever on the umbrella, sending the nylon canopy flying open.

"Shit!" she struggled to wrestle it closed.

Malcolm laughed, dropping the bags on the slick wood floor, and swept the umbrella from her hands, calmly snapping it shut. "There—no harm, no foul. Just a few years of bad luck and a pissed off god or two."

"Is that all?"

"I think there is a bit about welcoming ghosts into the house as well, if you really want to know."

"I really *didn't* want to know," Alex laughed, dragging her purse from around the Scotsman's neck. "Any further superstitions you can keep to yourself."

Turning to face the room, she blinked her surroundings into focus, the recessed lighting of the apartment a blinding contrast from the darkened vestibule. They'd come in through the down-stairs sitting room—a space Alex had never seen Catharine utilize —but tonight, to her surprise, she found the TV on mute, chairs drawn to the coffee table, the fireplace lit, and two sets of eyes regarding her—neither of which were Catharine's.

"Well, aren't you a sight? The state you're in, you may as well have swam across the Atlantic—you're positively soaked."

The haughty tone of Elle Kirkland swallowed the silence that had fallen, accentuating Alex's awkwardness at finding herself under unanticipated scrutinization. She'd not realized the woman would be here, expecting only Catharine and Nathalie, and at once found herself painfully aware of her damp clothing and grime-splattered shoes, and the wet hair that clung to her forehead.

"It's good to see you again, Ms. Kirkland."

"Miss Grey." Elle made a point of looking at her watch. "It was getting so late, I'd begun to fear we'd have to tell Catharine you'd run off with her driver."

"I guarantee she wouldn't be able to return him fast enough."

Alex turned to see Catharine leaning against the wall leading to the kitchen, the corners of her mouth lifted into a close-lipped smile. She looked as tired as Alex felt, but her eyes were warm when they caught her gaze, and the sight of her made the enervating past twenty-four hours feel worth it.

"Touché," Malcolm returned, unruffled to find himself the subject of Catharine's teasing. "On that note, I'll just drop these upstairs and see myself out."

With an obligatory greeting to Nathalie—the Frenchwoman's attention diverted between the muted TV and a game of Rummy spread across the table—Alex followed Catharine to the kitchen, taking a moment for just themselves.

"You made it." Catharine leaned back against the floating island.

"Did you doubt me?" Alex had meant it playfully, but the intensity behind Catharine's gaze turned the sentiment into something else.

"No," Catharine answered after a beat, the clarity of her blue eyes unblinking. "I didn't."

Alex wanted to reach out and touch her, but found herself unexpectedly trapped in her former tentative reservation, uncertain—after weeks of ups and downs—exactly where they stood. She'd meant to arrive confident, collected, leaving all the turmoil of the past month behind them.

Honour Stone. *Kickstar*. The election. The disappointment of her personal shortcomings in letting her team down.

She'd come here intent on being a steady foundation for Catharine—offering her whatever she needed to get through the election—helping her find strength for whatever the coming days would bring.

In the other room the voices of Elle and Nathalie elevated in an amicable dispute over the value of a sequence of cards, Elle's laughter stifling in the atmosphere. It was enough to shift the direction of the conversation. To alter the course of thoughts from wherever Catharine's mind had been.

"I'm sorry, about..." Catharine gave a subtle nod toward the sitting room. "The visit was unexpected. I tried to call you, but your phone is off."

Alex brushed away the apology. This was not a night for Catharine to worry about anyone but herself.

"How are you holding up?"

"I'm all right. Tired. A bit apprehensive—I suppose that's to be expected. More than anything, I just want the day to be over. I think the dread of anticipation is almost worse than the results." She reached out, collecting Alex's hand, stroking her thumb across her palm.

Around the corner the sound of the TV clicked on.

"Catharine—you must see this!" It was Elle over the chatter of American commentary.

Catharine's sigh was subdued, though everything about her broadcasted the exhaustion, the anxiety, the repressed emotion that she felt.

You don't have to do this, Alex wanted to tell her. She could walk out there, send Elle home, turn off the news, and find the peace she needed to get through.

But she knew Catharine wouldn't. So Alex kept her thoughts to herself.

"I'm glad you're here, Alex." Catharine gave her hand a squeeze, leaning forward to kiss the corner of her mouth. Then she straightened, found a smile that never met her eyes, and returned to the sitting room.

It was after midnight when Alex rejoined the small party downstairs. She'd showered and changed, and taken her time settling her things, hoping by the time she reappeared Elle Kirkland would have moved on. But by the sound of her conversation with Nathalie—a combination of acerbic sparring and unabashed flirting—and the news commentary droning in the background, Alex held little hope for her impending departure.

Carlton Cleveland's accentuated Southern drawl greeted her as she descended the staircase. It was seven p.m. in South Carolina. There were a couple dozen reporters huddling around the steps of Cleveland Manor, eager to get the senator's closing sentiments on Election Day. He took each query in turn, grandstanding with his Biblical quotes and blustering with uncharted arrogance.

How was he feeling? "'Thanks be to God, who gives us the victory through our Lord Jesus Christ.'"

The race had narrowed in several key states. What was his response to New Hampshire swinging against him? "'Blessed is the man who remains steadfast under trial.'"

Did he have any additional comment? "'I have fought the good fight, I have finished the race, I have kept the faith.'"

Alex stood in the dark of the hallway, watching the broken capillaries of his ruddy cheeks rise with his pompous smile. She marveled how any man could turn the *Second Epistle to Timothy* into a political platform. Her father had loved *2 Timothy*. Be loving and peaceful, patient and kind... that was the message. Not the seeping insolence of this man who'd sell his soul to the devil if it bought him one more vote.

"Il est con comme un balai," Nathalie waved her hand of cards at the TV—she, Elle, and Catharine all focused on the screen. "He has not finished any race yet. The prick is too stupid to count to two hundred seventy."

"Catharine," Elle's posh London accent had grown heady with whisky, "I have to say, it is genuinely revolting to think you ever wed and bed this man."

Catharine did not respond. Her gaze had turned from the TV to the windows, where the rain continued to hammer down.

"Tell us, Senator Cleveland," one young reporter egged, looking for a laugh, "how do you think your wife cast her ballot?"

There was uneasy chuckling around him. The more senior reporters appeared uncomfortable with the idea of chaffing the man who might next hold the power of admission to the Press Briefing Room at the White House.

"A better question," Carlton shot the reporter a scathing glare down the barrel of his nose, "would be to ask me if I care? The only thing Mrs. Cleveland should be worrying about is patching the holes in her sinking shipwreck in England—she'd do well to keep her own head above water."

Undeterred by the chastisement, the reporter persisted. "I take it it doesn't bother you, then, that Alex Grey was seen departing a flight bound for London early this morning?"

"The soccer player?" He tried for casual, but the shift toward ire was evident. "If my wife needs to comfort herself with trinkets and playthings while she swallows the reality that by morning I'll be one of the most—" he paused, considering his words as the smugness of his demeanor returned, *"influential* men in the world, so be it."

"He's not even subtle in threatening you." Nathalie tossed her cards onto the table. "I know you want to return to San Francisco, Catharine, but aren't you worried what he might do?"

From her refuge in the darkness, Alex watched Catharine's profile stiffen into annoyance.

"Like what? Put a hit out on me? Blow my car up? String me up in the street? Come off it, Nat. It's not as if we are living in a third world country where he can order my execution. He can't do worse than he already has."

"Exaggeration aside," Elle steepled her hands, clicking her manicured nails together, "her concern isn't without merit. I know you're intent on reestablishing yourself stateside by January, but it wouldn't hurt to allow things to settle, no matter which way this election swings. With the corporation in limbo, there's no rush, and even—"

Catharine opened her mouth to argue, but Elle continued, undaunted.

"And even if the gods grant you a windfall—if a bolt of lightning comes out of nowhere and strikes your father dead—you could resume command from here. There's no pressing necessity to rush back into shark-filled waters."

"I don't want to stay in London—"

"Oh, to live in a world with your particular set of problems." The lawyer gestured to the extravagance of the room surrounding them. "Can you imagine—the absolute atrocity of being forced to lay-low in these unbearable conditions? Christ, Catharine, give it a year or two. At least let your divorce finalize. It's not as if you're being marooned off to the hinterlands."

"I want to be home with Alex."

"For fuck's sake, do you think *that* is going to make things better? The whole world saw how he reacted to that photo of the two of you on your birthday—popping off on his ludicrous tangent about your lover—can you fathom how he'd respond—"

"You encouraged that! *You* told me to make things more public— to 'win' the people over."

"That was for the sake of your business—which is, I believe, exactly what you hired me for. I warned you at the time you'd need to shed some blood—"

"*My* blood. *Not* hers—"

"*Whose* is irrelevant. Things were always bound to get messy. Don't pretend you didn't know that. But this is all neither here nor there. The truth is," she pointed a pink nail toward the television, "that man you married is unhinged—and all we're asking you is to be reasonable. You don't have to relocate indefinitely, just let the dust settle. A couple years is hardly the end of the world."

"I told Alex—"

"Catharine—stop thinking with your libido for a minute and employ that acclaimed brain of yours instead. No one is saying you can't have your little affair. Alex is young, when time permits, she can fly here to see you. Have your fun, just do it at a safe distance. Given that pillock's imbecility," she took another glance toward Carlton on the TV, "he'll sink himself long before he ever has an opportunity at a second term. And when they throw him out on his ear, you can go home. Reestablish yourself wherever you want to be." She looked to Nathalie for validation. "Tell me I'm wrong?"

Alex stared at the Frenchwoman through the darkness, willing her to take a stand. To tell the barrister she'd overstepped her pay grade—that it wasn't for her to decide what Catharine did or didn't do.

It was news to her that Catharine planned to be home in San Francisco by January. They'd not spoken of dates—made no definite plans. But *years*... years had never been part of the discussion. Years seemed an impossible amount of time.

Lips pressed together, Nathalie exhaled. "You know how much I miss you—how much I want you home—but I do worry, Catharine. We both know what he's capable of. How vindictive he can be. Perhaps she's right..."

"You both talk as if he's already won the damn thing!" Catharine snatched her whisky off the table. "For Christ's sake, you're asking me to make plans four years from now when we don't even know what tomorrow will bring!" She set the glass to her lips, but returned it to the table without ever taking a sip.

In front of the trio of women, the election footage was showing a drone shot of Cleveland Manor. There, in the South Carolina sunset, was the opulence of the plantation home's massive columns and sweeping dome. The gardens, the pool, the Daufuskie Island coast. Alex numbly registered the dock was gone. The commentator was talking about Carlton's steadily rising electoral votes, but Alex tuned him out. She was thinking only of what Elle had said. Of Nathalie's agreement. Of what Catharine might agree to.

"Well, don't you look comfortable."

Lost in her thoughts, Alex hadn't noticed Elle look her way, finding her through the darkness and ousting her from her hiding place.

Not wanting to look like she'd been eavesdropping, Alex lunged into the light. "Hey," she said, too brightly, "sorry that took so long."

"Hey." Catharine's smile was tight, but by the time she'd slid over to make room on the sofa, the affability had returned to her gaze. "I wouldn't have blamed you if you'd called it a night. You've had a monstrous day."

Alex could feel Elle's judgment from beneath the thickness of her mascara-tinted lashes, sweeping her from head-to-toe. Taking in her t-shirt and joggers, lingering on her slip-on Vans.

"You've arrived just in time to help us settle a debate," the lawyer said, casting Alex a glance that told her she knew she'd been standing there far longer than the abruptness of her entrance. "Something tells me your vote will be the only one that matters."

"Elle," Catharine sighed, leaning back into the cushion of white upholstery, closing her eyes, "please. Enough for tonight."

As Alex took a seat beside her she tried not to dwell on how gaunt her face looked. How pale her skin. She'd lost more weight since she last saw her—weight she didn't have to lose.

"It's simply a discussion, Catharine. An open communication. The first step to a healthy relationship."

Catharine opened her eyes. "I hired you as my barrister, not my therapist."

"You'd be surprised the similarities—both require an in-depth knowledge of psychology, a critical understanding of the human thought process, and the majority of days spent dealing with

197

delusional clients with unrealistic expectations." She pinned Catharine with a pointed look, before turning to Alex. "Perhaps you caught the tail end of our conversation?" She tossed her auburn locks over her shoulder. "We're concerned for Catharine's safety. Should the worst happen, we were discussing how wise it might be for Catharine to stay in London for a while. To lie low and keep out of the limelight. She, of course, was worried how you would feel—but knowing how much you care about her, I've no doubt you share our apprehensions. I'm sure nothing is more paramount for you than her wellbeing."

Alex wanted to tell Elle to save her theatrics for the courtroom. That she wasn't one of her wig-wearing judges she could wrap around her little finger, to be manipulated into doing her volition.

Instead she opted to keep the peace. It was all a lot to digest, and none of it did she wish to address with anyone other than Catharine.

"I think only Catharine can say what is best for Catharine."

Elle's smile was cutting. "How diplomatic."

"Look." Nathalie diverted the attention of the room to the TV. "They've called Pennsylvania."

The screen flashed its red *breaking news* banner, adding the twenty electoral votes to Carlton Cleveland's ascending number. It was the first flipped state of the election.

"Tell you what," said Elle, tipping back the last of her glass before reaching to pour another. "This night is going to go how this night is going to go—we may as well make the best of it. I say we play a game of Whist. Nathalie and I against the pair of lovers. And to keep the night interesting, each time a state is called, we take a sip. Two if it's been deemed a battleground. Three if it's been flipped." She topped off Nathalie and Catharine's tumblers to the brim. "Care to join the fun, Alex? Or are you still America's favorite teetotaler?"

"She can share my glass," Catharine said, finding Alex's hand and entwining their fingers. "I have no desire to get as soused as the two of you seem hellbent on."

Two games of Whist and six states later, Alex found her patience growing shorter and shorter. Elle seemed to enjoy pressing her buttons, actively looking for ways to try and provoke her, but Catharine's presence—squeezing her hand, pressing her knee, leaning against her shoulder-to-shoulder—kept her grounded. With the anxiety of the day and the stress of long travel, Alex told herself she was just oversensitive. Exhaustion was closing in on her, and with it, her shortening composure.

"So Alex," Elle's blithe singsong warned of an impending jab as she opened another bottle of whisky. South Carolina and Georgia had just been called in quick succession, sending Carlton's numbers over two hundred. "You are—what—twenty-five? Twenty-six?"

"I'll be twenty-nine in January—"

"Ah, twenty-nine! Oh, to be your age again," she shot Catharine a wink, laying down the ace of hearts before resuming. "So at twenty-nine, what do you envision for your life once your football career is over?"

Alex was cautious, aware a trap was lying here somewhere. "I've not made any concrete decisions."

"No, no, of course not. Why would you, when you've got quite a—safeguard—to fall back on?" Her eyes shifted to Catharine, who had grown quiet over the last half hour, her attention waning from the conversation as Carlton's numbers climbed higher. She nor Nathalie appeared to catch the slight, and Elle plowed on before Alex could defend herself. "Mayhap coaching would be an option? Surely there are many youth teams that would benefit from a player with your experience?"

Alex was unable to think straight past Elle's suggestion she intended to *fall back* on Catharine. As if she were here for her money. Here for what Catharine could offer her.

"Or perhaps you could look into athletic training? Helping the next generation of stars rise to their full potential."

"I majored in architectural engineering—I don't imagine I'll return to school for kinesiology."

"An architect? My word. That's quite a stray from a career in sporting."

Alex didn't have a chance to tell her the majority of women on her team held degrees in advanced industries—that they weren't just dumb jocks who could kick around a ball. Hell, Molly Rodrigues had graduated from law school while playing professional soccer. But Catharine's phone rang on the coffee table, cutting off the conversation—the jarring peal of an unknown number.

Broken from her stupor, Catharine flicked mute on the TV and collected her phone, checking the clock on mantle. It was almost two in the morning.

"Hello?"

Through the silence of the room the unmistakable tone of Carlton Cleveland's Southern drawl filtered through the receiver.

"Are you watching this, Catharine?"

Catharine stood abruptly. "Why are you calling me?"

"I told you," he drew out the words, elongating every vowel, speaking to her as if English was her second language. "I want to know if you are watching?" He was drunk, no question, the derision in his laughter nauseating. "Are you and that little dyke enjoying the show? Have you seen those numbers, Catharine? Do you know what they mean?"

"How did you get this number—?"

"Now you're japing me, m'dear. I know the woman I married is smarter than that. Have you paid no attention? Do you think there is anything in this world I can't get? Has tonight proven nothing?"

Across the room Elle Kirkland sprung to her feet, striding around the coffee table far more steady in stilettos than Alex would have imagined possible after God-only-knew how much whisky.

"Hand me the phone."

Catharine cast the woman a quick glance, shaking her head, her attention on the other end of the line.

"Is that her? Put the little harpy on. I want to ask her a question." Alex could hear Carlton's sneer, despite the crescendo of blood skyrocketing between her ears.

For months he had badgered her, degraded her, taken shots at her in interviews and social media. But hearing his voice in the intimacy of this setting—with all the malice, all the disgust laced behind it—was more unsettling than the rest of it combined.

"Carlton, I'm finished—"

He cut her off. "Ask her for me then—ask her if it's all been worth it? Has slipping between your sheets been worth the shit-show storming down on her—"

"Catharine! Give me the phone!" Without waiting for consent, Elle snatched the phone from Catharine's hand, raising it to her ear.

"Hello, Mr. Cleveland." It was impressive, the unwavering command of her voice. "This is Elle Kirkland, Mrs. Cleveland's barrister. Unless you'd like your first headline as President to be for a suit thrown against you for harassment, I suggest you hang up and lose this number."

"Who the hell do you think you—"

"Listen, you half-brained muppet," the lawyer snarled, hovering on the brink of losing her countenance, "I don't give a twopence who you are—call my client again and you'll find yourself sodden with litigation before you ever take office. Now get stuffed!" She disconnected the call, pressing the phone back into Catharine's stunned hand. "He's got some bloody nerve, the wanker. Has he called you before?"

Catharine took a breath, composing herself, clearly shaken by the call and Elle's handing of the situation. "I can't believe you just did that."

"It's what you should have done months ago. Back to my question: has he called you before?"

"Yes. From time to time. Mostly when he's drunk. It's why I changed my number."

"Is your divorce counsel aware of it?"

"Yes. I was told to ignore it."

Elle settled onto the edge of the coffee table. "Fire the firm."

"I'm sorry?"

"Fire them. They aren't protecting you. I'll handle the case."

Catharine was reluctant. "That seems beneath you."

"Trust me, pay me enough, and nothing is beneath me." Elle crossed her legs, drawing her skirt up to fix one of her sheer stockings. "I've sat for the New York Bar Exam. I'm more than qualified. So trust me when I say cutting the President Elect of the United States off at the knees would be a pinnacle pleasure."

"I—" Catharine looked out of sorts, unusually rattled. The muted TV was showing the state of Arizona called for Carlton in the background. "I'm sorry, will you all excuse me a moment?"

Alex watched her leave, debating whether to follow her. If she needed a second alone to collect herself, she didn't want to intrude.

"I'm going to enjoy stringing that bastard up by his balls," Elle said after Catharine had disappeared down the hall.

"Have you worked in divorce court?"

From the stony look Elle shot her, Alex would have regretted the question, but she didn't want Catharine being bullied into a terrible decision. Changing counsel in the middle of the divorce proceedings seemed an irrational decision.

"I haven't. Have you, Miss Grey?" Elle elevated her pristinely shaped eyebrows, tossing out the formality of Alex's last name as if it were a slur. "Perhaps you snuck in a law degree between your Architectural Engineering major and your football career? A woman of many talents?"

Before Alex could determine how to form a response that didn't start with *fuck you*, Elle continued.

"No? Then perhaps allow me to be the judge of my suitability for the case. I assure you—business dissolution—domestic dissolution… it's all the same. As long as it's my client doing the destructing."

Fluctuating between infuriation and humiliation, Alex stared at the fraying cuffs of her Vans, devising her exit. As soon as Catharine returned she intended to excuse herself. She needed away from this conniving, belittling woman before she said something she shouldn't.

"He's unbelievable." Elbows settled across her abandoned spread of cards, Nathalie had paid no interest to the exchange between them, her focus fixed on the television. Her tipsy tone had mellowed, sobered by the phone call. "All these years he's gone out of his way to make it clear she meant nothing to him—yet here he is, about to get everything he ever wanted, and she's still the only thing on his mind."

"The *Catharine Effect*," Elle laughed, rising from the table. "I could see how she could be a real Svengali, that one. It's honestly a marvel you've resisted her charms all these years, Nathalie. The two of you would have made a smashing couple."

Alex tidied the cards on the table, refusing to give the lawyer the reaction she knew she was seeking. It was impossible a woman of

Elle's cunning observation had missed the signs that Catharine and Nathalie had once been lovers. It was just another punch thrown with intention. For whatever inexplicable reason, the woman was hellbent on getting under her skin. An objective she was readily achieving.

Utilizing the Queen of Clubs to flick away a crumb of biscotti, Nathalie shrugged. "Some relationships are better left as friends. Others," her lips curled into a suggestive smile, some of her playfulness returning, "I prefer to leave more open."

"C'est donc ainsi?" Elle smiled and Alex fought the urge to gag. Let Nathalie find out for herself that certain species were known to bite the heads off their lovers after mating.

Catharine reappeared by way of the kitchen, carrying a glass of water.

"I'm sorry—I don't know why I let that get to me." She offered a flustered laugh to hide her embarrassment, coming up behind the settee and setting a hand on Alex's shoulder.

"I can't speak from experience," Elle lounged back in her chair, kicking up a stiletto onto the table. "My former husbands are mainly a compilation of judges, commissioners, and a good-for-nothing oil baron, but I imagine having your ex a breath away from winning one of the most coveted elections in the world—then having him call to gloat about it—might do that to a person."

"You were married to an oil baron?" Nathalie was intrigued.

"Mmm. Unfortunately. Turns out my type of silk was better suited for his counsel than his bedroom. Certainly no loss there. Now I've got the best of both worlds—I still pick his pocket representing him on legal matters and no longer have to pretend to enjoy calling him *daddy* while down on my knees."

Nathalie's face twisted with a disgusted shudder. "I don't know how any of you tolerate it—being with a man. They're so primitive. So... boorish."

The corners of Elle's lips twitched. "Have you really never been with a man?"

"No. And I've no plans to change that."

"Oh, they aren't all so bad. Though I admit I've come to learn I prefer my husbands with the prefix *ex* in front of them. And what about you, Alex? Have you never been married?"

"No." The curtness of her answer made Nathalie laugh.

"Not that she hasn't been asked—"

"*Nathalie*," Catharine scolded, but the Frenchwoman dismissed her.

"What? The video is wildly funny. No doubt at this point Alex can laugh, too." She glanced at Alex. "Can you not?"

Without Elle Kirkland dissecting her every reaction, she may have found it more amusing. But underneath the strain of the shrewd woman's scrutiny, there was nothing funny about it.

"Video?" Elle's eyes shined.

"Alex's ex-boyfriend streamed a livefeed of his failed proposal —"

"Wait! The blighter with the jersey! I don't know why I never put two-and-two together! That was you! That footage bounced around the football forums for ages. There were all kinds of jokes that Amelia Walker should be placed on defense after that clip of her in the hallway." Elle's laugh was grating. "Oh, which reminds me—I had lunch with my friend Stanwick last week—the owner of Arsenal. He mentioned how disappointed the club was that Walker turned down their buy-out offer, deciding instead to return to the NWSL."

At Amelia's name, Alex stiffened, aware Catharine could feel her reaction from the hand on her shoulder. She hadn't told her anything about Amelia returning to Oakland. Or that she'd seen her the previous weekend. The omission hadn't been intentional, there had simply been no time for the discussion.

Now, however, she wished she had. She didn't want Catharine thinking she'd kept anything a secret. Or had anything to hide.

"Were they?" Alex tried for ignorance, immediately regretting it. There was a look about Elle that promised she was up to something.

"I'm surprised you didn't know. I understand you two were very close."

"We were teammates—"

"Is that what the girls are calling it these days?" Elle winked. "We just used the term fuck buddies, but I suppose that wasn't too original—"

"What are you getting at?" Alex was on her feet without even knowing how she'd gotten there. Behind her, she was vaguely aware of Catharine saying her name, trying to defuse the situation, but Alex had reached her tipping point. The wick of her patience had extinguished.

Elle smiled as if she'd won a contest Alex hadn't known they'd entered. "Easy, killer. I meant no offense. I just thought you two had been close—I figured she might have told you about her return to Oakland when she was at your match last weekend."

"What?" Alex barely breathed.

"I'm surprised you didn't see her. Stanley mentioned she was on three days excused absence to meet with your coach."

Alex was certain her heartbeat could be heard over the downpour battering against the windows.

She should have just told Catharine about Amelia. Instead she stood there, looking like she'd been caught in an indiscretion.

"I did see her." Alex looked at Catharine. "I just hadn't—"

"Was that why you stayed in Carolina?"

Alex was thrown by the sudden venom of Nathalie's accusing tone.

"What do you mean?" Her attention shifted to the Frenchwoman.

"Is that why you didn't come back to Oakland?"

"*Nathalie!*" Catharine was as furious as Alex had ever seen her. "*Don't.*"

Nathalie paid her no heed. "Is it?"

Why Nathalie would even know she'd stayed an extra day in South Carolina, Alex couldn't begin to guess. Why she'd care was even less comprehensible.

"I don't know what you're asking."

Across from her Elle was relishing the turmoil she'd caused, breaking in with a self-admonishing laugh. "Sorry, I hadn't meant to imply—"

"So you stayed in Carolina to hang out—or *whatever*—with your ex-girlfriend, while Catharine—"

"God damnit, Nathalie—"

"—flew halfway around the world to see you—only for you to never grace California with your presence!"

"Enough!" Catharine slammed her hands onto the back of the settee, spilling her glass of water. "You can never just leave well enough alone!"

Subdued by Catharine's anger, Nathalie fell quiet, the room silencing with her.

"What are you talking about?" Alex whispered at last, struggling to grasp an understanding. "When were you in Oakland?"

"It doesn't matter!" Catharine's vehemence was directed at Nathalie, but still it made Alex wince.

She thought about the night of her game—the missed calls, and then all the hours Catharine's phone had gone to voicemail. She thought about the conversation they'd had while she was sitting in Amelia's hotel room—how Catharine had reacted when she told her she wasn't in Oakland. She'd sounded so deflated.

It made sense, suddenly.

Horrible, collapsing sense.

If she'd just answered her call the night before…

But it was more than missing one phone call. It was more than just one wasted trip.

It was two years of miscommunication. Two years of turmoil, of tension, of being unable to express themselves. It was days of contentment followed by months of dissatisfaction. Hours of joy trampled by following heartache. It was never just easy. Never simple. There was always something pressing on them, hampering their happiness. Disrupting whatever normalcy they tried to find.

This evening was no different.

Unable to curb her frustration, Alex threw the cards she'd been holding onto the table, turning for the hall. She knew she should be the one apologizing to Catharine. She should be the one to make things right.

But she just wanted out of this conversation. Away from Elle and her endless provoking. Away from Nathalie and her accusations. Away from the banner rolling across the TV screen announcing another flipped state for Carlton. To pretend bright bold letters weren't predicting the bastard's unfathomable win.

Afraid tears were soon to follow, she bolted for the hall leading to the stairwell, no longer caring where she went.

Chapter Twenty-Two

Catharine heard the vestibule door slam shut, taking Alex's fading footsteps with it. She felt unsteady, as if the room was revolving in slow motion while she remained in a fixed position.

The strain of the night had been building. The pressure coming at her from all directions.

The election. Elle. Carlton and his phone call. Nathalie's inability to keep her brainless mouth shut.

And now, finally, the tension had imploded.

Across from her she registered Elle laugh, the woman kicked back with her stilettoed feet on the table.

"Ah, to be tetchy and volatile in youth again."

Catharine didn't answer.

Decorum demanded she laugh. Brush the contention off. Stay and smile or politely excuse herself to deal with the situation.

But decorum failed to matter. All Catharine could focus on was going after Alex.

Shaken from inaction, Catharine rounded the settee and headed for the lift, sparing neither word nor glance in any other direction. She hit the down button, then hit it again, her impatience elevating as the old conveyor made its leisurely rise from street level. For all the renovations the building had gone through, with its wealth of modern amenities and cutting-edge technology, she would have traded it all for having had the foresight to replace the laggard utility. It was too slow. Too fickle. And at the speed Alex was going, she'd have already reached the street.

"Honestly, Catharine," said Elle from across the room, watching her hit the button a third time. "Let her blow off some steam. A little fresh air will cool that choler."

Cursing the lift in lieu of the barrister, Catharine ran for the staircase, tracing the same path Alex had taken only moments earlier.

"Alex!"

It was only her own echoed voice that answered. She started down the stairs.

There'd been something in Alex's expression. Something that drove Catharine to abandon her heels at the next landing, freeing her to fly down the iron steps two-by-two until she reached the fire door of the Shad Thames alley.

It was the middle of the night. The shops were closed, the pubs buttoned up, the pedestrian footpaths vacant. The rain was coming down in a torrential mantle of water, making visibility nonexistent.

Heedless of her bare feet, Catharine ran down the stone steps onto the street, torn on which way to turn. The bite of the rain against her skin stunned her, stealing her breath with its arctic sting as she shielded her eyes from the downpour.

To her right were the lights from the bridge, distorted in a kaleidoscope of bokeh. To the left, the dark street running adjacent to the Thames, entirely deserted.

Catharine went left.

A hundred feet into her trudge down the pathway, she made out the outline of a person.

"Alex!"

The figure slowed, looking back, before continuing.

"Go back inside, Catharine." Alex's voice sounded choked, distorted by the slapping drops of water on the cobblestone.

Catharine picked up a jog to catch up with her.

"Please don't walk away from me."

Alex stopped, turning as she swiped a hand across her eyes, brushing away more than just the rain.

"Catharine, please go back inside."

"Not without you." They were both drenched, their hair dripping, their clothing sticking to their skin. Catharine tried to ward off a shiver, crossing her arms across her chest, shaking her head. "I'm not going anywhere without you."

"I don't know how to do this anymore." Alex's entire body slumped with the weight of the admission and Catharine forgot about the cold. Forgot about the discomfort of her bare feet as they stood, staring at one another.

"Talk to me. Please."

"About what?" Alex's laugh was as disconsolate as the weather. "About Nathalie being right? Is that what you came to hear? That I stayed behind in Carolina to spend time with Amelia? All the while never even knowing…" She hid her face behind her hands.

"It doesn't matter." Catharine filled the silence, uncertain she wanted to hear any further.

"Doesn't it?" Hurt crept into Alex's challenge, replacing the edge of her anger as her hands dropped to her sides. "Because I need it to matter."

Catharine revised. "It doesn't matter what Nathalie thinks—"

"It matters to me what *you* think. It matters to me if you think I spent the weekend fucking my ex-girlfriend—"

"I don't think that, Alex—"

"Would you even ask me?" Her bitterness returned. "Or is it just one more thing we'd sweep under the rug? Just move on and continue to pretend like everything is fine?" She looked away, once again abrasively wiping at her eyes with the heel of her palm.

The rain began to calm, turning into a steady drizzle, allowing their clouds of breath to fill the space between them. Space that felt like it was widening with every passing second.

Catharine wasn't certain how to respond, and in her indecisiveness, Alex continued.

"I didn't get your call that night because I *was* with Amelia. After the game she showed up at my hotel room—she'd seen the news about *Kickstar* and came to check in on me. She told me she was coming back to the NWSL. We talked; she left. After she'd gone, I tried to call you. I was depressed, upset about the game, angry about *Kickstar*, and there was no one I wanted to talk to more than you. But your phone went straight to voicemail—over and over. So I texted Amelia, asking if we could meet the following day. Not with any intention," she added, defensive, "I just needed a friend. Someone who understood. Who would listen." She took a breath, the plume of her exhale disappearing. "So the next day we hung out—we went back to her hotel. That's where I was when you called."

Catharine waited.

For a moment Alex was quiet, composing her thoughts, before looking directly at Catharine.

"She kissed me." She held her gaze, almost in a dare. "She kissed me and I didn't stop her."

"All right," Catharine said carefully.

"All right?" Alex's teeth were chattering. "How can you say that?" She quit bothering to wipe away her tears and Catharine suppressed the urge to console her. "How can you just—" she tried to regroup, failing to pull herself together, her thoughts shifting in a separate direction. "Do you know what it's been like for me these last few weeks? Having someone like *him* go after me on a personal level? In front of the *entire* world? Seeing thousands of comments from strangers online, belittling me, threatening me, calling for me to resign from my career?" The words tumbled out from between clenched teeth, her lips trembling as her chest heaved beneath her sodden t-shirt. "Having everyone around me whispering behind my back, steering clear of me for fear they'll get caught up in the crossfire? I'm not you, Catharine. I've never lived my life in the limelight—I'm not accustomed to seeing my photo in the papers or hearing my name on the news for any reason outside of soccer. For weeks now I've woken up terrified to find out what he might have said the night before and knowing there is nothing I can do to stop it. Do you have any idea how it felt—missing that penalty, knowing he was watching? Knowing half the country had taken an interest, just hoping to see me fail? When I walked off the pitch that night I felt like my entire world had shattered—and I was all alone—and Amelia—she offered me a lifeline." She took a shaky breath, closing her eyes and tipping her head toward the sky, allowing the rain to cool her burning cheeks. She'd stopped crying. "So when she kissed me, I let her." She opened her eyes, looking back. "But that was all it was, Catharine: a kiss. And that was all it took to remind me there was nothing more I wanted than you. Than *this*." She gestured between them. "And so I've told myself every day to hang on, to wait this out, that everything will get better. The election will be over. You'll get things worked out here and then you'll come home, and it will all be worth it." She let her shoulders fall. "So hearing you talk tonight about the possibility of years—I don't know how to do that." Her eyes brimmed again, her voice turning raw. "I don't know if I can."

"You won't have to." Catharine stepped forward, catching Alex's arm before she could turn away. "Nothing will keep me here, Alex. Not Carlton. Not this election. Not my father or Brooks Corp. I told Elle the morning I returned from my flight to California that I had to be home by spring—in time for your first game. And there is nothing—there is no one—that will change my mind."

"But what about—?"

"What about a million things? Carlton is going to do what Carlton is going to do. The courts will either rule in my favor over Brooks Corp. or they won't. The world will keep spinning either way—and the only thing I am certain of is that whatever happens, I'll be with you. I want to be together, Alex. I don't want flights every couple of months across the Atlantic just to see each other for a couple of days. I don't want a relationship built on midnight phone calls and good morning texts, uncertain when we might see each other again. I want to wake up with you. Have breakfast with you. I want you to get tired of me going to your games. I want to commit to the sides of the bed we sleep on. I want to argue over who is cooking dinner and decide on takeaway instead. If the media is going to badger us, we may as well give them something worthy to write. *US Soccer Star and President's ex-wife: Spotted Deliriously in Love.* That's the story I want to read about. Not this." She motioned to indicate their surroundings.

Alex's arm slowly relaxed in her grip, her expression softening. Catharine could feel the racing pulse in her wrist pounding against her fingers, coinciding with the rise and fall of her breath.

"You mean that?"

"Yes."

Alex laughed, stifling a sob, and drew the collar of her shirt up over her face to wipe her eyes. When she'd finished, a slow smile tugged at the corners of her mouth, her dimples appearing.

"So are you saying you want to move in with me?"

The dimples deepened at her enjoyment of Catharine's inability to hide her stunned reaction.

"I'd not—" Catharine began, flustered, "I'd thought, perhaps—"

"A whitewashed one-bedroom in Oakland not your style?" Alex no longer hid her smile.

Aware she was being teased, Catharine shrugged. "I understand you have a pool?"

Alex nodded, considering. "But yours has a garbage disposal."

"Yours offers free wifi in the amenities."

"Yours comes with a dishwasher."

"Oh, well, then" Catharine raised her brow, "that settles that." She brought her free hand to Alex's cheek, all jesting disappearing. "I mean it, Alex. When I get back to California, promise you'll move in with me. I want a life together."

Alex closed her eyes, the fluttering of her pulse slowing. "Okay." She let out a long exhale, the remainder of the tension in her body dissipating. "I would really like that." Opening her eyes, she laughed, her attention focused on the ground. "You're barefoot."

"Yes."

The two of them took stock of one another, for the first time seeming to notice the state they were in—the dripping hair, the goosebump-covered skin, the soaked clothing—standing in the middle of the street in the small hours of the morning.

"I've never had someone chase me through the rain before." Alex admitted with a smile.

"I've never chased someone through the rain before." Catharine entwined the fingers of the hand Alex tucked into hers, their steps turning toward her building. "As romantic as it sounds, I'd prefer it to be a one-and-done experience."

"I could commit to that."

Their steps slowed as they reached the narrow passage of the vestibule and Catharine reluctantly pressed the button for the lift.

Upstairs was the loss of this peace. This contentment. This moment of privacy. Despite the discomfort of the cold, Catharine dreaded leaving it, walking into the waiting blaze of upheaval. She didn't want to know the results of the election. To deal with Elle. With Nathalie. With whatever next catastrophe lay lurking around the corner.

But it was inevitable. They couldn't stay all night on the landing.

The doors creaked open and they stepped inside, still hand-in-hand, Catharine trying not to think about being barefoot on the decades old vinyl.

As the lumbering box began its climb, Alex leaned over, kissing the side of her neck, her lips drifting to her ear. "Sorry, but I've wanted to do that all evening."

"Don't start something you can't finish," Catharine teased, turning her head, finding Alex's mouth with hers. There was an immediate solace in the familiar nearness—the smoothness of her skin, fresh with rainwater, and the taste of her lips, still bearing a hint of salt from her tears.

All thoughts of the filthy tile and lurching pulley creaking above them vanished, replaced with a welcome warmth as Alex stepped into her, the length of her body pressing her against the wall.

"It's a slow elevator." The words were mumbled into her mouth as bold hands found their way beneath her saturated blouse, grazing her damp skin, drawing a different kind of chill. Alex's smile broadened as she ran the flat of her palms along Catharine's ribcage, down to the small of her back. "And I'm not a quitter."

Catharine was unable to hide the hitch of her breath as her muscles tensed, quivering beneath Alex's fingertips.

It was a mild touch to have stirred the intensity of her reaction, evoking a longing she couldn't conceal. But the stress of the evening had left her body on edge, her senses overly heightened, searching for an outlet of relief.

"Alex." The word was half admonishment, half invitation; knowing it could lead to nothing, but unable to resign herself.

The lift slowed, the whine of the cables increasing, indicating they were nearing their stop.

"Alex," Catharine repeated, trying to catch her breath. Alex's mouth had left hers, trailing down her jaw, her throat, pausing at the collar of her blouse. "We can't," she said, with no real conviction, even as she closed her eyes and dropped her head back against the tarnished metal wall, inviting deft fingers to work loose the satin clasps. The common sense side of her knew it was pointless. They were seconds from alighting the lift. But common sense had a way of fleeing when it was needed most.

Above them the blare of the TV filtered through the narrow shaft, joined by Elle and Nathalie's murmured voices. The floor beneath her feet shifted, preparing to settle, and then the motion ceased all together in an unexpected jolt. She opened her eyes to find Alex had pulled the red knob on the emergency stop, pausing them between floors.

Catharine couldn't help but laugh. "They'll notice." Alex's hands were already back on her blouse, resuming their endeavors, reducing Catharine to a whisper. "They'll probably call London Fire Brigade."

"Let them," Alex's lips followed the wake of her fingers—tracing the curve of her collarbone, the swell of her breasts, the sensitive skin along her ribs. "It's an old elevator, it's bound to get stuck."

The logical side of Catharine told her to end this. It was a ridiculous notion to even entertain the thought. They were almost to her sitting room. Her best friend and barrister were less than a dozen feet away.

In ten minutes she could have the situation handled. Go in there, send Elle home, call it a night. She and Alex could go upstairs, like any civilized couple. It was the proper thing to do. The responsible reaction.

One step ahead of Catharine's hesitation, Alex undid the last clasp, sliding the wet material off Catharine's shoulders, allowing the blouse to fall at their feet.

To hell with proper.

Catharine offered no resistance as Alex raised her arms up over her head, securing her wrists in her grip.

She'd been proper her whole life.

The fingers of Alex's free hand slipped beneath the silk material of her bra, working the fasteners loose.

Proper had gotten her nowhere.

Yielding to the demands of her body, Catharine's thoughts diminished to everything but the progression of Alex's mouth.

Above them the sounds of the sitting room carried on—the droning newscaster commentary, the fluttering of shuffled cards, French expletives from Nathalie, and Elle's abrasive laugh. But Catharine could isolate none of it. It became nothing more than background static, discordant to her staggered breath.

Despite the restrictions of their time, Alex's actions became slow, measured, her mouth lingering in its advancement, her enjoyment unmistakable in making Catharine wait. Aching with anticipation, it became impossible to remain still when Alex at last bent her head to run her lips across her breasts. Taunting her with her tongue. Toying with her nipples. Catharine twisted, arching against the confinement of her arms, no longer aware of the chill of the steel against the bareness of her back. The stress of the evening diffusing, falling away no different than the trousers Alex eased, one-handed, down around her hips.

Catharine's breath stilled as Alex's undertaking resumed, her fingers mapping a meandering path along her thighs, her thumb brushing against her, before slowly slipping beneath the remaining lace.

"You're shaking," Alex straightened, momentarily separating their bodies as she released Catharine's wrists, searching her face.

"I'm fine." Catharine didn't recognize her own voice, thick with desperation, impatient at the interruption as she took the moment to step out of her trousers. She needed Alex's mouth against hers, her fingers inside her, the comfort of her body against her skin. Modesty forsaken, she caught Alex's hand, bringing it back to her, and wrapped an arm around her waist to close the space between them. And in her haste Alex seemed to understand the urgency of her need.

Gone was the slow, teasing advancement. The playful, drawn out trifling. At once Catharine found her body weakening, seeking support from Alex's shoulders to keep herself from collapsing.

Somewhere above them a door slammed, rattling the panels of the lift, the voices growing more distinct. And then all at once there was silence, the commentary of the TV disappearing.

"Fuck all. That bastard's done it." Elle's voice cut through the quiet. "I'd really believed the polls were in the wrong."

"Fils de pute," was the response from Nathalie.

The conversation had diverted Catharine's attention, luring her out of the moment, but just as quickly Alex reached a hand to turn her face to her, seeking to reclaim the entirety of her focus.

And Catharine let her.

What was going on in the world around them would happen either way. Catharine couldn't stop it. Couldn't change it. Couldn't alter the shape of history. What would be, would be—it was out of her control. And that which mattered to her most was standing right in front of her.

"Shhh," Alex whispered, as if she could hear the furor of her thoughts. She shifted their bodies, raising one of Catharine's legs up over her hip, drawing an involuntary gasp as she pressed deeper inside of her. Catharine's inhalations grew ragged as she struggled to breathe, and in the final breaking of her tension, Alex's mouth covered hers, smothering Catharine's cry as her body collapsed in Alex's arms.

For one fleeting, perfect moment, the world was still around them, the only sound the erratic beating of Catharine's heart. And then, without fail, Elle Kirkland unwittingly trampled on their serenity.

"I'm off then. Unless…" Her smile was evident, even half a floor below. "You'd care to join me?"

Nathalie laughed. "Aren't you all the way across the river?"

"A thirty minute cab ride. I'm sure we could find a way to kill the time."

"A tempting offer." Their voices had neared the lift. "I should probably wait for Cate."

"Think of your absence as doing her a favor. Whichever way this night ends for her—fight or shag—there's nothing worse than the presence of a third wheel."

"When you put it that way… how could a girl say no?"

Alex stifled a laugh as Catharine panicked, trying to drag on her trousers. The rain-soaked material caught against her skin, refusing to pull up over her hips.

"Shit."

"Shhh."

The old conveyor groaned against the cables as Catharine hopped on one foot, trying to loosen her trousers while simultaneously dragging on her blouse.

"The bloody thing is stuck," Elle complained above them, and Catharine swatted Alex's hand away from the stop switch until she'd managed to get the offending slacks buttoned.

"You good?" Alex whispered, still laughing, leaning over to kiss her one last time.

Catharine had misbuttoned her blouse, her bra hidden beneath Alex's t-shirt, her hair a tangled wreck—but there was no time to tidy her mess.

"Fine," she resigned for Alex to depress the emergency stop, freeing the car to finish its climb.

"The left side, by the way," Alex said, just before the doors opened.

Catharine glanced at her, uncertain.

"I claim the left side of the bed."

Chapter Twenty-Three

Thousands of glittering lights illuminated the streets of Canary Wharf, casting a festive glow along the buildings and lampposts adorned with flocked wreaths and dangling ornaments in scarlet, gold, and silver.

The bitter cold of November had blown into an unexpected mild first week of December, drawing the stir-crazy city dwellers onto the streets of London in droves.

In a previous year, Alex would have found the chaotic fever of the holiday festivities draining. She would have hated the cramped ride on the standing-room only underground, and gone out of her way to avoid the weaving throng of bodies filtering along the shop fronts. But as they stepped off the escalator at Canary Wharf Station—Catharine's arm linked through hers, hips touching—Alex found it impossible to find any fault in the night at all.

The bustle of the streets gave them anonymity. The temperate weather offered a welcome change from the wind and sleet. The cheeriness of the twinkling lights and symphony of holiday sounds was infectious.

But more than anything, Alex was on a perpetual high from the three best weeks of her life.

Every day—spent with Catharine.

No drama. No heartache. No stress or conflict or strife.

Nothing but the two of them, shut away from the world.

Away from social media. From Carlton. From Elle. From football. From criticism. From fans. Whatever went on outside the glass walls of Catharine's Thameside apartment, neither of them knew. Nor cared.

Days of breakfast at noon and never finding a reason to pull on shoes. Nights intoxicated with pleasure, drifting into dawn wrapped in each other's arms.

It was a perfect, insulated happiness. A contentment Alex knew was unsustainable, yet one she clung to all the same. One that made the looming end of their cloistered days bearable as the reality of life took over again.

And the magic of it lingered as they navigated the overflowing streets of Canary Wharf on their way to meet Elle Kirkland.

Well, *Nathalie* and Elle.

The perfect storm, Catharine had labeled it, when Nathalie called the previous week from California to announce she was coming back out for Christmas—but no, she wouldn't be needing to stay in the apartment on Shad Thames.

"You spent two days with the woman and now you're jaunting back for an extended holiday? Jesus, Nathalie—why not just move in?"

Alex had been lounging beside Catharine on the sofa when Nathalie rang. Despite her uneasiness at the thought of the attorney and Frenchwoman teaming up together, continuing whatever they had started the night of the election, Alex couldn't help but laugh at Catharine's disgruntled reaction.

"*Jealous?*" Catharine had scoffed into the line, disgusted by whatever Nathalie had said. "I'd be more jealous of catching the flu. Are you entirely daft? She's my barrister, for God's sake—"

Cut off, she'd bristled, and rose to pace the room.

"Stop—*stop*! Do whatever you will, but for all that is holy, I don't want to hear about it!"

In the time that had passed since the phone call, Catharine hadn't warmed to the idea, but she had grudgingly agreed to meet the pair for dinner a couple days after Nathalie's return. And for once, Alex had found she didn't really mind. Despite the night of the election and Elle's endless barrage of insults, the weeks alone with Catharine had given her some peace regarding her place in Catharine's life. It didn't matter what the attorney thought, or what Nathalie thought, or whatever other opinions were shared. She'd finally found a sense of stability in their relationship, and while she didn't look forward to an evening of jabs disguised as repartee, it didn't trouble her as much as it previously would have.

"I just don't see it—the two of them," Catharine lamented as they crossed Upper Bank to Montgomery Square. "It's like tossing a keg of dynamite into an inferno."

"What is the saying?" Alex gave Catharine's elbow a squeeze. "Fight fire with fire? Maybe they're good for each other."

"Don't you dare join the lunacy of this bandwagon," Catharine bumped her with her hip, slipping her arm around her waist and tucking her hand into the back pocket of Alex's jeans. "You're supposed to be on my side."

The simple freedom of the gesture, with its unabashed display of affection and irrefutable intimacy, was so unexpected to Alex, she temporarily forgot the subject of the conversation. She could think only that this exact instant, strolling side by side—with the magnificence of Christmas in London surrounding them—was the most perfect moment in her life.

"Could either of you saunter any slower?"

Elle Kirkland's serrated jibe snaked through the chorus of *Santa Tell Me* humming from the speakers in Jubilee Park. Alex looked up to find the woman leaning against a tinsel-wrapped lamppost, the toe of one of her trademark heels tapping out an impatient tattoo from beneath the flare of black leather pants. Nathalie stood beside her, wrapped in a scarlet peacoat and cream beret, and Alex had to concede they made an eye-catching couple.

"I see the two of you remain pathetically besotted," Elle continued, unmoving from her position. "Considerate of you, Catharine, to have managed to don shoes and—I'll assume—arrive with all your undergarments in their appropriate locations."

The comment was not unexpected. The last time they'd seen Elle, the straps of Catharine's bra had been dangling out the bottom of Alex's t-shirt—an incident the attorney had been quick to point out, before Alex fled the scene of the crime, leaving Catharine to face the music on her own.

"Bold of you to make assumptions." The words tumbled out of Alex's mouth, drawing all three sets of eyes to her, the teasing retort surprising no one more than herself.

"I see keeping house for a few weeks has emboldened your paltry sense of humor." Elle's smile appeared almost genuine. "I didn't know you had it in you, Miss Grey. Now enough tosh," the woman clapped her hands as soon as Nathalie had kissed their cheeks in greeting, "I'm famished."

Dinner elapsed with a surprising level of amicability. The hostility from the night of the election had dissolved, and with

Catharine's strict demand that all talk of business be banned, the conversation drifted through relatively non-controversial territory.

Mulled wine or Winter Pimm's? The misery of the weather. Which city did Christmas better, London or Paris?—a debate that momentarily risked a spat between Elle and Nathalie, inadvertently diverted by Alex's acknowledgement that she'd never experienced either.

"What about Copenhagen? Vienna? Prague?" Elle drilled Alex as they received their coats from the doorman.

Alex shook her head.

"Tell me you've at least been to Rockefeller?"

She had, once, as a child. The last Christmas before her parents had died. A memory she opted to keep for herself.

"I'm afraid the majority of my Christmases have all been spent in Carlisle, South Carolina."

"Wherever the devil that is," Elle discarded the name with as little care as she did the lint she plucked from her coat lapel. "Come, then, we'll start with the Christmas Market in Montgomery Square. It's by no means as grand as Hyde Park's Winter Wonderland, but I guarantee it will supersede whatever it was you had in Carlisle."

"Winter Wonderland is for tourists." Nathalie finished buttoning her coat, her disdain muffled through the wrap of her scarf. "If you really want to impress our American friend, we should fly over to Paris for the weekend. Show her La Magie de Noël beside Place de la Concord."

"Only if we want our pocket picked by some riffraff—"

"Your weak English wine has addled your brain. You've confused Tuileries Garden with Leicester Square—"

As the two bickered on, Catharine turned to Alex, raising a gloved hand to adjust the knot of the scarf at Alex's throat.

"A pair of petulant children," she smiled, the reflection of the holiday lights turning the blue of her eyes to a patchwork of scarlet and emerald diamonds. "We should leave them to their squabbling and enjoy the festivities on our own."

"Hogwash," Elle cut back in, her attention diverted from Nathalie. "We can hardly risk the two of you getting booked for indecent exposure! Miss Grey is on her own—she can't afford my hourlies—but you, Catharine... as the unlucky sot charged with the impossible task of trying to keep your public image afloat, I simply cannot allow it." To Alex's surprise, Elle reached out and took her arm, leading her down the steps with her signature authority. "There's a booth at the market that makes the best mince pies in London." She shot a look over her shoulder. "That's something you certainly won't find in Tuileries Garden."

Nathalie's response in French made Catharine laugh and Elle glare, and not for the first time Alex tried not to imagine what exactly was the unifying attraction between them. It was clearly not the sparkling nature of their companionable personalities.

Dozens of market stalls and hundreds of brushed shoulders and *beg your pardons* later, Alex had come to discover roasted chestnuts were not her thing, but found a welcome relief in learning the majority of modern mincemeat pies contained no actual meat.

It had been fun, she had to admit. With Catharine's hand tucked in hers, the four of them wandering shop to shop, the crowds too dense for any outsider to pay them any attention, it had felt like an entirely normal outing. Something that had been in short supply over the course of their relationship.

They'd departed the outdoor market with powdered sugar-dusted fingertips and *Last Christmas* emblazoned into their brains, and wandered along the waterway until they reached One Canada Square. There, nestled amongst some of London's tallest skyscrapers—one of which housed *Crown Bridge Chambers*, where Elle kept her office—was a glass-domed ice rink flanked by an outdoor bar.

The glint in Nathalie's dark eyes turned mischievous as she grabbed Elle's lambskin-gloved hand. There was no question as to what she was thinking.

"Parfait!"

Fortunately, for potentially the first time, Elle and Alex were of one resolution.

"No. Absolutely not."

"You cannot skate?" Nathalie's chestnut eyes grew brighter, her grip on Elle's hand firmer.

"*Cannot* and *will not* do not share the same definition."

"You cannot skate," Nathalie laughed, walking backward toward the rink, dragging Elle along with her. "Imagine—there is finally something the esteemed polymath cannot do."

"I have not said I cannot—"

"If you could, you would. There is no chance you would miss an opportunity to show off your prowess." Nathalie's smile grew suggestive. "No matter what the skill."

"And what would you care to bet?" Elle matched her provocative tone.

Catharine made a mock showing of clearing her throat. "For the benefit of all of us, why don't you two call it a night and take it upstairs." She gestured in the direction of Elle's sky rise apartment, less than a block away.

Elle paid her no mind. Her fingers were toying with the tie of Nathalie's peacoat, her cherry red nails in contrast to the darker hue of the wool. There was something about her that reminded Alex of a cat playing with its kill. And Nathalie appeared a more than willing sacrifice.

"You'd have to be bold enough to find out." Nathalie gave a coy tilt of her head, withdrawing herself from reach. "But I can see you're not up for the challenge. Pas de problème." She looked to Catharine. "Cate won't let me down—she's an excellent skater."

"Somehow I doubt that."

Catharine had opened her mouth to decline, but the attorney's snub drew her up short.

"You doubt that?"

"Very much. You may be an expert at skating on thin ice, but when it comes to the literal sport of gliding across a frozen pool of water, I simply cannot bring myself to imagine a woman of your kind managing that with any manner of success."

"Well, then," Catharine drawled the words and Alex had to laugh. Whether Elle had been goading her, or truly believed Catharine incapable of the task, it wasn't clear—but it was obvious Catharine would not be walking away from the provocation. She turned to Alex. "Do you skate?"

She didn't. She'd never even tried. But there was something so satisfying about leaving Elle as the odd man out on the sidelines, she didn't care if she embarrassed herself on the ice.

"It seems as good a night as any to learn."

"Bollocks—you're going to break your ankle. That won't be suiting for your career." Elle motioned toward the bar. "Come have a drink with me whilst these two nitwits try to relive their youth."

"Preseason's eight weeks out—bones heal in four to six." Alex offered Elle a canned smile, before following Catharine and Nathalie toward the rink.

It came as no surprise Catharine turned out to be an elegant skater. Despite her whispered admission—as they laced up rented skates —that she hadn't set foot on the ice in over twenty-five years, it took her no time to find a graceful rhythm gliding across the rink. Alex opted to watch for a few minutes from the sideline, enjoying the carefreeness Catharine had embraced. The evening had given her a lightheartedness, separating her from the reserved, proper image that consumed her daily life.

Not far down the rail, Nathalie—less fluid, yet bolder in her speed and maneuvers—baited Elle from the rink-side wall, slowing only to steal sips from her steaming drink.

One foot onto the ice was all it took for Alex to rue her decision. Suddenly sipping spiked cider from the safety of her tennis shoes while sitting beside Elle Kirkland on a bar stool sounded less shameful by the minute. It was far more difficult to stand than she'd expected—let alone remain moving forward in an upright position—and she'd fallen twice before making it through the low swinging gate.

"Looking sharp out there!" Elle called as Alex eased back to her feet, both arms held out in a prayer to find an ounce of stability. "Perhaps you should consider a change in careers!"

Alex would have loved to have shot her the finger, but her concentration was dedicated to the frozen ground in front of her. She managed three short, shuffling strides, thrilled to not find herself flat on her back.

"You know what they say," Nathalie's taunting voice sang out in response as she skated backward past Elle, "those who can, do; those who can't, criticize."

"That is *not* the saying."

"No, but it's fitting. So much bluster—and nothing to back it up."

Lost in a sea of nimble, confident children that spun and weaved around her, Alex slowly found enough balance to manage the full circumference of the rink without having to grab for the rail.

On her third lap, a pair of hands found her waist, skating up behind her. "I didn't see you come out here."

Alex laughed. "I don't know how you missed me flailing along the wall."

Catharine agilely glided beside her, supporting her elbow. "You look good."

"You're a terrible liar."

Catharine smiled. "Well, you're still on your feet." Her glance swept to Alex's wet knees and the glistening ice shavings covering her forearms. "For the moment, at least."

"I've had a humbling lesson learning 'natural athletic ability' doesn't necessarily extend to other disciplines."

"You can't be the best at everything—it wouldn't be fair to the rest of us."

Alex intended to make the argument that the *only* thing she did well was kick a ball—and even then, that was sometimes questionable—but Nathalie's pealing laughter from across the rink cut through the music and cheerful chatter, drawing their attention.

Either by her own ego, or Nathalie's ribbing, Elle had been cajoled onto the ice—where she now stood, center rink, her poised demeanor entirely abandoned as she lurched and teetered, her arms swinging wildly trying to maintain her balance. All efforts from Nathalie to lend her a hand were warded off, before the attorney's legs splayed beneath her and her valiant fight with gravity was lost. She landed square on her butt, the blades of both skates turning skyward.

"Oof," Alex sympathized. "That's going to leave a mark."

Twice more Nathalie proffered an arm—her provoking remarks evident in the coyness of her smirk——and twice again Elle brushed her aside, only to find herself back on the ground, struggling to rise due to the snugness of her skintight leather pants.

"Oh, God." Catharine cringed.

Alex followed her gaze to where a rink attendant was gliding out with a skate-aid—essentially a large plastic penguin with handles coming out of its head—intended to accommodate unbalanced children.

"I can't watch this." Catharine tugged on Alex's elbow, reversing direction toward the break in the wall that lead toward the bar. "Have a drink with me?"

In the time it took to return their skates and order steaming mugs of spiked cider, the quarreling duo had finally made it to the exit. Elle had foregone the penguin, and relented to the indignity of clinging to Nathalie's coat.

"Tell me one of those is for me," the attorney huffed, heaving herself onto the stool beside Catharine when she finally arrived at the bar.

Alex slid her half sipped drink toward her.

"Oh, come on, I'm sure Alex thought you were looking sharp out there," Nathalie prodded, recycling Elle's earlier taunt. "Have you considered—"

"Don't you dare say it," Elle threatened, cutting her off, downing Alex's glass.

"I'm simply disappointed you declined the aid of the penguin," Catharine joined in, squeezing Alex's knee under the table. "That would have been the highlight of the evening."

Elle's intended retort was cut short by the buzzing of Catharine's cell phone, sitting face up on the bar top.

Emily Brooks. The name flashed on the screen, visible to all of them before Catharine snatched it into her hand.

"Why would she be calling?" Elle's amber eyes shifted from their embarrassed glower to intrigue.

"I've no idea." Catharine tucked the phone into her lap beneath the table, all the merriness of her demeanor lost.

"Perhaps your father wants to make us a more intelligent offer. Or," Elle mused, "even better: bit the dust. Either way, Catharine," she nodded toward the sound of the phone still buzzing, "you need to answer that."

"No, Cate," Nathalie's vehement disagreement did nothing to restore the lightness of the atmosphere. "You owe her nothing. Do not allow her to ruin the night."

Elle and Nathalie stared at one another, their inimical opposition resembling a pair of cobras in a standoff.

"It is my recommendation, as her *barrister*," spat Elle, pinning her lover with a withering glare, "that Catharine keep an open line of communication with her mother. The joyfulness of the evening is not of consideration when it comes to winning this trial."

The phone fell silent in Catharine's lap.

To Alex's astonishment, the headstrong Frenchwoman backed down.

"Perhaps she is right, Cate." Resigned, Nathalie dropped her eyes to the mugs of cooling cider. "You may as well find out what she wants."

Catharine's free hand drifted from Alex's knee before Alex had a chance to catch it.

The lightness of the holiday evening had suddenly worn off.

Chapter Twenty-Four

Slowing her steps down the unfamiliar gangway, Catharine trailed her mother and Alex by half a dozen yards. She could no longer make out the entirety of the conversation, but from the select words filtering across the breeze, she knew they were still talking about the white cliffs of Beachy Head, a topic that had carried over from the end of luncheon.

It had unexpectedly nettled Catharine, the easy way Alex had found around her mother. A resentment she knew was entirely unfounded, but one she hadn't been able to shake.

She'd found herself ridiculously bitter from the moment they stepped into the yacht club bar. Bitter at the way Alex had not shied away from her mother's welcome, allowing herself to be hugged. Bitter at the effortless way the pair had fallen into conversation, while Catharine remained predominantly silent.

She wasn't mad at Alex. She couldn't be. She wasn't entirely irrational. It wasn't Alex's fault she felt so displaced.

Alex had made the trip to support her, even when Catharine knew she'd rather have not been involved. After the catastrophe at Honour Stone, the last thing any sane person would care to do would be to attend another Brooks' family reunion, but Alex had offered to join Catharine all the same.

On the phone, Emily had asked to meet in Eastbourne over the approaching weekend. She'd given no reason beyond the vague "I'd like to see you again, if you'll allow me a second chance," and offered emphatic reassurance that Colonel Brooks would in no way be involved.

Catharine had wanted nothing more than to decline.

Her life had only just begun to level. Things had started to fall into place.

Allowing Elle and her associates at *Crown Bridge* to take over the dissolution of her marriage, the overqualified counsel had made surprising headway on her divorce.

The brutal stalemate with her father had forced her to accept, even after things went to trial, Brooks Corp. might never again truly be hers.

And even with that reality looming, she'd found she could still be happy. That she looked forward to the future. To starting a new life.

Allowing her mother into that safety felt like sipping from a poisoned chalice.

But she'd agreed to meet her anyhow.

The events at Honour Stone had not been Emily Brooks' fault. They'd been caused by the meddling of Elle Kirkland, and in extension, the blame fell to Catharine. She felt obligated to make up for that. To give her mother the chance she deserved.

So three days after the phone call, she and Alex had driven to the southern coast.

And as Catharine followed behind the two women, she scolded herself for her unjustified petulance and instead determined to be grateful for Alex's embracement of her mother. Grateful that she was able to do what Catharine was not.

"She is a beauty, isn't she, Catharine?"

Stepping onto the dock, Catharine came up alongside the pair, where they had stopped in front of the yacht Emily had chartered for the weekend. A stunning teak-decked Oyster sailboat—small enough to be sailed one-handed, but with plenty of size to tackle the waters of the English Channel.

"She is." Catharine forced the approving nod she knew her mother sought, trying to find some of the amicable tranquility the other two women managed to share.

"Mrs. Brooks?" A man—about Catharine's own age—appeared from below deck, greeting the three of them with a sun-weathered smile. His gaze lingered too long on Catharine, sweeping her figure from head to toe, before refocusing on Emily. "We spoke on the phone."

"Indeed." Uninvited, Emily mounted the step and boarded the sloop without waiting to accept his extended hand. "Thank you for your punctuality."

"At your service, Mrs. Brooks." His eyes drifted to where Catharine and Alex remained on the dock. "Are we waiting for…?"

"For?" Emily probed at his implication.

Catharine monitored the lift of her mother's brows, well aware of where this was going.

He tried again, more delicately. "Is it just the three of you?"

"Is there a problem, Mr.—" Emily glanced at the engraved name badge on his blazer, "Allan?"

"Certainly not, Mrs. Brooks. I just wonder if you and your daughters might prefer a skippered charter? It would allow you ladies to sit back, relax, enjoy the afternoon. Let one of the fellows do all the grunt work."

"Catharine is my daughter," corrected Emily, unblinking through her caramel stare. "Alex is her partner. And unless your proposed skipper intends to pour our drinks and make our sandwiches, I assure you, Mr. Allan, we are perfectly capable on our own."

Chastened by the older woman's reproof, and embarrassed by the implication of the term *partner*, the man gave an acquiescent nod of his head. "Of course, Mrs. Brooks." He stepped to the side deck, making room for Catharine and Alex to board. "If there is anything else I can do, please, don't hesitate to call."

After he'd gone and Catharine set to familiarizing herself with the vessel, Emily's bravado dropped down a notch.

"I should have asked you, Catharine, if that was all right."

Catharine looked up, her hands grazing across the lines running through the jammers above the companionway, her fingers pausing on the mainsail halyard. "We'll be fine. All her lines run aft. I can sail her singlehanded, if needs be."

"No, I meant…"

Catharine knew what she meant, she'd just pettishly chosen to not let her off so easy. "It's fine, Mum. Call us whatever you want." It came out too curt. She knew her mother was trying. Trying to say the right things. To offer the right support. "Partner is fine."

The older woman leaned forward, running the tip of an index finger along the clutch with the word *mainsheet* engraved across the top. The last time Catharine had seen those hands touch a line, they'd been without the wrinkles now creasing the back of the knuckles, without the thinning skin and thickening joints. Without the burden of twenty-five years crowding the choked cockpit.

"Shall we, then?" said Emily, when the silence threatened to go on too long. "May as well have a good look at the cliffs while the sun is still high."

By the time the sun touched the western waters, casting its mandarin glow across the chalky cliffs, the wind had abated, leaving the agile Oyster to cruise along at a laggardly pace. Catharine wanted to start the motor, to help fill the luffing sails, getting them sooner to shore as the temperature promised to drop with the disappearing daylight, but she could feel her mother's reluctance. Feel her mother's need to draw the day out as long as she could, to not rush to an end what little time they had together.

So she left the vessel to the mercy of the waning breeze, knowing the slow progress would put them in after nightfall, making it more difficult to navigate the unfamiliar waters and maneuver the marina. But the inconvenience was worth it. The afternoon had been pleasant. Enjoyable, even. As they'd traversed a course along the towering cliffside of Beachy Head, the strain of Honour Stone had gradually slipped away. Catharine had found a familiar comfort in working the sheets alongside her mother, and a nostalgic pleasure in listening to the warbled voice teaching Alex one line from another, the way she once had for Catharine long ago.

It had offered them a common ground—Alex as the denominator. Sailing as the sum.

The light fading, Alex worked her way aft from where she'd been sitting at the bow, treading light steps toward the cockpit where Catharine manned the helm, and Emily sat on the starboard bench, wrapped in a blanket.

Catharine watched her, the nimble shadow, the ease of which she moved so suiting to the swaying motion of the sloop, her confidence along the narrow side deck an enjoyment to regard. She was a natural on the water, showing an organic inclination for a sense of the wind, the tide, the rise and fall of the swells.

It made Catharine suddenly long for the bay, the bridge, the familiar outline of the Northern California coast. For time spent on her own yacht, just her and Alex. For their life together to begin.

Alex dropped into the cockpit, and without being asked drew in the mainsheet a handful of feet as Catharine nosed the bow further upwind.

"I'd say you've got the hang of this," Emily approved, her voice muffled through the layers of the linen as she rose to step through the companionway. "I'm going to put on the kettle." She disappeared below.

Alex smiled, settling onto the bench nearest the helm, her knee pressing into Catharine's thigh. "And what do you think? Could you make a decent sailor out of me?"

Holding the wheel steady with her hip, Catharine brought her free hand up to run her fingertips through Alex's wind-tussled hair, her thumb caressing the flushed skin of her sunburned cheek.

This was the life she wanted. This closeness. This nearness. This easy intimacy. A togetherness they'd only just begun to explore—afforded them by a short handful of weeks.

"Most certainly a better sailor than a skater," Catharine teased.

In the shelter of the shadow of the towering cliffs rising parallel their path, Alex caught her fingers, turning them over to kiss her palm, trailing her lips across the heel of her hand to the delicate skin of her wrist.

Catharine closed her eyes, leaning against her, contemplating the coming months.

January, Elle promised her. January, after the quarterlies were released, after it could be proven the colonel was purposefully capsizing the revenue, they would steamroll ahead. But what then? The foundation of Brooks Corp. was already splintering. The holes in the hull threatening to expand to the point of no repair. It could be months before they went to trial. Months of stress. Of travel. Of waging through a war she might never win.

And to what purpose?

For nights she'd found herself awake, staring into the darkness, questioning her motives for remaining in the fight. The jobs were already lost. The HOPE Foundation abolished. The company she'd loved teetering on the brink of collapse.

Her father's most recent buyout proposal had come back as a nearly reasonable offer, closing in on market value of what her shares were worth.

So why continue? Justice? Honor? Her integrity?

Did it matter anymore? She could no longer tell if it was worth it in the end.

Tomorrow she could call Elle. Tell her to contact her father's counsel—accept the settlement. Concede her defeat. She could refocus her life and build it anew.

The heat of Alex's body was warm against her side. A tangible happiness. The horizon of her future guaranteed.

Steps sounded on the companionway ladder and Catharine pulled her hand from Alex's grasp swifter than she intended, uncomfortable at the nearness of their bodies beneath her mother's gaze.

Emily averted her eyes toward the cliffside, aware of her interruption, but stayed her course, stepping down into the cockpit and resuming her seat. There was nothing else she could do without embarrassing them all.

"This must be the most mild December on record," she commented, resettling the lightweight blanket about her shoulders. "This time last year Dover was experiencing gale force winds and hail."

They sailed on, quiet in the setting sun, until the shrill whistle of the kettle sounded below deck. Emily, tired from the day, started to rise, but Alex beat her to her feet. "Stay—let me get it." She was through the hatch of the entry before the older woman could turn down the offer, leaving Catharine and her mother alone.

"Thank you," Emily broke the silence of the deck after a few moments had passed, watching the gentle swells of water cutting through the bow. "For today. For allowing me this. It's been a lovely afternoon."

The steel of the wheel whirred beneath Catharine's bare fingers.

"Yes." With Alex's absence came the stiffness between them. She tried again, hoping to alleviate the flatness of her tone and return her mother's sentiment. "I'm glad you called."

"I hope we might do it again."

"Perhaps." Catharine kept her eyes on the flashing signal of the lighthouse. The never-ending warning of danger ahead. "If I accept his settlement, will he leave me in peace?"

If her mother was surprised at the swiftness of the change in topic, she did not show it. She only followed suit in tracing

Catharine's line of sight, the brilliance of the white beam growing radiant with the impending darkness.

"I do not know."

Her honesty was cutting. Catharine had been seeking reassurance. Had wanted a modicum of certainty. Something to help her determine the best path forward.

Looping her arm through the spoke of the wheel, she turned to face her mother. There was something else she needed. Something more she had to understand.

"Why does he hate me?"

It was a question that had lingered her entire life, sealed behind her lips. Waiting. Hurting. Searching for resolution.

Her mother's placid brown eyes didn't falter from their watch on the lighthouse. "He hates himself."

The banality of the answer was infuriating. "Do not feed me platitudes! You owe me more than that."

"It is the truth." Emily did not flinch beneath her daughter's ire, her only tell of discomfort in the unwillingness to meet her eye. Instead, she followed the jagged shadow of the coastline as it disappeared into blackness. Her voice was steady when she continued. "Your unwavering resolution to stay true to who you are has long attracted the reflection of the hatred he feels for himself."

"I deserve more than riddles."

For a dozen beats of Catharine's racing heart, her mother remained quiet. She didn't know if she would continue. If she would grant her the justice of the answers she sought. And Catharine knew she would not be able to bring herself to ask again. Once was enough.

Emily exhaled, shrugging out of the blanket bundled around her shoulders, and allowed it to fall to her waist. Through the glow of the cabin light cast up from the companionway, Catharine could see her mother's fingers worrying her wedding ring. Resigned, she drew a second breath, and exhaled again.

"You are the living representation, Catharine, of who he will never be. Ever since you were a child he has resented your willingness—your desire—to be no one but yourself. And then, as you became a young woman… when you…" she trailed off, searching for the words, regrouping her thoughts. "He was invidious of your bravery. Your—" again she paused, "—your certainty."

"My bravery?" Catharine laughed, her anger climbing. "My certainty? Any *certainty* I ever had was stamped out of me! My entire life I have done everything ever asked of me! Everything he —everything the *both* of you—ever demanded of me!"

"Yes," her mother agreed, "you did as you were bade. But it's more than that, Catharine. More than that to him. You knew who you were. You always have. From the very start, you knew who you wanted to be. You didn't shy away from it. It didn't frighten you. And even after all these years you never let go of your verity. You never lost sight of yourself. Your father has never had that conviction—he is nothing more than the hull of a man—the husk of someone he was too afraid to be."

"What are you trying to say?"

Frustrated, her mother rose, steadying herself with the wire of the backstay. Whatever subtlety she wanted to cling to, whatever allusion she meant to employ, she abandoned. "Your father never wanted a *wife*—a *child*. He never wanted the domesticities his life entails. He had—he *has*—certain proclivities he hates within himself. Do you understand?" She finally looked at Catharine, still gripping the rigging, balancing her aging body against the rolling sway of the sea. "He, too, did what was commanded of him. But he never had your courage, Catharine. He never allowed himself to consider it could be any other way."

Catharine stared back dumbly, her full weight against the wheel, the flashing beacon of the lighthouse disappearing in her peripheral view. She didn't dare clarify, for fear she'd misunderstood. That her assumption had gone to one place while her mother was speaking of another.

But no—she could tell from her mother's face, from her mother's regret of the disclosure, the shame of what she considered a failed marriage etched across her brow—that she had not falsely interpreted the indication. She had correctly understood.

"So he resents my happiness, when he cannot have the same." Catharine spoke quietly, the words barely audible above the breaking of the water shedding off the hull. It was no longer a question. No longer a grasping for understanding after all the endless years. It was nothing more than a statement; the simplicity of fact. "And these... *proclivities*," she chose her words carefully, knowing the question was out of line, yet needing the answer. "Has he never entertained them?"

The caramel eyes staring back at her remained unblinking, the square chin tilting upward, contrary to her wounded pride. "He entertains them still."

The pounding of Catharine's heart slowed with the ceasing of her breath. Of everything her mother said tonight, this divulgence struck the hardest. Not the revelation of his inclinations. Not his unfaithfulness and betrayal. Not even the sanctimony of his actions.

It was the sheer hypocrisy of it all—the condemnation of her happiness while he engaged in his own covert affairs. She did not care that he was not happy. She did not care that he could not accept who he was. She cared only that he had spent her entire life condemning her for what he was himself.

"You have always known this?" Her voice came out far steadier than she felt.

"No." Emily was quick to answer, defensive. "Not for many years. Not until long after you had wed."

Would it have changed anything, if you had known before? Catharine wanted to ask—wanted to know. Would her mother have defended her, helped save her from her fate? She thought she knew the answer, but couldn't be sure.

But footsteps were on the companionway, and the clanging of mugs broke the brittle quiet as Alex climbed the ladder, appearing through the opening of the hatch.

"Sorry," she laughed, unaware of her accidental intrusion, the darkness concealing the anger—the betrayal—Catharine was certain was stamped across her face. "I had no idea how hard it could be to pour tea while in motion."

"Thank you, dear," Emily took the mug offered her, her tone resuming its practiced neutrality, with no indication of the conversation that had transpired.

In turn, Catharine focused her attention back to the lighthouse, back to the sea, following her mother's lead. It was what they did best—pretending nothing had ever happened. A Brooks' family tradition passed down, generation after generation.

Chapter Twenty-Five

"Get in! Well done, marra!"

Alex tried to keep her attention on the phone call, while motioning an apology to Catharine for their interrupted conversation. They'd just arrived at the apartment in Shad Thames. The trip to the South Coast had been intended for the weekend, but when they'd returned from the evening sail, Catharine had asked Alex if she wouldn't mind if they went home to London. Something had changed between her and her mother—the shift in the air had been evident—but Catharine had offered nothing on the two hour drive from Eastbourne.

It wasn't until they'd stepped out of the elevator into the apartment that Alex had tempted to ask what had happened. And then her phone had blown up with half a dozen calls in quick succession.

Halsey. Rodney Collins. Jill Thompson. Molly. Caleb.

It had been during her panic of attempting to send Caleb to voicemail that she'd inadvertently answered the sixth call, allowing Sam Huntley's unmistakable Newcastle accent to sound over the line.

"That's champion, that!" the loud, brassy voice continued, forcing Alex to recenter her focus, unsure of what the woman was indicating. "You must be chuffed."

"What are you talking about?"

Sam laughed. "Shut you!" It was silent a moment before she realized Alex wasn't teasing. "Hadaway and shite! You really haven't seen?"

Over the past couple of years those words had come to provoke a Pavlovian sense of anxiety in Alex, sending her heart racing and deploying an instant sense of malaise to settle in her chest. Her concern for Catharine's stilted parting with her mother was tem-

Jen Lyon

porarily abandoned as she found herself battling the familiar dread.

"Seen what?" It was the most she could manage.

"The shortlist."

"For what?"

Sam's hearty laugh made her wince as she pulled the phone away from her ear.

"C'mon, Grey! There's this little award in football…"

Her heart began to slow, even when it should have been the other way around. She should have been excited at Sam's implication. Over the moon. But all she could immediately process was that it wasn't about Carlton. She'd not been thrown into the fray of another media circus. Another nightmare wasn't waiting in the wings.

"The shortlist for…?" she asked calmly. She didn't dare guess. It felt too pretentious to assume.

"Oh, come on," Sam ground, "the bloody Ballon d'Or, ya divvy! Big to-do. Ring a bell?"

Alex risked returning the phone to her ear.

The *Ballon d'Or!*

The most prestigious award in all of football. Every year the best players from across the globe were narrowed onto a thirty-player shortlist by France Football, who were then voted on by some of the most respected journalists in their field. Attending the gala in Paris as a nominee was the highest honor you could receive in the sport. A concept that had once been too farfetched to even entertain in Alex's wildest imagination.

A literal dream come true.

"You're not fucking with me…?"

"You're a proper doylem, man, you know that?"

Alex sucked in a breath. "Who else is on it?"

"Cheeky—trying to figure if you'll win it already, eh?"

Winning hadn't crossed Alex's mind. She only wanted to know
—

Sam beat her thoughts to it. "Yeah, Walker's on it, Grey. Nominated for a fifth insane time. She's the only one who will give you a run for your money. Well, her, and Kelsey Evans."

Alex took a moment to process everything. Sam Huntley, arguably one of the most decorated players in the history of the

238

women's game, felt like Alex stood a chance at actually winning the trophy—narrowing it down to her, Amelia Walker, and Kelsey Evans.

"Wow."

"Tell me no one's ever accused you of being long-winded," Sam needled, but Alex ignored the jab.

She was still too stunned to find herself the third wheel to two of the indisputable GOATs of the game.

Amelia's record went without saying. Few players could hold a candle to her career—even Sam Huntley.

However, Kelsey Evans came a close challenge.

A star forward for the English national team, the decorated striker had broken goalscoring records at some of the most illustrious clubs in the sport. Barcelona. Olympique Lyonnais. Wolfsburg. Alex had recently read she was leading the season in both goals and assists at Chelsea, where she currently played.

The twenty-nine year old two-time FIFA Best winner was tall. Blonde. Movie-star pretty. A favorite of billboard sponsors, her face plastering the sides of buses, buildings, and trains. If England had a "Face of Football," Kelsey Evans was the cover queen.

"Still with me, Grey?"

Alex blinked herself back into live time. She shot a glance across the room at Catharine, ready to explain the call, but Catharine stood with her attention out the wall of windows, her thoughts elsewhere—miles down the road. Same as she had been all evening.

"Earth to Grey."

"Yes." It came out terser than Alex intended. "Sorry. I'm here."

"Ace. So, now that I'm done kissin' your arse with news of your accolades—the more important question awaits… do you want to take me as your date?"

"What?"

The level of shock in Alex's tone made Sam laugh.

"Howay, calm down, man," she hung on the words in her thick Geordie accent, singing a mild rebuke. "I'm not inviting you to hop in the sack with me—trust me, you'd bore me to my grave before the end of the night. I was simply offering my services as arm candy, given it's probably not your lass's bag to attend."

"She'll attend." The words were out of Alex's mouth before she had time to consider them. Before she'd remotely given it thought. With everything Catharine was going through—with the cluster of their lives—a trip to Paris to watch Alex *not* win a golden trophy was the last thing Alex wanted to put her through. The ceremony was just days away from Carlton's Inauguration. Catharine would no doubt have other things on her mind.

Still, Alex doubled down. "We're looking forward to it. But thank you."

"Pork pies," Sam tutted. "But suit yourself. You don't know what you're missing. Guess I'll just go stag."

Alex laughed. "You'll have a girl on your arm by the end of the evening. I've heard the stories."

"*A* girl? *Please*. Why limit myself to just one? Anyway, it's late, and I'm clamming, so I've got to run. But wanted to tell you canny job on cutting the shortlist. You deserve it, Grey."

Alex wished her Merry Christmas, and agreed to get together sometime before she headed back to the States for preseason, and then hung up. Looking around, she found herself alone in the living room, Catharine having slipped out sometime during the call.

For a few minutes she sat on the cream upholstered sofa overlooking Tower Bridge. She checked her voicemail—all congratulatory messages about the Ballon d'Or, deleted Caleb's plea to call him back, and then sent out a few texts, promising to chat with her friends in the morning. It was late—almost midnight—and she was tired from the day spent on the water.

It had gone so well, the meeting with Emily. Catharine had thawed over the course of the afternoon, coaxed into a tentative amicability, and for a time Alex thought there was a chance the two women could repair what had been lost. That they could rekindle the relationship that had once meant so much to both of them.

And then something had changed. In the minutes Alex had been below deck, something had been said. Something had gone wrong. And Catharine had resumed her defensive mask of detachment.

Alex took the stairs to the master suite, heading toward the bedroom they shared—the one that had begun to feel as much her own as Catharine's. In the hall she could hear Catharine's voice. Clipped. Unsettled. Brimming with frustration.

Alex forgot about the Ballon d'Or.

"No, it can't wait. If I thought it could, I would have waited to call you in the morning."

Alex paused in the doorway and Catharine looked up, meeting her eye, before continuing on her phone call.

"Yes, really." A short silence. Then, "thank you. Fifteen minutes."

She hung up and tossed her phone on the bed.

"What's happened?" Alex leaned against the doorframe, already knowing, by Catharine's guarded expression, she wouldn't elaborate.

"I need to go out for a little while."

"Will you tell me what's going on?"

"Yes," Catharine said, to her surprise. "But will it upset you very much if I ask to hold off the conversation until morning?"

Alex considered it. She'd not really expected Catharine to disclose whatever had happened between her and her mother. So seldom was she willing to discuss her dilemmas. Especially when it came to her family.

"Are you going to see Nathalie?"

"Yes."

It once would have upset Alex. To think whatever it was could be said to her friend, but not to her. That she would be left on the outside.

But it didn't feel like that any longer. She knew where she stood in Catharine's life. She knew her value. Felt secure in her place.

She also understood. There were times where she'd want to call Sawyer or Halsey—to discuss things with a friend, before talking them over with a lover. It was fair. And she trusted Catharine to tell her whenever she was ready.

"Morning is fine." She left the doorway, approaching Catharine in the middle of the room, and took her hands, squeezing her fingers. "Will you text me when you're on your way home?"

Catharine kissed her forehead. "Yes."

"Whatever it is, it's going to be all right."

Catharine took a step back, and for a moment the guardedness of her expression changed, altering into something Alex wasn't exactly sure how to read. An underlying fervency. A set determination.

"Yes," she nodded, her thoughts traveling once again. "I think it just might."

Chapter Twenty-Six

"This better be earth-shattering." Nathalie heaved herself into the empty armchair, her voice carrying across the vacant lobby of the Canary Wharf high-rise, where she'd made herself at home in Elle's flat for the last ten days. "You have no idea what you've just interrupted."

By the Frenchwoman's tussled hair and flushed cheeks, combined with the silk robe Catharine suspected wasn't her own, it didn't take much imagination to guess, but she wasn't in the frame of mind to play games.

"He's gay."

"Quoi?" Nathalie's russet eyes narrowed, some of her exaggerated fluster dissipating. "Who?"

Catharine crossed her legs, then uncrossed them again, leaning forward to rest her elbows on her knees. She'd gone over her mother's conversation a dozen times since leaving Eastbourne, trying to reconcile her feelings. A gamut of emotions had run her raw. Disbelief. Hurt. Incredulity. But the overwhelming sensation remaining was outrage. Outrage at the hypocrisy. Outrage at the betrayal. That he had blamed her. Guilted her. Forced her into denial. And all the while her sins were his own.

"My father."

To Nathalie's credit, she didn't laugh. Catharine thought she might have. The idea was so ridiculous. So preposterous. But Nathalie remained staring at her, unblinking, her lips drawn into a single line.

"Your mother told you this?"

"Yes."

"You believe her?"

"I have no reason not to."

"I suppose not," Nathalie conceded, sitting back in her chair. The concierge was still out on a smoke, the two women entirely alone. Still, Nathalie took a glance around, confirming their privacy.

"Is there proof?"

Catharine resisted the urge to stand. She wanted to pace. To kick the coffee table sitting between them. Anything to find an outlet for her frustration.

"I've no idea."

"What are you going to do?"

"I haven't decided."

"Well," said Nathalie, sitting forward, clapping her hands to her knees, "I should think it's obvious." As the impact of the information sank in, she grew more animated, her voice no longer tempered as it carried across the glass walls of the lobby. "This is your chance to force his hand! You can hold him at checkmate—threaten to expose him!"

Catharine didn't know why a part of her recoiled at the suggestion. She had known it would be Nathalie's answer. Sensibility had not been part of the midnight solace she'd come seeking. She'd needed someone to share in her fury, to understand her hurt, as only Nathalie could. And it *was* the obvious solution. Yet, still, she hesitated. It had been one thing to play out her rage-filled revenge in her daydreams. To imagine herself confronting her father, exposing him as a fraud, as a hypocrite, as the duplicitous coward that he was. On the drive home from Eastbourne she had contemplated the endless possibilities. She could demand immediate restoration of her position. Perhaps even more, depending on how he responded.

But to actually speak it out loud—to put it to plan—she wasn't certain she could do it.

There was a part of her that desired nothing more. That wanted to see him hurt. That longed to watch his downfall. But somewhere deeper, somewhere more rational, there was a side of her that questioned if it was truly what she wanted? She had been on the flip side of the situation. She had been exposed against her will, and knew what it was like to suffer the consequences—to watch those you loved suffer them with you. The repercussions of this would not affect only her father.

"I don't know if I could go through with it."

Nathalie's animation turned as quickly to exasperation. "You can't be serious. After all he's done—"

"It's not as simple as that—"

"It *is* as simple as that. He's a monster, Cate! He's made your life a living hell! I cannot believe you would sit here and pretend like it doesn't even matter—"

"Doesn't even matter?" The brittleness of Catharine's whisper stopped Nathalie short as Catharine leapt to her feet, her furor tipping her manners. "*Doesn't matter*? Do you have any idea what it was like—all those years—living under his thumb? What it was like to be forced to marry a man I didn't even know? The horror of that first night, married to a stranger—my body no longer my own!?" Her voice rose, strangled, hoarse, her fingernails biting into the flesh of her palms, all of her fury at her father—at herself— sparking anew. "And all the nights after nights, years after years, after?" She stared at her friend, struggling to calm her breathing, fighting off the threat of a sob. "Do not *ever* suggest to me that I feel it doesn't matter!"

Nathalie did not flinch under her rage, regarding her instead with an infuriating composure.

"Then it is as I said before—the answer is obvious."

Catharine drew a deep breath, leaning against the back of the chair, her legs weak with the waning of her anger. "I don't even know if it would work. I cannot begin to guess which is more important to him—his pride or his reputation. If he succumbs to threats, it is his dignity that is damaged. If he dismisses me and calls my bluff, he risks character annihilation."

Nathalie shrugged. "There is only one way to find out."

Across the lobby the front doors slid open and the concierge reappeared, rubbing his chilled hands together as he sulked toward his desk. He hardly gave the pair a second glance, his attention held on counting out his last remaining cigarettes, but it was enough to curb their conversation.

Nathalie stood. "Come upstairs."

"Why?"

"We'll get a third opinion."

"Now?" Catharine didn't have to look at her watch to know it was nearing one in the morning. "I'm not about to turn up uninvited—"

"Ma chérie," Nathalie waved off her protest as she doublechecked the silken tie at her waist, the hint of a smile lurking. "There are certain things money cannot buy—a middle-of-the-night consult with Elle Kirkland may be one of them. But there are other ways in which they may be earned—and *this*, I assure you, I have merited. Besides," she looked over her shoulder on the way to the lift, "I promise, she is not sleeping."

Elle Kirkland rifled through half a dozen boxes of tea in her cupboard before selecting the one she wanted.

"How do you take your tea, Catharine?" The question was terse as she grudgingly snapped the cabinet shut, looking over the center island into her sitting room, where Catharine sat stiffly on the edge of a leather sofa.

The barrister had been less than thrilled at the unexpected intrusion, immediately disappearing into her ensuite for the better part of half an hour. When she reappeared, the wildness of her fiery hair had been tamed, makeup touched on, and she'd donned a satin pajama suit Catharine imagined was making its debut out of a forgotten drawer in her closet.

Nathalie, perched on a barstool, still lounging in nothing more than the robe and pair of slippers, beat Catharine to an answer.

"Loose leaf, steeped four minutes, long pour of milk, one sugar."

"I'm not her fucking barista." Elle flung down a box of PG Tips. "If she wants her loose leaf, hoity-toity whatever stirred with a golden spoon, the two of you can piss off elsewhere."

"Whatever you have will be marvelous." Catharine shot Nathalie a pointed glare, which the woman blithely ignored.

"Sommelier." Nathalie leaned over the bar top, watching Elle pour the kettle of steaming water.

"What?" The barrister paused in her tea administrations.

"It's a tea sommelier. By definition, a barista deals in coffee."

Elle opened her mouth, shut it, then opened it again. "I swear, you are the most infuriating woman."

"That's not what you were saying earlier."

The pair of women shared a smile that made Catharine rue her imbecility of allowing Nathalie to talk her into stepping through the threshold of Elle's front door. It was a senseless endeavor as it was. She couldn't very well ask a Queen's Counsel barrister to assist her in coercion.

"Perhaps I should leave you two to it, and we can reconvene at a more reasonable hour?"

"Nonsense," Elle rounded the bar with two steaming mugs, taking a place on the L-shaped sofa adjacent from Catharine and sliding one of the teas along the table in her direction. "You're already here, and I'm already going to charge you for the bags I'll have under my eyes when I go into the office in the morning, so we may as well continue." She moved over half a foot to make room for Nathalie, who squeezed in beside her, and Catharine hated admitting to herself that they made a befitting couple.

Settled, Elle picked up a notebook, pulled on a pair of cat-eye glasses, and poised with her pen above the paper. "Now I understand you've had an interesting conversation with your mother. Please expand."

"There's little to expand on. Unbeknownst to me, my father has been carrying on clandestine relationships with men throughout their marriage, continues on with them still, and that is the extent of my knowledge."

Elle tapped the pen against the paper. "I see. When you say 'relationships,' do you mean long-term romantic connections, or casual trysts over the years?"

"I have no idea. What does it matter?"

"If you're going to barge in here at this God-awful hour of the morning, I'll be the one asking the questions, capisce?" Elle scribbled a few words, before looking up, the V between her brows deepening. "I imagine Colonel Brooks wouldn't take it well if this information became public knowledge?"

Catharine stared straight ahead, her gaze falling to Nathalie's hand, draped casually across Elle's knee. She thought about the morning her father had found the two of them together. His outrage. His threats. His repeated accusation that she had brought shame to their family.

How often as a child had she heard him condemn duplicity?

No. He would not take the shattering of his righteous image lightly.

At Catharine's silence, Elle continued, satisfied with the answer. "You realize blackmail falls under the Theft Act of 1968—carrying a sentence of up to fourteen years in prison?"

Catharine steepled her fingers, uncomfortable with the casual way the barrister tossed out the word blackmail.

"I do not wish to put you in a position that could jeopardize your integrity."

The merriment of Elle's rich laughter resonated through the room, humming across the porcelain tile, sweeping up the pale gray walls where the bourgeois art struggled to achieve the intended haute monde atmosphere.

"Oh, Catharine," the woman dabbed at her eyes with the corner of a linen serviette, "you cannot possibly be so naive to think I've reached my place in life by maintaining my integrity. Who am I to stop you if you choose to present your neck to Madame la Guillotine?"

"Understood." Catharine rose, further regretting having entertained the notion that this small hours visit would bear any worthwhile revelation. "Well, thank you—as enlightening as this tête-à-tête has been, I think it is time I—"

"Oh, sit down," Elle waved her off with her pen, "don't be so dramatic. I'm just taking the piss out of you, Catharine. I did not come to wear the silks by being foolish enough to risk my neck for the whim of every high-dollar client. The only thing he'd have against us is invasion of privacy—difficult to prove, and even more difficult to prosecute. I have to admit," she tapped the lipstick stain on the rim of her cup, "you surprise me. I pegged you as too much a Goody Two-Shoes to be up for a round of behind-the-barn tactics. Now," she collected her cooling tea, "let's get down to business."

Catharine remained standing. "I'm not even certain where I'd start. Or if it is even feasible."

"Which is exactly why you pay me." Elle turned serious, discarding her tea to resume her notebook. "Is your mother returned to Henley?"

"I've no idea. Why?"

"We're going to pay her a visit."

"Absolutely not!"

"*Catharine.*" Condescension dripped from the word as Elle offered an affected yawn, leaning back and crossing her arms behind her head. "If you'd ever allow me to do my job, you'd be surprised to find I do it very well—"

"She does," Nathalie slipped in, her smirk accentuating the innuendo. "And it's not the only thing. She's a multitalented individual."

At Catharine's lour of annoyance Nathalie's smile spread. "Don't have such a filthy mind, Cate. I was only referring to her well-rounded skills at law. She's a proven business expert. Divorce specialist. Extortion extraordinaire. Give her the opportunity and she'll serve you your father's manhood on a silver platter."

"Classy." Elle pinched Nathalie's exposed calf. "Eloquence is not your forte."

"I make up for it in other ways."

Catharine tuned out their banter. "What do you hope to gain from speaking with my mother?"

"Insight."

Catharine shook her head. "I don't want her involved in it. If he found out she's the one who told me—"

"Collateral damage." Elle brushed her off. "It's not as if she's in the running for Mother of the Year. I'd have taken my own mother to trial if the chance presented itself."

"I don't want her part of it!"

"My mother?" drolled Elle, mocking. "Don't worry, she's dead." The barrister sighed at Catharine's lack of amusement. "Listen, I need somewhere to start. We need proof of your father's... indiscretions. A name, a place, something."

"I know a man who could—"

"Please," Elle rolled her eyes. "I have a dozen such *men* at my disposal. With enough time, they could uncover Cleopatra's Tomb. The thing is, time is not in our favor. We're due to pre-trial review week after next—we need to act before that." She deliberated for a moment, before decidedly scribbling another notation in the margin of her notebook. "Tomorrow I will call his counsel, set a meeting to discuss acceptance of the buyout. We'll lead him to believe we've decided to settle. It will be the best way to gain his captive audience. And then we'll approach him from there." She tossed the pad onto her table. "In the meantime, I need something solid—compelling—that he will be unable to sidestep when the time arrives. Which is exactly where your mother comes in."

"She won't say more than she's already said."

"Did you ask her?" Elle's perfectly shaped brows elevated behind her reading glasses.

"No. But I know her well enough to know she won't betray him, and I will not ask her to."

Nathalie shrugged. "She betrayed you." As soon as the words were out of her mouth, it was evident she regretted them. Her expression shifted, her dark eyes widening at her own tactless transgression. "Cate, I'm sorry—"

"Do not apologize for being right," Elle snapped, never taking her eyes from Catharine. "Nathalie's correct. Here's the truth, Catharine: you may have convinced yourself that you think you want to do this, but you don't have the backbone. The first rule of blackmail is not to make threats you aren't willing to bring to fruition. And let's be honest, we both know you don't have the nerve. You've hardly maintained the fortitude to face him in court, always wanting to crumble the moment things get hard. So go home. Sit on your high horse and ride your ethical merry-go-round. Sign the bloody settlement for all I care. Move on. You've never had the courage for a proper fight. There's no reason to expect you to find it now."

"*Conneries!*" Nathalie leapt to her defense, but Elle silenced her with a hand on her arm.

"Tell me, have I read you wrong, Catharine? If he forces you to show your cards, do you have the mettle to throw him to the wolves? Or has your sense of familial loyalty made you too soft?"

Catharine's rage radiated through the ticking of her jaw. She knew the woman's game. She knew she meant to get her goat, to goad her, antagonize her into action. With the latest buyout pro-posal approaching fair market value, she'd grown increasingly concerned Catharine would settle. A result which would be felt as a loss for the trial lawyer. This outlet offered her a different way to win—even if it was via so-called *behind-the-barn tactics*.

But it didn't change the fact that her accusations were off the mark. It was not Catharine's courage that was lacking, nor was it loyalty that wavered her resolve. There was so much more to it than that. She did not owe this woman an explanation. She could tell her to go to hell, and simply walk out the door.

Yet pride was a perilous mistress, with ego an ardent accomplice at its side. So instead of following her gut, acknowledging her hesitations, Catharine allowed her vanity to step through Elle's set snare.

"My mother is off limits. Find another way, and we'll move forward."

Chapter Twenty-Seven

Taking a seat on the edge of the bed, Alex was careful not to wake Catharine. It was midafternoon, but the room was dark, the lights off and the sun blocked by the tightly drawn curtains.

Alex had heard Catharine return late the night before, but when she hadn't come to bed, she'd gone downstairs to find her standing, aimless, in the middle of the kitchen. Startled from her thoughts, Catharine had laughed, before dissolving into unchecked tears, unable to hide the frustrations of her evening.

They'd talked for hours over a shared bottle of single malt, sitting on the kitchen floor like a pair of freshman their first semester at university.

Catharine had told Alex about her father. About her anger—her admitted hurt—over his deceit. She told her about the conversation with Elle, and how she had previously been considering accepting the settlement, but now, with the opportunity to press him for reinstatement, she was no longer sure. She did not know if she could bypass the chance to regain control. To take back what was hers. But there would be risk in threatening him. Risk she wasn't certain would pay off in the end.

And then—sipping whisky straight from the bottle, her head thrown back against the cabinets of the kitchen island, her golden hair hanging in disarray—Catharine told Alex about her childhood. About her father's endless wrath. About the struggle through her youth with his inexplicable hatred. And lastly, about the morning it had fallen apart, when he had caught her in Henley.

Throughout her soliloquy she hadn't been looking for sympathy, nor had she been seeking advice, and Alex had offered none. She'd just listened and let her talk, sitting shoulder-to-shoulder, until the sun had risen and the sleepless night had taken its toll, Catharine growing a little drunk with the passing hours.

"I'm sorry," she'd said, more than once, as Alex steered her up the stairs and into the bedroom.

Sorry for what, Alex wished she could ask. Being human? Having emotion? Allowing herself to hurt like every mortal person? But she'd left it alone, instead helping her undress and slipping into bed beside her.

"I don't know what I should do." Catharine's words sank through the dark, her despair heavy as an anchor.

"You don't have to decide tonight."

"If I go through with this, does it make me as bad as him?"

Alex rolled onto her side, wrapping her arms around her. She knew, after meeting Benjamin Brooks in Henley, how much Catharine feared they were alike. That she had, by pure genetic default, become more like her father than she ever wanted to acknowledge.

In looks. In temperament. In actions.

But she was wrong. The two may have shared features. Shared brilliance. Shared ambition and drive. But they were not the same.

Alex pressed her face into the back of Catharine's neck. "You are nothing like him."

Catharine let out a slow, surrendering exhale, relaxing into the comfort of her embrace. "Thank you," she whispered. "For loving me."

Alex had hugged her tighter until she could tell, from the steadiness of her breathing, she was finally asleep.

Now, eight hours later, Alex studied the serenity of her slumber, and debated whether or not to wake her.

Sawyer had called late last night, while Catharine had been at Elle's. Alex had assumed it would be in regards to the Ballon d'Or, but had instead been surprised when her friend told her she'd be in London the following afternoon.

"Arsenal vs. Chelsea at Emirates Stadium," the familiar midwestern tone had lured as airport announcements echoed in the background. "I have two tickets center circle, and expect you to fill one of them."

"You're flying in to watch the match?"

"Not exactly, but I can explain the rest over a beer when your sweet ass meets me in front of the stadium. Don't even dream of telling me no."

And Alex hadn't.

But now, sitting on the edge of the bed watching Catharine sleep, she felt bad about leaving her alone.

"Hey." Alex gently brushed her fingers down the exposed skin of Catharine's arm.

Her eyes fluttered, the touch stirring her to wakefulness, and Catharine blinked into the dark.

"What time is it?" Her voice was hoarse, riddled with confusion.

Alex smiled. How it was possible, even in the throes of sleep, hungover, her hair tangled and face puffy from crying, for her to still be pure perfection, Alex would never understand.

"A little after four."

"What?" Catharine struggled to sit up, immediately regretting the quick movement, and flopped back down. "In the afternoon?"

Alex reached to brush back the stray hairs that fell across her face. "The good news is it's still Saturday."

"In December?"

"If I said January, would you panic?"

Catharine's smile was weak. "No. I think that would be quite fine by me. To just wake up and have it all be over."

Alex stroked her cheek. "How do you feel?"

"Like I drank a bottle of Macallan by myself."

"I helped, I promise."

The smile across her exquisite lips grew more genuine. "Not by much, based on the evidence that you're up and dressed, and all I want to do is sleep for another week."

"You could at least sleep for the rest of the night." Alex dropped onto her elbow beside her. "I have to go out." She told her about Sawyer's call, and the invitation to watch the game.

"Where's she staying while she's in town? You should invite her to stay with us."

Alex kissed her forehead. "I'll ask," she said, knowing she wouldn't. Not now. Not with everything going on. But the use of the word *us* still brought a tightness to her chest—a welcome ache of the best kind.

Resigned to leave, she sat up. "You'll be okay while I'm gone?"

"I'll miss you, if that's what you're asking." Catharine pushed herself up against the headboard. "But yes, I'll be fine. Go have fun —please tell her I said hello."

As soon as the whistle signified the half—Arsenal leading Chelsea one-nil—Alex tugged down her scarf and pushed back her cap, fixing Sawyer with an expectant stare.

"Okay, Abby Sawyer, enough's enough. Spill the tea."

Sawyer had run late to meet Alex at the gates, the Piccadilly Line experiencing an interruption in its service, and by the time they made it to their seats, the teams were preparing for kickoff. It had been too loud—the rivaling chants too boisterous—for any meaningful conversation, and so the pair had settled for shouted clips of *missed you* and *I can't believe you're really here*, interspersed between cheers for various plays and players.

With the halftime break underway, however, Alex was ready for answers.

"What if I just flew out to see you?" Sawyer's dark eyes glinted beneath her beanie.

"I'd say you were full of shit," Alex laughed, "but thank you, I like the sentiment. Now—the truth."

"O ye of little faith. For the record, if time permitted, I *would* have flown out just to see you. I miss your pretty mug. But alas, I cannot tell a lie. You were only a fraction of the driving force behind my arrival."

"Ouch."

"I know, sad story. But anyway," Sawyer winked, tugging on the lapels of Alex's coat, "I do have some big news."

"I feel like I might be an old lady by the time you tell me."

"I've come to play a little footy."

Surprised, Alex straightened. "Here? For who?"

Sawyer twirled her fingers toward the red and white banners hanging across Emirates Stadium.

"You've gone on loan for Arsenal?"

"Yes. But," Sawyer said, a little more carefully, "not on loan."

"What?" Alex's heart sank.

"Don't look so glum, Dove. It's a good thing, really. I've got a two year contract. It's the best salary I've ever made."

"Right," Alex slumped a little lower in her coat, trying to wrap her mind around her friend leaving the NWSL. "Of course. It's just... I'll miss you. I know we haven't gotten to see each other much since I left Rage, but, still... It seems so far away."

"Nonsense." The tight spirals of Sawyer's curls bobbed with the tilt of her head. "A short plane ride. Besides, you'll be sick of me come summer. We've got a gold medal to bring home!" She patted Alex's cheek. "It's a good move for me. For my career. To grow my game."

Alex knew she was right. But she was still loathe to see her leave.

"Annnnd…" Sawyer drawled out the word, her ruby red lips puckering into a secret smile, "there's something else."

"Something?" Alex studied her face. She knew her too well. Knew exactly what that look entailed. "More like *someone*. Confess!"

"She's going to meet us for a drink after the match."

"Ah, so I am right." Alex's smile widened. "Local girl, then?"

"I can't be leaving all the Londoners to you."

"Ha! So what came first—the girl or the transfer?"

"Wouldn't you like to know?"

"I can't believe you didn't tell me!"

"In fairness, the transfer just finalized. It won't be released to the press until Monday."

"Yeah, but this mystery woman…"

"We've been a bit on the down low. But," Sawyer consoled, "you are the first to know!"

"I'd better be!"

The match resumed and for a while Alex's attention returned to the pitch.

Amelia, still playing out her final games for Arsenal, was in top form, as always. If at thirty-three her age was slowing her down, she never let the fans know it. She lead the WSL in assists, and trailed Kelsey Evans in the Golden Boot race by only one goal. If she won it, she'd be the first player to come out as the top goal scorer in two different leagues in the span of a single year. An impressive feat for anyone—but even more so as a central mid-fielder.

"Hell yeah!" Sawyer suddenly leapt to her feet, cheering after Chelsea winger, Rani Bains, drilled the ball between the posts off a perfect cross from Kelsey Evans, leveling the score.

"You forget what team you signed with?" Alex yelled over the commotion of booing from Arsenal fans.

"What?" Sawyer finished her whooping and sank into her seat. "It was a beautiful goal. Besides—aren't you supposed to root against your ex? You can't tell me you're really hoping Arsenal come out with the win?"

It still felt weird to have Amelia referred to as her ex. Even by Sawyer.

Alex shrugged. "She's still my friend. I'll always cheer for her to win."

"Not this summer," Sawyer's eyebrows did a double wag. "Her Australian ass is going down. I want that gold medal on my mantle."

"From your lips to God's ears," Alex laughed.

"Hell nah, from your boot to the back of the net." Sawyer dragged off Alex's cap and ruffled her hair. "My little lucky charm."

Twenty minutes later, despite the reverberating chant of "Oh to be a Gooner," ringing through the stadium, the match ended in a draw. A disappointing result for both sets of rivaling fans.

Skirting toward a rear exit, hats pulled low, scarves up over their chins, Alex and Sawyer managed to reach the crisp December air of the exterior stadium grounds without drawing any recognition. Less fortune followed them to the Tube, where a couple of teenage Gooners spotted them on the carriage and begged for photographs. They posed, arm-in-arm, as Sawyer signed a McDonald's napkin and Alex wrote her name across the back of a Nando's receipt.

"So why didn't mystery woman come to the match?" Alex asked over the rim of her beer after they'd settled into a pub on an off-the-beaten path in Hoxton.

"She was tied up with a prescheduled engagement."

"She live around here?"

"God, no," Sawyer glanced around the pub. *The Battered Wren* was an appropriate name, as the place looked like it had been through the wringer, but it was quiet and unobtrusive, and the patrons at the bar paid them no consideration. "She's got a place over in Kensington. She just felt this would be a good spot to meet in the middle, so you wouldn't have such a long trip back from the West End."

"How'd she know where I was staying?"

"*Sugar*," Sawyer shot her a look of incredulity, "you're living with Catharine Cleveland. The whole world knows where you're staying."

"That's comforting."

"First World Problems of the rich and famous." Sawyer flicked a stream of foam from her beer into Alex's face. "Speaking of— we've talked enough about me. Fill me in on you! Tell me everything!"

Alex's version of *everything* was narrow. Yes, she was happy. Yes, the election was stressful. Yes, the sex was excellent. Yes, it got old hearing herself referred to as "the president's wife's girlfriend," yes, they both planned to return to California, no, the CEO thing hadn't yet been sorted.

Sawyer had just asked her about her plans for Christmas when her gaze flicked over Alex's shoulder, her lips slipping into a grin.

"Well, well, look what the cat dragged in."

Alex turned to find herself stunned by a shock of wild blonde hair and a familiar, sauntering gait as Amelia Walker navigated between the tables to join them. For a horrifying second she stared, mouth gaped open, as her brain tried to process her arrival.

She couldn't—she *surely couldn't*—be the mystery woman they were waiting for. But then a taller, more slender, more effeminate figure emerged in the space between them, and Alex felt an entirely different form of surprise—this one reaching a more welcome conclusion.

"I see you brought along a straggler." Sawyer stood, greeting Kelsey Evans with an unapologetic kiss on the lips. The woman laughed—a lower, raspier sound than Alex would have imagined from her—and slid her arm around Sawyer's waist, before turning to Alex.

"The infamous Alex Grey." She held her free hand out. "I know we've said hello in passing—but it's a pleasure to officially meet you."

"I—" Alex shook her hand, "wow, Sawyer didn't mention—"

"That she was sleeping with the enemy?" Amelia cut in, flashing Alex her uneven smile.

"Hey," chided Sawyer, "I don't pull on the Arsenal kit until Wednesday. Until then, I'm The Blues' biggest fan."

The remainder of pleasantries were skipped as the four settled at the table, Amelia giving Alex a half hug as she took a seat beside her.

"I see you've been catching up with my midfield replacement," the Australian kicked back in her chair, tipping her chin toward Sawyer.

"Replacement? Oh please, honey," Sawyer hummed, "I'm your upgrade."

Amelia's smile remained amicable as she stole a sip of Alex's beer, and Sawyer and Kelsey launched into the story of the evolution of their relationship.

Assigned to the same table at The ESPYS over the summer, a few too many Long Islands at the open bar, a shared cab ride back to Kelsey's hotel... and the rest was self-explanatory. Alex was too polite to ask about Kelsey's split from her former girlfriend, Dillon Sinclair—an Olympic triathlete who she had made the cover of *Sports Illustrated* with two years earlier in an edition celebrating *The Most Athletic Power Couples in Sports History*—but Amelia'd not had the same reservations.

"So you and Sinc are officially no longer a thing?"

Kelsey's expression hardened. "We haven't been for over a year. We just didn't feel the need to project it to the masses."

Amelia waved off her defensiveness. "Fair dinkum, no judgment. Just asking."

Kelsey glanced at Alex. "I know you're friends with Sam. Sinc's her best friend. If you could, perhaps, not say anything about me and Abby just yet—I'd appreciate it. It's just—we just—"

"Not a word," Alex assured her. "Trust me, I get it." She knew the look of someone not wanting to hurt someone else... even when you were done and over.

"Speaking of exes," Sawyer filled in, untroubled by the conversation, "I'm sure you've already heard about Ass-by?"

"Heard what?" Alex asked. She could tell by Amelia's heightened interest, she hadn't heard, either.

"Ohhh," Sawyer blew out a low whistle, "I figured Caleb would be blowing up your phone by now."

Alex waited. Caleb had called her twice—once last night, amidst the succession of calls after the announcement for the Ballon d'Or shortlist—and again this morning, which she had similarly sent to voicemail. His messages had been rambling, begging her to call him back. She'd only tolerated listening to the first few seconds.

"Weren't they supposed to get married this weekend?" Amelia said, in Sawyer's prolonged dramatic silence.

"Keyword: *supposed*," said Sawyer.

Alex hadn't even realized the wedding was this weekend.

"And?" Amelia prodded.

"She left him at the alter."

"What?" Alex cradled her warming beer.

"Well, not literally. I guess more specifically she left him in the parking lot of the venue. According to Bree, who heard it from Valerie—Monica's maid-of-honor—the pair had a screaming match in front of the entire wedding party. Monica called him a 'demented psycho still obsessed with *that bitch*'—I think we can all guess who she was talking about—and apparently told him she'd rather marry Satan—as if the devil would want her," Sawyer added as a side note. "Anyhow," she continued, "Monica had Valerie drive her from Temecula all the way back to Oakland, still wearing her wedding gown. I guess the entire way up the coast he called her, threatening to sue her for the seventy-thousand dollars he financed for their "fairytale" ceremony—horse, carriage, cake in the shape of a castle, the whole-shebang—and all she told him was she was going to hock her engagement ring to the first pawnshop she found." Sawyer made no effort to hide her amusement as she took a long sip of her beer.

Kelsey broke the commencing silence. "Please tell me there's a video posted on YouTube."

Alex tried to join their laughter, but it came out weak, her thoughts too scattered.

She hated that a part of her felt sorry for him. That even after everything, she'd hoped, with his new direction in life, he might be happy... he might move on and find some happiness of his own.

But happiness, she'd begun to learn, was what you made of it—it took work. It took effort. It was a choice you had to make every day while you sat up and pulled your shoes on. Even when it was easier to give up, even when it was easier to feel down. It was a journey you had to take, and one you often had to take alone.

Caleb, she suspected, might never find that. For as long as Alex had known him, he'd depended on other people to determine his worth—to show him his value.

And she couldn't be that person for him anymore. This time, whatever his troubles, he had to face them on his own.

Amelia caught Alex's eye, and gave her a nudge with her toe beneath the table. It was just a *hey.* An *I get you.* An *I know where your thoughts have gone.* And the affection behind the gesture was palliative in its nature—a soothing balm to the disappointing knowledge that when she got back to the States, Sawyer would be gone. But Amelia would be there—and somehow, despite everything, Alex felt certain their friendship would survive. That they could get back to wherever it was they'd been before things went wrong.

"So you know we need to post a photo of the three of you," Sawyer said, digging her phone out of her purse and flipping the camera on. "The three best footballers of the year, sharing a pint in a dingy pub."

"Hard pass." Amelia sat back and crossed her arms. "It would destroy my image as an arrogant bastard."

"Trust me," Alex laughed, dragging her closer by the collar of her shirt, "your image is in no danger of being tarnished. But I want a photo of the four of us, just because. So suck it up." She snagged Sawyer's phone and swiped it to selfie-mode, the four of them pressing their heads together, making faces as the flash went off.

After a couple more beers, Kelsey reluctantly called for the ticket to close her and Sawyer's tab.

"Early morning tomorrow," she lamented, swiping her card. "FA has me scheduled for a charity match with a few of the guys from the men's side. They're forcing us to play in Santa hats."

"You better send a photo," Alex lipped in a stage whisper, pulling Sawyer into a hug.

Goodbyes said, Kelsey and Sawyer hailed a cab toward Kensington, and Amelia walked Alex to the Shoreditch High Street Station.

"See you at the awards ceremony next month in Paris?" Amelia asked, as they paused at the top of the stairwell.

Alex hesitated. "I was hoping maybe a little sooner? I've got to get into preseason shape, and thought you might be looking for a running partner?"

"You know, the key to getting into preseason shape is—"

"—I know, I know, is never falling out of it." Alex rolled her eyes. "Cut me some slack, will you?"

"Never." Amelia smacked her back, walking away, before glancing over her shoulder. "Mondays, Wednesdays, Fridays, six am, Hampstead Heath, southeast corner."

Chapter Twenty-Eight

"Six men!" Elle said without preamble, "though I suspect there are probably more. Still, it's a number we can work with."

Catharine slowed her steps along the riverfront walkway, pausing to lean against the railing overlooking the Thames. The path running parallel her building was growing crowded on the Sunday afternoon, the pubs and eateries lit with cheerful lights and tinseled garlands. Christmas was little less than a week away.

"Are you there, Catharine?"

Catharine suppressed a sigh and readjusted the phone against her ear, watching as a cormorant landed on the crumbling stone of the abandoned dockyard jetty, spreading its wings to dry.

"Yes." Her voice was lost in the hum of traffic commuting across the bridge.

"Have you read the report I sent you?"

"I glanced it over." It was an understatement. She had read the encrypted files from the private investigator line for line in its entirety, but she wasn't willing to admit it. She wouldn't give Elle the satisfaction. A coolness persisted between them since their middle-of-the-night meeting the previous weekend. Elle's biting comments about Catharine's lack of courage had not been something Catharine was willing to easily brush aside, even if the accusations were proving to hold some validity. Her conviction to pressure her father continued to vacillate, but it hadn't kept her from reviewing the information the barrister unearthed—or dedicating to it the consideration it deserved. No matter how little she truly wished to know the finer details of her father's private life.

"I'm glad you could be so inconvenienced to *glance* over the miracle I pulled off. You're welcome. Now, as you've read, we have proof—solid, irrefutable proof. No risk of *he said, she said*. If we play our cards right, I promise, he will be open to… negotiation."

"Blackmail," Catharine corrected, knowing the word had been chosen to appease her.

Elle's tsk of disapproval scratched across the line. "Don't plague me with semantics, I have no time for your holier-than-though rhetoric. You won't convince me you've earned your fortune keeping the conscience of a saint."

"Then let's call a spade a spade."

"Catharine, don't be difficult!" Elle's annoyance simmered, her temper growing short, but she seemed to reconsider, and in an attempt to mollify the discord between them, subdued the admonishment of her tone. "I know we've been at odds this past week. I will concede, what I said was harsh—even if it was in your best interest—but let us put that behind us. It's time to stop mucking around. In sixteen hours we'll be sitting down with your father and his counsel and I must know we are of one accord."

Catharine pushed off the railing. The sleek black bird startled from its sunning, gliding across the river to find a more peaceful place to dry. Catharine turned from the river. She needed to get away from the Christmas music humming through the overhead patio speakers, chorused by the upbeat chatter of dinner patrons huddled beneath the orange glow of terrace heaters, their laughter swelling with uncorked bottles of wine.

She debated asking Elle to postpone the meeting. To cancel their pretense of signing the settlement in order to give her more time to think. But she knew if she put her father off—if she gave any indication as to a change of heart—he'd shut her out, and her opportunity to gain his audience would be indefinitely lost. She couldn't risk that. Not now. Not when it was so close to being over.

"Catharine?" the barrister pressed in her silence. "Are you still there?"

"Yes." Catharine breathed in the quiet as she stepped into the narrow alley leading to Shad Thames. Above her the lamplights flickered on one-by-one, illuminating the glistening cobblestones as it started to rain. "We're of one accord," she said, trying to muster enough conviction to at least convince herself.

"Good. To reiterate: tomorrow we go in, we muck them around a bit to get him flustered, then we tell them we've reneged our decision to accept his offer. Instead, we demand reinstatement of your position—when asked why, we give Colonel Brooks the opportunity to clear his counsel, suggesting we speak in private. When he does not comply, you show him the list of names, giving him time to reconsider. At which point, I feel certain he will grant our request to speak in confidence. And then you allow me to handle it from there. Understood?"

She said it as if it were all so simple. As if it were like any other meeting, on any other day. Business as usual.

"Understood." Catharine could rally none of the barrister's confidence, but agreed all the same. "I'll see you in the morning."

"Cheer up, Catharine. This time tomorrow, you'll have your company back."

Chapter Twenty-Nine

"Calla lilies in winter?"

Alex looked up at the sound of the voice muted over the cascade of water pouring into the tub. She caught Catharine's eye in the reflection of the bathroom mirror and smiled.

Catharine looked tired. The wool of her coat glistened with the dampness of the evening rain and her flaxen hair had turned dark as droplets of water streamed down her face. Still, Alex was relieved to see her eyes brighten as she glanced around the ensuite. She took in the drawn bath. The candles. The unopened bottle of Macallan resting on the stone tile floor, two snifters turned up beside it.

"You've been busy."

"I thought you could use a quiet evening." Alex's gaze dropped to the bouquet of flowers she'd been placing into a vase, trying without success to arrange the mismatched blossoms into harmonious balance. They were too out-of-sorts, too contrasting to compliment one another. She gave up, leaving them as they were. "I think I can mark myself safe from having anyone ask me to arrange the flowers at their wedding. These didn't come together as I'd planned."

"I think they're charming," said Catharine, ignoring her self-deprecation. She came up behind her and leaned over her shoulder to get a better look at the quintet of cut blossoms. "Tell me about them."

Alex felt her self-consciousness for the odd bouquet dissipate. Catharine knew, then. She understood Alex had chosen each with specific consideration. That it wasn't just a bunch of clashing blooms she'd grabbed on her way home from the old man at the corner market. It was so typical of Catharine's keen perception. It made the trek across the whole of London to find exactly the flowers she wanted worth every missed train and stepped-in puddle.

Reaching an arm around her, Catharine touched the nearest vertical emerald spire, stroking the satin smooth calyx between thumb and forefinger. "How wonderfully unique."

"Bells-of-Ireland," said Alex, still watching Catharine's reflection in the mirror. "Meant to bring luck to whomever they are given."

"Luck I could use in abundance." Catharine rested her free hand on Alex's hip, both of them knowing she was referring to her meeting with her father in the morning. Her expression remained thoughtful as she turned her attention to the adjacent contrasting fuchsia flower.

"A snapdragon, for strength. A lily-of-the-valley," Alex indicated a hanging bell the color of a pearl, "for happiness. And this one, as you already pointed out, is a calla lily." Her fingers brushed the sturdy, trumpet-shaped petals.

"Faithfulness?" asked Catharine.

"I chose it in recognition of divine beauty, but I guess it's suiting for either."

Catharine leaned against her, resting her chin on her shoulder. "And the last one?"

"A coxcomb." Alex lifted the undulating crest of scarlet from the center of the vase, turning to face her. "The promise of everlasting love."

"The only thing I need." Catharine cupped her chin and in the close proximity of their faces Alex was surprised to find the blue eyes staring back at her were glistening, the golden sweep of her lower lashes damp from more than rain. "Thank you." She brushed her thumb across Alex's lips, drawing a shaky breath. The stress she'd been under for the past week had been harrowing, and Alex had hated seeing her so anxious and on edge.

Fitting of their life, Catharine's phone rang inside her coat pocket, interrupting the peace.

Without pulling it out, Catharine silenced the call, but already the moment had been lost. Her exhale was long and deep, and there was no question where her thoughts had drifted. Back to the approaching morning. Back to the decisions she had to make.

"I'm sorry," Catharine's jaw clenched with her frustrated apology, aware of the inadvertent shift she'd brought to the evening.

"You've gone to all this trouble, and I... here I am, ruining the entire thing."

"Don't be silly." Alex kissed her palm before dropping the coxcomb back in the vase and crossing to turn off the running water. The tub was full, the bubbles she'd added popping and fizzing in accordance with the dancing flames of candles lit around its rim. With a swipe of her hand, Alex dimmed the overhead lights, returning to Catharine. "Do you want to talk about it?" She reached up, brushing the loose strands of hair behind Catharine's ears, her fingers finding the hairband securing her bun and tugging it free.

"No." Catharine unbuttoned her coat and tossed it toward the end of the long marble vanity, where the weight of the wet wool dragged it to the floor. To Alex's astonishment, she left it in its disorderly pile. "Let's not." Drawing another breath, her fingers moved to the ivory clasps of her blouse as she stepped out of her heels. Despite the preoccupation of her thoughts, she glanced up as she undid the last button, meeting Alex's eye with a suggestive smile. "I'm certain we can think of better ways to spend the evening."

More than willing to play into her game, Alex leaned against the counter, watching her undress. Appreciating the beauty of her flawless complexion as it was unhurriedly revealed. It still stunned her, sometimes, that she had touched every part of that body. That she knew it as well as she knew her own.

With the same unrushed leisure in which she'd discarded her clothing, Catharine stepped into the deep basin of the corner tub, sinking gracefully beneath the steaming surface, the soapy suds enveloping her neck and shoulders, leaving only her upturned face exposed.

"Join me?" She didn't open her eyes.

The lights of London kaleidoscoped through the rain streaked window as Alex pulled off her clothes with none of Catharine's elegance, and tossed them to the tile. The water was hot. Hotter than she'd anticipated, and she had to stand, knee-deep, allowing herself to acclimate as she poured a measure of whisky into the empty glasses she collected from the floor.

Across the room, Catharine's phone chimed its indication of a voicemail, the sound muffled in the pocket of the coat.

"Do you want me to get that for you?" Alex set the whisky down.

Catharine shook her head, her eyes still closed. "It's just Nathalie. I'll call her later."

Sliding into the blanket of bubbles, Alex tucked herself behind Catharine, watching as the waterline rose, the suds of soap flecking her golden crown of hair. The heat, more bearable now, melded their bodies together, their limbs no longer distinguished one from another. It was an intoxication that never seemed to wane—this contentment they found in each other. The simple pleasure of the way Catharine leaned into her, settling in her embrace.

"Let's just run away," Catharine murmured, tucking her head beneath Alex's chin, a trickle of steam zigzagging down her cheek, disappearing into the water.

Alex ran her lips across her temple, stopping at her ear. "I hear the Maldives are nice in winter," she whispered, her thumb beginning the path of a lazy circle around her navel as she found one of Catharine's breasts with her opposite hand.

"Hmm," Catharine sighed, the weight of her body sinking deeper against her, "too many people. I was thinking more along the lines of somewhere uninhabited. The middle of nowhere."

"South Pole?" Keeping in accordance with the suggestion, Alex's hand at her belly ventured further south.

"Too cold." Catharine's breath hitched as she tried not to squirm, feigning indifference to Alex's wandering hands.

"Tibetan Plateau?" Alex stirred one nipple to attention, and then the other, her lips working a slow course along the line of her jaw.

"Too high."

"I see." She smiled as Catharine lost her battle with self-possession, arching against her, seeking her roaming fingers. "Somewhere lower and warmer. Let me think." Momentarily persisting in her present occupation, she enjoyed Catharine's responsiveness to her, before abruptly withdrawing her hands, running the flat of her palms down Catharine's hips, along the outside of her thighs, stopping only when she got to the mundane safety of her knees. She racked the index of her brain, trying to recall the name of the lowest point on earth. The Dead Lake? The Black Sea? Something along those lines, if high school geography served her memory correctly. She hadn't cared much at the time.

"The Black Lake?" she took a stab at it.

"I think you mean The Dead Sea." Catharine's amusement was limited, her body taut with the sudden absence of Alex's previous undertaking.

"Too low, too high, too hot, too cold," Alex sing-songed, her hands inching up the inside of Catharine's thighs as her lips explored the soap-dried skin of her shoulder. "If you're not careful, you're going to be labeled as difficult."

"So I've been recently told." Catharine twisted in her arms, finding her mouth, slipping a hand between them, forcing Alex's thoughts in a different direction, her teasing coming to a close. But as Catharine shifted to straddle her, they were once again interrupted by the ringing of her cell phone. "*Fuck!*"

The frustrated word sounded so foreign, so out of character for Catharine, it jarred Alex more than the high-pitch of the ringtone.

"I'll grab it for you—"

"No," Catharine stayed her, her body slackening as she slumped back against Alex. "It's Nat. She wants to know *ma stratégie*." She stared up at the ceiling. The bubbles had diffused, leaving only a frothy tinge of soapy water covering the surface. "I swear, she has the most outrageous sense of timing."

In a fleeting attempt to resume where they'd left off, Catharine bent her head to kiss the arm Alex had draped over her, but abandoned the effort just as quickly, the atmosphere sufficiently derailed.

"I don't know what to do," she said, returning her stony gaze forward as she sank lower in the tub, out of Alex's embrace, her face disappearing beneath the cloudy sheen of soap. Her halo of hair floated out around her, catching Alex in an uncanny feeling of déjà vu—memories of their meeting on Daufuskie tugged from the corner of her mind.

As she resurfaced, the voicemail tone chimed again.

"I don't know if I want to do this," Catharine said plainly, propping her head in Alex's lap, her body buoyant in the water.

Alex waited. Despite Catharine's reluctance to discuss her troubles, she knew it would do her good. To get it off her chest. To sort out her uncertainties before the morning came.

"I wish I could tell you my resolve was wavering for the proper reasons," she continued after a laden silence, her eyes unreadable amidst the glowing shadows flickering across her face. "I wish I could say that I was a better person than I am. That I could lay claim to unimpeachable ethics that have given me pause, swaying my conviction to move forward with tomorrow's plan. I've spent the last week telling myself I'm above this—above using deceit to get what I want. But in truth..." She didn't finish the sentence, each word growing softer as her thoughts carried her back to whatever internal battle she endured.

Alex knew better than to argue her merits as a person. To tell her, without question, she was one of the most ethical people she'd ever known. In her present headspace it would have fallen on deaf ears. Instead, she took the opportunity to continue the line of thought, hoping to keep her talking. To keep her from shutting down.

"What is it you hope to gain tomorrow?" she asked, tentative, reaching for the bottle of shampoo and squeezing it into her palm. She knew it hazarded on a rhetorical question. It should have been obvious. She wanted the return of her company. Reestablishment of her life. But for some reason, it didn't feel as straightforward anymore. At least not to Alex. Nor, she suspected, to Catharine herself.

A fact underscored by Catharine's lengthy delay to respond.

"I'm not sure," Catharine finally said, closing her eyes as Alex worked the shampoo through her hair. "Peace, I think, more than anything else."

This was an answer Alex could relate to. An answer, she felt, that cut closest to the heart.

"My entire life," she continued, as Alex retrieved a bar of soap from the edge of the tub, "has been comprised of Brooks Corp.— for more years than I can even recall. It's been my first thought in the morning. My focus throughout the day. The constant pressure that has kept me up for nights on end." Her eyes remained closed as Alex made slow, even circles across her shoulders, working the lather along her skin. "It's so ingrained in me, that without it, I don't know who I am."

Alex considered it for a moment, her thoughts straying to a cold day in a snowy park in Washington DC. To a time when it felt like soccer was the only thing to live for. That her life was comprised of nothing more than her career.

"I was reminded once," she said, slipping her hands beneath the surface of the water, running the bar of soap along the ridges of Catharine's ribs, the smooth plane of her stomach, the soft underside of her breasts, "that, no matter how much I'd allowed soccer to become my identity, there was more to me than it. More to my life. More to come. At the time," she couldn't keep the smile from her voice as she playfully pinched Catharine in the crease along her thigh, aware it harbored her most ticklish spot, "I admit, I thought the advice was a load of bullshit. I mean, the advice-giver *was* trying to get into my pants—"

"Oh, please, I was *not* trying to 'get into your pants.'" Catharine protested, pushing herself upright to face Alex and using a slender finger to flick her with the last dying suds of soap. "You could have only hoped."

"I *did* hope," Alex said slyly, splashing her back, laughing as Catharine lunged for her hand. "My *point*," she continued, her superior strength winning the grapple, despite inadvertently dislodging the drain plug from the tub, "was that it turned out to be decent guidance, after all. Perhaps you should consider it yourself."

"Take my own advice?" Catharine arched a brow, her smile subtle. "Surely it can't be as simple as that?"

"I promise you, Catharine Brooks, there is not one thing about you I would ever call simple." Alex raised her hand to her lips, turning it over to kiss her wrist. "Tomorrow, however, I do think the answer may not be as complicated as it seems. You need to do what's best for you. No one else. Not Elle. Not your father. Not your mother. Not even Brooks Corp. Just you."

"Just *us*," Catharine corrected, rocking forward to kiss Alex's forehead. "Because I hate to tell you, come hell or high water, you're stuck with me now."

"Believe me," Alex leaned back as the water drained around them, drawing Catharine on top of her, uncaring that it was cold and they were covered in soap, "there's no place in this universe I would rather be."

Chapter Thirty

At a quarter to eleven, Catharine watched out the window through a rivulet of raindrops as Malcolm pulled past the iron gateway and onto the tree-lined drive. Half a mile in the distance Honour Stone unfolded amidst an ocean of fog, the manor stark and unwelcoming, caught in the unfeeling grip of winter. The tires grated across the frost-covered ground, the woodlands rolling out pale and barren, the only sign of life apparent in the pair of black sedans parked in the turn-around of the front entry.

In the seat beside her, Elle let out a low, bemused whistle, and not for the first time since they'd left London, Catharine regretted agreeing to meet her father and his counsel in the country.

It was typical of Benjamin Brooks. His turf. His upper hand. Demand she come to him, that he might maintain each aspect of control. She had considered refusing him, requesting to parley in the city, at a more neutral locale, but it had seemed somehow appropriate, closing this chapter in Henley-on-Thames. It was where it had all begun. It felt fitting it should be the place where it ended.

"I once attended a banquet at the Duke of Colville's estate in Stirlingshire," said Elle, clicking her jeweled fingers together. "It was the most magnificent manor house I'd ever seen. Gilt-bronze and cut-crystal chandeliers. Mulberry drapes. Hand-carved Brazilian mahogany handrails." Her amber eyes flicked from Catharine back to the looming rise of Honour Stone, where its limestone pilasters and voussoir arcades gleamed a cruel facade through the midmorning haze. "This place makes that one look like an abandoned summer cottage, twice forgotten. I will say it again, Catharine," she gathered her purse, extracting a compact to examine her hair, "I grossly undercharged you. Had I known you came from this—"

"*This* is not mine, I'll have you recall." Catharine yanked open the door handle as Malcolm slowed to a stop, not waiting for her father's valet who had promptly appeared at the foot of the landing.

"Then perhaps I chose the wrong client to represent."

Elle's parry remained unanswered as Catharine stood, smoothing nonexistent creases from her coat, while glancing at her reflection in the passenger window. She'd chosen the simplicity of a somber charcoal suit, aware of her father's outdated distaste for women in trousers.

"Remember, I do the talking. It is what you pay me for." Elle stood at her shoulder. "Now," the barrister turned for the stairs, "let's go hang the bastard."

Catharine willed her feet to obey her brain, passing Malcolm on the way to the stairs. The Scotsman leaned against the hood of the car. "A whistle away," he whispered his reassurance, offering her the encouragement of a nod.

Inside the manor, the valet led them through the grand foyer and down the long, broad corridor, past the formal dining hall and music rooms, the art gallery and sun parlor. It was the route to the west wing, where Catharine knew her father would be waiting in his library.

The further they traversed into the house, the more she could feel Elle's intrigue growing. Her astute gaze flicked across the gold-trimmed French wallpaper and masterfully crafted moldings, her attention sweeping the open door of the palatial ballroom with its Palladian windows and Italian murals spanning the cathedral ceiling. It was the life of luxury she knew the barrister saw. She could not see the hurts and heartlessness that lurked behind its enigmatic walls.

"Madames," the valet paused at the end of the hall and swung open the familiar blackwood door—a door Catharine had learned to loathe as a child. Without hesitation, Elle marched through the threshold, her heels clicking resoundingly across the Macassar ebony flooring.

Catharine followed behind her, finding herself more composed than she'd anticipated. More certain of herself than she'd felt in weeks. Months. Maybe longer. As they approached the far wall where her father sat at his desk, surrounded by his trio of counsel, she felt none of the trepidation of years past. There were no faltering steps as she'd taken in her youth, no racing heart to evince her discomfort.

"Ms. Kirkland." Colonel Brooks stood, a cold figure amidst the warmth of the hearth and amenity of the leather-bound volumes lining the walls from the floor to the vaulted ceiling. His gaze swept across the barrister, making no effort to hide his disdain. He took in the ruby red of her heels that matched her lips, accenting her copper hair. His judgment slid over the unorthodox fit of her low-cut blouse, the snugness of her skirt, the sheerness of her stockings, and, with a tilt of his chin Catharine knew all too well, he dismissed her relevance, relegating her to unworthiness of his consideration.

The casual discreditation of the woman enlivened Catharine, temporarily underscoring her misgivings that Elle would not be given the chance to take him to trial. To dismantle his arrogance. To fluster him, infuriate him with her calculating, scheming mind. To give the barrister the opportunity to beat him in the open, turning the tables on his own game.

"Catharine." Her father acknowledged her with a curt nod. There was a glint of victory in his callous expression, the cerulean of his eyes alight with anticipation. "You may sit."

"Mightn't we?" Elle bristled beside her, her hackles rising at the blatant condescension dripping from his intonation. "How charitable."

"Do as you please, Ms. Kirkland. Sit. Stand. Kneel? However you are most comfortable, it matters to me not at all." He dismissed her, resuming his seat on the opposite side of his desk. "Mr. Liebermann has prepared the documents for signing."

"Ms. Kirkland," Gordon Liebermann cut in, trying to get ahead of Elle's anger at his client's flippant degradation, "if you and Mrs. Cleveland please," he gestured toward the two high-backed chairs. "I realize this is a difficult situation, and I assure you, I will make this as concise and uncomplicated as possible."

For the first time since they'd entered the room, Catharine looked at the attorney. She'd known he would be there; he led the legal team for Brooks Corp., after all. But it still stung to have him present. To see her old friend—the man *she* had hired—standing at her father's elbow, his sharp mind employed to engineer her downfall.

"Do complexities intimidate you, Mr. Liebermann?" asked Elle, still standing.

"I meant no offense, Ms. Kirkland." The attorney lifted a handkerchief from his pocket and mopped at his brow. On another day, in another place, Catharine would have felt sorry for him. Despite his brilliance at law, he was not a confrontational man, and had always maintained undue respect for his opposition.

"Cut the show, Elle." One of the two men sitting to the left of her father snapped shut a silver cigarette case he'd been trifling with. "Save your theatrics for your next trial. There's none of us here who are going to be impressed by your blather."

"Oh, Marcus," Elle fixed the man—a fellow Queen's Counsel colleague, no doubt—with a frozen smile. "So quick out the gate. It's just like you to jump the gun and rush to a premature finish." She sank into her seat, crossing her shapely legs, a smugness tugging at her lips as she pulled her Buccio briefcase into her lap. "However, since you are in such a hurry, there is a bit of a snag I suppose we ought to discuss."

"A snag?" Gordon Liebermann's handkerchief crumpled between his fingers. "If you're still unsatisfied with the language of article II, section VII, I assure you, the ambiguity has been clarified. I'm happy to go over any areas of concern, certain we can reach a favorable agreement."

"Tell me, Mr. Liebermann: if Mrs. Cleveland were your client, would you find any of this favorable?" She gave him no time to answer. "Of course you wouldn't. So don't blow smoke up my arse. As I was saying—we've hit a snag, though perhaps that choice of wording is an understatement." Elle casually unbuckled the straps on her bag, taking evident pleasure in her opposing counsel's mounting consternation.

"If you've come here with your smoke and mirrors, intent to jerk us around—" Marcus started, but Gordon silenced the younger barrister with a firm hand on his shoulder.

"Mrs. Cleveland?" His focus shifted to Catharine, appealing to her on their familiar level. "I was under the impression we had achieved satisfactory terms?"

It had come to the point of no return faster than Catharine anticipated. She'd hoped for more time for preparation, more time to gather her thoughts, to convince herself she was making the right decision. But what difference did five minutes... ten minutes... an hour make? She'd known stepping through the Honour Stone threshold what she was going to do. And the immediacy of the unraveling situation kept her resolve from wavering.

Resisting the urge to apologize to Gordon, Catharine addressed her father, breaking her silence for the first time since she'd entered the manor. "I would like to speak to you in private."

Colonel Brooks leaned back, folding his hands across his lap, his ankles crossed in disinterest. "Cut to the chase, Catharine. You were not raised to muck around in circles. Say what you will and let's be done with it. I have no care to have this turned into a spectacle."

"Nor do I. Which is why I would like five minutes of your time —just you and I."

She could feel Elle's eyes snap to her, her fingers ceasing the fiddling with her briefcase. This was not part of their plan. This was not something the barrister would approve of. Elle had not felt Catharine capable of handling her father on her own. It had been her intent to control the conversation.

On the other side of the desk, the two counselors to the left of the colonel exchanged a hasty whisper.

Catharine's attention remained on her father, maintaining his unblinking glare.

"I have no time for this," Benjamin Brooks uncrossed his legs, the only tell he'd grown uncomfortable. "Sit down, Catharine— sign the bloody settlement. I've been more than generous—"

"*Make* time or I will walk out that door."

Beside her, Elle went rigid. "What my client means to say, Colonel Brooks—"

"I do not need an interpreter, Ms. Kirkland." Rocking upright in his seat, Benjamin Brooks flicked two long, slender fingers in the direction of the hall. "You can show yourself out, Catharine."

Despite his bluster, Catharine could see his apathetic arrogance dissolving. She knew an idle threat when she saw one.

"So be it." She drew the strap of her clutch taut across her shoulder, turning and striding across the floor. She'd set only one foot on the knotted silk rug ornamenting the center of the library when she heard his chair scrap across the hardwood.

"Wait." His voice was low, the simple syllable laden with so much disgust, she almost kept walking. Instead, she forced herself to pause, her heels sinking into the intricate design of the hand spun carpet.

"Colonel Brooks!" it was Marcus, his voice risen in pitch as he battled desperation, "this is preposterous. She cannot come in here and dictate—"

"Get out."

"I'm sorry?"

"You heard me. Give us the room."

"They are playing games, Colonel—"

"I will not tell you again."

Catharine turned, watching as the young man sulked behind his associate toward the hall. Gordon was the last to leave her father's side, coming to a stop at the edge of the mahogany desk, making a point to wait for Elle.

"After you, Ms. Kirkland."

Elle didn't budge. "Catharine," she began, forgetting her propriety in her mounting confusion, "this is not—"

"Thank you, Ms. Kirkland," Catharine interrupted, "I will handle things from here."

Fury fringed on the woman's expression, her brightly painted lips disappearing into the thinnest of lines. She swallowed, biting back words she could not utter, held hostage to the present company in the room. Finally, ignoring the American attorney's offered hand, she rose, collecting her briefcase, and stormed for the door.

"Suit yourself," she snapped, brushing past Catharine, unwilling to meet her eye.

When the door had shut, when the footsteps had been absorbed by the seventeenth century walls, Catharine forced herself from her frozen position, choosing a path along the perimeter of the room. She slowed in front of the built-in bookshelves, running her fingers across the spines of books she'd known since she was a child. *The Wealth of Nations. Principles of Logic. The Richest Man in Babylon. The Prince.* Theories drilled into her. Economics. Capitalism. Free enterprise. She could quote the greatest business philosophers—Carl Icahn, Herbert Allison Jr., Gerald Levin. She spoke six languages and could calculate future and present values, compound interest, and exchange rates in her head. By the time she'd learned to talk, her days had been filled with the finest tutors Europe had to offer, brought up in an elite world few ever really understood.

Her father had given her that. Given her purpose. Given her drive. Given her an unattainable appetite for success. Her twenty hour work days, her obsession with perfection, her tunnel vision on the next acquisition, the next merger, the next deal to be made or gain to be had—she had him to thank for that.

But what had he stolen from her in return? What had she been forced to give up?

The carefree nature of childhood. The acceptance that it was innately human to make mistakes. The sense of satisfaction with the simple things in life.

She'd been raised with the inextinguishable feeling she would never be enough.

Running a finger along the gold engraved letters of a century-old copy of *The Art of War*—one of her father's favorite texts—a passage crossed her mind she hadn't read since her first year of university. It hadn't meant much to her then. She hadn't lived enough to understand.

"'There is no instance of a nation benefitting from prolonged warfare.'" She spoke aloud, turning from the shelf to face her father. He'd resumed his seat behind his desk and was watching her through the mask of his inscrutable stare.

"Sun Tzu. What of it?" Atop the finished mahogany, his fingers began a familiar cadence, tapping out a slow tattoo. Born of neither anxiety nor boredom, but a practice formed from long hours in thought. A habit she recognized in herself.

How much of him had she unknowingly inherited? How much of himself did he see in her? Beyond the blueness of their eyes, the high set of their cheeks, the brow that had been passed down from the generations of Brooks that had come before them.

Her mother said he had never wanted a child. A wife. A family. Did it irk him, then, their similarities? Did he look at her and see a reflection of himself? Her simple existence the legacy of his lies. Alike in more than visage. Alike in ways neither of them could deny.

She crossed the room, taking up the chair Elle had been forced to vacate, aware in the back of her mind she'd likely never earn the barrister's forgiveness. A thought, for now, she put to rest.

"I am tired of fighting."

The drumming of the colonel's fingers ceased. Without taking his eyes off her, he reached for the prepared paperwork his counsel had left behind, and slid it across his desk. "Then sign."

Catharine leaned forward, scanning the first few lines of the contract she knew inside and out, start to finish. The contract that would dissect her from her life, cutting out a part of her as if it were an imaginary limb.

She took up her father's Visconti pen from where it lay in its crystal stand, slowly unscrewing the hand-carved cap to reveal the rose gold nib.

"Did you think I would never find out?" Her thumb brushed the honed tip, drawing a bead of ink.

If he suspected the direction of the conversation, he gave no tell.

"I've warned you already—I will not tolerate your equivocal nonsense."

She persisted. "All those trips to Liverpool. Summers in Amsterdam. Unexplained business in Barcelona. You were careful, I'll give you credit. I never would have suspected. But—*know thy enemy*. You hammered it into me as a child. How often did I hear you quote *'the opportunity of defeating the enemy is provided by the enemy himself'*. And in the end, Sun Tzu was right—and you were not careful enough."

Through the peripheral of her vision—her attention held to the intricate art of the pen—she could see his hands tense, his forearms going rigid. She had touched the chord she was aiming for, and there was no turning back.

"Are you threatening me?" His voice, though still measured, had lost some of its command.

It did not surprise her he did not deny it. That he made no excuses. Rushed to no defense. He was too proud for that. Too arrogant. Too categorical in his self-assurance. And he knew her well enough to know she would not strike at him without indisputable evidence. She had been raised to be too astute, too prudent for that.

She sat back, recapping the pen. "My entire life I've wondered what it would take to gain your approval. To earn your respect. I didn't need your love—I'd given up on that long before it actually failed to matter. Long before I'd come to realize it was something you were not capable to give. But I never did learn how to lose the desire for your admiration. I always thought if I found a way to work harder—expand wider—build higher… that one day you'd notice. One day you'd acknowledge my success. That you might even appreciate the effort I'd put in."

"Is that what this is about?" he scoffed, derisive. "You needing a pat on the back?"

"No, no," Catharine half laughed, her own malice seeping through, "we're past that now. I've come to understand that your contempt… your loathing… your hatred… has never been about me. It was merely a reflection of yourself."

For a second his body jerked, pitching forward, and he was half risen before he decided better of it and slowly resumed his seat.

"You think yourself so clever. That you've got me so sorted." He crossed an ankle atop his knee, forcing a nonchalance she was certain was not felt. "What is it you want, Catharine? Are you so keen to keep your power? So desperate to be returned to your position? Fine," he shrugged as if it was no matter, as if she could not see the seed of fear that had sprouted behind his facade of indifference, "so be it. Take it. That's what you've come for, is it not? Come to drag me down. Come to reclaim what you feel is yours."

And there it was, everything she'd wanted—all uttered in a single breath. If she asked him for more, she would get it. Majority claim. Sovereign authority. The power to control the corporation as she saw fit. All she had to do was reach out and take it.

"No." Once again she uncapped the pen, her gaze returning to the contract acting as a barrier between them. The signing page was upturned, her father's neatly scripted name already inscribed above the blank line waiting for hers. "I am finished living my life for you, bound between your four walls. I have lived for Brooks Corp., given it everything I had to give, and still it has never been enough. You've stripped from it everything I loved. I don't want it anymore." She pressed the nib to the paper, waiting for the ink to form, before executing her signature. "It's yours. It's always been yours. It can die with you."

He stared at her drying name as if it were foreign. As if it were not the one he had given to her. "What's the catch, Catharine? You didn't tell me all this just to walk away."

"That's where we differ, you and I. I could have destroyed you. I could have done what you did to me. And I wanted to, to tell the truth. I wanted to watch you suffer—to know what it was like. But I won't. Because I am not you. I never will be."

He laughed, all of his contempt through all the years bottled into the sound. "And what are you expecting? My gratitude? I don't owe you a God damn thing." He swiped the crystal penholder from his desk, where it shattered against the floor. "You are a fool, Catharine. Like all women, you are weak. Incapable. I gave you the world and you flung it in my face. When you walk out of here you will be nothing. No one. And no matter what you do— what you try to build—you will never come close to having anything like this again."

She stood, stepping over the broken fragments of crystal. "No. I might not. But I will have my freedom. And I will have my happiness. And those are two things you will never know."

Chapter Thirty-One

"There is no way I'm wearing this."

Alex stared at herself in the fitting room mirror, eyeing the plunging neckline that fell midway to her sternum. The shop attendant clucked and hummed as she adjusted the shoestring straps, until Nathalie grew impatient with the woman's fussing.

"*Ça suffit! Très bien!*" she said, brushing the attendant aside and sweeping Alex's hair into her hand, lifting it to reveal her bare shoulders. "*Cette tenue est superbe!*" Still holding her hair up, Nathalie examined her from both sides, nodding with approval. "It is as if it were made for you. You must buy it!"

Twenty minutes earlier Alex had been in her favorite pair of worn out jeans and one of Catharine's waxed cotton jackets, perfectly comfortable as she and Nathalie made their way toward Elle's high-rise office. The Frenchwoman had invited her to lunch, the two of them killing time while Catharine met with the barrister.

It had been a mistake—in the middle of picking croutons off her caesar salad—to mention the Ballon d'Or ceremony taking place in Paris. And it had been an even greater error to admit she had no idea what she'd be wearing.

After putting up no resistance when Alex offered to pay the tab, Nathalie had suggested they walk back by way of the underground mall, insisting it would be warmer. Alex had agreed, not realizing the outing would present the opportunity for the notoriously meddling woman to assume the self-appointed duty of dressing her.

"I'm not exactly the type that can pull this off." Alex smoothed the ruched fabric that clung to her silhouette, leaving no imagination to the outline of her slender figure.

"You are either deserving of an Oscar for your portrayal of humility, or our next stop needs to be at the optometrist to pick you up a pair of glasses, because I promise, there is not a soul with decent vision who cannot see this dress has your name all over it." Nathalie looked to the attendant for confirmation, receiving an enthusiastic nod of the woman's loosely spun curls.

Given the staggering sum of the price tag—and commission that undoubtedly accompanied it—Alex couldn't blame her.

"Does Janet Jackson and the Super Bowl Halftime show ring a bell?" she asked, turning sideways in the mirror, testing out exactly how much of her modest cleavage was on display. "Because it is exactly something like that that would happen to me."

Nathalie tugged at the satin material, dragging it half an inch lower. "All the better. Free publicity."

"*That* is the last thing I need."

Four dresses later, Alex swiped her card at the register, finally conceding to the purchase of the gown with the plunging neckline. She'd been saved from trying on heels by the sales associate's erroneous assumption that Nathalie was her mother, a blunder which had sent the delicate ego of the actress into a tailspin.

"What did she think?" Nathalie ranted long after the glass doors of the luxury retailer had closed behind them. "I mysteriously gave birth as a child?"

"Is this a bad time to point out that you would have legally been an adult when I was born?"

"The only reason the authorities won't be dragging your lifeless body from the Thames this evening is because Christmas is in two days and I'm in a forgiving mood. Besides," she added as they stepped off the escalator, resurfacing to the foggy streets of Canary Wharf, "I'll have you know I am only twenty-one months older than Cate, which means I was still seventeen when you were born."

Their banter dwindled as they stepped through the glass doors of the lobby sitting fifty-two floors beneath Elle Kirkland's office inside *Crown Bridge Chambers*. The security guard looked up from the desk, giving the pair a disinterested glancing over, and then resumed her FaceTime call discussing an upcoming Ugly Jumper party.

"I imagine if the two of them had killed each other up there, we'd have heard about it by now?" Nathalie thumbed in the direction of Elle's top floor office, settling into a plush armchair as Alex folded the garment bag onto the black marble coffee table and pulled out her phone. There were no messages from Catharine, and Alex wasn't about to be the one to interrupt. Nathalie's teasing of homicide aside, the impromptu meeting had not come with a warm welcome. Catharine and Elle had not been on speaking terms since their return from Henley four days earlier. An untimely inconvenience, given the necessity of their forced communication due to Carlton Cleveland's latest stunt in their divorce case.

"Perhaps the common enemy will unite them." It came out more hopeful than Alex felt.

"You must admit," said Nathalie, finding a segue into a subject Alex suspected she'd wanted to discuss all afternoon, "it wasn't fair on Cate's end. What she did."

Fair, maybe not. Alex understood the barrister's resentment over being caught unaware. But Catharine had done what she needed to do.

"I think she did what she felt was best for her future," she said, simply.

"She could have done it without blindsiding Elle."

"Elle would have tried to talk her out of it."

"As she should have!" Nathalie defended. "Look where her impulsive behavior has gotten her!"

It wasn't an unjust assessment. Catharine's timing on her acceptance of her father's buyout had thrown a wrench in her divorce with Carlton. After word of the purchase of her stocks had reached her husband's attorney, Carlton had withdrawn from their negotiated settlement, claiming the sale removed the corporation's immunity in division of their assets, and was now eligible for equitable distribution in the case of their separation.

Catharine had appeared unperturbed when Elle called her that morning. "Leave it to Carlton to think he is above the laws of an irrevocable trust," Alex had heard her say, before citing a handful of exemptions that were well over Alex's head. But the barrister had not been as unconcerned, with Alex catching the words *South Carolina, marital property, consent, appreciation,* and *timing* amidst her demand that Catharine make an appearance in her office at two pm.

It was now after five-thirty.

The security guard wrapped up her FaceTime call and flipped on Christmas tunes which hummed through her iPhone speaker.

"Did you know she was going to do it?" Nathalie probed over the chorus of *Frosty the Snowman*. The question was bitter, and one, based off the honed glint in her expression, Alex imagined cut nearest the root of her resentment. Less that Elle had been taken by surprise, or that Carlton had found a loophole to further contest the divorce and try and milk Catharine for more money, but more so that *she* hadn't been privy to her best friend's plans. That *she'd* been left in the dark.

A hurt Alex could understand.

"No." It was mostly the truth. She hadn't been certain what Catharine would do. She wasn't even certain Catharine knew what she was going to do before she'd left for Honour Stone. They'd talked all night about the various possibilities, but never once had Catharine come out forthright and said she'd sign the settlement. Even if Alex had had her suspicions, Nathalie didn't need to know that. "She didn't tell anyone."

For all her impressive acting skills, the actress was unable to hide her visible relief, clearly grateful she hadn't lost her place as best-friend-confidante to a mere girlfriend. With Catharine and Elle at odds, it had put Nathalie precariously in the middle, and by the simple rule of alliance based off whose pillow you were sharing, she and Catharine had been on frosty terms. It had to kill her, Alex knew, to be forced to ask her for crumbs of information.

"Well," Nathalie fiddled with a leather bracelet hung loosely around her wrist, "she certainly led us all up the garden path, didn't she? I suppose there's no reason to be surprised. Once Cate gets something into her head, there's little to talk her out of it." She gave another twist of the braided leather. "Is she happy, do you think? About... with her decision?"

"Yes." Alex didn't elaborate. She didn't tell Nathalie for the past three days Catharine had been nothing short of elated. That she'd told her over and over how relieved she felt to be so completely unencumbered. She hadn't stopped talking about the plans she wanted to make for the future. Formulating new ideas, new dreams, a new life—one where she didn't have to answer to any-one.

She would leave that for Catharine to share. For her and Nathalie to discuss once they'd made amends with each other.

"Good." Nathalie shrugged, as if the answer hadn't meant much to her, though Alex suspected it meant everything. "I mean, it's not like she's been left desolate. Not too many people can say they've been forced into a ten figure settlement. We could only hope for such misfortune, no?" Her attention momentarily flicked to the security guard, where *I Want A Hippopotamus For Christmas* had begun its obnoxious refrain, the woman's cell phone speakers rattling on full volume. Annoyed, Nathalie glanced toward the elevators. "She'd better be up there groveling for forgiveness. She owes Elle that much. She wouldn't have come out with half of what she did without her. And if nothing else, she owes it to *me* to smooth this over. I like Elle. A lot. More, I guess, than I've liked anyone in longer than I can remember," —it came out an admis-sion— "and I refuse to choose between the two of them."

Alex did a poor job of hiding her smile.

"Oh, don't you dare look at me like that," Nathalie jumped to the defense. "I'm not saying I'm in love with her. We're just—we get along, that's all. We get each other." Despite her tone, the corners of her own lips turned, her eyes growing warmer. "She's going to come to my season opener. Perhaps, while she's in Cali-fornia, she'll come to one of your games."

"Only to root against me," Alex laughed.

"Would it be Elle otherwise?" Nathalie gave a flippant wave of her hand. "So you head back after New Year's?"

At lunch they'd both discussed their imminent return to the States. Alex had been called to a US National Team camp preced-ing two friendly matches in Chicago and Fort Lauderdale—her offseason cut short as they geared up for the Olympic year. She would be gone for ten days, and then return to London, where she and Catharine would spend her final weekend of downtime together before she headed to Paris to attend the ceremony for the Ballon d'Or. And then it would be back to California, back to the Sirens, back to the grind—and, if luck and hard work proved to be in her favor, come late September she would be in Australia where the US would vie for gold. The perfect year, made all the better by the knowledge that this time, Catharine would be with her. That their lives would be intertwined. No more clandestine nights spent looking over their shoulder. No texts without the promise of knowing when they would next see each other.

The anticipation of it—the excitement of it—had made it all so easy to forget she would be returning to a country who had elected a monster into office. That her first preseason game kicked off the same night as his inauguration.

A recollection that was quickly returned to the surface when Catharine exited the elevator into the lobby looking like she was prepared to commit murder.

"He is such a blithering ignoramus," she said to Alex, once she'd given Nathalie a brusque farewell and curt *Merry Christmas*—not the smoothing over the Frenchwoman had been hoping for—and they'd stepped into the damp chill awaiting them along the waterway. "He's not going to win another bloody cent from me, and he knows it—the law isn't on his side. But while he's spinning his wheels fighting this, all it does is push back the final decree. One would think he'd have wanted to go into his presidency a free man —or at least not looking like the leech that he is!" Her steps slowed as they reached the entrance to the underground, and only then did she notice the garment bag Alex had slung over her arm. "I thought you were going to lunch? Leave it to Nathalie to turn a meal into a miserable afternoon of shopping."

"I mentioned Paris and I don't think she would have slept tonight if we hadn't determined what I'd be wearing. We had fun, actually." Alex shouldered the garment bag, digging out her Oyster card and swiping it to gain access through the turnstile, Catharine's heels following in the wet footprints her tennis shoes left on the floor. "She's worried what will happen if you and Elle don't reconcile."

"Whatever for?" Catharine reached to move a newspaper from the seat on the Tube carriage, then thought better of it, and instead unfolded it with a fingertip, leaving it as a barrier between her skirt and the grungy checkered fabric. "Nat heads back to California next week, and, God willing, my divorce will eventually be finalized, and then Elle Kirkland can wallow in her wounded pride while sitting atop the exorbitant sum of cash she's made off me.

No doubt the zeroes will help mend her ego. And we'll all go on with our merry lives."

"I take it the two of you still aren't seeing eye to eye."

"I've just spent the past three hours being berated by a woman who's technically employed by me, amidst being informed Carlton's attorney has now demanded a deposition in effort to justify suing me for half of everything I own, so forgive me if I'm not too concerned with Nathalie's feelings for her Shag of the Week."

Alex tabled the mention of the deposition in order to stay on the topic of Nathalie, while trying to hide her amusement at the word *shag* falling from Catharine's lips.

"I think she's more to her than that."

"I'm sorry?" Growing frustrated with the crinkling of paper, Catharine pulled the newspaper from beneath her thigh and tossed it onto the adjacent seat. "Nathalie has a tendency to fall in love with everything that slips between her sheets. This one's not special, I promise you."

"Shall we make a bet on it?" Alex attempted to turn Catharine's testiness into a game, luring her from her mood. By the rise in the angle of her brow, she felt confident she could succeed.

"What shall this bet entail?"

Alex shrugged. "I bet in six months they're still together."

Catharine laughed as if it were the most entertaining joke Alex had ever told. "Six months? With Nathalie returning to San Francisco at the end of next week? I won't give them six weeks."

"If I'm right, what do I get?" Alex prodded, bumping Catharine's ankle with her toe.

"Hmm." Catharine's teeth grazed her lower lip in thought. "What would you want?"

"A weekend with you, somewhere… anywhere. Forty-eight full hours with no phone calls, no emails, no correspondence with the outside world. Just your undivided, devoted attention."

"What if I said I wanted the same thing from you if I win?"

"You can't!" Alex chided. "I have to feel like I won something."

"So competitive." Catharine's blue eyes glittered in the glare of LED lighting. "Fine, I'll think about what I want when I win. And I *will* win. I know Nathalie well enough to know she'll be on to the next flavor by the time her feet hit California soil."

"Which will make my victory all the sweeter," Alex quipped, tugging her garment bag into her arms as she gave up her seat to an older patron. She stood in front of Catharine, their knees touching, trying to balance as the carriage lurched toward the next station.

"So when am I going to see this dress so I know best how to complement it?"

Alex laughed. "You aren't really wanting to come, are you? It's a silly soccer award ceremony." *Silly* wasn't the right word. It was the most prestigious award in all of football. But it still felt minuscule compared to everything Catharine was going through. "One —I promise you—I will *not* be winning."

"*The Athletic* feels otherwise. They've got you ranked in the top three candidates."

"You haven't honestly subscribed to *The Athletic*?"

"Of course I have," Catharine said, "don't be ridiculous. I swear, it is absurd and nearly maddening how little credit you give me when it comes to caring about your career."

"It's not that I don't think you care," Alex braced herself against a hard stop of the carriage, "it's just... a nomination for a trophy seems so... trivial, in the long run."

"Are you going to invite me as your date or not? If you don't," Catharine chastised, accepting Alex's hand as she got to her feet, the doors sliding open at Tower Hill Station, "I'm going to start to think you are embarrassed to be seen with me."

"It's black," said Alex, following her out the carriage door and slipping her arm through hers as they shuffled through the holiday crowds, beginning the walk toward Bermondsey. "And leaves little to the imagination."

"I see." Catharine's smile was subtle as their eyes met in periphery. "Then I expect a private showing when we get home so I can determine just how much of you I'll be sharing with everyone at this 'silly soccer award ceremony'."

Chapter Thirty-Two

Time passed too quickly for Catharine. Christmas came and went, the perfect day together—just her and Alex. The two of them had dwindled away the morning hours, lounging on the sitting room sofa, watching holiday classics until they dosed off to black and white credits and empty glasses of spiked mulled cider. By evening, Catharine had laughed until her sides ached as Alex talked her into attempting to build a gingerbread house, scrounging makeshift material from the kitchen cupboards, the pair of them finding themselves sticky with molasses and blanketed in powdered sugar, both a little drunk and high off each other.

The days leading to New Year's slipped away like sand through a sifter. Alex ran with Amelia in the mornings and Catharine pieced together the details of her financial portfolio. There were Zoom meetings with *Nike* while Alex worked out her springtime schedule, and endless phone calls with Nicole as Catharine began the process of reestablishing her life stateside. On New Year's Eve Catharine stayed home to comb through the dozens of questions Elle sent in preparation for the deposition while Alex was reluctantly convinced to go out and celebrate with Abby Sawyer and her girlfriend. Ten minutes to midnight, however, Catharine was startled from her paperwork to find Alex standing behind her, unwilling to miss a kiss to bring in the New Year.

The following day, she drove Alex to Heathrow, where they hugged goodbye on the sidewalk of the departure terminal, before Alex boarded a plane for Chicago.

The peaceful lull they'd enjoyed had ended. A week later, Catharine was forced to follow across the Atlantic, joined by Elle and Malcolm, as she traveled to South Carolina to be deposed by Carlton's legal counsel.

"I would have shed no tears of regret if I'd gone to my grave without ever setting foot in this parachronistic cesspool," Elle hissed as they were ushered through customs at Charleston International and greeted by the blinding flash of cameras and chorus of questions from lurking reporters. The interest from the media in the high profile divorce had been soundly reinvigorated since news of the coming deposition reached the headlines.

"You can hardly judge an entire city based off a walk through the airport." Catharine found herself defensive of the southern metropolis. Port Charleston had been one of her earliest North American accounts, and she was fond of the personnel who operated the harbor.

"I can judge an entire *state* based off its backward legislature," Elle said, ducking into the waiting car. "Are you aware it took over fifty years for South Carolina to ratify the 19th Amendment? How's that for the Americans pounding their chests for freedom? Combine it with this state's piss poor track record in electing senators, and I will reiterate, the place is a brassbound rubbish tip."

Catharine had no argument for the latter.

That evening, after they'd settled into an adjoining set of suites at Hotel Bennett, Elle strode uninvited through the connecting doors and made herself at home on Catharine's settee, overlooking Marion Square.

"They're going to tear you apart tomorrow." The barrister browsed the room service menu, stifling a yawn.

"Isn't that the purpose of you being here? To see that they don't."

There'd been no amenability between the two of them since Henley. Beyond the necessity of a handful of brusque phone calls and laconic exchanges in preparation for the deposition, they'd hardly acknowledged the presence of one another.

"I can keep his counsel in-check—the better question is if I should be made aware of any intent for my own client to sabotage her future? Your recent history isn't exactly stellar."

"Elle," Catharine tried to be reasonable, "I realize you've been less than thrilled with my decision to settle, and I'm sorry for the way I allowed it to play out. It wasn't fair, and for that, I do regret —"

"*Fair*?! We had him! We had him and you cut him loose!" Elle flung the room service menu to the floor. "You made me look an utter fool! I don't want your twopenny apology—it's neither here nor there. Cause and effect has had its say, and as the laws of life have proven, you reap what you sow. All I want to know now, is: have you made any plans to throw yourself off the proverbial cliff tomorrow? Because if that is the case, I am resigning as your counsel—"

"The only person I want to throw off a cliff is Carlton," Catharine hurled with more venom than she realized she'd been suppressing. "I want to *annihilate* him!"

Four days. From the time she'd left Honour Stone to the morning Elle had called her to her office—that's how long her respite of tranquility had lasted. She'd signed her life's work away to buy her peace, and within ninety-six hours, Carlton had come knocking. He'd smelled blood in the water, and, as always, wanted a share of what wasn't his to take. She'd been more than fair; she'd been excessively generous, offering well beyond what he deserved, and still, it wasn't enough. It would never be enough. He'd broken his word, defaulted on every deal they'd made, and she was finished with being his patsy.

"I want to get through tomorrow, and as soon as we step out of that office, I want to take back every offer on the table. Leave him as desperate and desolate as he was the day we were married. He can get exactly what he deserves from me: *nothing*." Catharine stepped over the discarded menu. "I have to win this case, no matter what it takes. I will not allow him to continue to try and press me."

"Well," said Elle, her tone snide, her jaw set in a challenge, "I was led to believe you wanted to win the last one."

"I did win, in my own way—though it's not something I expect you to comprehend. Your only victories come by the digits preceding decimals." Catharine crossed to the threshold of her bedroom. "But even still, let's not pretend you haven't come out with your share of the spoils. So save the bullshit, Elle. Just do your job tomorrow." Catharine slammed the door

"Before we get started, is there anything I can get for you, Catharine?"

The man settled himself at the far end of the table with all the grace of a felled log. Carlton sat beside him, an ankle crossed over his knee, his polished derby shoe bouncing out an irregular rhythm. It had been more than seven months since she'd been forced into his proximity. Seven months since she'd been reminded just how much oxygen he sucked out of a room. He looked scant in comparison to the hulking frame of his attorney. Older. Grayer. His tie barely concealing the strain of the ivory buttons above his gibbous gut.

He'd not taken his eyes off her since she came through the door, his thin lips twisted in the subtlety of a smile. It was a game he liked to engage in. A power play to force the subject of his attention to be the first to look away.

Catharine did not oblige.

"My client has resumed use of her family name. As such, you may refer to her as Ms. Brooks." Elle took the chair beside her.

The lumbering attorney laughed, the deep baritone of his voice surprisingly melodic as it echoed off the bareness of the walls.

"Elle—I may call you Elle, mightn't I?—we're all friends here. There's no need for such formality."

The honed tone of Elle's posh London accent clashed against the lawyer's heavy Southern drawl.

"I prefer formalities, Mr. Alden. And let me be clear—we are not friends. Now, shall we begin?"

"You're used to calling the shots, aren't you, Elle? Maybe you walk into the courtroom with your pretty smile and that come-hither swing to your swagger, and that judge looks you in the eye —imagining all sorts of possibilities—and jumps to do your bidding? Well, let's set things straight, shall we? This is *my* domain, and you're only here with my permission. You're not licensed in this fine state of South Carolina—"

"Which is exactly why I've been granted *pro hac vice*. Now, let's move forward and get on the record, or my client and I will be leaving."

The attorney's eyebrows crept up his too-large forehead as he tried to conceal his surprise with a smile. It was doubtful any person spoke to him like that very often, let alone a woman.

"I love my ladies with a little fire in 'em." He blew imaginary smoke from a finger gun, before twirling his hand toward the waiting videographer, and loosened his tie.

A Blue Hose class ring adorned his little finger. Carlton's alma mater.

"Now, Mrs. Cleveland—is that suitable for today's purpose, given you *are* still legally *Mrs. Cleveland*?—I'll ask again, is there anything I can get you before we get started?" He rose, his voice slick with saccharin suavity, a man accustomed to performing for the camera.

"No. Thank you." Catharine at last withdrew her attention from Carlton as she settled into her seat and folded her hands across her lap. She'd sat through depositions before as witness—cases related to WorldCargo, where her testimony was little more than routine. But she'd never gone through discovery as party, and was not relishing the coming hours.

The attorney nodded toward an older woman who'd kept her silence at the end of the table.

"Mrs. Farrow."

"Mrs. Cleveland," the woman addressed Catharine, "please raise your right hand. Do you solemnly state that the evidence you shall give in this matter shall be the truth, the whole truth, and nothing but the truth, so help you God?"

Catharine wasn't sure God had much to do with the situation, but did as she was told.

"I do."

"Excellent," Carlton's attorney—Jim Alden—clapped his hands together, dragging his expansive frame to his feet. "Now, Mrs. Cleveland, today I'll be asking you some uncomfortable questions, questions you might wish to decline—but I'll remind you that because you are under the penalty of perjury in a legal proceeding, you are obligated to answer, do you understand?"

Catharine nodded.

"I will need you to audibly articulate each and every answer, Mrs. Cleveland."

"Yes," said Catharine, flatly. "I understand."

After she'd stated her full name and address, the attorney began a deliberate pace around the conference room, his hands entwined behind his back.

"How long have you been married, Mrs. Cleveland—how old were you, do you recall?"

"Objection to the form of the question; compound." Elle's delicate assemblage of golden bangles clicked against the oak table top.

Mr. Alden's smile confirmed his pleasure in goading Elle. He was figuring her out; testing the waters.

"My apologies, Ms. Kirkland. How many years have you been married to Senator Cleveland, Mrs. Cleveland?"

Senator. The word had once grated on her, but today it came as a consolation. Had the deposition been held little more than two weeks later she would have had to sit through listening to him called President Cleveland. An unfathomable title she hadn't yet learned to stomach.

"Twenty-four."

"At what age were you wed?"

"Twenty."

"Ah," he chuckled, looping the room and giving Carlton something of a congratulatory clap on the back as he passed. "Tell me, Mrs. Cleveland—what were you worth at the time of your marriage?"

Elle's nails clicked together. "Object to form; vague."

"On the day of your nuptials, what amount of monetary value did you bring to your marriage?"

"I could not give an exact figure."

"I've been told that you never forget a number. Is that true?"

"Someone has more faith in my aging memory than I do."

"Mrs. Cleveland—"

"I do not often forget numbers, Mr. Alden. But I cannot say it has never happened."

"I'll return to the former question: would it be safe to say your worth was in the millions on the day you were wed?"

"Object to form, leading."

"Of course, Ms. Kirkland," the attorney gave a mocking half bow. "Mrs. Cleveland, would you say the value of your assets over the past twenty-four years have increased?"

"Yes."

"Could you estimate by how much?"

"I am not fond of estimations, Mr. Alden."

The fullness of his lips thinned as he feigned a smile. "And I am not fond of repeating myself, Mrs. Cleveland. To what degree has the value of your assets increased over the course of your marriage?"

"In the realm of nine hundred percent."

"Nine hundred percent?" He let out a smart whistle. "That's something. You must be a clever lady."

"Is there a question, Mr. Alden?" Elle pressured.

"Just an admirable observation, Ms. Kirkland. Like I said, we're all friends here." His elevated confidence in representing the future President of the United States gave him an unmistakable sense of latitude he felt entitled to exude.

He pressed on, questioning figures, balances, projections for future income Catharine knew they already had the answers to. *How long had she financially supported Carlton? What had been the disparity in their incomes at the time of their marriage? Who had been the breadwinner throughout the years? Who had carried the responsibility for funding their lifestyle?* Questions, Catharine felt, any man worth his salt should have found humiliating—but when it came to seeking alimony, Carlton knew no shame.

But none of it was the driving purpose for the discovery. Catharine was well aware the South Carolina counselor was merely flexing his legal muscles before he got to the reason for calling her in.

Several hours into the procedure, they took a break, the attorney jesting that it was no doubt past their time for High Tea.

"I do not think that means what you think it does, Mr. Alden," Elle said on her way out the door, Catharine close on her heels.

In the break room, Elle poured them both a mug of black coffee as Catharine glanced through the notifications on her phone. Three missed calls from Nathalie, with three new voicemails in her inbox.

She'd have expected the deposition to be over by now. She'd want the details.

Catharine swiped the notifications away. She could get her drama fix from Elle, who Catharine was certain paid little mind to client confidentiality when it came to the pillow talk the two women shared.

"How are you faring?" It was the closest thing to Elle showing a modicum of sympathy for the grueling hours of questions Catharine had endured.

Catharine accepted the coffee. "Fine."

"Is there anything I can get you ladies?" Mr. Alden poked his head in through the glass doors, where he and Carlton had been chatting in the hall, flanked by a pair of men in suits.

They were secret service agents, Catharine realized. Gone were her husband's two-bit private security details and mall cop bodyguards. In were the stone-faced officers with their concealed firearms and flashing eyes, ready to lay their lives on the line. It would be a dream come true for Carlton; 24/7 protection with the full weight of the US government in his corner.

At least it was one less bill she'd have to pay.

Above them, on the overhead flat screen, someone had switched on the channel airing the US Women's National Team match underway in Chicago. It was thirty minutes into the game. Knowing it had not been turned on inadvertently, Catharine tried to pay it no mind.

"We have all that we need," said Elle shortly, annoyed by the intrusion.

"We've got sandwiches. Salads. Cookies—what do you call those? Biscuits?" he laughed. "I suppose you wouldn't want gravy on those." He rambled on until Catharine gave in to the temptation to glance over his shoulder at the TV, noting the score was 1-0.

"Should I postpone our plans to reconvene, Mrs. Cleveland? Perhaps you'd care to stay and watch the game?"

"I am ready when you are, Mr. Alden." Catharine did not return her gaze to the screen.

"I wouldn't want you distracted, Mrs. Cleveland. After all—"

"Let's get on with it, shall we?" Elle pushed her way past him, brushing through the pair of Secret Service agents and into the conference room.

Once the video camera was recording and they'd all resumed their seats, Jim Alden spent a few minutes browsing through his notes before looking up, putting on a show of surprise that all eyes were on him.

"Oh, we're all here. Let's see, where were we?" He shuffled his papers, stacking them in front of him, and rose. "Mrs. Cleveland, I realize your counsel may be unfamiliar with our procedures here in South Carolina, but has she made you aware of the four qualifications this state recognizes for fault-based divorce?"

"Objection," droned Elle, unbothered by his dig, "privilege."

"You just enjoy objecting to object, don't you, Ms. Kirkland?"

Elle stared back at him, impassive. "Objection, argumentative."

Mr. Alden laughed, a full, throaty, deep-barreled guffaw that made Catharine's jaw tense. She had no trouble understanding why Carlton had chosen him. The pair shared countless despicable attributes.

"Mrs. Cleveland," the man continued once he'd regained his breath, "are you familiar with the term fault-based divorce?"

"Yes." Elle had prepared her for this. This was what she'd been dragged across the Atlantic for.

"Peachy." He strode across to his whiteboard and uncapped a marker. "Mrs. Cleveland, please accept my apology in advance for this next line of questioning. I realize these proceedings can feel like a personal violation. This isn't a part I particularly enjoy."

Catharine doubted that very much.

He reached up and drew a rudimentary sad face on the surface of the whiteboard, followed by two stick figures; presumably a man and a woman.

Out of the corner of her eye, Catharine watched as Elle opened her mouth, then closed it, then opened it again, disbelief strewn across her expression. It took little imagination to guess that the barrister had never experienced the condescending level of unprofessionalism the good-old-boy American lawyer exhibited.

In the end, the University of Cambridge-educated Queen's Counsel barrister sat back and said nothing.

"Have you slept with other men besides your husband, Mrs. Cleveland?"

"No."

"Never?" The coarse patches of peppered grey hair met as he knit his brows together.

"Objection—" Elle started, before the attorney cut her off.

"Yes yes, asked and answered." He drew a line through the stick figure of the man, then tapped the woman with the end of the marker. "How about women?" He drew the three words out, every vowel elongated.

"Is there a question in there, Mr. Alden?" Elle's nails drilled into the table.

"Have you had sexual intercourse—er, sexual *relations*, I guess would be more fitting—with women, Mrs. Cleveland?"

"Yes." Catharine held his gaze. If there was one thing she refused to lose throughout this process, it was her dignity.

"More than one?"

"Yes."

He conveniently did not ask her how many, intentionally disallowing her the opportunity to clarify the answer was two.

"At any point throughout your marriage did you enter into a sexual relationship with any person other than Senator Cleveland?"

For the first time, Catharine hesitated. "We had already separated."

"That was not the question, Mrs. Cleveland." He circled the crudely drawn figure of a woman on the board before turning back to face the room, clearly enjoying his own performance. "Has there been any period of time throughout your marriage that you engaged in sexual activities with someone other than your husband? Yes or no, Mrs. Cleveland?" He tossed the marker into its holding tray. "I should take this time to remind you that this is a deposition in a legal proceeding. You gave an oath to tell the truth under the penalty of perjury."

"Yes."

"Please clarify the answer, Mrs. Cleveland."

"Yes, I was involved in a relationship whilst still legally wed to Carlton Cleveland."

"*Was*, Mrs. Cleveland? Indicating you are no longer?"

"*Am*." Catharine could feel her temper heating. "I *am* in a relationship after nearly two years of separation from my husband."

"If only we could adjust the laws of heaven to suit our lustful urges on earth—it would certainly make my job a lot easier."

Catharine laughed, disbelieving, shaking her head.

"Is there something you find amusing about adultery, Mrs. Cleveland?"

"Only that you mean to pin it on me," she said, looking directly at Carlton. That he could sit there, smug, self-righteous, while every person in the room knew who he was—*what* he was. A man who'd been accused of sexual assault more times than she could recall, yet never officially charged. A senator who had made the "Creep List" on Capitol Hill, an unofficial warning passed by word of mouth from female staffers. A candidate who had slept with his own colleagues wives, yet still managed to win their vote when it came to supporting their party.

And yet she was the one to blame. She was the one receiving the wag of his finger, even as he held out the opposite palm for a handout.

"Does the name Alex Grey mean anything to you?"

"Form—"

He rephrased, responding to Elle with a patronizing smile. "Mrs. Cleveland, are you familiar with Alex Grey?"

"Yes."

"In what capacity?"

"I'm sure you're a subscriber to the *Wall Street Journal*," said Catharine, referencing the front page photo the conservative paper had run of her kissing Alex after the World Cup win.

"Mrs. Cleveland, at any point during your marriage did you engage in sexual acts with Alex Grey—"

"Objection to form, privacy—"

"Relevance to the timeline. Please answer the question, Mrs. Cleveland."

"Yes."

"And when did this *relationship*," he struggled with the word, as if it were a foreign concept, "with Miss Grey begin?"

"I am uncertain of the day."

"I doubt that," he muttered under his breath, shooting a look at the court reporter. "In your best estimation," he projected, back on the record, "how long ago would you say your involvement with Alex Grey began?"

"Two years ago, March."

"You've indicated you were separated from Senator Cleveland, yet you did not file for divorce until May of last year."

"I'm sorry," said Catharine, "was that a question, Mr. Alden?"

"You began your sexual engagement with Alex Grey over a year before you filed for divorce, is that correct?"

"I informed my husband of my desire to divorce many months before my involvement began with Alex."

"Yet you did not file."

"I made an agreement with Carlton to delay filing until the primaries were concluded. I did not wish to damage his campaign." By the subtle disappearance of Elle's lower lip, she knew she'd volunteered too much information.

"I see," said the attorney, resuming his chair, flipping casually through a handful of papers. "And yet you *did* end up filing months before the primaries—an event which was turned into a media circus. Are you in the habit of going back on your word, Mrs. Cleveland?"

"Do not answer that, Catharine." Elle dropped her elbows onto the table, the tension in her forearms betraying her anger. "Mr. Alden, your client made threats against his wife, her company, her employees, and Alex Grey—all of which she had to assume were with intent, given his previous history of violence. She wasn't about to stick around and put herself in the position to be on the receiving end of another one of his beatings."

"You little—" Carlton began, hurling the words at Elle, but was silenced by the heavy hand Jim Alden dropped on his shoulder.

"You can save your hearsay for the judge to handle, Ms. Kirkland," the attorney dismissed her with the contempt of his composure. "But since you brought up the subject—it's been well-established that on the night in question, my client was at no point alone with his wife, as his security detail was always with him. In fact—the only person the hotel staff saw entering or exiting Mrs. Cleveland's room alone was none other than Miss Grey."

"That is only because I did not think to pay off the staff to omit her presence as my husband did his," Catharine snapped, staring at Carlton.

"Do you make a habit of resorting to bribery often, Mrs. Cleveland?"

Catharine's pulse quickened, the top button of her blouse suddenly restricting. Had her father said something?

She decided he was grasping at straws. He had nothing.

"I do not."

"Not often? Or not ever?"

"I am not in the habit of resorting to bribery."

He jotted a note in the margin of one of his papers. "Earlier this year did you not offer to buy Senator Cleveland's silence in an effort to cease his lawful right to express his sentiments about Miss Grey on Twitter? *'What's it going to take for you to leave her alone?'* Is that not something you said?" He flipped through his notes. *"'What's your price, Carlton?'* Shall I read to you the definition of bribery?"

"Objection to the form!"

"Object all you want, Ms. Kirkland." He winked at her. "We're almost done here." Sitting back, the attorney picked a crumb off his cashmere suit jacket, and flicked it onto the table. "Do you have any history of mental health issues, Mrs. Cleveland?"

"What?" Catharine's shock beat Elle to whatever form of objection she'd been planning. "No."

"On the day you met Miss Grey, had you not tried to drown yourself off the coast of Daufuskie Island?"

"I—" Catharine laughed, incredulous. "That's preposterous."

"That is how you met Miss Grey, however, is it not? Unconscious in the water?" He didn't wait for an answer, forgoing the propriety of the deposition. "It seems odd, a capable sailor such as yourself, nearly drowning a quarter mile from shore, while your husband entertained guests in your garden."

"It was nothing more than an accident."

"Noted." He made no move to write down anything. "I have only a few more questions, Mrs. Cleveland. Do you need a glass of water?"

"I'd prefer we finish."

"I do appreciate a woman with your kind of stamina." He smiled to cover his innuendo. "Thank you for your perseverance, Mrs. Cleveland. In that case," he leaned forward, collecting his notebook, "let's get down to it. Is it true you recently sold your shares in Brooks Corporation?"

"Yes."

"And the money earned from that sale—where is it now?"

"In my trust."

"And who put it there, Mrs. Cleveland?"

"I did."

"I see." He scribbled what looked little more than a doodle on the bottom of the page. "Did you inform Senator Cleveland about the sale of your stock?"

"I did not."

Another scribble. "Was the senator aware of the funds transferred into your trust?"

Elle rapped a knuckle to the table, her bangles clattering against one another. "Objection, speculation—my client cannot guess what your client does and does not know."

"Did *you* tell Senator Cleveland you were transferring the funds from the sale of your corporation into your trust?"

"He is not a beneficiary on the trust, nor has he ever been."

"That was not the question, Mrs. Cleveland. When you sold your company, did you tell your husband where you were depositing the profits of the sale?"

"No. I did not."

"Thank you, Mrs. Cleveland." He tapped his pen against his notebook, sending a splattering of ink across the open page, going out of his way to draw Catharine's attention to his scribbles.

CHECKMATE he'd written in all caps, triple underlining the word. Once he was certain she had read it, he scooped up the tablet, popping to his feet faster than a man his size should have been capable. "Your time has been appreciated, Mrs. Cleveland. Ms. Kirkland." He doffed an imaginary hat. "We're all done here."

Catharine waited in the lobby overlooking Citadel Square Church as Elle remained in the conference room to discuss details of the handling of the transcript.

She could feel Carlton's presence a breath before he defiled the space with his raucous laugh, parading into the room with his posse in tow.

"Stellar," he barked at his assistant, Matthew, who looked as stressed and enervated as ever. "Get Congressman Johnson on the line—tell him to meet us at Halls. We can't come this far into Charleston without stopping for that braised quail I'm so fond of."

"Sir, Halls requires advanced reservation—" he cut himself off beneath the sear of the senator's glare. "I'll see what I can do, sir."

Carlton gave him no acknowledgement as he fished a handkerchief from the breast pocket of his jacket. "You're too thin, Catharine," he criticized, dabbing at the sheen of moisture beneath his nose as he turned his sights on her. "You should join us for dinner—have one of those famous key lime pies—for old times' sake."

Catharine was saved from the necessity of a response by the buzzing of her phone. Again, it was Nathalie.

She would have sent her to voicemail, delayed calling her back until she reached the privacy of her hotel, but given the options of being stuck in forced conversation with Carlton or answering the call, she opted for the latter.

"Nat—"

Before she'd managed another word, she was met with a flurry of hysterics, Nathalie shouting in French in such a frenzy Catharine could barely understand her.

Feu. Dégâts. Pompier. Fire. Damages. Firefighters.

"Nathalie, slow down," Catharine demanded, cupping her hand to her opposite ear to try and drown out the chatter of Carlton's entourage. "What's going on?"

"Have you listened to none of my messages?" the Frenchwoman screamed, on the brink of tears.

"I just got out of the deposition—"

"It's gone!"

"What is?"

"My theatre!"

"Nathalie! What are you talking about?" Catharine pushed her way through the half dozen men orbiting her husband and found her way to the hall. "What is going on?"

"It burned! It's completely destroyed!" The tears had finally won out, the words muffled through a garbled sob on the other end of the line. Catharine could make out the sounds of traffic, the city alive in the background.

"There was a fire?" Catharine wasn't sure she understood. "Is everyone all right?"

"I wasn't here—the theatre was empty. We finished rehearsals at noon."

Catharine was still reeling too much from the unexpectedness of the situation to find much relief. "Do they know how it started?"

"There's too much damage. They think it started near the front." Beginning to get a hold of herself, Nathalie let out a shaky breath. "They said it could be weeks before they know."

"And it's—it's gone?" Catharine was hoping her friend was being dramatic. That it was a small ordeal, a little smoke, nothing more.

"Destroyed." The waver to the word brought tears anew. "They said with how hot it burned—how fast it happened—an accelerant must have been used."

"An accelerant?" After hours of questioning with her nerves on high, Catharine felt slow to comprehend. "They think this was intentional?"

"I don't know! Jesus, Cate! I don't know what happened. Can you just come home?"

"I—" Catharine could hardly remember what day it was, let alone where she was meant to be next. "I'll—yes. Let me talk to Elle. I'll be on a flight tonight."

When she hung up, she turned to find Carlton had followed her into the hall. He stood, a hand propped against the textured wall, watching her.

"Something wrong, my dear?" His eyes were hooded beneath his heavy lids, a simpering smile playing at the corners of his lips. She knew that look. She'd seen it throughout his career. It was one he reserved for when he'd completely fucked someone over. One he liked to employ while they were still unaware. One she'd seen on him when he'd reneged his support in the eleventh hour of a legislative proposal he'd sworn to uphold. One he'd worn while standing in their garden in Daufuskie, drinking shandies with the Speaker of the House, while the man didn't realize Carlton had orchestrated a coup to oust him from his chair. Or a favorite of his when he found himself the deciding vote on an adversary's battle to get a bill to pass the floor.

Yes, she knew the look, and in that second, knew exactly what it held.

"Nathalie, I presume?" He made no effort to hide his growing pleasure, emboldened by their isolation in the hall. "How is my favorite cadger? Still leeching off your tit, no doubt."

"You did this," she said, and wasn't sure why she found herself so full of disbelief.

"Has something happened?" He righted himself from where he was leaning and folded his arms. "I'm afraid I'm a little behind the times, given I've been tied up here with you all day."

"You think you're so untouchable." Catharine felt like her mouth was full of sand. The way he looked at her. The confidence. The composure. The certitude of his impunity.

"Think?" he laughed. "My dear, can you really be so obtuse?"

She went to step past him, back to the lobby, but before she'd made it to the threshold, he grabbed her arm.

"You listen to me, you little bitch," he hissed, crushing her forearm in his grip, "let this be a reminder—"

"Step away from my client, Senator Cleveland." Elle appeared from the opposite end of the hall, where she'd come from the conference room. Without a particle of hesitation, the barrister strutted straight to Carlton, squaring up in front of him. "Lay a hand on her again and you'll be heading into Inauguration Day whilst sitting on a restraining order and saddled with charges of assault." Her voice, assertive, amplified into the lobby, catching the attention of his waiting parade of fools. He backed away, aware of his growing audience.

"You heard me, Catharine," he hissed between clenched teeth, his shoulder colliding with hers as he ambled in the direction of his security detail, "you've been warned." Pausing in the threshold, he turned back, offering her a greasy smile. "Take care of yourself, Catharine," he sang loudly, a show for the entirety of the floor. "I'll be praying for you, dear."

Chapter Thirty-Three

Alex's cheeks ached from smiling for photo, after photo, after photo. From the moment she'd arrived at the hotel in Paris, to the hours-long makeup session, and bus ride to the Théâtre du Châtelet, she'd obediently posed, smiled, answered journalists' questions, posed, smiled, walked down the red carpet through a burst of cameras flashing, posed, smiled, sat in the front row of the awards ceremony, and then been forced to smile some more as Kelsey Evans took the stage to receive the Ballon d'Or.

Her disappointment for herself had been minimal. Of course, it was only human to have held onto a sliver of hope that she'd done enough to warrant hoisting football's most illustrious award. It was the most coveted individual title of every athlete who laced on cleats. But even though her year had held the highest of highs with the World Cup win, it had also come with the lowest of lows. Her preseason red card expulsion and crashing defeat after missing her PK in the NWSL championship would be analyzed, and she knew it was the latter that was most likely to be the most recent memory on the voters' minds.

And it was okay. The mere fact that she'd not only made top ten —narrowed down from the initial shortlist of thirty—but actually come in third place amongst the best footballers in the world, had felt like enough. It had been an honor to get the nomination. To find her name on the lips of journalists across the globe. To know she'd been in true contention to actually win the Ballon d'Or.

But there was another, she felt, who *had* done enough. Who truly earned the right to be called The Greatest Footballer in the World. And her heart had broken for Amelia Walker when Kelsey Evans' name was called to the podium.

The Australian was the only player to have been nominated for the award every year since its inception into the women's side of the game six years earlier. In turn, she was the only athlete with the unfortunate record to hold six top-five finishes, always just shy of claiming the trophy. It was an injustice, this year's second place finish—her third time coming runner-up—and though she sat attentive in the audience, clapping for Kelsey at all the appropriate moments, Alex could tell the snub had not come without a sting. This was Amelia's year. She'd captained her team to a World Cup Final. Won FIFA Best. The Golden Ball. Dominated not only one, but two club leagues. There wasn't a better player on the planet. And still, the accolade eluded her.

She'd lost by only a handful of votes.

"What'd you expect, Grey?" Amelia brushed off Alex's quiet condolence when she'd found a moment alone with her friend in the hall leading to the grand ballroom of the hotel hosting the after-party. "I mean, we both come from countries who still call it soccer."

Alex didn't dismiss the Australian's loss as casually. "You know, even Kelsey told Sawyer she knew you'd bested her this year."

"*This* year?" The shrewd green eyes shifted from where she'd been studying one of the statues adorning the hall—a caryatid supporting an entablature of gilded marble, the minimally clad figure stark against the scarlet tapestries lining the walls. "That sounds like her. As if it were a one-time affair." Amelia scoffed, but remained in good humor. "She'll be apples, Grey. I don't need a seven kilogram ball of plated gold to remind me I've outscored Kelsey Evans every year since she joined the WSL. I'll admit she did look hot tonight in that sequined number, though—so you can't blame *France Football* for wanting that photo on their cover."

"You hate sequins," Alex jabbed her beneath the black floral-printed suit jacket she'd unbuttoned since leaving the awards venue.

"It's not like there were enough of them to find objectionable. In fact," one side of Amelia's mouth turned up, her smile growing rakish, "between the two of you, if you sewed your gowns together, you might just have enough material to swath a small child. Infant, maybe." She flicked the exposed stone nipple of the marble sculpture in front of her. "You almost gave this ol' dame a run for her money."

"Oh, shut up," Alex rolled her eyes as heat singed her cheeks, her self-awareness having been on high all evening due to the extreme décolleté of the dress Nathalie'd pressed upon her. "You're such a twelve-year-old boy." She chastised the desecration of the centuries–old statue.

"Sticks and stones, Grey. Sticks and stones."

Amelia headed for the towering archway door where the warm lights of the glittering chandeliers lit the parade of mirrors circum-navigating the ballroom. It was a uniquely stunning visual, with its soaring dome and exquisite nineteenth-century detail, dripping in the excessive opulence of the Second Empire. She couldn't help but feel her father would have loved it—architecture of a time long past, when artists had leant their meticulous perfection to the awakening of a masterpiece.

Taking a moment in the threshold, Alex surveyed the room for Catharine. They'd not seen each other since the morning Alex left for training camp two weeks earlier.

She'd been waylaid in the states. First, by the tragedy of Nathalie's theatre. An act, Alex had read in the *Bay Times*, blamed on the growing vandalism of San Francisco's downtown districts. Catharine had been less forthcoming on the situation, saying only that it was under an active arson investigation, and she had to stay a few extra days to deal with insurance. And then, on the morning she was meant to fly back to London—where Alex had already arrived—leaked statements from her deposition had turned up in the media. Cherry-picked details intended to smear Catharine's public image, the intent obvious to exalt and exonerate Carlton prior to his inauguration. Quotes were printed painting Catharine as a serial adulterer, a villainous money launderer, a woman of unstable mental health with a grievous vendetta against her distin-guished husband. It had come as a severe blow to her impending divorce trial. A maneuver Elle immediately moved to parry with gag order filings against Carlton's counsel, but one that kept her delayed all the same.

But even with it all, she'd made it to Paris. And despite Alex having been detained by interviews and photos and the pre-and-post ceremony socializing that had come as an obligation with her nomination, she'd known Catharine was in the audience. That she'd come to support her. That she'd be there waiting for her in the magnificent French ballroom.

She scanned the scene that lay before her. Glamor. Luxury. Affluence and influence. All of it swirling across the room with an electric vigor. With the official ceremony for the Ballon d'Or over, the highest profile athletes had made their way to the exclusive after-party—the *real* event, Sam Huntley had emphasized—where the crowds had mixed, the footballers interspersing amongst celebrities, captains of industry, even European royalty descended from the blood of families extending back through the millennia.

"Getting to be your regular scene, eh, Grey?" Amelia teased, keen to her sudden reluctance to enter the fray. "Hobnobbing with the lush and loaded."

"I'd prefer the pajama-clad and placid," Alex countered, searching the sea of faces, yet still coming up short of the one she sought. "I've still got a full season of *The Witcher* to catch up on before preseason starts."

"Yeah, well, Netflix and Chill isn't on your calendar. That's not how being the face of *Nike*-Poster-Girl-All-American-Soccer-Star Alex Grey works, mate. You should know that by now." Amelia took her elbow, steering her onto the parquet floor—the same floor, Alex considered absently, that Napoleon III had once tread upon.

Scanning the room, the Australian's gaze landed on the center of the dance platform, where the flash of Kelsey Evans' sequined strapless gown caught the reflection of the overhead chandelier, turning her into a living, breathing disco ball.

The leggy blonde was surrounded by a gaggle of admirers fawning over her every move, but the English striker appeared blissfully unaware of the audience she had gathered. Instead, her focus was honed only on the woman in front of her, matching every shake of her hips, every twist of her torso, their silhouettes swinging to the techno beat of *Take My Chance* humming off the golden walls.

It was Sawyer, resplendent in burgundy, her gorgeous hair left loose, cascading in a crescent of dark ringlets flowing across her shoulders. She was laughing, her entire being radiating her joy of the evening.

"I guess the *hush hush* part of that relationship was short lived," Amelia commented, the two of them watching as Kelsey's hands found their way to Sawyer's backside, the previous song ending and the synthetic strains of *I Need Your Body* vibrating through the speakers. The pair ground against one another to the suggestion of the lyrics, blissfully lost in their champagne-induced oblivion.

By morning, the couple would be the online football community's latest *TikTok* obsession.

"Excuse me?" Alex turned toward the voice, finding herself looking up into the sculpted face of an extremely tall, extremely handsome woman. Her black hair was cut short into a side-parted pixie, the ends frosted an incandescent blue. She looked very chic, and very modish, and though Alex was certain she had never met her, there was a familiarity to her features.

"It's nice to finally meet you, Alex." She held out her hand, her long nails exaggerating the lean dexterity of her slender fingers. Her voice was smooth, the annunciation bordering on affected, as if she were putting on a performance. "I'm a big fan."

"Thank you." Alex shook her hand, desperately trying to place her face, and where she'd seen it before. It was obvious she was expected to recognize her without introduction.

"You were bonzer in that last *Marvel* film," Amelia supplied, throwing a lifeline to Alex's floundering. "Supermodel turned superhero—not a bad transition."

Xia Wen. Alex mentally kicked herself for not making the connection. She loved her work. She'd seen at least a dozen of her movies. Her face was currently plastered all over the billboards, the overground carriage cars, the train stations, advertising her current role as the newest Avenger.

The model-turned-actress gave Amelia nothing more than a passing glance with her onyx eyes, her interest solely invested in Alex. "You should have won tonight. I am inclined to give Matteo Giordano a piece of my mind."

Alex laughed, as equally flattered as she was embarrassed. It wasn't every day the woman who'd won an Academy for playing Wu Zhao—the first and only female emperor of China—threatened to go to battle on her behalf with the President of FIFA. She didn't have the heart to tell her FIFA had nothing to do with the Ballon d'Or.

"I'm honored you feel that way, Miss Wen."

"I only state fact. You were done an injustice."

Out of the line of sight of Xia Wen, Amelia rolled her eyes. "Maybe we should start a movement? #justiceforalex?"

Before Alex could decide on how best to strangle her friend without causing a scene, a hand was placed on her arm and another voice—this time familiar—spoke close to her ear.

"I'm sorry to interrupt, Miss Grey—but I simply cannot wait a moment longer to tell you how stunning you look tonight."

Alex turned quickly enough to threaten her balance atop the staggering height of her lace-up stilettos—her *fuck me heels*, Sawyer had dubbed them—and forgoing what was probably proper etiquette for being in the middle of a conversation with a movie star, wrapped her arms around Catharine.

"I've missed you," she whispered against her cheek, breathing in her presence. "Thank you for making it here—after everything."

"I would never have missed it." Catharine kissed the corner of her mouth, before gently extracting herself from Alex's embrace as she commenced her own good manners and redirected the conversation to Xia Wen. "Please, forgive my interruption."

The actress turned up her chin, elongating her graceful neck, and peered down at Catharine from her impressive height—a feat which wasn't easy, given Catharine's own imposing stature.

Xia paid her more mind than she had Amelia, making no effort to hide the critical sweep of her head-to-toe assessment. It wasn't an appreciative glance, as so many did upon meeting Catharine. There was no lascivity to her appraisal, but instead the haughty evaluation from one beautiful woman to another.

"If you don't mind...?" Her articulation grew even more pronounced, an effort to match the posh tone of Catharine's accent. "We were in the middle of a conversation."

"By all means," Catharine made no effort to step aside, her hand falling from Alex's forearm to find a place at the small of her back, "please continue."

Xia's shrewd eyes followed the path of her hand, noting its intimate comfort against Alex's bare skin, and looked up with a close-lipped smile. "I see. You must be the girlfriend." The coolness of her demeanor did not falter as she slid her eyes to Alex. "I'd heard rumor you were attached. Well, I'm glad your date is here. It eases my conscience asking you to dance. I'm certain she won't mind, will she?" It was a challenge flung in Catharine's direction.

Alex wanted to laugh at the absurdity of the situation. Was this woman—this famous, gorgeous, silver screen queen—really picking a pissing match over her with Catharine? In the heart of Paris? In a centuries–old ballroom? At an after-party for the Ballon d'Or?

Whose life was this, really?

One look at Amelia's arched brows and curled lip assured her she hadn't misinterpreted the burgeoning contest between the two glamorous women.

"Gag me with a spoon," the Australian lipped to her, swiping a flute of champagne off the tray of a passing server and disappearing into the throng of bodies milling around them.

Alex mustered an apologetic smile. "As much as I'd love to, Miss Wen, I'm afraid my lack of talent for grace would put everyone at risk on the dance floor."

"Rest assured, I am skilled at making anyone look a natural. Come," she held out her hand, her heart-shaped lips pursed in her simper, "allow me to show you the perfect dancing partner."

Before Alex could again decline, Catharine said something in what Alex could only guess was Mandarin.

Xia Wen's head snapped up, her smile pinching into a tight line. Her eyes locked on Catharine, she responded curtly, and was given a brusque reply, before her hand—frozen in midair—dropped to her side.

"Well, I am afraid my time is short, and I am sought elsewhere," she sniffed, looking down the line of her nose, having regained some of her dignity. "It was a pleasure to meet you, Alex."

Without waiting for a response, she pivoted on her heels, and waltzed across the room to where a man in a purple suit abandoned his conversation with the Count of Paris to devote to her his whole attention.

"I…" Alex laughed, finding the hand Catharine pressed against the bare skin of her back, intertwining their fingers. "Do I even want to know what just happened?"

"I'm afraid my tolerance for impertinence is at an all time minimum."

"What did you say to her?"

"I simply asked what sort of dancing partner she was seeking: horizontal or vertical?"

"And she said?" Alex raised an eyebrow.

"Something along the lines of 'what's it to you, old woman?'"

"She didn't!" Alex covered her gaping mouth to hide her smile. "I'm never going to be able to watch one of her films again. What did you say to that?"

"There's an old Chinese proverb: *when on a tiger's back, it is hard to dismount*. It essentially means—"

"—the American equivalent of *fuck around and find out*?"

Catharine's laughter was rich, the timber of a harbor bell. "Yes. I imagine that is a fair translation."

Alex reached up to adjust the single asymmetrical strap crossing Catharine's shoulder. It needed no adjusting. She wore the midnight blue of her satin gown with effortless perfection. But Alex wanted to touch her. To run her fingertips along the groove just above her clavicle, aware people were watching. It was the first public event they'd been to together. The first time they'd attended anything as a couple. It was unbridling. Liberating. Cathartic. To know they would be photographed. To know they would be talked about. And to no longer care.

"Why, Catharine Brooks," she teased, giving a gentle tug on her pearl earring, "I do believe you're jealous."

"Incurably so."

"Oh, I think I can find a cure." Alex held her gaze, provoking her with a slow, alluring smile.

"Do you, now?" Catharine elevated what was meant to be a lofty brow, but was not entirely successful at maintaining the mastery of her nonchalance. "And what, pray tell, might that be?"

"I *could* tell you," Alex trailed a knuckle down her arm, drawing goosebumps in its wake, "but it would be so much more fun to show you."

It never ceased to thrill her—the effect she had on this woman. The way this woman affected her in return. Even jostled amongst hundreds of people, surrounded by the insistent drumming of a techno beat, she could feel the increase of the pulse at Catharine's wrist, hear the subtle halt of her breath, sense the magnetic current that ran between them.

Catharine stepped closer to allow a tuxedoed waiter to pass with a tray of hors d'oeuvres, taking the opportunity to whisper in her ear. "Come upstairs with me."

How badly Alex wanted to kiss her. To abandon the party, disappear from the spotlight. Find themselves alone.

But there were people she needed to see. Faces she had to put on. The party was work as much as it was pleasure, and an immediate exit after her arrival wouldn't show well.

It didn't, however, mean she couldn't find a way to amuse herself while waiting for the minutes to dwindle down.

"Such a hurry, Ms. Brooks. Whatever is the rush?" She stepped back, taunting, just out of reach. "What if I said I wanted to dance first—with Xia Wen—since she asked me so nicely?"

"Well," Catharine's eyes ignited with the challenge, "I could always go alone."

Alex smiled over her shoulder as she headed to the dance floor. "Ten bucks says you'll wait for me."

Through the windows of the corner suite, an incandescent light radiated off the rooftop of the Opéra Garnier. Above it, clutching his golden lyre, the copper statue of Apollo kept sentry over the heartbeat of Paris.

Alex would have appreciated the unstinting decorative details of the majestic building. The eclectic ornamentation. The heavily bracketed cornices, ornate balustrades, and symmetrical quoins. She would have been mesmerized by the glittering view of the River Seine from the master bedroom—had they made it that far.

Instead, the luxury of the sprawling suite was lost on her, fading to a blur of white and beige. She was tipsy—a conservative assessment—reeling with armagnac and French champagne. But it wasn't the alcohol that made her head spin, or the grandeur of the penthouse rooms that stole her breath away.

She'd kissed Catharine in the elevator as soon as the doors had closed on the lavish foyer, and kissed her again on the way to their room, uncaring of the woman wrapped in mink who'd gawked at them in the hall. And Catharine had kissed her back. Kissed her until she was dizzy. Kissed her until she could think of nothing else besides getting behind closed doors.

They were half undressed before the tile of the vestibule had transitioned to the plush carpet of the living room, grappling with silk and lace and satin. One heel on, an earring missing, a zipper caught between shoulder blades.

"Shit," swore Alex, laughing after she'd pried the offending fastener on Catharine's dress free, and pulled her into the darkened room, stumbling backward onto the cushioned alcove of the bay window. Catching Catharine's hands, she dragged her down with her.

"You are irredeemable." Catharine's smile neutralized the admonishment.

"You're only saying that because you owe me ten dollars." Alex laid back on the narrow recess, reaching up to trace a line from her ear to the corner of her mouth.

"You could hardly expect me to leave you there with Xia Wen draping herself all over you." Catharine's hands worked their way up her calves, easing her legs apart as she settled to kneel between them.

"Oh please," droned Alex, "it was one dance. Like I said: you're jealous." Her jesting reproof dwindled into a sharp intake of breath as Catharine's fingers continued on their upward path.

"A fact we've unequivocally established. And, if memory serves me correctly—a malaise you promised to rectify."

Alex's ability to return a sensible response was assailed by the brush of fingertips—soft, gentle.

Too soft. Too gentle.

She lifted her hips, reaching for Catharine, intent to draw her closer, to find more of her, to ease the desperate need she felt, but before she'd found her hand, Catharine sat up straighter, pulling away further, and laughed.

"Such a hurry, Miss Grey. Whatever is the rush?"

Alex's body slumped deeper into the silk upholstery. "You're evil," she muttered, slinging an arm across her eyes in defeat. "You've been waiting to use that against me all night."

"Just deserts." The smirk to Catharine's tone was unmistakable as her hands continued to dally. "You're a tough girl—I'm sure you can take what you dish out."

Alex dropped her head back against the hard wood of the alcove joist.

All night she'd teased Catharine. Dancing with Sawyer. With Kelsey. With Kylian Mbappé, and the head coach of PSG. When she'd danced with Xia, she'd never taken her eyes off Catharine, ever aware of her return gaze. Their hands had brushed in passing while Catharine was held captive to small talk with the wife of the Prime Minister of Spain, and when Alex had been cornered by the manager of Barcelona Femení—dead set on trying to get her to join his team—Alex had surreptitiously tapped out an inappropriate text while the man pontificated the benefits of the chance to play in Champions League. The entire evening had gone on as such, in between glasses of champagne. Glances. Touches. Discreetly whispered suggestions on how their night might be better spent when they finally escaped.

And now, with Alex at her mercy, Catharine had seized control of the game.

Brushing her thumbs along the tender backside of Alex's knees, she leaned to kiss her belly. "Who the hell does she think she is, anyway? A supermodel? Oscar-winning actress? Daughter of Guo Wen, famed *Global 500* financier?"

Alex laughed, despite her efforts not to writhe when Catharine trailed her fingers down the ticklish groove of her ribcage. "Oh, it's that last thing that gets to you, isn't it? Here I thought you held a grudge against her for relegating you to the lowly title of '*the girlfriend.*'"

"*That* title," Catharine's lips grazed her breasts, "is a promotion. Her father, on the other hand, is a clever, corrupt bastard…"

"Can we *not* talk about Xia Wen's father?"

"I suppose we can table the talk of illicit hidden revenue corporate structures until later." Despite her teasing, Catharine's voice grew headier as she drew one of Alex's bent legs around her waist.

Alex couldn't respond. Aching with anticipation, her arm still shielding her face, she waited. Waited as Catharine's fingertips drew an agonizingly slow map across her body, leaving no twist or turn unexplored. Waited as her lips skimmed a path with chaste leisure, from shoulder to palm, hip to the arch of her foot. And then her touch withdrew all together, the suite ebbing into silence.

"What are you doing?" It came out no more than a whisper as Alex opened her eyes to peek out into the faint glow of darkness. Catharine was sitting up, her silhouette haloed by the dim lights of the opera house shining through the window. She was watching her in that way she had—regarding her as if she could see straight to her core.

"Why are you staring at me like that?" Alex laughed, growing self-conscious beneath the intensity of her gaze. She grabbed for her hand, wanting to pull her to her, to kiss her, to feel the weight of her body against hers, but again Catharine leaned back, remaining just out of reach.

"How could I not stare at you?" Her voice was low, intoxicating, as equally arousing as the consummate sweep of her eyes that studied her from head to toe. How a simple glance from her could make Alex feel like the most beautiful woman in the world, she would never understand.

Without another word, Catharine bent to her, and in the absence of her idling, Alex had to press her palms against the windowpane, centering herself by the chill of the glass. She had to convince herself to breathe, her body shivering as Catharine led her to the precipice, and then held her there, but didn't let her fall.

And when at last—with her desire nearly blinding—she could take no more, Catharine released her, allowing her to plummet over the ledge. To spin. To float. To fade into the burning lights of the Paris skyline, beneath the watchful gaze of the statues of Harmony and Poetry atop the Opéra Garnier.

Muted light from the overcast morning spilled through the window onto the linen duvet. Alex blinked at the unfamiliar ceiling, before squeezing her eyes closed, trying to judge the intensity of the pressure threatening behind her forehead. It was dull. Nagging. But nothing worse than she deserved. The result of a night of overindulging on champagne on a day where a single banana was all she'd remembered to eat.

Her feet, on the other hand... She winced as she stretched, taking stock of the pain. Her toes felt blistered, her arches throbbing. The consequences, she lamented, of dancing in heels intended for a journey no longer than the traipse down a catwalk. But it was a marvel, really, that she'd survived the evening without breaking an ankle. So she'd chalk off bruised soles in exchange for bruised pride, and consider the night a win. And perhaps make a mental note to leave the *fuck me* stilettos behind for the next red carpet ceremony.

But they'd served their purpose, hadn't they?

The thought brought her full circle to the morning, and once again she gingerly opened her eyes, smiling when she found Catharine sitting up beside her. There was another ache, a subtle ache, accompanying her growing consciousness, and as fragments of her night replayed, Alex briefly wondered if it was possible for a heart to ache of happiness?

"Good morning." Her voice was hoarse and full of sleep, underscoring how little of it she'd actually gotten. A worthy repercussion. One she'd gladly repeat again.

Catharine's fingers stilled on the keyboard of her laptop as her attention shifted from the screen.

"Good afternoon."

"It isn't that late!" Alex checked the window for any tells from the sun, but found only clouds settled across the beauty of the city.

Snapping the computer shut, Catharine slid it to her nightstand. Her fair hair was damp from her shower, tied up into a mussed bun, and she'd pulled on a t-shirt Alex recognized as her own.

Following her gaze, Catharine ran her thumb across the *Nike* logo. "I hope you don't mind? Without the time to stop in London, my wardrobe options this morning were limited."

The corners of Alex's lips turned up into a sly smile as she dwelled on the implication of the word *limited* and what that may have entailed. She propped herself into a sitting position. "Just don't let the *Nike* reps see you in it. They'd be bound to sign you instead."

"Ha," Catharine scoffed, her fingers trailing the curve of Alex's bicep. "Only if they want to narrow their market to middle-aged housewives everywhere."

"Shut up!" Alex laughed, though her thoughts strayed as Catharine's finger glided from her bicep, to her shoulder, to the base of her throat, and then down to her navel.

"You should do that cover they called you about," Catharine said.

"The *ESPN Body Edition*? God, no." Alex couldn't even think about it without feeling her cheeks go scarlet. Posing nude for a sports magazine was not in her future. Like, ever. No matter how tastefully it was done. No matter how many zeroes came with it.

"I guess I get to keep you all to myself, then," Catharine leaned over to kiss her. "Do you want to go out, or shall I order breakfast?"

Alex had to reel-in her thoughts from the trajectory of Catharine's fingertips to the sudden switch to room service. It hadn't been the first thing on her mind, but based off the alcohol-induced uneasiness of her empty stomach, she imagined Catharine's line of thinking was headed in the more appropriate direction. But the thought of getting dressed, of pulling on shoes, of leaving the luxury of the ridiculous comforts of the Parisienne penthouse, were out of the question.

"Let's order in. Wait," she paused, realizing Catharine had suggested breakfast. "I thought you said it was afternoon?"

"It's after nine—it may as well be."

"I bet you're fun at parties," Alex rolled her eyes, and upon seeing Catharine's confusion, rolled them even harder. "It's a phrase. Not literal. It means…" she shook her head. "Never mind."

"What?"

"It's just—a different generation."

"And what exactly is that supposed to mean?" Catharine took a playful swipe at Alex, who swung her legs over the side of the bed and tentatively climbed to her feet.

"I bet Xia Wen could tell you," she said over her shoulder, before launching herself for the safety of the ensuite, narrowly avoiding the throw pillow that whizzed past her onto the limestone tile.

Forty-five minutes later, showered—one cup of coffee down, a second in progress—Alex found Catharine on the window nook settee, and settled down beside her. Through the broad bow of glass, Place de l'Opéra unfolded into the streets of Paris, the River Seine snaking through the city in the background.

"I didn't realize you could see the Eiffel Tower from here." The iconic iron structure stood erect in the distance, framed—Alex realized as a threat of heat flushed up her neck—by two smudged palm prints on the windowpane.

"Oh?" said Catharine with contrived disinterest, not looking up from where she'd resumed work on her computer. "Too consumed with thoughts of Marvel superheroes?"

"Frosty," Alex laughed, forcing her way beneath Catharine's arm, interrupting her typing. "And a pop cultural reference to boot. Look at you, all hip with the times."

"I'll have you know that it was not your generation that invented Marvel Comics."

The idea of Catharine having ever picked up a comic, even in her youth, was unfathomable—but Alex decided to let that one go; she was in enough hot water.

"What are you working on?" Alex dropped her head onto her shoulder. The computer screen was sans its usual tables and columns of numbers. There were no stock market line charts, nomograms, or scatter plots. No endless list of emails or odd hours phone calls in languages Alex couldn't decipher. There hadn't been for a while now. It was mainly just Zoom meetings with her assistant, Nicole, or online banking portfolios viewed on encrypted browsers. Alex knew the idleness was maddening to her, as little as she spoke about it. Even the exploration of new nonprofits and analysis of potential charitable organizations didn't fill the void of the life she was missing.

"Research."

Alex turned her attention to the open tab, which Catharine didn't minimize. It was Reuters News Agency, and in the top corner of the screen was the National Women's Soccer League logo. Scanning the first lines in the paragraph, Alex realized it was an article on the process of NWSL expansions—the steps to add a team to the league.

She sat up, out from under Catharine's arm, still reading the story. When she'd finished everything she could see on the page, she turned to look at Catharine.

"Research for…?"

"Investment." Catharine was nonchalant.

"In…?" Alex prodded.

"Possible opportunities."

"*Catharine*," Alex goaded, trying to wrap her mind around the idea. "Are you honestly looking into…? I mean… Most teams historically don't make much money—"

"—only when they haven't been invested in properly. HEG turns a profit, for example."

"But, it's…" Alex didn't know how to put it another way. "Sports. That's not really your wheelhouse."

"*Women's* sports," Catharine clarified, "and believe it or not, cargo freighters and shipping containers were once not exactly my cup of tea, either. But I think I muddled through all right in the end. Besides," she closed the laptop, "this time I'd have an in-house specialist to help guide me."

Alex sat back against the cushions of the settee, the Eiffel Tower forgotten on the horizon. "Are you really serious about this?"

Catharine's delayed response was answer enough.

"How long have you been looking into it?"

"I'd browsed the possibilities last year—but in earnest? The last month or so."

"You didn't say anything."

Catharine drummed her fingers on the case above the Apple logo. "I wanted to see how logistically feasible the idea was first."

"And?"

"It's feasible. With your blessing, I'd like to pursue it."

Alex laughed. "You hardly need my blessing—"

"Don't be daft. Of course I need your blessing. This is your world, Alex. I don't want you to feel like I am stepping into some-place I don't belong."

"It's not that at all! It's just…" Alex's head spun with the thought of it. The idea that she'd even be interested in investing in women's soccer… "What if it lost money?"

"It's an investment, Alex. The entire laws of investing are based off a well-analyzed gamble. I could reinvest in shipping and still fall flat on my face. That's the excitement of it, I guess. That you never know the outcome. Play your cards right and…" she shrugged, "it just might pan out. One never knows." The corners of her mouth rose. "I do promise you, however, it's the same as I've told you before: I've not gotten where I am by investing in anything I don't believe in."

"And," mused Alex after a minute, "what about…? Are there…?"

"There are oddly no laws that prevent owner/player relation-ships, if that's what you're asking?"

"Even if one day we…" Alex cut herself off. She didn't know where the presumptuousness of her thought had come from, or why she'd almost voiced it.

Catharine, fortunately, didn't grasp her question, or, if she had, was gracious enough to let it pass unmentioned. "And even if there was a legality against it," she continued, "it wouldn't apply, given that the involvement would be between two separate teams."

"So there are no league rules that would prevent you owning a team and me playing for another one? It isn't a conflict of interest?"

"Legally, no. The only conflict would be between us. And I don't personally see that as being an issue."

Alex smiled. "You might think differently the first time my team stomps yours."

"Nonsense. There's no point in debating hypothetical situations that aren't ever going to happen. If I invest in a team, be reassured, I have no plans of leaving them vulnerable to stomping. Most certainly not to a club owned by HEG."

Laughing, Alex shook her head. "You know, I take back what I said. This may be entirely your wheelhouse. I don't think I've considered until now how competitive you might be."

"Trust me, you're not the only one who plays to win." Catharine folded her legs up onto the settee and leaned back against the window, her expression growing serious. "So honestly, what are your thoughts on me moving forward? If you need to consider it for a while—"

"I love it. I mean, there's nothing to consider. This sport needs successful, driven, forward-thinking people at its helm. You're perfect for it. And even if it means you force me to sleep on the couch a night or two a year—because I'm warning you right now, I *will* score against your team—it's worth it in the long run."

"Well then, before I launch into a market analysis and start looking at potential cities, I suppose I should make two things clear."

Wary of the sudden severity of her tone, Alex waited.

"One—I don't care how many goals you score, you are *never* sleeping on the couch. At least not without me," she added, tucking her cold feet beneath the warmth of Alex's thigh.

"Fine," Alex drew out the word as if it were a tremendous sacrifice, relieved at the frivolity of the condition. "We can sleep back-to-back, pretending like it's an accident when we wake up in each other's arms in the morning."

"Deal."

"And the second thing?"

"One day, when the time comes for you to retire from the pitch —happy, healthy, many years from now—I hope you'll consider it *our* team. Not *my* team. I was hoping this could be something we do together. *Build* together."

Alex stared at her. She'd long grown accustomed to the idea of a future with Catharine. What they had together no longer felt fleeting, no longer wavered on unsteady ground. But it had never felt clear what that future would look like. What life would resemble years down the road. But this offer—this reality—gave birth to a subsistence, a realness she hadn't been able to pin down. She had to swallow away the tightness that crept up her throat, certain if she allowed it to linger, she'd embarrass herself and cry.

A knock at the door saved her from awkwardly diverting the subject, or asking something ridiculous, like what they would name the team.

"Breakfast," was Catharine's answer to her glance of inquiry. "I thought we might eat on the balcony."

"If you snuck a parka into your carry-on, sure."

"The balcony is heated."

"Of course it is," Alex laughed, pushing herself to her feet. "Better get used to a shoestring budget if you want to get involved in women's sports, Ms.-I-Like-My-Hotel-Balconies-Heated-And-Expect-Turn-Down-Service-At-Night. You can trade that in for Motel 6s. Honda Civics. Top ramen. Mac and cheese when you want to splurge."

"Or perhaps we should raise the bar instead?"

"Bentleys for the Starting XI? Mercedes for the B Team?" Alex teased.

"I was thinking more along the lines of a living wage, healthcare, and a 401K with matching contributions."

There was nothing jesting Alex could say to that. Catharine *was* exactly what the league needed. Someone who believed in female athletes enough to put their money where their mouth was. To lead others to follow suit. To build a safe environment and provide a winning culture. An owner who didn't just want to sit in their box and sip cocktails and write a check only once their arm was twisted. One who would take a boots-on-the-ground—or *heels*, in the case of Catharine—approach, to give their team the tools to succeed.

"Thank you," she said instead.

Catharine caught her hand before she could turn to get the door.

"Do you know that I love you, Alex Grey?"

The tightness returned. She did know. There was no question. But a second knock at the door stole the earnestness from Catharine's face, and instead of allowing Alex the opportunity to return the sentiment, Catharine waved the moment away.

"Breakfast awaits."

Taking the cue, Alex padded barefoot to the entryway and pulled open the door.

A man in a well-tailored three-piece suit stood in the hallway. A glance at his engraved name badge read *Maurice Bonfils—General Manager*. It seemed significantly below his station to be making room service deliveries, nor was there a food cart in sight.

"Hi?"

He looked past Alex. "Madame Brooks, s'il vous plaît?"

"Um, she's..." Alex glanced over the partition to where Catharine had risen from the couch. The manager gave her a deferential nod, waiting for her to approach.

"Madame." He pulled a card from his vest pocket, presenting it to her with a flourish. "A gentleman in the lobby asked me to deliver this."

Catharine took the folded card and flipped it open. As she read the handprinted text, her entire body stiffened.

"Quand t'a-t-il donné ça?" she demanded, snapping the card shut and tossing it onto the low partition wall.

"Just now, madame," he responded in English.

"And he is there still?"

"He said he would wait for your reply."

"Tell him—" she looked at Alex, her jaw taut, all the tranquility of the morning gone. "Tell him I will be down in ten minutes." Without waiting for a response, she closed the door.

"What is it?" Alex didn't dare pick up the discarded card.

"My father is in the foyer."

Chapter Thirty-Four

Colonel Benjamin Brooks stood with his back to the lifts, observing a painting hanging above the hearth in the foyer. He was unmistakable in his Harris tweed suit and Herringbone flat cap, the supple leather of his Chelsea boots unblemished despite years of wear. Dressed for the country, Catharine suspected he'd come down from his villa in Chevreuse, where he was known to spend the holidays. Why he had sought her out—the purpose of his unwelcome visit—she could hardly begin to fathom.

There was one possibility, however, that had obliged her to appear.

"Has something happened to my mother?"

He turned, the militant severity of his movements unchanged from his younger years, and cast the intensity of his deep blue eyes down upon her.

"No."

Relief she hadn't realized she was seeking flooded her.

Followed by anger.

Once again she'd jumped at his bidding. Allowed him to draw her from the comfort of her morning by the simple snap of his fingers. One final display of the dominion he'd held over her.

But enough was enough.

"Then our conversation here is finished."

"Catharine." The authority of his voice followed her across the pillared hall of the grandiose lobby. When she didn't turn or slow her steps, she could hear the lug-soles of his boots glide across the polished marble. "I gave you five minutes of my time. I ask the same of yours."

She paused with her fingers waiting to illuminate the button on the wall, ready to leave him standing there—however far-traveled —no longer holding the ability to bend her to his will.

He came up beside her. "I have not come, Catharine, to make you my friend. Nor am I here under any guise that we are family. We are neither, and I have no ambition or desire to remedy the past. But I am not a man who leaves my debts unpaid. You know me well enough to know that."

"Debts?" She slapped the button with the heel of her hand, whirling on him as she waited for the door to open. "Is that what this is about? Your guilty conscience? You can pack your contrition out the door. There is *nothing* I want from you."

"When you hear what I have to say," he followed her into the waiting lift, "I think you will reconsider."

She glanced toward where they had drawn the attention of a passing bellhop. The young man stalled within listening distance, catching Catharine's eye. A gesture from her, she knew, and he would call for security.

The colonel lowered his voice. "It's about your husband, Catharine. Spare me your time; it will be in your best interest."

The mention of Carlton stayed her.

Forcing a reassuring smile to her lips, she sent the bellhop on his way, allowing the doors to close and shut them off from the lobby.

"Fine." She couldn't walk away. Not now. Not without hearing what he had to say. And what, exactly, he had to offer. She selected the button for the rooftop café. "Five minutes."

The line was out the door of people waiting to be seated. After a brief exchange of words and a sleight of hand between her father and the host, Catharine found herself at a table-for-two in front of a window with a view of Opéra Garnier. No one paid them attention, and beyond the immediate arrival of two demitasses of coffee, the servers kept their distance.

Rigid in his posture, the colonel administered a level teaspoon of sugar into his espresso, before taking the petite cup between his thumb and forefinger. Catharine hated his mouth. The way he held the drink to his lips. The way both reminded her of herself.

Her coffee untouched, she leaned deeper into the wicker chair and crossed her arms.

"The clock is ticking."

"Sit up, Catharine—your slouching is as unbecoming as your petulance. I did not raise you a spoilt brat."

"*You* did not raise me at all." Raising suggested the nurturing of life. The careful tending of something fragile with the intent to help it flourish. He had done nothing but diminish her. Stymy her growth. Pare her down to keep her small. She sat forward, dropping her palms to the edge of the table, and challenged his imperious glare. "Now cut the rubbish. Why are you here?"

He hated Paris. He'd always hated Paris. An irony, she realized now, given its inclusivities toward his very nature. But all the same, he loathed the city, so the timing of his presence had not come by happenstance.

"I've had a recent conversation with your husband." He recentered the sugar in the middle of the table. "He's taken an interest in your shares."

Catharine wasn't sure if she laughed. If she did, the sound was eclipsed by the tidal wave of blood rushing between her ears. She didn't know what outraged her more—that that insipid, officious, esurient cretin she still had the misfortune to call her husband had found a way to ferret himself into yet another place he didn't belong, or that she hadn't seen it coming.

Of course Carlton would still be after Brooks Corp. Of course he couldn't let it go. She had lived and breathed her empire. Built it brick-by-brick with her own blood and sweat and tears, allowing it to enslave her. And here he was, wanting to crown himself as Emperor without ever having hefted sword and shield.

"He couldn't afford them," she finally managed, resorting to taking up the demitasse and sipping the bitter brew black. Anything to keep her hands from betraying her. From giving him the satisfaction of her hurt. "If he's counting on funding his new endeavor by winning this divorce settlement, you might tell him not to count his eggs before they've hatched."

"Based off his offer, he wasn't in need of cash."

Catharine's eyes darted over the rim of her cup before she could govern her face into its impenetrable mask. The same mask, the same absent emotion, reflected to her across the table.

"But of course." She set down the espresso. How had she not foreseen that Carlton would try and bargain with her father? With his newfound position, with his rising power, an entire world of underhanded negotiation had opened like a blossom to his beckoning.

"By the laws karma," she continued, sliding her hands beneath the tablecloth to conceal her shaking fingers, "I suppose it's only fitting that you should have the final laugh." She dug her nails into her thighs to try and keep her tone in check. "Well, suit yourself. You're no stranger to making deals with the devil. May you both get what you deserve." She stood, slowly, steadying herself with the table's edge. "In the best interest of the corporation, however, I do feel obliged to suggest you pay special heed to the Ocean Shipping Antitrust Enforcement Act currently sitting with the House Judiciary Committee. Even Carlton won't be able to side-step that one once it goes to the floor. So when it all goes south—which, it *will*—there will no longer be the safety net of antitrust exemptions to catch your fall. And," she dropped ten euro on the table, "trust me—when it implodes, don't expect Carlton to come out with any muck on his shoes. He's perfected the art of stepping around shit, my husband."

"Are you quite finished?"

Catharine slung her purse over her shoulder. "Entirely."

"Good." The colonel suppressed a yawn. "Now sit bloody down. I didn't accept his offer, Catharine."

Vacillating between embarrassment and surprise, Catharine took a moment to straighten her blouse, hoping he could not read into the relief she felt. She remained standing.

"I don't know what you want, then. A clap on the back? A well done, perhaps, for your episodical display of ethics?"

"*That*," he spat, the growl to his voice the only tell she'd touched a nerve beneath his impervious facade, "is a falsity, and you know it."

As little as she cared to admit it, she did know it. He was not, as a habit, unethical. Ruthless? Yes. Cruel? Yes. An opportunist with no regard for who he crushed beneath his heel? Yes. But he was not dishonest. His business practices, his principles, remained above-board.

She kept silent.

"I recorded the conversation." He extracted a slim brown paper package from inside his jacket and set it on the table. "Along with several others. I have included various forms of correspondence with the senator over the course of the years. Some of which, I think, you might find beneficial."

"And what exactly do you expect me to do with that?" she asked, attempting to temper her interest.

"I do not think I need to spell it out for you."

His insouciance was infuriating.

"If you really think I'm going to get him to back off this divorce case by threatening him with an illegally recorded tête-à-tête with his father-in-law about joining the family business, you're more out of touch than I imagined. Nothing sticks to him, or perhaps you haven't noticed?" Her volume had crescendoed over the din of their surrounding tables' conversation, and as she felt eyes drawn to her, she slipped back into her seat, hoping to dissuade their curiosity.

Unfazed by her outburst, the colonel dabbed at a fallen grain of sugar with the corner of his napkin. "Your squabble regarding your divorce," he drawled, "is of positively no interest. You are an intelligent woman, Catharine. Set your sight on the bigger picture."

She almost laughed at the irony of his idiom.

Those fucking words were forever going to haunt her.

With her lack of a response, her father continued. "You know, for a woman who's been hailed for her avant-garde vision in industry throughout the years, it astounds me, your myopic perception." He tapped the package. "Do you understand what kind of leverage I am talking about, Catharine?"

This time she did laugh as it slowly sank in what he was getting at. "Did you not hear me the first time? *Nothing* sticks to him. Voter intimidation, campaign fraud, domestic abuse—nearly a dozen women came forward and accused him of sexual misconduct, for God's sake, and *still* they elected him—"

"It was circumstantial evidence, all of it! That is not what I'm offering you, Catharine!" His cheeks had turned ruddy beneath his fair skin, anger in his eyes smoldering. For all of his failings, he was not a man born of fanciful whims, and an uneasy apprehension began to spread through her.

He was serious. He believed, with utter certainty, that whatever was in that package was enough to crucify Carlton.

"Why?" she finally asked, unable to find the comfort of a full breath as her thoughts were reeling. "Why now, after everything? You are, after all, the one who helped create him."

"Your husband mistook me for a man who could be bought." He shrugged as he sat back, once again calmly regarding her. "It was a mistake you nearly made yourself, but alas, you didn't. So it is as I said: a debt is owed. Not so much for me, but for your mother. It would have ruined her. Amongst various others." His voice dropped as he looked away, his fingers turning to toying with his demitasse spoon. It was the first she'd seen him uncomfortable, both of them knowing his acknowledgment of these *others* was in itself an admission of their existence.

He pushed the package across the table. "We are level now, Catharine. The arrears have been settled."

Catharine stood, picking up the parcel, poised to leave, then turned again to face him.

"Was there ever anything I could have done that would have been enough for you?" She hated that it mattered. Mattered enough to her to ask him. That even now, amidst the entire lunacy of this conversation, it remained her burning question.

For a long moment he looked at her—looked at her, she felt, as if he'd never looked at her before. As if she were someone he'd never met. A person he'd never known. And then, without so much as a hint of regret, he gave an indifferent shrug of his broad shoulders and rose to pull on his coat. "No," he said, tugging on his cap, and walked out the door.

Catharine's legs felt unsteady as she stepped from the lift into the fifth floor hallway. Trying to regain her composure, she paused on the way to her suite, staring out the window overlooking the Place de l'Opéra. The plaza was crowded, the Sunday afternoon streets lively despite the chill as an open-top tour bus slowly glided through the sea of pedestrians.

A deep russet overcoat caught her eye, its inhabitant concealed by a Herringbone cap, and she watched her father's familiar stride as he disappeared down the avenue, fading out of her life once more, back to nonexistence.

It was madness, all of it. Madness to have met with him. Madness to have heard him out. Madness to find herself hurt by his continued unwavering detachment.

She leaned against the hand carved molding of the arched window and forced herself to set aside the vortex of her feelings.

There would be time to analyze sensibilities later. For the moment she had to focus on the choices that had been presented to her.

Her father's certainty of the strength of proof of Carlton's misconduct was as frightening as it was compelling. The power of it came with a peril she wasn't sure was worth risking.

But on the latter hand... the idea that she might truly have been given the means to expose him—to cut him off at the knees—raised a sense of vindictiveness in her she didn't know how to extinguish. The opportunity to annihilate him. To metaphorically hang him with rope he himself had provided.

The longer she considered it, the more the thought of retribution outweighed the fear of Carlton's reaction, her desire for retaliation edged aside only by the slowly rising concern that her father could be mistaken.

That his smoking gun would turn out to be little more than a children's toy. Amounting once again to nothing.

She turned the package over in her hand. It was a memorable weight, one carrying a sense of familiarity.

Slipping her fingers under the tie, she eased the cord off to one side and worked open the brown paper. Inside was a folded manilla envelope, sealed with no markings on its exterior, and beneath it, making up the bulk of the parcel, her father's beloved leather-bound edition of *The Art of War*.

The sight of it struck her, somehow—the gift, if she could call it that. She shoved the envelope into her purse, and ran her fingers over the gold engraved letters of the title. Had it been just weeks ago she'd held it last? And then decades before that? She flipped it open, thumbing its pages, finding a passage marked with a scrap of paper.

Rewards for good service should not be deferred a single day. The words were lightly underlined. In the margin, her father's meticulous handwriting: *I owe you this, Catharine.*

Her body sank a little heavier into the window frame. She didn't know how he'd meant it. She never would. She'd never ask him. Was he referring to her keeping of his secrets? Was it in reference to the dedication and years of her life she had given him? Was it of little thought, meaning next to nothing?

It shouldn't have mattered to her so much. And it shouldn't have hurt even more not to ever know.

Skimming the ancient text, she found one more underscored citation.

When you surround an army, leave an outlet free. Do not press a desperate foe too hard. And again, her father's script tucked neatly underneath it. *Be smart, Catharine.*

She snapped the book closed, shoving aside her analysis of the cryptic messages. There would be time for that later. For now her only focus had to be on the contents of the envelope.

Chapter Thirty-Five

"I've seen tectonic plates move faster!" Amelia heckled from the comfort of the bleachers. The Australian had spent the afternoon watching her teammates bust their asses while she sat, bundled in a scarf and beanie, her foot propped up in an ankle boot atop a bag of pinnies. The repercussions of a misstep the day before during their first training scrimmage.

Alex flipped her the bird and then proceeded to come in dead last in the preseason Beep Test, designed to assess an athlete's aerobic capacity. Unlike most of her teammates, Alex had never dreaded the grueling endurance evaluation, and had never, at any point in her professional career, finished in the bottom of the pack. Until today.

"You, uh, forget how the whole running thing works, mate? One foot in front of the other?" Amelia hobbled along on crutches next to her as they filed out from the end-of-day team meeting.

The walk across the training center to the parking lot seemed infinitely longer in the settling dusk than it had in the rising sun ten hours earlier. Alex's entire body hurt. The ball of her left foot, which had threatened to blister from dancing in heels in Paris, had finally succumbed to bleeding.

But it was none of that that she could blame on her miserable results. She simply couldn't focus. Not since boarding a flight from France to California five days earlier. Not since Catharine had returned from the unexpected meeting with her father.

"That's rich coming from someone currently hopping on one leg," she deflected to Amelia.

"Yeah, and I still would have leveled higher than you just did. Fuckin' oath, Grey. What was that?"

Alex deliberately picked up her pace, forcing Amelia to limp along in double-time. "I don't know, jet lag, a blister the size of the

Great Barrier Reef on the bottom of my foot, preseason jitters? Take your pick." She left off the option of the mounting concern that her girlfriend was going to end up checked off her soon-to-be-ex-husband's hit list before he was sworn in the following week as President of the United States.

"We've been running together all winter—"

"It was just a shit day, Amelia! It's not the end of the world. I'll be match fit by season opener, so lay off, will you?"

Surprised by Alex's uncharacteristic irritability toward her, Amelia fell silent.

"I'm sorry," Alex apologized as they crossed the dirt track at the far end of the training field. "It's just.. I'm not..." She trailed off. She couldn't tell her. She couldn't begin to explain.

"Ei vacas!" Molly Rodrigues rolled her window down as she, Halsey, and Jill Thompson slowly drove by. "We're going over to *Barney's* for a burger. Meet us there?"

Amelia waved them on. "Nah, hot date with a couple Advil and my couch."

"Knock yourself out." Molly looked to Alex. "Join us after you ditch grandma?"

Before Alex could decline, her attention was pulled across the parking lot in the opposite direction.

"Alex!"

The voice didn't belong to this facet of her life, and even with her customary too-tall heels and nonconservative length of her skirt, Alex had to do a double take to identify the speaker. It was Elle Kirkland's chestnut hair, unruly in the breeze off the bay, that gave her away as she picked a careful path across the slick sidewalk heading in Alex's direction.

"I need to speak with you," she said, once she'd stepped onto the safety of the asphalt, her heels finding more reassuring purchase. "I've called you several times." It was more accusation than observation.

"I'm sorry. I've been busy." Alex gave a half twirl of her finger around the training center to indicate the obvious.

But they both knew the obvious had nothing to do with it.

"*Un*busy yourself." Elle shot Amelia an impatient glare, followed by a darting glance toward Molly's idling car. Three sets of eyes from inside the dented Honda stared back at her, the looks ranging from intrigue to amusement. If Halsey catcalled, Alex was going to break the goalkeeper's nose. No questions asked. Or answered, for that matter.

"Could you…?" Alex offered Amelia an apologetic cringe. "For just a minute?"

"Rack off so you can shoot the shit with the pom? Yeah, sure, Grey." Amelia met Elle's rancorous expression with the classic apathy of her own. "Old man Stanwick warming his lap with another skirt these days?"

It wasn't surprising Amelia had recognized Elle. The attorney frequently boasted about sitting in the owner's box at Arsenal, and was photographed often with playboy billionaire, Stanwick Koehler, the team's majority shareholder.

"Do I know you?" Elle peered down through the caked-on paint of her lashes. "Oh, wait," she faked sudden recollection, "Walker, right? I believe I read an article about you this weekend. No other footballer in the world holds the distinction of coming in runner-up on more occasions. Quite an achievement."

A car pulled up behind Molly, and Nathalie's face appeared through the driver's side window, as if on cue for the closing act of a dark comedy.

Amelia looked between the pair, then at Alex, drawing a linear connection. "Ah." Her chapped lips twitched. "New lap, different venue." She swung herself off the curb with her crutches, motioning for her teammates to wait for her. Before folding herself into the backseat beside Halsey, she looked over her shoulder. "Has she shown you that thing she does… you know, with her pinky…?" Amelia gave Elle a smug smile. "The French—never short on imagination."

When Molly's beat-up Honda had finally cleared the parking lot, Elle rounded on Alex. Incensed, Alex imagined, as much at Amelia's parting shot as the reason for her visit, the woman wagged a reproachful finger in her direction.

"What is she up to?"

So the cat was out of the bag. And it wasn't Amelia she was asking about.

Alex slung her backpack over the opposite shoulder, watching Molly's taillights disappear. She should have taken them up on going for the burger.

"I don't know what you're talking about." She practically choked over the words.

"You're as good at lying as you are at PKs. Now don't toy with me, Alex. She hasn't returned my calls all week, and this morning I get an email asking me to hold off on noticing Cleveland's attorney? I smell bullshit. So quit with the games—"

"I'm not playing any fucking games!"

Ever since leaving Paris, Alex had been struggling to maintain the waning grasp on her temper, but it was starting to come apart at the seams. She'd spent days trying to change Catharine's mind —to make her see reason—but reason wasn't what Catharine wanted to hear. Had she been seeking logic, she would have told Elle about the conversation with her father. Sought her advice. Examined whatever legal avenues there were to explore.

Instead, she'd told no one but Alex—forcing a burden of secrecy on her she hadn't wanted to bear.

They'd sat inside the penthouse suite on the pearl upholstered sofa, overlooking the charm of the Ninth District of Paris, listening to the files on the flash drive. Much of the conversations had been all but Greek to Alex. Good-old-boy chatter surrounding words like *deregulation tariff* and *expedited backhaul* and *fostered channels of distribution* interspersed between Carlton's repeated phrases of *c'mon, Brooks—help me help you,* and *oblige me, Colonel, I'll make it worth your while.* Nothing quite as damning as Catharine had hoped for, Alex could tell by her frustrated pacing that had begun minutes into the recordings. But then she'd browsed the printed pages, stopping on one in particular. It had been a query from the senator's private email, soliciting the colonel's assistance in a 'ghost freight' shipment from the Philippines, promising a 'lucrative yield' for 'turning a blind eye.'"

"Arms-trafficking, most likely," Catharine had said, unfazed, citing the cargo's departure from the Port of Manila as her thesis for that deduction. "Common in the industry." She'd looked up to find Alex staring at her with alarm. "*Not* something WorldCargo has ever participated in," she clarified. "My father is a bastard, but he's never caved to running illegal lines. It just goes to show what a complete pillock my husband is."

She'd studied the page again. It wasn't the contraband she was interested in, but rather the chain of email addresses at the top.

There were three additional CCs between the correspondence of the senator and the colonel, one of which she underlined. *StellarM@gmail.com*. "Matthew," she shook her head, tapping the French tip of her nail to the page. "The imbecile."

"The arms-trafficking—" Alex had started, still hooked on the potential charge. "That has to be—"

"It's nothing in the scheme of things," Catharine had waved her off, but Alex noticed she'd dog-eared the page.

On the way to the airport the following morning, Catharine had said, very simply, "I'm going to meet with him."

A declaration which had evolved into their first official fight.

She'd given no definitive reason for why, or what she hoped to gain. She'd said herself there wasn't enough condemning evidence to see Carlton charged with any crimes, or call him out on foul play. But all the way across the Atlantic—six miles above sea level —she'd held fast to her determination to meet with him all the same.

Subdued by their first-class surroundings, tones never breaking a whisper, Alex had pleaded with her to let it all go. Whatever advantage she felt the confrontation would give her wasn't worth the gamble.

That had been five days ago. And this morning she had left with Malcolm to fly to Washington DC.

Carlton would kill her if she pushed him. Alex felt certain of it. He had implied it before, over less consequential matters, and if she tried to force his hand, he would make good on his threat. And there was nothing she could say—could do—to stop it.

Standing in the cold, on the empty sidewalk, Alex felt suddenly deflated. The stress of the entire week was catching up with her, and she knew it wasn't Elle who deserved her anger. Given she'd been concerned enough to show up unexpectedly in Oakland, they were on the same side.

"She's going to DC."

"What!" It wasn't Elle, but Nathalie, who'd unfurled herself from the open door of her car. "Why?"

"I don't—she doesn't—"

Fuck. It wasn't like she'd been sworn to silence, but Alex knew it had been implied. If Catharine had wanted Elle or Nathalie to know, she would have told them herself.

But it wasn't fair, forcing her to carry this. Forcing her to worry alone.

"She's going to meet with him."

Nathalie's ballet flats were sinking in the wet grass. "What do you mean?"

Alex couldn't tell them about the meeting with the colonel. Despite her desire for support—for guidance—for the simple comfort of sharing the albatross; knowing someone else knew—it felt too much a betrayal.

"I don't know why." It wasn't entirely untrue.

"Get her on the phone." Elle stuffed her hands inside the pockets of her suit jacket, stamping against the chill. "Now."

"I can't."

"You *can*. She'll answer your call."

"She's already there."

"Get her on the phone. One word from you and she'll change her mind. You share her bed. You have her ear. It's the benefit of sharing one's pillow."

The attorney was wrong. Catharine had listened to her. Listened to her plead her case that she should just walk away. Leave things as they were. It wasn't worth the peril. Nothing was. She had listened and nodded and allowed Alex to go on. And when she was finished she'd acknowledged she understood her concerns, but would be going to DC anyway. For the first time in their relationship, Alex knew she held no influence at all. Catharine's mind had been made up back in Paris, and nothing Alex said would persuade her otherwise.

"Listen, Alex," Elle continued, taking a step forward, so close Alex could smell the hint of whisky on her breath intermixed with the florals of her shampoo. "She may think she knows what she's doing, but she has no business meeting with him alone. Unrepresented. He's bound to try and take her for all she's worth if she tries to make a deal."

The momentary relief of solidarity crumbled. Elle hadn't comprehended the seriousness of the situation. This wasn't about the divorce. This wasn't about the settlement. It was so much more. And Alex couldn't begin to explain, because she herself didn't understand. She just knew, whatever Catharine wanted, whatever she was hoping to achieve, wasn't worth the risks she was willing to take.

"I'm sorry," she said instead, taking a step away. "If you want to talk her out of it, call her yourself."

"Alex—"

"I have to go. I have to meet my teammates."

Chapter Thirty-Six

The bags under Matthew Stellar's bloodshot eyes darkened as Catharine spoke, an illusion amplified as his lean face shed the last of its color, turning another shade grayer. Sweat had broken out along his stubbled upper lip, which he wiped at absently with the cuff of his sweater.

"I can't. He'd kill me. He'd kill me if he even knew I was sitting here talking to you." He'd moved from picking his cuticles to working on the lashes of his left eye—a habit Catharine had witnessed over the years since he'd turned up as an intern in her husband's office a decade earlier. He hadn't made Executive Assistant due to his exceptional abilities as a staffer. He'd simply outlasted all the others.

"It's possible, yes." Catharine leaned leisurely against the back of the café chair, her legs crossed and voice collected. As if it were the most natural thing in the world to be discussing the very realistic terms of homicide in a back alley coffee shop a few hundred yards from Dupont Circle. She regarded him a second, feeling almost sorry for the nightmare she was about to turn his life into. She'd never disliked the nervous young man. She'd sympathized with him, on most occasions. He'd been her husband's peon, his lackey, his whipping boy when he needed one. And he'd taken it all like a loyal dog, devoted to its master. But then she remembered how he'd avoided her eye while her face had been caked beneath layer after layer of makeup, hiding the souvenir of Carlton's outrage on the top floor of the Fairmont. And how he'd stood unwaveringly in front of the cameras and verified Carlton's lies that she'd fallen in the shower.

"But," she forged ahead, "if you take this route, at least it's not a certainty."

He quit plucking his eyelashes long enough to blink at her. "What?"

"Matthew," she took her time withdrawing a stack of papers from her tote, tidying the edges before dropping them in the middle of the table, "what do you think he'll do to you when I tell him these came to me by your hand?" On the top of the pile was the printout from her father, Matthew's personal email highlighted in the top left hand corner.

She'd debated her method of attack. Start slow and build momentum—or spring on him the lethal blow, and taper off gradually, making the palliative option appear more appealing? She'd decided on the latter. Fluster him without allowing enough time to find an escape and human nature would default him to the less painful option.

"I—" he gave an anxious, distrustful glance toward the papers. "What are those?"

"Years of life with Carlton Cleveland."

His fingers fumbled with the neckline of his sweater, searching for his glasses. Catharine reached across the table and edged the thick black-rimmed spectacles in his direction, from where they'd been sitting right in front of him.

"Have a look. Take your time."

He didn't move, resorting to refusing to acknowledge the pile. "I didn't give you these."

"Obviously." *God, he was slow.* "But that's your name there, is it not?"

"I—" he sputtered, risking a squinted glance at the top page, scanning it from top to bottom. "I know nothing about this!"

Catharine tapped one of the two addresses beside Matthew's inside the CC column. "Albert Flemmons says otherwise." She hadn't spoken to the Georgia congressman. She wasn't even certain the public server email account belonged to the slime ball representative. But it didn't truly matter.

"He's lying!"

"I believe you," Catharine raised a dismissive shoulder, "but that makes no difference. Tell me—who do you think is going to take the fall when Carlton's backed into a corner? Flemmons?" she laughed, leafing through the papers, careful to avoid the blank fillers she'd stuffed in the center. "They drink bourbon together on

Tuesday nights and regale each other with conquests of skirts in their office." She set the stack down and looked at Matthew directly. "You think Carlton will accept responsibility?"

He stared at her. The underarms of his sweater had darkened, the sheen around his pallid face glistening as he perspired. "Why are you doing this, Mrs. Cleveland? A few emails won't stop him."

"You've known me a long time, Matthew—you really think I'd be here without incontrovertible evidence?" She hid her bluff in the undertaking of gathering her paperwork, certain he was too rattled to think much further than trying to save his own skin. "Let me worry about that. In the meantime, I'm offering you an opportunity. Help me with this simple task and your name slides under the radar. When all is said and done, no one will be looking at the former senatorial executive assistant Carlton Cleveland found so insignificant he named him as a third-level staffer to the White House Office." She stood, looking at her watch. It was a quarter to eleven. "I meet with him at Blair House at noon. Schedule it for half after."

"I can't do this, Mrs. Cleveland—"

"You can. And you will. Self-preservation is a basic human instinct."

At a quarter to twelve, Catharine found herself flanked between two uniformed Capitol Police officers as she and Malcolm were escorted up the staircase to the broad entry of Blair House. She had often passed the four-story residence—situated directly across the street from 1600 Pennsylvania Avenue—but never paid it significant attention. For the better part of a century the home had been known as the President's Guest House, welcoming foreign dignitaries and royalty from around the globe, but it had never held particular interest to her. She'd found it gaudy. Antiquated. Rich in history, but teeming with a garish opulence which gave it an artificial charm.

It was everything Carlton would love in a building.

Over the years it had become tradition for the incoming president and his family to take up residence in the nineteenth century dwelling the week prior to Inauguration, and so, she imagined, her husband must have been in a state of rapture when three days earlier he'd been permitted to move into the temporary lodgings.

A stone's throw from the White House. The final step—less than a hundred yards—from the realization of Carlton Cleveland's once-upon-a-time pipe dream.

"I think my gran's gran had this same wallpaper in her kitchen," Malcolm teased of the vibrant flowers climbing the walls through a backdrop of turquoise. They'd been left to wait in a room off the foyer, their every breath scrutinized under the watchful eye of a taciturn man in black who stood unmoving in the doorway. "Do you know, pal, if they've got this print on a postcard?"

On another day Catharine might have smiled at the Scot's raillery, but her only focus was on resisting the urge to check her watch for the hundredth time as they waited on her husband.

It was a quarter after noon when Carlton sauntered in through an adjacent hallway, appearing to be in a state of mid-dress. The top buttons of his shirt were unfastened, his tie draped slackly around his collar, the laces of one polished Oxford slapping loose around his trousers.

It never ceased to dumbfound her that this man had garnered enough votes to win a seat in the senate, let alone clinch the role of leader of the Free World.

"Catharine." Her name rolled off his tongue like a stale draft. He stifled a yawn, a display intent to prove how inconsequential he found her visit. "Come, come."

She followed him through a series of halls until they reached a room painted in radiant scarlet, where an enormous antique table extended across the paisley-covered carpet. Beside a double-hung window overlooking the White House on the southern wall, three men in suits huddled around a desk, their faces buried in the screens of their computers as they spoke in animated tones.

Carlton cleared his throat, announcing his arrival as he lumbered through the door.

"Gentlemen."

The trio looked up, their conversation abruptly ceasing.

In the center sat Matthew Stellar, whose eyes darted everywhere but to Catharine.

"Sir." Carlton's recently appointed Chief of Staff, Martin Kilmore, gestured toward an iPad that was propped up between them, his face lit by its fluorescent glow. "Tuesday's seating chart has been leaked on Twitter." He gestured toward his earpiece.

"I've got the Clintons' aide on the line. They're unhappy with their proximity to—"

"Tell Clinton he can lick my boots." Carlton strutted straight to the drinks trolley, uncorking a bottle of bourbon. "If he doesn't like it, tell him I'll sell his seat on eBay. We'll call it charity; donate the money to his next piece of ass—"

Kilmore's palm flew to cover the speaker. "Inform Mr. Clinton we'll work on the arrangement," he said quickly, before disconnecting the call.

"Bunch of pansies, the lot of you." Amused with himself, Carlton dropped an ice sphere into his tumbler. "Jesus, Stellar," he barked at his assistant as he turned to stroll to the conference table, his heavy steps creaking the two hundred-year-old floorboards. "You look as if I've just invited John Wilkes Booth to the theatre. Buck up, boy—Clinton's been out of the Oval Office for over twenty years. We don't need him as a friend."

"Yes, sir." Sweat trickled down Matthew's temple, where he sat, hunched in his chair. Of all the people Catharine had to count on, she would not have chosen her husband's neurotic toady as her man.

"Carlton." Still in the threshold, she drew his attention to her. "If we might proceed?"

"Yes, yes," Carlton swirled the ice in his glass, indulging in another sip. "Gentlemen—it appears my impatient wife is anxious to get me alone."

Kilmore offered a stilted laugh as the three men rose, gathering their work.

Catharine could see Carlton's temper edging on the brink of annoyance as Matthew was the last to tidy his workspace, straightening his things.

"Let's go, chop, chop!" He clapped his hands together, startling his assistant, who lost hold of the file folder he'd been carrying, scattering its contents across the carpet.

"Oh, for fuck's sake, Stellar!" Carlton tossed back the remainder of his glass before strolling to where Matthew had dropped to his knees, swiping at post-its and paperclips with visibly trembling hands.

"You're pathetic!" He ground his heel onto one of the errant papers Matthew was retrieving, slowly dragging it out of his reach. "Just leave it—I've not got all day!"

"Yes, sir." Not needing to be told twice, Matthew shoved himself to unsteady feet.

"Stellar!"

Matthew's entire body lurched on his way to the door, slinging around like a hooked fish who'd been set loose, only to be reeled back harder.

"Sir?"

"I need you to push back the President of Belarus an hour. You think you can handle that?"

"Yes, sir."

"Good. Now get out."

As soon as his assistant cleared the threshold, Carlton ambled back to the trolley and refilled his glass.

Catharine stood, unmoving from the center of the room, staring at the bottle of bourbon, absently wishing she'd beat Carlton to the cart.

"Lose your dog, Catharine."

She blinked herself out of her stupor. If Matthew had come through for her, she didn't know. But there was nothing left to do but move forward with her plan.

"No." She watched the back of her husband's head. She'd known he'd insist on sending Malcolm from the room. It was exactly what she had counted on. She checked her watch. It was a few minutes before twelve-thirty. Right on time. "He stays. Non-negotiable."

"Excuse me?" Carlton spun, bourbon sloshing over the rim of his tumbler onto the boteh-patterned carpet. "You think you can waltz in here and tell *me* what is and isn't negotiable?"

She had no intention to negotiate. Negotiation was long behind them. It was lost somewhere between publicly humiliating Alex and the smoking pile of rubble that was all that remained of Nathalie's theatre. All talk of compromise abandoned amidst threats, Tweets, black eyes, bribery, and greed.

But he didn't realize that. Which was the leading asset of his pompous, vainglorious, self-serving ego. When she'd called three days earlier to tell him she'd reconsidered moving their divorce forward to trial, he'd believed her. Believed that she'd still be willing to bargain. That he could still cut a deal.

And so, without suspicion, he'd thrown open the gates of Troy to accept her gift of a wooden horse.

"*Fine.*" She waved a hand toward the door. "Malcolm."

The Scot's pewter gaze touched a beat too long on Carlton, his challenge unmistakable, before he did as he was bade and exited the conference room.

"Ah," sighed Carlton, his exhalation brimming with mockery as the door clicked shut, sealing them off from his ever-looming entourage, "see, my dear—isn't that better? Just you and me, alone."

Casually, he began a slow orbit around the table, clinking his glass to the back of each antique chair as he drew closer to where she stood.

"You know, I'll still let you take me up on my offer, Catharine. We may be a few days shy of the Oval Office, but this is a fair alternative." He stopped a few feet from her and ran his palm across the polished surface of the wood. "Imagine the things that have taken place on this table—treaties, treason," he shrugged, "trysts."

"Don't attempt to wax poetic, you'll just embarrass yourself."

"Oh, don't be shy." His laugh was coarse and throaty. "There's no one to see us but this old broad—" he tipped his glass to the hanging portrait of the Empress Dowager Cixi of China, "—and I assure you, she won't mind. What do you say, let bygones be bygones?" With a flick of his wrist, he threw back the remainder of bourbon in a single swallow. "Just think, tonight at dinner, when the Prime Minister of Syria is kissing my ass, he'll have no idea a few hours earlier I fucked my wife in the very spot where Truman smoked cigars with Churchill."

Atop one of the curio cabinets housing a wealth of vintage china, a mantel clock chimed the half hour.

Catharine smoothed the pleated silk of her blouse, aware of the dampness of her palms. She was certain, the way her heart was pounding, that her pulse had become visible at the base of her throat.

It didn't matter. It was now or never.

Foreging acknowledgment of his crassness, Catharine slipped around him to put herself on the opposite side of the table. "Are you familiar with the penalties for trafficking in firearms?"

The unexpected question stripped the sneer off his lips. "What?"

"Specifically 18 USC 933?" She pulled her phone from her pocket—the only item she'd been permitted to bring past the foyer—and thumbed in her passcode.

"What are you talking about, Catharine?"

"How about the Federal Trade Commission Act? Or perhaps the Ocean Shipping Reform Act might ring a bell?"

"What the fuck are you going on about?" A mist of spittle flew from his lips to the floor.

"And then of course there's Chapter 96—but I already know you're well versed in RICO charges, given you campaigned for stricter reform during your first run for senate."

"Are you fucking threatening me?" Carlton slammed his tumbler into the smooth walnut finish of the table, shattering the glass. "Is that why you think you've come here?"

Silently commending herself for neither flinching nor dropping her phone, she drew a forced breath as she selected the file she wanted, and set the mobile on the table in front of her.

"No threats, Carlton," she said, waiting while the file loaded. "A threat would indicate I want something from you—and there is nothing left for which I would care to bargain."

Through the speaker, a clipped segment from a conversation with her father began to play—Carlton's hubristic laugh unmistakable as he propositioned the colonel. It was no more condemnatory than it had been the first time she heard it. A slap on the wrist from the feds, at best.

"This?!" he scoffed after listening for a moment, "this is what you think you've got on me?" He'd sidestepped slowly around the table, inching himself closer to where she stood, his movements measured, like a grizzly on the hunt. "You are a fool," he spat, lunging suddenly, springing forward, moving faster than a man of his constitution should. He seized her arm—and though she'd stepped back, making a half effort to avoid him, she'd deliberately not moved far enough. "Are you wearing a wire?" He dragged her to him, tugging at her top, patting down her chest. "Is that what this is? You think you're going to incriminate me? You stupid, *stupid* bitch!"

The recording had switched over to the next conversation, an offer of preferential shipping lanes and expedited break bulk in exchange for ten percent of shares.

"Where is it?" he demanded, continuing to grope at her back, her hips, her calves.

"There's no wire," she hurled, indignant, shaking herself free of his grasp and staggering back a step. "I needn't bother, it's all there already—and by this time tomorrow, those recordings will have made every headline across the globe. You'll never set a foot in that Oval Office—"

He took a swing at her, but one she'd been expecting, and before he'd made any contact, she was able to maneuver herself around the Queen Anne dining chair.

"You are out of your fucking mind!" He took another step forward, a crimson blush burning up his neck. "You think they'd indict me? You think I don't own them? That there's a single half-brained, cocksucking judge or dumb fuck jury who can't be bought? That I don't have down on their knees?"

"I think your party will abandon you once they see you for the incompetent, cataclysmal failure you've always been. They'll rally around Sherwood—"

"That senile bastard couldn't win the votes of those leather-necked knuckle draggers if he offered them lifetime welfare. You're delusional—you and your old man—if you think any of this will take me down." He charged again, this time his fingers finding purchase on the collar of her blouse, yanking her forward across the chair. "I gave you fair warning to leave well enough alone. My message of the theatre was loud and clear. But I've had it, Catharine—you've made your last mistake. Do you know what happens to whistleblowers? You think when you walk out of here I won't find you?" He curled his free hand into a fist in her hair, dragging her face inches from his. "I swear to you, I'll slit your throat myself. And when I'm done, and your body's feeding fish at the bottom of the Potomac, I'll pay a little visit to your girlfriend."

She turned her face away, recoiled as much by the stench of his breath and the nearness of his body, as she was the realness of his threats. If she had misjudged Matthew Stellar... If she had gotten it wrong...

In the hall there were voices. Men's voices, rushed, inaudible, subdued over the bounding of her pulse.

Carlton had heard them, too, because by the time the door was flung open—without fanfare, without a knock—he'd released her from his hold and backed a half dozen steps away.

"Kilmore!" he snarled at the intrusion as his Chief of Staff bolted, uninvited, into the room. "What the hell do you think you're doing?"

The man stood, momentarily transfixed by the setting around him, before fixing his sights on the desk in front of the window that overlooked the White House lawns. In only a handful of strides, he'd catapulted himself through the maze of displaced chairs and snatched the iPad from its cradle. The screen briefly illuminated the pallor of his face, before he hurled the device to the floor, where it bounced harmlessly against the plush cushion of the carpet.

"*Fuck!*" The word was a half growl of fury and howl of dismay. Shell-shocked, he finally turned his attention to Carlton, who stood with his mouth agape, his instinct sensing the impending implosion of his world around him.

"Sir." Kilmore looked as if he might pass out. "We have an issue." Unable to look Carlton in the eye, he cast his gaze back to the iPad and took a rasping breath. "You've been broadcasting live on *Twitter*."

Chapter Thirty-Seven

"Gooooood morning!"

Alex opened her eyes to the singsong voice with only enough time to catch the tail end of Halsey's leap before the weight of the sagging mattress pitched, the cheap hotel bedframe threatening to collapse beneath them.

"Do you know what day it is?"

Christmas, based off the goalkeeper's overtly exuberant enthusiasm.

But no, despite Alex's addled state from the abrasive awakening, she knew it was March, she knew she was in Texas, and she knew it wasn't even a game day. Which left her roommate's oh-dark-thirty intrusion all the more confusing.

"Erin." She dragged the polyester comforter up over her head. "Go back to sleep!"

"Not a chance!" The keeper dropped back against the laminate headboard so hard she shook the paper-thin wall. "Sawyer and Molly are on their way over."

Alex uncovered her face. "Why?" The gap between the window curtains revealed only the faintest glow of the unrisen sun.

It was a recovery day. They'd flown in from the National Team training facility in Colorado late the night before, after a week long camp, and arrived in Frisco, Texas, where they would kick off the SheBelieves Cup the following evening in a match against Japan. There was absolutely no reason to be doing anything other than watching the back of her eyelids.

"It's Arraignment Day!" Without allowing time for a response, Halsey rolled her six-foot frame over the top of Alex, seizing the remote control from the nightstand. "Homeboy 'bout to go down!" She flicked on the TV.

"You didn't seriously wake me up to watch this." Alex couldn't help but peek over the rumpled comforter toward the footage on the flatscreen bolted to the dresser. There, in block letters, was the CNN news ticker: *Indicted Former President-Elect Carlton Cleveland Arrives at Presentment Hearing.*

Two days earlier, the first—of what was anticipated to be many —charges were brought against Cleveland, and every major news station across the globe had headlined the disgraced politician's mugshot from where he'd been booked at the Metropolitan Police Department.

The dark-haired reporter looked anything but grim as he gesticulated over his shoulder toward the courthouse steps where Carlton Cleveland had stepped out of the back of a black sedan.

"Little more than two months after Congress were called together in a shocking special session, following the condemning livestream due to a staffing error of then-President-elect Cleveland's volatile altercation with his estranged wife, Catharine Cleveland, we await today's presentment—which comes less than forty-eight hours after his indictment of *Felony Threats.* This morning we will find out if the former South Carolina senator will be released on bond, or held in custody pending a full detention hearing."

Alex tuned out the garrulous reporter as he went on, rattling off the more than half a dozen expected charges across four different states for a plethora of felony and misdemeanor offenses.

She knew the impending charges. Elle had practically created a powerpoint presentation on everything she felt the DOJ would pin on him. *Felony Threats. Threats to do Bodily Harm. Arson. Bribery. Criminal Collusion. Campaign Finance Offenses.* A list nowhere near exhaustive as the jurisdictions involved continued to build cases against him.

As it turned out, publicly labeling judges as *half-brained cocksuckers,* and inferring they could be *bought—while down on their knees—*won a person very few friends in the judicial system.

"Oh, just in time!"

Alex's attention resurfaced to find Sawyer standing in the threshold of the narrow hall, still in her pajamas, with Molly and Jill Thompson crowding in behind her. On the TV, as Carlton was being escorted into the courthouse, a woman was shown amidst the mass of bystanders wearing a shirt that said "Recovered Leather-Necked Knuckle Dragger." Beside her, a green-haired teen waved a sign with a caricature of Cleveland in an orange jumpsuit, and below it, printed in cheery bubble letters: "The Hazards of Boomers and *Tweeting*: 'oops, is that recording?'" Another sign, panned over quickly by the camera crew, read "I wanna be on your *dumb fuck* jury!"

Sawyer dropped herself onto the foot of the bed, using Halsey's bent knees as a backrest as Molly crammed into the space between the wall and Alex.

"Make room!" Jill prodded at Alex's outstretched legs.

"You realize there is an entire empty bed three feet away, right?" Alex chucked her thumb toward Halsey's vacant mattress, even as she sat up and drew her knees to her chest.

In truth, she didn't mind the company.

It had been two months of turmoil. Of ups and downs.

She'd been getting taped in the recovery room when Catharine had called her. When she'd told her, very succinctly, very matter-of-factly, what had transpired, and what, presumably, would follow. Alex had listened, knowing little of what to ask, other than if she was okay and when she would be home, and then hung up the phone. The magnitude of it—the immensity of the repercussions—hadn't really struck her until an hour later, when Rod had called her off the pitch and into his office, where two plain clothes police officers were waiting for her, offering a security detail.

And the nightmare had commenced from there.

She'd been angry at first at Catharine. Angry she'd put herself in danger. Angry she'd stirred the hornets' nest when things had settled down. She hadn't been able to stomach watching the full *Twitter* broadcast, despite being subjected to it every place she turned. The media. Well-meaning friends. Every social platform, her phone notification banners, the story making the front cover of every newspaper at the grocery store.

When Congress was called to session the day after the infamous broadcast—just two days before Inauguration Day—and found themselves forced to make the unprecedented decision to terminate Cleveland's nomination and name Bill Sherwood acting-president in his place, Alex's anger had begun to recede. Only to be replaced by a well-founded fear instead.

It would take months, Elle had prophesized, for the Supreme Court to establish a ruling on how to proceed. It was uncharted territory—having an incoming president determined unfit to serve —and the debates would be longstanding. During that time, while awaiting not only a verdict for the presidency, but for charges to be brought forth to Carlton, Alex worried for both Catharine's safety as well as her own. What was left for Carlton to lose? Colonel Brooks' highlighted passage from the Art of War had not been unwarranted—*do not press a desperate foe too hard.* Catharine had left that advice unheeded, and pressed as hard as she could.

But as the weeks had passed and Carlton remained sequestered in his manor on Daufuskie Island, desperate to avoid the media who haunted his every emergence, Alex slowly became accustomed to the idea that for once, it might actually be over. That the black cloud of their lives that had hovered over them in the shape of Carlton Cleveland had evanesced for the final time. And with her abating anxiety came forgiveness of Catharine. Understanding that, had she not done what she'd done, he'd have always been looming. Always been waiting. Just one endless, unrelenting threat away.

"It's too early for popcorn, but…" Molly dragged a bag out from what appeared to be her sports bra. "I brought chocolate covered espresso beans."

"Disgusting." Halsey made a face.

"Who the hell doesn't like chocolate?" Sawyer snatched the bag from Molly's hand.

"I like chocolate—just not where that particular chocolate came from."

Sawyer popped a handful in her mouth. "Says the girl who I've seen snag a Pop-Tart straight out of the bin."

"It was still in the *wrapper*," Halsey defended. "Besides… *bin?*" She rolled her eyes. "Four months in the UK and you're already turning into a Brit."

They bantered on about Sawyer's move to England, and her ridiculously cutesy relationship with Kelsey Evans that had taken WoSo by storm. As the conversation jumped to the upcoming tournament, it naturally segued to who they felt would be most likely to earn a spot in Melbourne for the Olympic Games. With only room for eighteen on the roster—the fewest of all major tournaments in the sport—nearly every position felt up for grabs.

"I can tell you who's *not* going to make it," Molly muttered through a mouthful of espresso beans.

Her teammates eyed the defender, awaiting whatever gossip she had to share.

"Ashby."

There was a collective groan. The rumor was neither fresh nor exciting. Monica Ashby's apparent elimination from the Olympic roster had been made obvious by Izzy Atwood excluding her from every National Team camp that had been held since the previous summer's World Cup. After her antics in the final, her days of wearing the Stars and Stripes appeared to have come to an end. At least while Atwood remained in command.

"Well, thank you, Captain Obvious." Jill picked at an unraveling thread on the comforter. "Anything else you care to tell us that we don't already know?"

Molly humphed. "I suppose you also know that she's decided to retire from club ball, then."

This regained everyone's attention, none more so than Alex's.

"Retire? At the end of the season?" Monica was only twenty-six years old. Three years younger than Alex.

"Nope." Molly hiked one broad shoulder, peacocking in her moment of glory while she held onto the top secret intelligence to which no one else was apprised.

"You win." Jill flicked her leg hard. "Spill it."

"Handed in her resignation to Rodney yesterday. She's finished."

"How the hell do you know that?" Halsey flipped the TV volume to mute, where dozens of reporters were still gathered on the courthouse steps, awaiting news from the closed session inside.

Alex didn't care how she knew. The more burning question was *why*.

Jill was of the same mind. "That makes no sense. Why even start the season then?"

"Rumor—on good authority—" they all knew she meant Monica's bestie, Valerie Sims, "—is that she's gotten engaged."

"*Again*?" Halsey bumped her elbow against the headboard, cussing as she sat up straighter, fully invested in the drama. "She just ditched the last one at the alter—what, three?—four?—months ago?"

"Three," said Alex, not that she'd been counting. She just knew it had been a blissful few months since Caleb's most recent drunk dial.

"Brazilian businessman. Wants a dozen babies, wife home barefoot in the kitchen on his ranch in Niterói—not," Molly clarified, "that there's anything wrong with that... I just prefer my days spent in cleats on the field. And, as rumor has it, it seems like they may have gotten their little family started early... like *before* she dumped Caleb wearing her virginal wedding gown."

A lengthy silence ensued before Sawyer suddenly snorted, unable to quell her laugh. "Are you even kidding? She strung that boy along for over a year with all her *lets-wait-until-we-get-married* bullshit, which she felt the need to preach to the *entire* locker room, and yet she was hooking up with some guy that *wasn't* her fiancé, and still had the audacity to plan an entire wedding, before jilting him while carrying this other dude's child?"

"Someone call Jerry Springer," Halsey cackled, rubbing her hands together with glee. "The fucking hypocrisy is epic! Alex, please, *please* promise me you'll unleash a vague social media reference about our departing teammate's *Core Christian Values* and questionable *ethical depravity*."

"Turpitude," said Alex. Monica had called her out on her 'ethical turpitude.' She shook her head without laughing, still wrapping her mind around the information. She wanted to care that Monica was a hypocritical bitch who'd been living a total lie—but the only thing she really cared about was that she'd played her last match with the girl who'd made her life a living hell, and the little twit would soon be living sixty-five hundred miles away.

"Oh!" Sawyer interrupted the conversation by gesturing wildly at the TV. "Erin, turn it up!"

Cameras had panned in on the limestone courthouse doors, where Carlton and his counsel had emerged onto the landing. Contrary to what had been expected, the former senator didn't stop and orate to the crowd, and instead hid behind the upturned collar of his coat, and remained surrounded by his security as they pushed their way to the waiting cars.

He looked old. Older than sixty-one. Grayer. Thinner. A shell of the man who'd been caught on camera threatening to slit Catharine's throat. There was none of his bravado or bluster. For the first time since Alex had known him, he actually looked the part of the insignificant, pathetic deadbeat who'd fooled an entire country into buying into his farcical lies.

Microphones were shoved in the face of the prosecutor from the United States Attorney's office as she followed her team out the door. Unlike Carlton's counsel, she was smiling, and was more than willing to stop for an interview. She answered basic questions —what had Cleveland plead? *Not guilty.* When was the trial due to start? *Four weeks from Tuesday.* Were there charges beyond Felony Threats? *Not from her office, but she could not speak for other jurisdictions.* But the question Alex cared about most was answered in a banner across the bottom of the screen: *Judge commands Carlton Cleveland to house arrest until trial.*

"Homie's gonna jingle jangle in that ankle bracelet!" Molly gave Alex a triumphant slap on the back.

It wasn't where Alex wanted him—behind solid block walls and two inch bars would have been preferential, if only secondary to six feet underground—but home detention would do. It was better than being released to his own recognizance, which was what they'd been expecting. Which also gave a strong indication that the court system intended to make an example out of him. There would be no buying his way out this time.

Her phone buzzed on the nightstand, but before she could pick it up, Halsey got to it first. "Ohhhh," she cooed, "I knew it would be the missus! Can I answer it?"

"No!" Alex lunged, but the keeper's massive wingspan easily kept the phone aloft as she rolled with ridiculous agility off the bed to her feet.

"Heyyy, *Portland!*"

"Erin—!" Alex struggled to disentangle herself from the bodies strewn across her bed.

"Yeah, yeah, she's right here. We're having a little party." She held the phone up to a chorus of hellos from Sawyer, Jill, and Molly. "Anyhow, we were just thinking, maybe you could help us out and make an emergency flight out to Frisco to see Alex, because she is taking herself way too serious and *really* needs to get la—"

The word was cut off by a sharp elbow to her gut as Alex recovered her phone.

"Hey," Alex escaped through the narrow hall to the bathroom and locked the door. "Sorry, they…" She dwindled off. She was far past explaining the idiocy of her teammates. Catharine was used to it by now. "Anyway." She leaned against the fake glass surrounding the shower. "Good news today."

"Ah—the presentment, yes. I'll be more satisfied when he's behind bars." Catharine sounded disinterested, yet cheerful. "But on a more interesting note—I've just had a call from Kathy Grimes."

"Oh?" Kathy was the commissioner of the NWSL. She was also the woman who held the majority of power when it came to determining eligible bids to buy into an expansion team. "And?"

"She liked my bid. A lot. I think they're going to accept it."

"Fantastic!" Alex took a seat on the closed toilet lid. For months they'd been waiting to hear if Catharine's proposal would make the short list of prospects to build into the league the following year. It wasn't surprising to Alex. The ownership group Catharine had put together, the plan for investment, the future she'd mapped out for a successful club, was top tier. She'd doubted any others could surpass what Catharine brought to the table.

"She loves the idea of Southern California."

"Who wouldn't? We knew the prospect of a west coast rivalry would sing their tune."

Catharine sighed on the other end of the line, but it was a happy sigh. A contented sigh. The sigh of life moving forward. Of things falling into place.

"Now," Catharine changed the subject, her voice growing teasing, "about what Erin said…"

Chapter Thirty-Eight

"It really is audacious to call this the *Summer* Olympics! For one thing, it's October. And for the other, it may be spring in this hemisphere, but it hasn't stopped raining since I got here!" Nathalie's complaints were muffled beneath the hood of the yellow slicker that had turned her into a life-sized replica of Big Bird.

Catharine tuned her out. For three days she'd been listening to the Frenchwoman's griping, ever since Nathalie'd arrived in just enough time to watch the States beat Sweden in the quarterfinals.

And as luck would have it, the foul weather continued. On the field, through a never-ending downpour, the US now took on Great Britain, both teams vying to secure a spot in the gold medal match the coming weekend. As it stood, a few minutes before the half, the Americans were up, one-nil.

Over the top of an obnoxious Stars and Stripes fan dressed as Uncle Sam, Catharine watched—with less than a minute left in stoppage—as a poor clearance inside the US box allowed Jamie Fisher, an English midfielder, to seize on the error and hammer the ball past the diving form of Erin Halsey. There was a moment of uncertainty as VAR determined if the play had been off-sides, and then the ref was signaling the goal was good, and Great Britain had leveled the game. Seconds later, the whistle blew for halftime, and the players cleared the pitch. Team GB, elated—the Americans, disheartened after giving up their lead.

"Damnit." Catharine's eyes followed Alex as she disappeared into the tunnel.

"Can we get under the cover now?" Nathalie pestered. Raindrops were dripping off her chin and nose, despite her nylon slicker, and her makeup had given up on its waterproof rating as gobs of black mascara streamed down her cheeks. "You realize there are perfectly good boxes in a perfectly dry concourse where we could be watching in comfort?"

Catharine hadn't cared if she watched in comfort. She wanted to be close to the pitch. She wanted to be near Alex. To to cheer her on, even if she knew her voice would never carry over the crowd.

The only thing she cared about was seeing her get through this elimination round.

The Americans had a chance to make history the following weekend—no team had ever won the World Cup and Olympic gold back-to-back—but first they had to get there. Which, at the moment, tied one-to-one, left it anybody's match.

"I could really go for a whisky and cider," Nathalie continued to bemoan.

"Then go up yourself!" Catharine snapped, flinging off the hood of her coat, as if that would help change the score. "I'll be staying here."

Caught off guard by the unexpected irascibility, Nathalie abandoned her nagging and gave Catharine's arm a conciliatory squeeze.

"Cheer up, Cate. They'll pull it off. They always do."

"Are you even rooting for her?" Catharine knew she sounded petulant, but she couldn't help herself. Despite her intent focus on the game, a part of her was still processing the bombshell Nathalie had dropped on her over lunch that afternoon.

"What?" Nathalie's russet eyes narrowed, disappearing into the dark streaks of smeared eyeshadow. "Are you serious? You think I'd be sitting out here, soaked to the skin, freezing to death, if I wasn't rooting for Alex? Jesus, Cate—you can be so petty! I flew all the way here, for God's sake—"

"Oh, please, you only flew here to tell me you are moving to England."

There, she'd said it.

Hours earlier, over flat whites and banh mi sandwiches, she hadn't found an acceptable way to express her hurt. So instead she'd let it fester, eating at her until she said something she'd regret. She had a knack for that.

"I flew here," Nathalie said, very slowly, very deliberately, "because I wanted to support you—*and* Alex. I consider her my friend as well, thank you very much. I only told you about England because I didn't want you to feel like I'd been withholding something from you when we got home. Which you absolutely know you would have accused me of."

She was right. Nathalie had been damned if she did, and damned if she didn't. Catharine would have been hurt either way.

"I just think it seems very drastic." Catharine looked away from her, pinning her gaze on the stands across the field. "You've known her what, half a year—?"

"Ten months—"

"Ten months." Catharine scoffed at the number. "Nat, she's—"

"I'm not even moving in with her, at least not yet. We just want to—"

"You're tossing aside everything you have to start a theatre company in London—"

"*Yes*. And I have you to thank for that. Without my success in San Francisco, I never would have been given this opportunity with Royal Court." Nathalie reached for Catharine's frozen fingers, enfolding them in her own. "I know you'll miss me—which is what you're unwilling to say—and that right now your feelings are hurt. But I think you'll come to understand, Cate—you don't need me like you once did. You've got Alex now. You've got a new adventure on the horizon. And it's time I set out on my own." She leaned her shoulder against her. "We'll still see each other, as we always have. You'll still be my best friend, my confidante, the one person I know I can always count on. That will never change. We'll just be a little further away." Nathalie pressed her hand. "Be happy for me, please."

Catharine watched a Union Flag fluttering across the stadium, its cloth weighed down by the continued onslaught of the downpour. The Great Britain supporters section was gearing up for the start of the second half, their bass drums issuing a muffled echo in the rain. On the opposite side of the circular stadium, a USA chant had risen up in the crowd. The players were jogging onto the field, their boots disappearing into the flooded grass.

"You're right, I will miss you," she admitted, returning the squeeze of Nathalie's hand. "But you're wrong to think I don't need you. That day will never come."

Nathalie said nothing, and simply slipped an arm around her, giving up on her hopes to find a dry place to watch the remaining forty-five minutes of the match.

With ten minutes remaining, the score still one-to-one, Catharine began to worry the game might go to extra time. Two fifteen minute periods of play, before—if neither team was ahead of the other—it would come down to a penalty shootout.

Every footballer's worst nightmare, albeit a thrill for the fans.

Catharine, however, was not included in those spectators who enjoyed the high intensity drama finale. Not when Alex was on the field. Not when she knew how much Alex struggled with the thought of letting down her team again. It left too much to luck. And placed too much weight on individual shoulders. The US team needed to find a way through Great Britain's unbending defense—and soon.

On the pitch, the players on both sides looked increasingly exhausted. With only three days between matches, there'd been no time for recovery, and as they progressed deeper into the tournament, it began to show.

Jill Thompson—captaining in the place of Kristin Salter, who'd come up with a minor hamstring injury earlier in the tournament—was beginning to lose speed, and when she was clipped from behind on a run toward goal, she laid on her back on the soggy pitch, clutching her calf. As the yellow card was issued and medical helped Jill to her feet, Catharine watched—temporarily forgetting her anxiety of the dwindling clock—as the winger handed off her captain's armband to Alex. In the team's last camp before leaving for Melbourne, Alex had texted Catharine that she'd been voted second vice-captain. An honor, she imagined, she'd never get to exercise. But an honor she'd been thrilled to have bestowed upon her all the same.

Three rows down from where Catharine was sitting, a familiar figure jumped to her feet, spinning to shoot Catharine a broad grin. "Tickle me pink, that's our girl!" shouted Clancy Halsey, her round face a glistening, swirled mess of red, white, and blue paint. With double thumbs up, the Mississippi woman let out a piercing whistle, swinging her *I Believe* scarf in an arc above her head.

"Good work, Jill!" she hollered as the winger hobbled off the field. "Let's do this, Captain Grey!"

How full circle it felt, watching Alex pull on that armband. A girl two seasons earlier who'd never played a single minute wearing a US jersey—who'd thought her chance at an international career had long passed her by—now given the privilege to lead her team on the world's biggest stage.

Catharine joined in the rallying applause as the free kick put the game back underway, and tried not to dig her nails too deeply into Nathalie's thigh.

The minutes ticked down. Eighty-eight. Ninety. Then five minutes of stoppage. Catharine grew antsy, unable to watch each time Great Britain found space and sent a ball toward the US goal frame. The US clawed back, the game turning frantic as the fatigued players became more careless, more brutal. It was a relief, almost, when the whistle was blown to end the second regulation half, allowing both teams a few minutes of rest before moving into extra time.

Atwood would pull Alex. Catharine felt certain of it. She'd played every minute of every match leading into the semifinal. But when the game resumed, Alex—still wearing the captain's armband—was back jogging through the ankle deep muck, ready to resume from the kickoff.

Two more yellow cards—one for each team—were administered in the first few minutes. And then a Hail Mary of a ball from Molly Rodrigues found Sawyer in the box, who shot it off the crossbar. She'd missed only by centimeters.

The crowd grew louder, more raucous, the hundred-thousand fans building into a frenzy as rivaling chants drowned out the shouts of the players as they continued back and forth across the slick grass.

Another shot from Sawyer was deflected by a Welsh defender, earning the US a corner in the last minutes of the first fifteen. Shrouded by the curtain of rain, the players jostled one another, shoulder-against-shoulder, until the ball was floated too far past its intended target of Rodrigues, arching to the far post, where Alex stood ready.

Her eyes never leaving the ball, Catharine watched as Alex threw herself into the air with full velocity, knowing the outcome of her header could be the game changing play. At the same time she left the ground, Kelsey Evans, England's biggest star, leapt to clear the threat, both players unaware of the other.

Catharine couldn't hear the collision, though felt as if she had. The two women missed the ball between them as their heads slammed into one another and they tumbled to the ground. It wasn't unusual. Hard impacts were an unavoidable risk of any contact sport. Catharine had watched countless numbers of rough tackles and heavy challenges lay players flat out. Alex included.

But this time was different. This time, as the pair collapsed, Alex didn't move. She just laid in the mud as Kelsey rocked to a sitting position beside her.

Catharine's heart plummeted. There were no elongated moments of slow motion. No spells of hyperfocus that allowed her to hear individual voices on the field. Instead she just felt numb, her thoughts addled as she watched the ref waving wildly toward the sidelines, beckoning straight for a stretcher, forgoing an initial medical assessment. Whatever had happened, the official, the players on the pitch, all felt it was bad.

Halsey sprinted all the way across from the opposite goal, her goalkeeping gloves discarded to the mud by the time she dropped to her knees at Alex's side. Sawyer, joined by a slow moving Kelsey Evans, blocked Catharine's view as they gestured teammates out of the way to make room for the arriving medical staff.

Excuse me. Sit back. Watch your toes. A familiar Mississippi accent roused Catharine from her stupor as Clancy Halsey wedged, sidled, and hoisted her plump frame across various laps and legs, making her way over the three rows of seats until she got to Catharine.

"It's okay," she cooed, soothing. At some point Catharine realized the older woman was holding her hand. "She's done gone and got herself knocked out—that's all. She's going to be okay, Catharine." But there was worry behind the rising lull and fall of the Southern drawl. "C'mon now," she picked up Catharine's purse and stuffed it into Nathalie's arms. On the field they were fitting Alex in a spinal collar. She still wasn't moving. "Let's just get on over to the tunnel. With a good knock like that, they'll be taking her over to the clinic to get checked out. Just routine."

Catharine obediently followed Clancy up the steps to the concourse, vaguely aware Nathalie was trailing behind them. When she got to the top, she turned back to the pitch and saw Alex was moving. Not much. Just a hand. Catharine realized she was trying to pull off the captain's arm band and give it to Sawyer. She wasn't sure whether to laugh or cry at the gesture.

"There, now, see, I told you." Clancy sounded as relieved as Catharine felt. "She'll be fine and dandy in no time. Now let's skedaddle on over and see if we can get you a ride in the wagon."

By the time they'd reached the exit, a roar went up from the stadium, and Catharine paused along the top row of seats long enough to see Alex had been loaded onto the stretcher and was lifting a hand in acknowledgement to the crowd, who clapped her off the pitch with a standing ovation.

Clancy tracked down a security guard, speaking to him briefly, before returning to Catharine's side. "Come, come, this gentleman will escort us."

"Clancy, you'll miss the rest of the—"

"Honestly, Catharine—my niece would be madder than a wet hen if she knew I didn't make sure you got to Alex. They'll be another match—have faith!" With that, the woman was off again, bossing the tolerant stadium guard to *hustle his bustle* along the way.

They didn't make it in time to the ambulance. The labyrinth of guarded doors leading to the cordoned-off *personnel only* areas of the stadium were slow to access, and by the time they got to the private exit nearest the dressing rooms, they were informed Alex was already on her way to the polyclinic in the Athletes' Village.

"Then I suppose you can give Ms. Brooks a ride to the clinic," Clancy said, squaring up with a man a head taller than she was who had the Olympic logo emblazoned on his black polo and appeared to be in charge.

"I'm sorry," he said curtly, "the Village is only accessible to athletes."

"I imagine there are exceptions for significant others under extenuating circumstances, such as life-threatening injuries." Clancy rolled her shoulders back.

"And her husband is...?" He made a sarcastic sweep of the hall, aware it was only Clancy, Catharine, and Nathalie present. "If he shows up, we will consider it."

"Ms. Brooks is her girlfriend."

"I see." His lips turned up in a mordant smile. "I'm sorry, I cannot help you. Once treatment is provided, her team liaison will contact the family."

"You know," Clancy took a step back to better see his face, "my niece is down on that field keeping goal for the US. She's got a few million followers on her Instagram who I am sure would love to weigh their opinion to the Olympic Committee about how they feel that one of their employees denied access to an athlete due to discrimination against—"

"Only one of you," he gruffly cut her off. "Whichever one." He yanked open the door.

Catharine sat in the waiting room of the polyclinic in front of a door labeled *triage area*. It had been difficult, despite the circumstances, not to find herself impressed by the state of the art facility; an entire hospital built on a micro scale. There was every type of specialist and care provider an athlete could possibly require.

Alex was currently being assessed by the neurology team as they reviewed the results of her cat scan.

"Fuck!" The man sitting beside Catharine—an athletic trainer from the USWNT who had accompanied Alex to the clinic—doubled over in his seat, his head briefly disappearing between his knees as he agonized over the livestream on his phone. He'd been watching the remainder of the match, while Catharine kept tabs over his shoulder. "No! Fuck, *no!*"

Catharine grabbed his arm, pulling him upright so she could see the screen. The Brits were celebrating, huddling around an English player Catharine recognized as Jordie Dobson, their brick wall center back. The women were high-fiving her, swinging her in circles, ruffling her platinum blonde hair. In the upper left hand corner the timer indicated they were twelve minutes into the last fifteen minute half.

For the second time that night, Catharine felt her heart sink, the cavity of her chest filling with an indescribable despair. They couldn't—they simply *couldn't*—lose. Not now. Not like this—without Alex even there.

But five minutes later, as both extra and added time ran out, the Brazilian ref raised the whistle to her lips and blasted it three times, ending the match. Team Great Britain had beaten the Americans two-to-one to move onto the Gold Medal final. The US were out, their only remaining chance to podium by playing for bronze in the third-place playoff. History would not be made. At least not this year.

Catharine set a hand on the back of the athletic trainer, but the man was too distraught to find comfort, instead hurling himself to his feet and pacing the room.

"Fuck," he repeated, over and over, the rubber soles of his damp shoes squeaking across the scrubbed tile floor. "I can't believe this."

Catharine could only stare at the *triage area* sign. Her phone was in her purse with Nathalie. She would have liked to have texted Clancy. She wasn't even sure why.

"For Alex?"

A stately young woman suddenly stood in the threshold with a clip board. Catharine hadn't even processed the door opening.

The athletic trainer was still pacing. Still cussing. Still typing furiously on his phone.

"Yes." Catharine stood.

"And you are?" The young woman was businesslike, but warm.

"Catharine Brooks. Her girlfriend." Catharine hated the diminutive sound of it. As if it were something new or temporary. As if it held no currency and was less than it was. The word had never bothered her until the black polo shirt dismissed her at the stadium.

"Excellent." The woman smiled and held out her hand. "I'm Dr. Adeyemi, Alex's neurologist. I'm sorry for the wait."

Neurologist. The woman had seemed so young. Catharine shook her hand.

The athletic trainer quit his pacing and came to a stop beside Catharine.

"I need to tell her we lost," he blurted. "That we're not moving on."

"I'm very sorry to hear that." Dr. Adeyemi seemed genuinely sympathetic. "Coming from Nigeria, I was disappointed to have the Super Falcons defeated in the quarterfinals, but I have great respect for your US team."

"I have to tell her we're fucking going home."

The man was crass, too frantic to be professional, and it would be over Catharine's dead body before he was the one who broke the news to Alex.

"I'm sorry, Mr.—" she searched for an embroidered name on his warm up jacket, but found only the US crest. "Look," she began again, more emphatically, dropping any attempt at formalities, "I think it would be better if she heard it from me—"

"It's my job—"

"Ms. Brooks is right," Dr. Adeyemi cut in. "Alex has taken quite a hit, and I think it might be better if the news came from a more —" she searched for the word.

Tactful, Catharine imagined, but kept her own mouth shut.

"If it came from her family." The doctor tread prudently. "It might soften the blow."

"Yeah, sure, doctor's orders," the man shrugged, indifferent. He looked at Catharine. "You going to stay here with her, then? Because I gotta get out of here. I gotta call my girlfriend."

He was gone, out the door, before Catharine could even respond.

Dr. Adeyemi motioned Catharine to follow her through the threshold.

"The good news," she said, once they were in the privacy of the hall, "is that Alex should recover well. Her CT showed no abnormalities—which is, of course, what we always hope for. She is certainly experiencing signs of being concussed—headache, nausea, some confusion—but I understand she was unconscious for several minutes, which—though of course is of concern—explains her current symptoms. I would like to see her back here again before she flies home." Dr. Adeyemi jotted something onto her chart. "I realize—with the unfortunate loss—her teammates will likely head back to the States earlier than planned, but I would be more comfortable if Alex didn't fly for the next ten days. Do you think she will agree to that?"

"Yes." Catharine tried to focus on the doctor's words, but all she could think about was that in a matter of minutes, she was going to break Alex's heart. Deliver her a hurt far more painful than any concussion she'd experienced.

But—she was okay. She would be fine. And that, really, was all that mattered. Because, having watched her lay motionless on that field, the outcome could have been... unthinkable.

Dr. Adeyemi was staring at her expectantly, and Catharine realized she'd asked another question.

Would she be the one staying with Alex? She would be willing to release her from the clinic once the worst of her symptoms had subsided as long as she was supervised.

Again, Catharine nodded. "Yes. Yes, of course."

"Wonderful." Dr. Adeyemi hung up her clipboard. "She's in the room on the left at the end of the hall. Don't switch on the light. Just come out and get me when—well," she hesitated, "when she's up for it. Again, I'm sorry for your loss."

Chapter Thirty-Nine

The morning after the loss to Great Britain, Alex laid on the couch in a hotel suite overlooking Victoria Harbour, and watched the replay of the second semifinal match that had been played simultaneously with her own.

Australia vs. Colombia.

She'd known the results before pulling it up on her computer—the hazards of a hundred phone notifications awaiting her when she woke—but had still wanted to watch the game. It promised a distraction from the splitting pressure in her head, overpowered only by the colossal weight of disappointment following her team's elimination.

The Matildas had defeated their South American rivals, sending Australia for the first time in history into the Olympic Final. It was a chance for redemption after the World Cup loss—a chance to win a gold in front of their home country. And despite her own misery, Alex found herself happy for her friend—rooting for her as she lead her team to a shutout victory against a sharp Colombian side. The Aussies had made a clear statement they 'weren't here to fuck spiders,' as Amelia had so casually dropped in the post-match press conference—much to the delight of the spectators, and horror of the international media.

Alex felt guilty, finding herself unable to curb a smile at her friend's unfiltered interview. It felt wrong to find any source of happiness, any form of enjoyment, so shortly after her own heartbreak. They'd lost. They'd given everything they had—pushing themselves both mentally and physically to the brink, and come up with nothing. There would still be the upcoming Bronze Medal match, but at the moment, even that opportunity felt conciliatory. The only thing worse than coming in first loser was—lo and behold—coming in second loser. Which also meant losing the Bronze Medal match was not an option.

But it wasn't something Alex had to worry about, because she knew, based off the pear-shaped lump on her forehead, and consequent black eye, she wouldn't see the pitch again in Melbourne. She remembered that much from the doctor's discharge instructions. Even if the rest of the night was veiled in haze.

She pulled off her headphones and snapped her laptop shut to find Catharine brewing tea in the kitchenette.

When Alex had first woken amidst a fog of dizziness and nausea, she'd found Catharine asleep in a recliner pulled close to the sofa. It had taken a moment to recollect the night before, to even realize why she wasn't on her polyethylene mattress with its cardboard bed frame, sharing a room with Halsey, Sawyer, and Rodrigues in the spartan accommodations of the Athletes' Village. And then, even before her recollection of being discharged from the polyclinic, and of the doctor's recommendation that she depart the team setting and recover in a quieter atmosphere, she was struck again with the realization that their gold-medal quest was over.

She remembered, then, why Catharine was on the recliner. Why her head was pounding and her body felt as if she'd been struck by a Freightliner. She remembered, with a twinge of embarrassment, that she'd made it out of the Athletes' Village, to the hotel, and through a shower before she'd broken down in sobs. And that Catharine had sat on the floor beside the couch, stroking her back and smoothing her hair, until she'd finally fallen asleep from exhaustion.

"How was the match?" Catharine sat down beside her, balancing two ceramic mugs and a bottle of ibuprofen in one hand, and a plate in the other.

"Australia won." Alex eyed the plate skeptically, her queasy stomach uncertain of its contents. There was a cut apple, a handful of blueberries, halved walnuts, trimmed broccoli, and what looked like a piece of dark chocolate.

"An article from the Mayo Clinic recommended antioxidants, fiber, vitamin K, and magnesium." Catharine set the odd assortment onto the arm of the couch, and handed Alex her tea, along with the anti-inflammatories. "So Australia versus England, then. That sounds like quite a match."

Alex downed the Advil and cringed at the green tea.

It would be quite a match.

Amelia Walker vs. Kelsey Evans.

There was a sliver of Alex that found relief in the knowledge she didn't have to face Amelia on the pitch again. Not because she didn't relish the challenge—when it came to football, there was nothing she craved more than pitting herself against the best. But because, no matter how much she'd wanted that gold, fighting for it against Amelia somehow felt like a losing battle. No matter which way the game unfolded.

Alex picked up an apple slice and tentatively put it in her mouth. Eating did not feel like a high priority, but the way the room swayed around her said otherwise.

"I'd like to go to the game."

"Of course."

Alex pushed the walnuts around the plate. "I'll be rooting for the Matildas." She didn't look at Catharine.

"I would expect nothing less. You need to support her."

Alex looked up. It was a relief to hear her say that and know that she meant it. The topic of Amelia had long hung between them, never festering, but always with the hint of a sensitivity lying beneath it. It was never that Alex had felt Catharine was jealous, or disapproving, or that she didn't trust her—on the contrary, she had been nothing but supportive of the friendship they'd rebuilt. But still, the nature of the matter had remained a fragile subject, as Alex supposed came natural with the territory.

"Thank you."

The chasmic empathy behind Catharine's sea blue gaze turned bright, her smile playful.

"I hope you'll forgive me if I root for Great Britain."

"I'd be skeptical of your heritage if you didn't—football at the crux of your English soul and all," Alex teased her.

"I wasn't going to bother you with it this morning, but I should warn you—Elle has decided to fly over to watch the match."

"Ah." Alex instantly regretted the tightness in her jaw as it made her swollen face ache. "Well, no question who she'll be rooting for."

Catharine offered a sympathetic grimace.

"I know. I'm sorry." She reached up, gently running the tips of her fingers across the angry lump on the side of Alex's forehead. "You know, you really scared me last night."

Alex mustered a smile. "I'm sorry. I think I took *go big or go home* too literally." Her smile slipped. "I guess *go home* was all that was in my cards this time."

Catharine's own smile was small, understanding. She said nothing, and simply leaned forward and kissed Alex's cheek.

Alex appreciated that she didn't try to placate her, or chastise her for her self-deprecation, or minimize her disappointment by telling her all those things well-meaning people think a defeated person needs to hear: *oh, but you did your best. You tried so hard. You'll win the next one.* Instead, she simply allowed Alex her grief, aware that sometimes the best support to be offered was empowering another to hurt without trying to fix it with words.

Aussie, Aussie, Aussie, Oi, Oi, Oi.

"Have you ever heard such a vapid chant?" complained Elle two seats down from Alex as a sonorous chorus of Australian voices welcomed their players back from the half. "At least we English have imagination."

Alex leaned over Catharine. "What, like: *we love you England, we do, oh England, we love you*? Or: *we're England, we're gonna score one more than you*? Both very original."

"Careful there, Miss Grey—you look dreadful enough with one black eye."

Malcolm, on cue, leaned down from his seat in the row behind Alex, offering Elle a thorny smile.

"Imagine how chippy the lasses are bound to get when they realize 'it's not coming home,'" he said to Alex, making certain the attorney could hear. He'd made it apparent as soon as they entered the stadium he'd thrown his support behind the Australian team. Despite representing all of Great Britain, Team GB was made up of primarily English players—with only two from Scotland and one from Wales. Not enough, the Scot had made clear, to disgrace himself and cheer on the English side.

"It's a shame they don't teach basic arithmetic in Scotland." Elle turned her head sharply away from him, viewing the field over the top of her narrow nose. "Catharine, have pity on your man and explain to him the score is one-nil."

"Least in Scotland we know the game consists of two halves," Malcolm whispered, giving Alex a cheerful clap on her shoulder, before sitting back, and in his strident Scottish brogue, shouting "Aussie, Aussie, Aussie," to which a sea of green and gold enthusiastically responded *oi, oi, oi*.

As the game commenced, Alex's attention returned to the field.

The atmosphere of the stadium was galvanizing. It was a complete sellout, with all 100,024 seats filled, the match setting a record as the largest attendance ever in women's football history. Outnumbering the English in droves, the Australian fans hadn't let the Matildas down, and even with the score against them, had not for a single second given up on the gold.

But the Great Britain fans—though fewer—were boisterous and making themselves known. Somewhere across the pitch, in response to the Australian cheers, someone had struck up the refrain of *Rule, Britannia!* as Sarah Lee, an Australian winger, took a long range strike toward goal.

The defense, caught off guard by the distance shot, were out of position, and despite a full stretch effort from Great Britain's goalkeeper, it sailed past her outstretched fingertips and into the upper pocket of the net.

Alex had experienced the wild frenzy of Wembley during the World Cup. The feel of the grass quivering beneath her feet as ninety-thousand fans shook the stands. But she wasn't certain it matched the pandemonium of the Australian celebration as the host country watched their team level the score. The horns. The drums. The hoarse screams from young and old. The man in front of her in a *Walker* jersey hoisted his toddler over his head, expletives flying from his mouth as the child waved her homemade sign.

On the field Alex could see Amelia yelling at her team mid-celebration. She couldn't hear her, but knew, based off her animated body language, what she would be saying: *Let's go, let's go, let's go! We're not fucking done yet!* Alex knew the demanding clap of those hands, the bark of that voice. The endless determination and drive.

Play resumed, battling back and forth across the pitch. The Australians had found renewed energy, the momentum shifting as Team GB fought to defend. A foul was called on Emma Wright, an English midfielder, resulting in a chant of *I'm blind, I'm def, I wanna be a ref*, from the Great Britain supporters.

The Matildas' quickly executed free kick sent a whistling shot toward the goalkeeper, which caught a jumping English defender in her outstretched arm.

"Bloody rubbish!" Elle was on her feet, her nails painstakingly painted with Saint George's cross shaking a wild fist through the air. The boos from the primarily English fans were drowned out by a seismic roar from the Australians as the official blasted her whistle and pointed to the penalty spot.

Sawyer, to Alex's left, clawed her friend's shoulder. "Bullshit! Her arm was in a natural position!"

VAR felt otherwise, and, as every spectator in the stadium anticipated, Amelia Walker stepped to the ball.

Alex sat down. She couldn't watch.

The Matildas' captain hadn't missed a penalty shot in her storied international career. There was something programmed in the Melbourne native—a steeliness that shouldn't have been human to possess.

"Admit it, even you get nervous," Alex had once insisted, the pair of them laying on their backs in Estuary Park across from their apartment building. They'd been watching the cargo ships cross beneath Bay Bridge.

"Nope," Amelia had said simply.

"Lies. *Everyone* gets nervous. You just deal with it better than others."

"Pig's arse." Amelia had turned onto her side. "I'd only be nervous if I thought I was going to miss."

Alex had rolled her eyes.

Now, she forced herself to peek toward the pitch. Amelia didn't look nervous. She stood with her hip cocked, waiting for the ref to blow her whistle, as if she were unaware that tens of thousands of her countrymen were screaming her name. As if the chance to put her team in the lead at the Olympic Gold Medal match in front of her hometown didn't lie at her feet.

The whistle blew, and Alex snuck a hold of Catharine's hand. And a breath later, with four quick, confident steps, Amelia drilled the ball to the far upper corner of the net.

And missed.

The shot ricocheted off the post and back into play, where the goalkeeper managed to scramble to her feet and pounce on the ball before the stunned Matildas' players could capitalize on the deflection.

"Hang up your boots!" Elle shouted over the subdued Australian crowd, as the Matildas' captain jogged—refusing to hang her head down—back toward the middle of the field.

Amidst her devastation for her friend, it crossed Alex's mind to leap up and put the disrespectful bitch in her place. To tell her exactly what she thought of her and her obnoxious mouth. She was no longer technically Catharine's attorney. Not after the jury had ruled in Catharine's favor of the divorce settlement two months earlier, determining a spouse with an abusive history ineligible for alimony. So there was no longer that conflict to keep her mouth shut and be polite. There was, however, the high likelihood she'd end up caught on video and posted on *TikTok* by a surrounding fan. All night long cameras had been pointed in her and Sawyer's direction, and she knew, if she caused a scene, it wouldn't go unnoticed. But whatever. Some things were worth it.

But before she could get to her feet, before she could assemble the exact way she intended to tell the woman where to go and how to get there, two dozen Australian voices rained down on the Englishwoman, snapping at her to *shut the fuck up and sit bloody down.*

To Alex's surprise, the attorney complied, cowed by the fury behind the demand.

Alex spent the next thirty minutes of the match in her seat, unable to keep herself from praying to whatever soccer Gods might be listening to give her friend another chance. Even though she knew no deities were responsible for sports, and that Amelia would have laughed at her for thinking any God favored the outcome of one team over another.

The Australian goalkeeper, a golden glove winner who played for Barcelona, was put to the test twice by Kelsey Evans, sending

Sawyer launching to her feet and shrieking praise on her English girlfriend.

"Let's fucking go, Kelse! Bring it home!"

Alex was too disheartened by the minutes dwindling down to raze her friend on her liberal definition of *home*, given three days earlier she'd hated Great Britain just as much as any of her teammates donning the US crest.

On the pitch, Amelia's work rate had increased, contrary to the fatiguing players surrounding her. At thirty-four years old, her younger teammates and opponents should have been running circles around her. But Amelia wasn't like other players. Where someone else would have been rattled by their failure, shaken by the missed PK, by the gutting disappointment of the knowledge she'd failed to give her team the lead, Amelia was only fueled by the missed opportunity. It was what made her special. Made her who she was. Indefatigable. Indomitable.

Another shot on goal brought a whoop from the Australians, and Alex caught Catharine squeezing her hand.

"If you're not careful, you're going to be accused of being a traitor to your country," Alex whispered with a smile.

Catharine pressed her lips to Alex's ear. "I want whatever makes you happy." And the next time the Australians pressed down the pitch, she cheered.

In the ninety-third minute of the match, with only three more minutes of stoppage on the board, Alex held her breath as once more the Matildas gained possession of the ball. They worked it patiently, systematically—under their disciplined captain's guidance—into their attacking third. Alex could tell Amelia had worked out space between her two opposing center backs, finding she could draw them out of position and leave an opening for her right winger at the far side of the eighteen. She'd been experimenting with it each run into the box, figuring out an angle, determining the best way through.

From two hundred feet away, Alex could read Amelia's body language, and see the play developing one step ahead of Britain's back line.

Split the defenders, draw them off their mark, pass it to her right winger, Jenna Campbell, and make the run to receive the cross back toward the near post. It would work. Five seconds before she put her plan to action, Alex could already see the winning goal.

But to Alex's surprise, Amelia kept the ball longer than she needed to, dribbling it deeper into the box. A simple chop and cut, a shoulder feint, and she'd found herself with space without ever having to release the ball. A clean shot Alex had seen her make a dozen times before. But instead of taking it, she flicked the ball with her heel to Jenna Campbell, who'd been making the run from the outside, and handed the twenty-two year old winger the keys to the late minutes lead.

The young up-and-coming Matildas' forward didn't miss, chipping the ball directly into the net.

Jenna was swarmed by her teammates, disappearing into the fold of gold and green, a hero to her country. The entire stadium was on its feet, and despite every effort from Great Britain to level the score and force the match to extra time, Australia's momentum dominated the ball with what felt like the entirety of Melbourne cheering them to victory.

"Well, the Aussies wouldn't last a day in the Euros," Elle said, snatching up her rain jacket and motioning Nathalie toward the stairs.

Beside Alex, Sawyer slumped in her seat. She sympathized with her friend. She knew from experience it was sometimes worse seeing the person you love lose the thing they wanted most, than losing it yourself. Sawyer had wanted this for Kelsey. But Alex knew she'd be okay. They'd dust themselves off—both the US and Great Britain—and set their sights on the next four year cycle. Besides—it wasn't a complete loss. Team GB had earned their first silver medal, and the US would come home with bronze. Thanks, in part, to Sawyer's winning goal in the third place match the night before.

"Sorry, friend," she said, putting an arm around her shoulder.

"Win some, lose some." Sawyer ran the back of her hand over her eyes, climbing to her feet. "I guess we should get ready for the ceremony." She managed a small smile. "Give me enough conceal-er and I can probably make that look almost presentable." She gestured at Alex's black eye.

"Trying to cover up your girlfriend's handiwork? No way, I earned this memento and I want it memorialized on that podium."

Alex winked, then winced, the eye still sore from cheekbone to forehead. "Meet you up top in a few minutes?"

When she'd gone, Alex kissed Catharine goodbye, knowing she would see her after the medal ceremony, and worked her way through a throng of elated Australians down toward the pitch. The Matildas were doing their victory walk, flags slung across their shoulders, waving to the fans. Alex almost felt guilty squeezing through a horde of children, but then got called out by a teenager who recognized her, and paid her penance for her push to the railing by signing a dozen various objects, from cleats to headbands.

Sheer luck gave her the opportunity to catch Amelia's eye as the team made a slow navigation of the stadium, taking photos and signing jerseys. With her trademark grin, the Australian leisurely climbed the barricade to get closer to the rail.

"That's a helluva ugly shiner," she greeted, raking back her sweat-drenched hair from her eyes. "You know, you didn't have to go to quite such drastic measures to avoid me on the pitch."

"Please, I did you a favor. Besides, winning gold would have made me look greedy. Had to spread the wealth around." Alex smiled, looking across the field to where Jenna Campbell was being interviewed, her name being announced on the Jumbotron as Woman of the Match. "That was some assist," said Alex, the both of them knowing assist meant *gift*.

"Yeah, well, she had the cleaner shot."

She hadn't. There was no question Amelia'd had an empty frame and acres for space. But there were other things that set Amelia Walker apart from the rest. It wasn't just her never ending work ethic, her incomparable athleticism, or her uncanny ability to find the back of the net. She knew how to raise someone up. To push them forward. To get the best out of someone who needed a lift.

She'd done it for Alex. Pulling her up by her bootstraps in the NWSL. Driving her with relentless encouragement to better herself on the National Team. Holding her head above quicksand when her entire life had been sinking into an unrecoverable mess.

She'd made the choice to give Jenna Campbell a boost, knowing the younger player was the future of her country's team. Knowing she was giving up her own opportunity to redeem her missed penalty kick.

And she'd never admit the selflessness of her actions. She'd just shrug it off as the best play in the moment.

And *that* was what made her irreplaceable in this beautiful game.

"Don't get too carried away celebrating that gold medal," Alex said, knowing their time was running short as she was jostled by a dozen children wearing *Walker* jerseys, clamoring to get a photo with their idol. "We still have a playoff berth to clench back home."

"I just happen to have a Sirens Championship on my bingo card," Amelia smiled, reaching up to hug Alex. "Thanks for being here, mate," she hugged her tightly. And then she was gone, off with a sharpie and her crooked smile, basking in the success she deserved.

The following evening, after Nathalie and Elle had departed back to England, and the remainder of the US team was on a flight to the States, Alex walked hand-in-hand with Catharine, browsing the aisles of Queen Victoria Market.

There was a lull that came with the closing of any major tournament; a letdown, after the months and months of preparation, regardless of results. It was the same sensation of the day after Christmas, after the excitement of anticipation had waned, the gifts had been opened, the friends and family who had visited were returned to their lives, leaving a somewhat gloomy hole in their wake.

Alex paused in front of a market stall selling colorful street art graphics. There, amongst the Sydney Harbour Bridge, and Webb Bridge, was Tower Bridge, and directly beside it, the Golden Gate.

She stared at the gleaming red towers rising out of the fog laden sunset. Everything had been so push and grind for—well, almost for however long she could remember—she hadn't realized how homesick she was. How ready she was to be surrounded by familiar places and friends.

Tomorrow she expected to be cleared to fly by the neurologist when she went in for her checkup at the polyclinic. Her symptoms had subsided, her appetite returned, and despite the ugly shade of mashed pea green that had taken over the bruise on the left side of her face, she felt almost normal. Normal, with a side of Bronze-Medal-melancholy, and fatigued relief, interspersed.

Home didn't necessarily mean rest. The Sirens were a week out from securing a spot in the playoffs for the third year in a row, and this season, she felt, they might just lift that trophy.

She'd better, Catharine had teased her throughout the season, informing her it would be her last chance for a while. Because she had every intention of seeing her Southern California club dominating the top of the tables for the unforeseeable future.

Alex loved the way Catharine had fallen head-over-heels enamored with the game. The way she studied the sport, using her influence to network resources, and put her entire heart into finding ways to improve not only the NWSL, but the world of women's professional sports in general.

The endeavor had given her a new sense of purpose—and with that purpose, a happiness that was beginning to feel lasting.

"*Firebirds FC.*" Catharine had woken Alex in the middle of the night several weeks before the Olympics. "A reference to the mythical phoenix and its ability to rise from the ashes. What do you think?"

Even in her disoriented state after being unexpectedly woken, Alex had loved it. The name was perfect. And suiting for Catharine.

"For both of us," Catharine had been adamant.

Moving on from the painting of the Golden Gate, they'd strolled leisurely down the aisle, stopping at the next booth to browse the display tables filled with delicate handcrafted jewelry. An old woman sat at a work table, her gnarled hands twisting wire into what Alex assumed would be a bracelet. Diamonds, turquoise, opals, and emeralds adorned the various custom pieces.

A man from behind the rear curtain appeared, taking one look at Catharine, and steered her toward the flashiest, most intricately cut diamonds. A mistake, Alex thought to herself, as she left Catharine to the overeager salesman and watched the woman turn a boring strand of copper into a work of art. If the man had had any sense, he would have noticed Catharine's appreciation for the subtle, and turned her in the direction of the more exclusive, but equally expensive black opals.

As it was, Alex browsed the array of gemstones, appreciating the vibrant blues and greens and oranges that came from the mineral crystals unique to Australia, and then bought the copper wire bracelet as a keepsake of Melbourne.

"Coffee?" asked Catharine. They'd passed an Airstream-turned-food truck with a line fifteen people deep, promising the best flat whites in Victoria.

As they waited to order, Catharine got a call relating to the *Firebirds*, and stepped away from the crowded clamor of the night market. Alex waited through the slow moving queue, passing the time as she cleared the zillion phone notifications that had been quickly amassing. It was the first she'd logged into social media since arriving in Australia.

There were endless messages—most of them she'd never open. Friends. Fans. Angry supporters of teams they'd beaten in the group stage. Some were kind. Many were ugly. Offers of hookups, business opportunities, and queries begging her to come coach middle school soccer. The ones that surprised her most—the ones she scrolled past the fastest—were of so-called proud US citizens cheering on the American team's early exit in the Olympics. Labeling the team traitors to their country. Out of touch. Woke. All because the team stood in unison for equality.

Alex flicked out of Facebook and logged into Twitter. The first news article she came across was about *Firebirds FC* announcing their partnership with *Woodrow West*, a global real estate conglomerate who had pledged a ten million dollar per annum front shirt sponsorship. More than four times greater than the next highest major investment deal of any NWSL team in history.

That was what Catharine had the power to do. The people she had the ability to attract. *Woodrow West*, Alex knew, was Richard Woodrow—Victoria Woodrow's father. But his cash was as green as anyone else's—even if he had raised a heathen as a daughter.

She got to the front of the line and ordered a pair of flat whites and a box of donuts—a far cry from the recovery-conscious health food Catharine had imposed on her—and scrolled a little longer while she waited by the condiments bar.

Another headline caught her eye.

Carlton Cleveland behind bars: unprecedented multi-jurisdictional case ends with 43 year consecutive sentencing.

Alex stared at the photo accompanying the article. Carlton had only been behind bars for his arson conviction in California for two months, but if the photo hadn't been attached to the headline, Alex wouldn't have recognized him. He was completely gray. His face was gaunt, the skin of his jowls hanging in double arches beneath his chin. It seemed impossible that this was the man who had terrorized her, threatened her, cost her her sponsorships, her endorsement, and almost her job. A man who had humiliated her to a nation, and rallied his band of psychotic followers to engage in an online smear campaign against her. He seemed so weak. So insignificant. So... *nothing*, now.

Alex's finger hovered over repost. She wanted to write: *For he who does wrong will receive the consequences of the wrong he has done, and that without partiality. Colossians 3:25.* She had her own few million fans who would enjoy the irony of the jab.

But she swiped the screen closed instead.

That wasn't her. She wasn't him. He was serving his punishment, and the price had been steep. It had cost him everything.

"I believe sugar was listed as a pro-inflammatory molecule."

Alex paused with a donut midway to her mouth to find Catharine emerging through the slowly wandering flock of shoppers, carrying a parcel wrapped in brown paper. The string of old-fashioned lightbulbs hanging across the narrow market alley lit her hair, turning the golden flaxen to an iridescent hue of platinum.

"Was it?" Alex returned her slow smile, before taking a massive bite of the donut.

"You, um..." Catharine tapped the corner of her own mouth. "A smidge. Right there."

"Oh yeah?" Alex's smile broadened as she took another bite, certain to leave powdered sugar on the opposite side. "Did I get it?"

"Hmm." Catharine's eyes flicked to her lips.

"No? Still there?"

"Still there."

"I might need your help with it," Alex baited, pushing herself away from the coffee condiment bar, closer to Catharine. But she was foiled at her own game when Catharine surprised her by leaning forward and kissing her, soundly, wholly, without a single care for the people milling around them. Alex laughed when

Catharine finally took a step back, both of them catching their breath.

"Well, I think you got it."

"Ask and you shall receive." Catharine gave an insouciant shrug of one shoulder.

"What's in the package?" Alex handed Catharine her cooling coffee.

"That print of the Golden Gate. I'm going to send it to Nathalie."

"Something to remember you by so she won't forget you all together?" Alex teased, knowing Catharine was struggling with Nathalie's planned move to London.

"Don't be mean." Catharine bumped her hip as they worked their way out of the market.

"I'm going to give you a hard time until you come to your senses. Nathalie adores you. I wager you'll see as much of her while she's in London as you did when she lived three blocks away in San Francisco."

"Another bet?"

"Not a chance—you still owe me for the last one!"

"I do, don't I?" Catharine stole a donut from the box as their steps turned toward the waterfront. "What was it again?"

"Forty-eight hours of your undivided, devoted attention."

"And what exactly do you call these last few days?" Catharine goaded.

"Oh no you don't, Catharine Brooks! No chance in hell you're getting off that easy. You owe me something spectacular. Something creative. Somewhere we've never been—or something we've never done."

"All that because Nathalie's gone and decided to shack up with her next bad decision?"

"A hundred percent. The forty-eight hours for winning the bet. The spectacular part for all the interest that's accrued in late payments."

"You drive a hard line."

Alex kissed her cheek, leaving a fresh print of powdered sugar. "I learned it from the best in the business."

Two Months Later

The bow of the boat briefly disappeared beneath the white-capped water, before shooting back toward the sky, sending a spray of seawater over the side deck and directly into Alex's face. Her gloved fingers tightened around the helm.

"Catharine." She hated that the single word revealed the entirety of her mounting anxiety as they rounded Pyramid Rock on the way past Lands End. It was the furthest she'd ever been from the protected waters of the bay. The furthest she'd been along the rocky shore. The Golden Gate was slowly shrinking behind them, its regal towers framing the rising sun as the skyline of San Francisco disappeared with each rolling swell.

"Just hold that course," Catharine called back, casually skirting across the foredeck, entirely unfazed by the crashing waves. "It'll flatten out as soon as we round Point Lobos. We'll stay jib and jigger 'til then."

Alex didn't ask what jib and jigger was. She really didn't care. She only cared that the shore was growing further and further away as the swells seemed to be gaining height and momentum.

"Can she withstand this?" Alex finally asked, after the ketch had suffered a particularly hard impact with a cresting wave. Catharine nimbly dropped into the cockpit.

"Withstand what?"

"Uh—" Alex twirled her finger around them, before immediately regretting taking her hold off the wheel. She doubled down on her grip. "This."

Catharine laughed. "This weather? *Alex.*" She came up behind her, resting her chin on her shoulder and placing her hands over the top of Alex's own. "This is mild. She's made for this." She found a space between Alex's beanie and the unturned collar of her nautical coat, and kissed her cheek. "You said you wanted to do something we've never done before."

"Dying in a shipwreck off the coast of California wasn't quite what I had in mind."

"It's still something you've never done before. You should have been more specific." She moved her lips to her neck. "But honestly, tell me sailing under the Golden Gate on the dawn of Christmas Eve isn't spectacular."

Alex couldn't deny it. They'd glided by sail power across the protected waters of the bay through the waning minutes of twilight, then watched the sun rise over Bay Bridge and Berkeley. There had been no one else on the water. Nothing but the festive lights of San Francisco and the invariably awe-inspiring shadow of the Golden Gate singing its sirens call to the expanding stretch of sea. It was, indeed, spectacular.

But as soon as they'd passed beneath the bridge and lost the protection of the headlands, spectacular had taken on a different meaning.

"Quit," Alex made no actual effort to pull away, "I can't think when you're doing that."

"Less thinking might do you good." Catharine gave a playful swat to her hip, before dropping onto the bench seat to look at the chartplotter. "As soon as we clear Seal Rocks the wind should die down and we should be able to unfurl the main. It'll level out from there."

"And you still won't tell me where we're going?"

"Sailing."

Alex released her death grip just long enough to flick the water dripping off her gloved fingertips into Catharine's face, but the effect was lost as the ketch careened down another rising swell, diving into the trough and drenching them both in the bone-chilling sea spray.

An hour later, the entire coastline had disappeared, the winds had calmed, the seas had flattened, just as Catharine had predicted. They raised the main and turned south.

Relaxing in the more favorable conditions, Alex flipped on the autopilot and took a seat across from Catharine. It had grown warmer as the morning grew later, allowing the two of them to strip off their hats and unzip their coats.

Winter would not have been Alex's most favorable season to be on the water, but it had been the only window of time that worked. After the Olympics in October, she'd come home to spend the entirety of November in a postseason push. Amelia had not been wrong—in their third year chasing a championship, the Sirens had indeed had an NWSL title on their bingo card. And then there'd been the early December international friendlies, and Catharine tied-up by back-and-forth trips to LA. So when, a few days earlier, Catharine had proposed the idea of the last minute sailing holiday, Alex jumped at the opportunity. Cold weather and all.

Two hundred and sixteen hours, Catharine had promised her. The first forty-eight in payment for her debt. The remaining one hundred sixty-eight to make up for what was promising to be another hectic, nonstop year.

They both knew the nine days would likely be the longest consecutive time they would have together, when, come February, the season was in full swing and *Firebirds FC* took on its inaugural year. But it would give them Christmas Eve to New Year's Day. And that, alone, was more than Alex had bargained for.

"I don't have an exact agenda," Catharine admitted later in the afternoon as they ate peanut butter and jelly sandwiches and kept watch for traffic in the shipping channels. "I thought we might cruise down the coastline. Maybe get all the way to Morro Bay?"

It was the coastal trip they'd planned to drive two years earlier, almost to the day. The trip they had never gotten to go on after Carlton showed up at Alex's apartment Christmas Eve.

Catharine's eyes followed the path of a cargo ship heading toward the bay. It wasn't one of *WorldCargo*'s. For that, Alex was grateful.

"So what do you think?" Catharine's attention returned to the cockpit. "Will that satisfy my debt?"

Nine days on the water with the person she loved more than anyone—anything—else in the world? Alex smiled. "Yeah, that should suffice."

For the next week they sailed along the California coast. Pescadero. Pigeon Point. Carmel. Big Sur. San Simeon. Cambria. Morro Bay. From the water, Alex took in the raw beauty of the California coastline, with its untamed woodlands and violent palisades, and long stretches of sandy, serene beaches in between. The weather remained forgiving, the nights clear, and when they made love beneath the blanket of stars, Alex could watch the burning meteors falling into the earth's atmosphere.

On the eighth day—New Year's Eve—when they'd long turned back from their southern destination, and the coastline had re-sumed its more rugged desolation of the northern terrain, Alex fought off a brush of dolefulness. Her spirits dampened by the knowledge that by the following night they would be stepping back into reality. Back to civilization. Responsibilities. Life. The stars would fade into the glow of the city. The sound of waves lost to the inevitable reentry into the rat race. She knew Catharine felt it, too. She could tell in the way she sat on the bow pulpit, her legs swinging over the side, her thoughts turned inward as the spray of the sea coated her neck and face.

"Do you know where we are?" asked Catharine, rousing Alex from her daydreaming in the cockpit. Alex sat up, realizing their blue water course had turned shoreward, the cliffs and barren beaches growing definition as they drew nearer to land.

"Strait of Gibraltar?" Alex teased, rubbing salt from her sun-burned cheeks.

Catharine shot her a look over the top of her sunglasses. "You wanted to abandon ship in eight foot swells coming out of the bay." She trimmed the jib and began to furl the mizzen. "Now you're ready to take on Gibraltar?"

"Hey, I made it the entire week without getting seasick. I think that counts for something." Alex reached across the cockpit and took over the mizzen halyard Catharine was struggling to unjam. She gave it a tug, easily outmuscling the line, and handed it back to Catharine. "See, you need me on your crew."

Catharine tsked. "Only for your muscle."

"Only that? You sure?"

"I don't know," flipping open the jammer, Catharine allowed the line to slip through her fingers, "you might be good for a few other things." She looked over her shoulder and gave Alex a coy smile. "Like pulling the dock lines out of the aft locker and tossing the bumpers over the side."

"Oh, I'll remember that," Alex playfully returned, climbing to her feet to comply.

They passed through an outer seawall, the shore surrounded by farmland, before a harbor appeared, tucked inside an inner break-water. It was an unfamiliar marina to Alex—a couple hundred small craft slips, most of which appeared to be commercial fishing vessels.

Stenciled letters on the dock lockers read *Pillar Point Harbor*.

"Do you fancy a night ashore?"

They'd tied up in a guest slip and spent a few minutes straight-ening up the deck and cabin. Alex glanced toward the parking lot past the harbor office. There appeared to be a strip mall featuring a fish and chips hut, a kayak rental, and a housing tract—but not much more.

"If you'd like, sure." It was their last night together on the water, and part of Alex didn't want to spend it away from the cozy intimacy of the aft cabin. She'd grown accustomed to falling asleep to the gentle sway of the ocean, and sound of the water slapping against the hull. But Catharine seemed intent on the prospect, and Alex had to admit the thought of a lengthy hot shower held its allure.

"Excellent." Catharine was already throwing a few things in a waterproof duffle. "I hope you don't mind that I took the liberty of making dinner reservations for us for New Year's Eve?"

"Here?" Standing in the companionway, Alex shot another glance toward the parking lot. The fish and chips joint had two outdoor tables with plastic checkered tablecloths. A half dozen men in overalls and waders were lounging in Adirondack chairs.

"Nearby." Catharine's smile was furtive, even if it was slight.

Alex took the bag from her and slung it over her shoulder. "Now I'm intrigued."

That evening, Alex found herself sitting at a windowfront table, dining on a three-course prix fixe menu, overlooking the serrated cliffs of Half Moon Bay.

She'd not recognized the small coastal town on the fifteen minute ride from the marina until the Uber driver had pulled into the long, winding driveway of the Ritz.

"I know the rules specified no places we'd ever been before, but tonight," Catharine said as they stepped out under the porte cochère, "I hope you'll make an exception."

"You already know, for you, I'd make any exception," Alex whispered as they passed through the front entry doors.

It was an admission she'd momentarily reconsidered when she felt the entire front desk staff staring in their direction as they'd waited to check-in. Despite having shed their waterproof sailing attire, Alex knew their hair was wild, their lips chapped and cheeks sunburned, their bodies carrying a coat of salt, shimmering white beneath the glowing lights of the overhead chandeliers. Catharine, ever poised, ever self-assured, remained impossibly unaffected by the looks—which in turn gave her the presence of belonging. Alex, however, knew she stuck out like a sore thumb. Not, she thought with rueful amusement, much different than the first time she'd stood in the same hotel lobby almost three years earlier.

Only this time, there was no secrecy to their relationship. No clandestine effort to conceal their identity or connection. When, at dinner, the waiter asked if—aside from the New Year—they were celebrating anything special, Catharine looked directly at Alex and toasted her glass in her direction, saying simply "the best days of my life."

After a shared dessert of a fig and pistachio glazed pear, Catharine suggested a walk along the cliffside, to which Alex happily agreed. It felt good to be on solid ground. Good to be showered. Good to be walking hand-in-hand. The familiar path to the steep switchback stairs leading to the beach below brought with it a wave of reminiscence. A night that had changed Alex's life—her view of the world—and everything she knew within it. A night, at the time, she'd worried might never be repeated. A night when she'd thought she understood the struggles that might lie ahead—but thinking about it now, what she thought she knew then hadn't even scratched the surface.

Yet they'd survived it all. Somehow. Someway. Survived it, and, as the proverbial saying went, come out stronger on the other side.

As they reached the white sand beach, Catharine once again stepped out of her shoes, and Alex followed suit, trailing her to the water.

"Are you cold?" Standing beside her on the compressed damp sand, frothy water lapping at their feet, Alex could feel an unfamiliar rigidity in Catharine's body. "We can go back in—"

"No." The syllable was short, definitive.

Alex eased the hold on her hand, considering bending to retrieve a flat rock that was gleaming in the moonlight, but Catharine's grip tightened.

"Alex." It was a tone she'd never heard from her. Nervous. Apprehensive.

Alarm filtered through her body.

"I want to give you something."

Alex wasn't certain how to respond. She couldn't read Catharine's expression from the shadows, she could only feel the increasing tension in her fingers and hear the pinch of her habitually melodic voice.

"It's... I don't..." Catharine started twice, before giving up on an explanation, and instead pressed something into Alex's free hand.

It was small. Cold. She knew at once what it was, but her necessity for logic required more detail. She opened her fingers, allowing the ring to sit in the center of her palm. She recognized it. The white gold band with its teal and orange inlay. Not dark teal, as in turquoise, but light—harboring the greens and grays of seafoam. It was the ring she'd admired at the Victoria Market in Melbourne.

"What is it?" Now it was her own voice that was strained.

"A black opal."

"No, I mean..."

From the expression on her face, Alex could tell Catharine knew what she'd meant, she just wasn't certain how to respond.

"It's whatever you want it to be," she said at last, unable to avoid the sensibility of her ingrained rationale. In Alex's stunned silence, she continued. "I don't know if... If you'd want... We've never talked about it." She ran a frustrated hand through her hair. "It could be a promise. It could be—a guarantee. A future commitment. A change of names. Or it could just be a gemstone on your finger on a night where a black opal matches your earrings—"

"Catharine." Alex cut her off, unable to bear her uncomfortable stumbling. "Do you want me to marry you?"

"I—" again her fidgeting fingers went to her hair, pushing back locks that hadn't been out of place. "I don't know if you find marriage antiquated. I don't know if you think it is—"

"Would you answer my question?"

"I—" the word hung for a second, lost in the rhythm of the water at their feet, before she seemed to regain her composure. And with it, her steadfast certainty. "Yes."

"Then ask me."

Catharine released a thin exhalation, before drawing a forced breath. "Alex, I would like you to marry me."

Alex laughed. "That doesn't sound like a question."

"Questions leave room for a variability of answers. I prefer a predictable outcome."

"And did you really come here uncertain of the outcome?"

"I'll admit, I've had my hopes that the odds would be in my favor."

"Don't you always get what you want?" Alex smiled, collecting Catharine's hand, allowing the redolent question to rest between them. She'd asked her that once before, in a room two hundred yards away. On a night that felt like it belonged to another lifetime. Years had past. Miles had been traveled. Hurts, heartaches, wins and losses, happiness and sorrows, and everything in between. In that room they'd been shackled to an insurmountable number of hurdles. The stability of their future as uncertain as the shale beneath their feet. At that time, neither had ever realized the consequence of the disastrous collision course they'd headed down, or imagined the magnitude of the storms they would face.

Yet somehow, they'd kept each other's heads above water. They'd weathered through and held on tight.

And tonight, when Alex leaned in to kiss her—she felt certain they'd ended up right where they belonged. Certain, regardless of every obstacle that had been thrown at them, it had always been intended that they circle back to this place.

Fate? Divine intervention? Happenstance? That's what Catharine had asked her. And today, Alex's answer would remain the same. She would stick with fate. Because, of one thing she was certain—this was meant to be. *They* were meant to be.

Alex could feel Catharine smile against her lips, responding to her question.

"In most cases, yes."

So she hadn't forgotten. She remembered that night as much as Alex. Remembered how far they had come.

"Then you already know my answer."

Catharine took a half step back, her smile subtle. "I'd like to hear you say it."

Alex raised her eyebrows. "I'd like to hear you ask."

Catharine laughed, collecting the ring from Alex's palm and turning it over in her fingers. "Fine," she finally said, giving in to their stalemate. "Alex Grey, there is nothing in existence that would make me happier than to spend the rest of my life with you. Please say that you will marry me?"

It was almost a question. *Almost.*

Alex gave in. "There is nothing I would love more."

She held her hand out, inviting Catharine to slip the ring on her finger. The hue of the stone was luminous in the glowing starlight. Original. Unique. As nonconforming to convention as their relationship had been. Spectacular, in a sense.

She loved the weight of it on her finger. Its unobtrusive presence. The promise of where they were going; the reminder of where they had been.

They were both silent for a moment, unmoving, absorbing the fraction in time they'd never have back.

Alex finally smiled, moving in closer, entwining both of her hands with Catharine's. "So—Alex Brooks, number 11—it has a nice ring to it."

To her surprise, Catharine didn't return her smile. "I was actually thinking, perhaps, you might be willing to share Grey?"

Despite being caught off guard by the request, Alex squeezed her fingers and didn't ask her why.

She knew. She understood.

Catharine had never been a Cleveland. And had never been allowed to be a Brooks. Catharine Grey offered a clean slate, opening the doors to a new identity. Allowing her to become whoever she wanted to be.

A fresh start to a new year. A new future. A new life.

"Catharine Grey." Alex tested it aloud. She realized it would take some time to get used to. Time to reconcile all of the women Catharine was—who she had been—and who she'd become.

But time was on their side.

Forever, they'd agreed.

Together.

No longer facing life 1v1.

ACKNOWLEDGMENTS

This series has been the culmination of the last five years of my life. It was something that started as a pastime, and then slowly evolved into a round-the-clock passion. To say that I've left my heart on these pages is an understatement.

However, one thing needs to be made clear: I may have written the words, and dreamt up the world of Catharine Cleveland, but these books wouldn't exist without my wife. Since day one, Donna has been not only my source of inspiration, but also my greatest cheerleader, my rock, my shoulder to cry on, my first reader, my gentlest critic, and simply the behind-the-scenes force that led these books to publication. So for every reader who has enjoyed this series —it's truly Donna who is due the praise. Otherwise, I guarantee, these books would still be sitting in a file on my MacBook, collecting dust with all the other cobwebs in my head.

To my mom, Melodie—thank you for your continued encouragement, and endless support. And for never freaking out that your introvert daughter preferred hiding in her room with her computer, world-building page-by-page, instead of being as outgoing as I'm sure you and dad would have loved me to be. For just letting me be me.

Dad—I know it's been a tough year. But thank you for keeping your chin up. For letting me drag you to all the soccer games. For putting on a smile when I know it was hard. I sure love you. Let's turn 2024 into another adventure.

Lara—sorry I'm such a bitch when I'm writing. ;-) Thanks for being understanding. And for taking the time to read everything I write. It's been great to have my big sister around.

Shawnee and Jesse—now that this series is done, maybe I'll actually get to see my best friends again? Can I take you guys up on the last five years of missed hangout time?

Charlie and Jules—your friendship has been one of the best things that has come out of this whole experience. Thank you both for your encouragement, your humo(u)r, your much needed kicks-in-the-ass (sorry, arse), and all the time you've taken to helping me try to get this last book right.

Thank you, Daisy, for the long walks while contemplating; Josey, for the foot-warming; and Piper, for the endless snuggling through a dozen revisions.

And lastly, to every reader who has picked up one of these books and given it a consideration—you've helped make a dream come true. Because of your support, and the incredible love you've shown this series, I've been given the opportunity to turn to writing full-time. Which, truly, has been a lifetime aspiration. I look forward to getting out my next books for 2024, and hope you will join me for the ride.

Cheers!

Jen

COMING SOON BY JEN LYON

The Unfinished Line
Curse of Queens Trilogy
Let Them Burn

Planned standalone books also in the works for: Amelia, a young Catharine and Nathalie, and Elle.

ABOUT THE AUTHOR

Jen Lyon is an avid lover of sports, travel, theatre, and the ocean. When she isn't writing, Jen can be found sailing, browsing the shelves of her local bookstore, cheering ardently at an NWSL soccer match, or training horses at her Southern California horse ranch, where she lives with her wife, Donna, and their dogs and horses.

Follow Jen on IG @jenlyonauthor where she unapologetically spams her page with photos of her corgis, dachshund, horses and obscenely large Maine Coon cats.

Printed in Great Britain
by Amazon

36262750R00229